ACCLAIM FOR

JEFF ABBOTT'S
SAM CAPRA THRILLERS

DOWNFALL

"Abbott packs a lifetime of thrills and suspense into a mere five days…Abbott excels at spinning complex webs of intrigue combining psychological twists and abundant action…Sam is both pawn and knight in an exciting chess game."
—*Publishers Weekly*

"Action-packed, never-stop-for-a-breath storytelling."
—*Dallas Morning News*

"Filled with action, intrigue, twists, and a variety of locales… It's perfect for a summer weekend's reading pleasure."
—*Fort Worth Star-Telegram*

"[A] whirlwind ride…*Downfall* moves like a juggernaut out of control and is impossible to put down…a torrid read that grabs the reader by the throat and never lets up."
—BookReporter.com

"Often wildly entertaining…a ton of action."
—*Austin American-Statesman*

THE LAST MINUTE

"An explosive cocktail."   —*Washington Post*

"Engaging from the first paragraph, terrifying from the second page, *Adrenaline* accomplishes what most modern thrillers can't. It makes us care about its characters even while we're speeding headlong down the ingenious rabbit hole of its plot. Well done!"

—Eric Van Lustbader

"Engrossing...flows rapidly from page to page...definitely a page-turner...wonderful descriptive writing... Abbott's demonstrated ability creates a highly recommended 5-star book."

—*Kingman Daily Miner* (AZ)

"The title of this book pretty much sets the pace for this action-packed thriller. Within its pages are all the best aspects of a very enjoyable good versus evil plot: intrigue, spies, double crosses, foreign locales, technology used for nefarious purposes, a good-hearted hero, and the obligatory nasty bad guys."   —*Suspense Magazine*

"Sam Capra is the perfect hero—tough, smart, pure of heart, and hard to kill. And *Adrenaline* is the perfect thriller. Taut and edgy, with breakneck pacing and perfect plotting, it's a breathless race from the shocking, heart-wrenching opening sequence to the stunning conclusion. Jeff Abbott is a master, and *Adrenaline* is his best book yet."

—Lisa Unger

"Hero Sam Capra likes to unwind with parkour, leaping from building to building, clambering up walls and hurtling through space across the urban landscape...The sport's a fitting metaphor for Abbott's style, tumbling from page to page with the frantic inevitability of Robert Ludlum... It all works beautifully."   —*Booklist*

A KISS
GONE BAD

JEFF ABBOTT

GC

GRAND CENTRAL
PUBLISHING

NEW YORK   BOSTON

Grand Central Publishing
Hachette Book Group
237 Park Avenue
New York, NY 10017

www.HachetteBookGroup.com

Printed in the United States of America

OPM

Originally published in 2001 by Dutton

First Grand Central Publishing Edition: April 2014

10 9 8 7 6 5 4 3 2 1

Grand Central Publishing is a division of Hachette Book Group, Inc. The Grand Central Publishing name and logo is a trademark of Hachette Book Group, Inc.

The Hachette Speakers Bureau provides a wide range of authors for speaking events. To find out more, go to www.hachettespeakersbureau.com or call (866) 376-6591.

The publisher is not responsible for websites (or their content) that are not owned by the publisher.

In Memory of
PATTI STANFIELD
who so loved the waters
and a good laugh

Perhaps villages fill their own quotas in mysterious ways, so many mayors, so many idiots, so many murderers, so many whores.
—JOHN D. MACDONALD,
A DEADLY SHADE OF GOLD

A KISS
GONE BAD

1

WHEN THE BLADE (as he secretly called himself) felt blue, he liked to relax behind the old splintery cabin, where his three Darlings were buried, and feel the power of their vanished lives pulse through him. It was quiet in the shade of the laurel oaks, and on lonely evenings the Blade pretended that his Darlings lived with him, with their cries and pleadings and wet, fearful eyes. His kingdom was small, twenty feet by twenty feet, and he ruled over only three subjects. But he ruled over them completely, life and body and soul.

Today, with his portable tape recorder playing a worn Beach Boys cassette and the clear harmony of "God Only Knows" drifting up into the oaks, he sat down between two of the unmarked graves: one of the mouthy carrot-topped girl from Louisiana who had fought so hard, the other the young woman from Brownsville who had cried the whole time and hardly deserved to be a Darling at all. He had selected a new Darling, a prime choice. But fear made his spit taste like smoke, because he had never wooed near Port Leo, much less wooed anyone ... famous.

He had followed her for a daring ten minutes yesterday, sweat tickling his ribs, idling near her in the grocery store while she shopped with the big-shouldered boyfriend who had brought her to Port Leo. The Blade didn't like the boyfriend named Pete, not one bit, although he liked to think about all the mischief that Pete had been up to, starring in those nasty movies. The Blade had eavesdropped in the grocery, pretending to inspect the jug wines while the couple selected beer. She fancied Mexican beer, one that folks drank with a lime slice crammed down the neck of the bottle, and he wished he knew its taste; but Mama didn't let him drink. The Blade hoped they would talk about sex, being their vocation, but Pete and his Darling talked about grilling shrimp, the rainy autumn, how irritating his Godzilla-like ex-wife was.

His Darling's voice sounded edgy, and impatient. *I'm tired of us sneaking around this town and you pissing off these idiots. Let's go to Houston to write your movie. I'm in big favor of Plan B*. The hint that his Darling was making a movie, here in Port Leo, tightened his throat with desire. The boyfriend muttered no. Then she'd said, *Let this crap with your brother go*.

The sweet agony of being close to her flamed into fear. He'd grabbed a gallon of cheap cabernet in terror and bolted for the checkout lines, crowded with new winter Texans. He'd fled to the cereal aisle and shoved the jug behind the Cheerios and waited until his Darling and her boyfriend left the store before venturing out.

They hadn't seen him, known him.

Pete was writing a movie? He didn't think that the films those two did involved screenwriting. Didn't they just point the camera, clamber on the bed, and do their artful moaning and thrusting with all the sincerity of professional wrestlers?

Last week he had driven into Corpus Christi when he learned that his soon-to-be Darling did movies, of an extremely dubious sort. He frequented adult bookstores, driving the two hours to San Antonio or the thirty-odd miles to Corpus Christi, avoiding the few establishments that were too close to Port Leo along the ribbon of Highway 35, never going to any single store too often, paying with bills worn thin from lying under Mama's mattress. He never asked the clerks for recommendations—he didn't want to be remembered—and tried to fit in with the faceless men who wandered the too brightly lit aisles of the porn stores. He was unremarkable: just another lonely guy with eyes only for the bosomy models on the video covers.

His research uncovered that she had acted in only a few movies; she had directed far more. He almost felt proud of her. On his last jaunt, off the sale table, he bought a video she had headlined five years ago, her last acting job. She went by the name Velvet Mojo, an appellation the Blade found tasteless. The tape was called *Going Postal*. He suspected the post office would receive a satirical treatment. Perhaps even a deliciously violent treatment. But the movie disappointed. No violence. And while his Darling was versed in erotic tricks involving stamps that made his tongue go dry, her friend Pete performed with her, which seemed...wrong. The Blade watched them couple again and again until the world's edges grew soft and his mind napped. He heard Mama cursing. When he awoke, he felt bleary and offended. She deserved rest with the pleasure of his company.

He could save her from this sordidness. He would.

That little shady spot under the old bent oaks, it would be perfect for her. But winning her would be tricky. Wooing

other Darlings and avoiding suspicion had been easy.
Louisiana and Brownsville and Laredo were far away. She
was within a mile or so. And he would have to wait. He
could not truly enjoy her now, but he could in a few days.
His hunger sharpened, and he imagined her lips, speckled
with her own blood, tasted of copper and strawberries.

The Blade stood with resolve. He would make her his.
But first he would have to make sure that no one cared if
she was gone.

2

THE PHONE JARRED The Honorable Whit Mosley awake at ten-thirty at night, out of a dream that melded campaign signs, incomprehensible legal mumbo jumbo, and his stepmother in a sheer nightgown. He cussed quietly and grabbed the receiver.

"This is Judge Mosley," Whit croaked.

"This is Patrolman Bill Fox, Judge. Sorry to wake you, Y'Honor, but we got a dead body we need you to certify."

Whit sat up in bed. "Where?"

"At Golden Gulf Marina."

Whit blinked and stretched. Golden Gulf was the rich-boy marina in Port Leo—no boats under fifty feet need apply. "You got ID?"

"According to a driver's license his name is Peter James Hubble."

Coldness settled in his stomach. *Oh, no way. No way.*

Fox took his silence as an invitation for details. "A girl showed up at ten, found the fellow dead, shot in the mouth."

Well, this would make a splashy headline. All over the state of Texas.

"Okay, I'll be there in a few minutes." Whit got up out of bed, a book tumbling to the floor. He'd fallen asleep trying to charge his way through the *Texas Civil Practice* text, the world's surest cure for insomnia.

"I'm wondering if this guy might be related to Senator Hubble," Officer Fox mused.

You think, Sherlock? Whit wanted to say, but Fox was a smiling, amiable man and he said nothing. Fox was also a voter, and Whit needed every vote he could muster. "Pete's her son. He's been away for several years." Whit managed to keep his voice neutral. "If we're sure it's him, someone's got to call the senator."

"Yes, sir. I'll talk to the chief about it."

"Okay, thanks, Bill, I'll be there in a few." He hung up.

Call the senator? How about calling the dead guy's ex-wife? He picked the phone back up, started dialing Faith Hubble's number, and stopped. No point in freaking her out until he was sure it was Pete.

Please, don't let Faith have had anything to do with this.

Whit pulled on the wrinkled khaki shorts, a clean T-shirt, and the parrot-covered beach shirt he'd worn earlier in the day. He locked up the guesthouse behind him, hurried barefoot across the cement decking around the pool, and by the back door to the main house found a worn pair of Top-Siders in a pile of pool accessories. Through the windows Whit saw his father assembling a sandwich in the kitchen, no doubt needing nourishment for another bout of nuptial bliss. His father noticed him rooting for the shoes and opened the back door.

"Who called?" Babe Mosley asked. He wore a silk robe Hefner would have approved of.

"Dead body, Daddy," Whit answered.

"Ah," Babe said, watching Whit. "You're not wearing that, are you?"

"Why?" Whit stuck his feet into the old boat shoes. A hole at the front of one showed a sliver of his toenail.

"Well, son, there might be some voters there. A crowd. You ought to look more judicial. Maybe a suit."

"Daddy, I don't have time to change." Whit kept his voice in check. Thirty-two and still his father lectured him. "The corpse sure isn't gonna care what I'm wearing." He pushed past his father and pulled a beaten navy baseball cap that commemorated a Port Leo fishing tournament (PRAY FOR MARLINS) off a hat tree on the kitchen wall.

"See, this hat's all civic. I'm set," Whit said.

"Whit?" Irina called to him from his father's bedroom. He crossed the kitchen and glanced down the hall. She stood in the doorway, sporting a flouncy little peignoir that a hearty sneeze would send drifting. Living at home was a bad idea, and as soon as the election was over he was *so* out of here.

"Who rang, Whit?" Voice like warm caramel drizzled on skin.

"I got to go certify a dead body," he answered, not looking at her.

"Tell him to put on a suit," Babe hollered from the kitchen.

"A dead person? Who is it?" *Eet,* she said. Her Russian accent grew more feathery in sleepwear. She came from a cold climate. Didn't she believe in flannel?

"I don't know," he white-lied. If the son of the most powerful woman in the Texas Senate lay dead on a boat, Whit wasn't going to breathe one word before any official announcement.

His stepmother—twenty-five—gave him a smile that nipped the edges of his heart. "Shall I make you some coffee to take with you? A sandwich?"

Yeah, if he was going to work a corpse with a bullet blasting open its head, he wanted a snack. But he smiled, grateful for the kindness.

"No, thanks. Be back in a bit." Whit jingled his keys in his pocket.

"Be careful," Irina called as he stepped out onto the grand front porch. Good advice. The previous three nights he'd dreamed of Irina in the most unmotherly ways. Be careful, right. He might mumble *Irina* in his sleep, and Faith Hubble would justifiably castrate him with her bare nails.

The night sky glowed with far-off lightning. A freshly brewed storm hovered over the western Gulf of Mexico, scudding dark clouds over Port Leo. The October air blew heavy with the promise of rain.

Whit eased his Ford Explorer down the crushed-oyster-shell driveway. He sped down Evangeline Street, past the old Victorian homes, till he reached Main Street, then headed north, threading through downtown, toward the marina.

The Port Leo storefronts catering to the winter Texans and tourists stood dark. He sped past Port Leo Park and its attendant curves of grass and beach; past the dour, guano-grimed statue of St. Leo the Great, the town's namesake because of his reputed ability to calm storms; past a line of trendy galleries selling the wares of the town's many artists. The large shrimpers' fleet docked at the downtown marina bobbed at rest. A couple of nightclubs, with cheesy names like Pirate's Cove and Fresh Chances (for what, Whit wondered—to catch syphilis?), remained open, strobe lights flashing against the windows, but few cars were parked in the lot.

A red Porsche 911, blaring K.C. and The Sunshine Band's "I'm Your Boogie Man," bulleted past him. In his rearview mirror, Whit saw the wink of the roadster's solitary taillight as it braked to swerve onto a side street. *See you in traffic court soon, and I may double your fine for your music,* Whit thought.

Main Street merged into Old Bay Road, which snaked alongside St. Leo Bay. A modest strip of grayish white beach, the color of dirty sugar, lay along the bay's rim, then there was the road, and then a line of rental cottages and retiree homes. Across the expanse of St. Leo Bay the jeweled lights of several pleasure boats cruised past. Whit lowered his window and breathed in the coastal perfume of dead fish, weathered wooden docks, and salt wind caught in high grass. A clump of signs along the road read ELECT BUDDY BEERE JUSTICE OF THE PEACE.

Campaigning sucked. Whit hated it. Election Day loomed just over two weeks away and Buddy, his esteemed opponent, had littered Port Leo with enough flyers and signs to endanger a forest. Whit had slapped several magnetic signs on his Explorer (Whit rechristened his car "the Vote Mobile") and erected twenty small post signs at major intersections around the county. He had not made time to phone, knock on doors, and shake hands for votes, hating the idea of begging strangers to put him in a job. If Buddy Beere—who Whit considered to have an IQ lower than a swarm of gnats, even a big swarm—defeated him, Whit's local career options included scooping ice cream, working a fishing boat, or frothing lattes at Irina's.

He drove past a huge sign asking him to REELECT LUCINDA HUBBLE TEXAS SENATE. The pictured Lucinda waved with her trademark big red hair and her bright blue eyeglasses, simultaneously evoking a kindly aunt and a confident leader.

If this dead guy was Pete Hubble, *mess* wouldn't begin to describe it.

Whit wheeled into the crushed-oyster-shell parking lot of Golden Gulf Marina. The main building was a faded sea-green with white trim, now ablaze in the spinning red-and-blues of the police cars. This death had drawn an array of authorities: Port Leo police, Encina County sheriff's deputies, Texas Department of Parks and Wildlife cruisers, and the highway patrol. It looked like a law-and-order convention. The Hubble name must've gotten mentioned over the police bands and all came running for a quick peek.

Whit cursed under his breath.

A small crowd of marina residents had been ousted from their boats and milled in the lot, dressed in robes and shorts, watching the proceedings in the glow of the mercury lights.

Whit parked and grabbed a notebook full of JP forms, a pair of latex gloves, and a flashlight from the death-scene kit he kept in his car. Fox, the patrolman who had summoned him, stood watch by a swath of yellow police tape and nodded.

"Hey there, Judge Mosley." Fox blinked at the tropical shirt and disheveled shorts. "Come from a party?"

"No." Whit grimaced. "Down there?" At the farthest tip of the docks, an officer climbed off a hefty cruiser.

"Yes, sir. Damn nice boat."

Whit ducked under the yellow police tape. *Maybe I should have worn the suit.*

3

WHIT HAD SERVED as justice of the peace for only six months, since the previous justice died in a car crash after several years in office. He'd accepted the appointment from the county commissioners, all cronies of his father's, because he needed Direction. Over the past five years since he'd shuffled back to Port Leo, his jobs shared only their brevity: photographing sports part-time for the paper, managing a defunct fifties-themed ice cream parlor with the ill-advised name of Shimmy Shimmy Shakes, and running a messenger service that never delivered profits.

His father measured success by oil leases, acreage, investment income, and wifely pulchritude, and believed in Direction (especially for English majors who had cost him fifty thousand dollars to educate at Tulane). Babe cajoled his buddies into appointing Whit to the remainder of the dead JP's term. Whit decided to give it a shot. *Judge* would make the most respectable addition to his crazy-quilt résumé.

Whit pored over justice court law but felt awkward and stupid every time he had to consult a book during a hearing, impatient litigants tapping their feet. He bought some dime-store eyeglasses to smarten his appearance and cut his blondish hair short but wore his beach-bum clothes (polos, shorts, and sandals) beneath the black sobriety of the robe. To Whit's surprise he liked the work: he adjudicated small claims and traffic court, which could be dishwater dull or raucously entertaining (depending on the cases), but he also issued arrest and search warrants, magistrated the arrested into jail, signed commitment orders for the insane, ordered autopsies, and conducted death and fire inquests.

With Encina County too small for a medical examiner of its own, Whit served as the first line of forensic defense. So far in his six months this unpleasant duty had reared itself four times: once with a car crash at the edge of the county, twice with drownings on St. Leo Bay, and once for an elderly suicide who, his insides gnawed with pancreatic cancer, washed several fistfuls of Valium down with a fifth of vodka while listening to Hank Williams CDs.

Another death, and the whole county would be watching. All the attention could make or break his anemic campaign. *Great. Your lover's ex-husband is dead, and you get to rule on cause of death. Congratulations.*

Whit headed past the long line of docked boats on the T-head, most shrouded in bright blue coverings. Weekend boaters from Corpus Christi or Houston owned these craft. A few folks lived on their boats full-time, retirees or trust-fund babies. Whit ducked under another banner of crime-scene tape taped right at the boat's stern.

"Hello, Honorable." Claudia Salazar, a Port Leo police detective, stood on the deck of *Real Shame,* watching him scale the ladder. A gust whipped her dark hair around her face, and she yanked it back over her ears. She looked decidedly more official than he did in her black slacks, white blouse, and a PLPD windbreaker.

"Hey," Whit said. "I heard this may be politically testy. No press yet?"

"We have a short grace period before they swarm, once it gets out that Senator Hubble's son is dead," Claudia said. "Get your quotes ready."

"Has anyone called the senator?"

"Delford is," she answered. Delford Spires was the longtime police chief in Port Leo. He had a full ruddy face and a natty mustache that made him look like a chunky catfish.

He followed Claudia across a pristine deck down to a living area and galley filled with clutter: a thick paperback propped open with a carton of Marlboros and an empty wineglass. On the floor a pizza box lay open with torn cheese and pepperoni glued inside. Two empty bottles of cheap cabernet stood on the coffee table. Each label had been peeled away from the bottles; little curls of paper dotted the floor. On one side of the den a series of windows faced the gunmetal waters of the bay. On each end, small stairs led to sleeping cabins. Claudia went to the aft stairs.

"Here's where he was found." She stepped aside so Whit could enter the tiny stateroom.

The dead man lay naked on the bed, lying on his back, arms and legs spread, the sourness of death-released waste scenting the close air.

"I haven't seen him in many years," Whit said. "But that's Pete Hubble." He did not add that Pete Hubble had skinny-dipped with Whit's older brothers and once you saw Pete naked you were unlikely to confuse him with someone else. "It might be best to get a formal ID from family or friends."

Eddie Gardner, another police department investigator, stood in the corner of the bedroom, snapping photos. An evidence-collection kit lay open at his feet.

"You were supposed to wait for Judge Mosley to get here," Claudia said.

"Sorry." Gardner shrugged. "Just taking some photos. I didn't disturb anything for the judge." Gardner made *judge* sound like *dog turd*. He wore his thinning hair pulled in a short ponytail, aiming for and missing the surfer dude look. He was a recent hire from Houston and had tried too hard to go coastal with the flowered shirts and baggy shorts.

"Why don't you get started on searching and cataloging the rest of the boat?" Claudia suggested in a patient tone. Gardner went up the stairs with his smirk.

"Houston know-it-all," Claudia muttered.

"Eddie's got to stop those public displays of affection for me," Whit said. He pulled on latex gloves and switched on an overhead light. A bit of bedsheet was wrapped awkwardly around Pete's upper torso, a gun loosely gripped in his right hand, his mouth a gaping hole. His eyelids stood at half-mast, rimmed with blood.

"This is awful," Whit said.

"Did you know him well?" Claudia asked.

"He was friends with a couple of my older brothers. I knew his brother Corey better than him."

Claudia cocked her head. "Corey. He went missing, didn't he?"

"Yeah. About fifteen years ago."

A hoarse voice called down to Claudia. "I'll be back in a minute," she said.

Whit probed—gingerly—Pete Hubble's throat for a pulse. Nothing, obviously. He poked the paling skin: cool but not cold, and rigor mortis had not yet begun.

The windows were shut in the cabin, but the boats at Golden Gulf were docked in neat succession. Surely someone would have heard the fatal shot. He raised the blinds on the windows. The two berths next to *Real Shame* were empty. On the other side was the open bay and the long pall of night.

Whit opened his notebook to a blank scene-of-death form. He heard more officers boarding the boat, into the galley and living area, Claudia greeting them, dividing responsibilities. Whit wrote: *Oct 12, 10:45 P.M. Peter James Hubble, male, age 40, brown hair, brown eyes, six-six, around 220 pounds, nude except for gold chain with lion's head on it around neck, red-and-green dragon tattoo on right forearm, lying face up on bed, sheet wrapped partially around chest, Beretta 92 in right hand, bullet wound in mouth, blood spray on face.*

Whit peered inside Pete's broken mouth, bringing his flashlight to bear on the damage. The tongue, the back teeth, the palate, the uvula, the smooth pink walls looked exploded. The back of the mouth was a gruesome tunnel boring to the brain. Pete had his lips wrapped neatly around the barrel when the gun went off.

"Ate the gun, didn't he?" Eddie Gardner asked conversationally. He had returned with his camera.

"Apparently."

"Sheriff's deputies are helping Claudia, so you and I can get the body done." He spooled film into the camera, still smirking. "Love the shirt. Parrots are you."

Whit ignored the jab, leaning close to the gun. "Odd. The safety is on."

"I pulled the gun out of his mouth so I could engage the safety. Standard procedure." Gardner explained this in a tone usually reserved for addressing toddlers. "Wouldn't expect you to know."

Great. A Buddy Beere supporter. "Did you take a picture first, with the gun in his mouth?"

"No. Forgot. Just trying to secure the scene, Judge."

Whit wrote in his notebook: *Gardner didn't take requisite pictures, mention THAT in the inquest report.*

"So you knew this guy?" Gardner asked.

"Ages ago."

"There's a whole bunch of adult movie videos in a cabinet by the television. And this guy's picture is on some of the covers."

Whit stared at him. "Please be kidding."

Gardner grinned. "Not kidding at all. You could hold a blue film festival with all the porn up there." He pointed at the dead man's prodigious organ. "A horse would be jealous. Makes sense he might make some money off of that."

The son of a prominent state senator starring in porn films. The imagined headlines took a greasy turn in Whit's mind. He wondered if Faith knew.

He watched Eddie Gardner snap photos.

"Eddie," Whit said, "please photograph the gun. I'm going to need those for the inquest." Gardner took several shots of the pistol from different angles. Neither man spoke for a minute until Gardner finished the roll.

"You thinking suicide, Judge? Looks that way to me."

"Why?" Whit asked.

"Big-built guy, no signs of struggle. It's hard to stick a gun in the mouth of a guy this big."

At one corner of the bed stood a sleek video camera, mounted on a tripod, aimed at the bed. Gardner watched Whit examine the camera.

"Maybe he was shooting a home movie with that little gal out there and things got rough," Gardner said.

"Little gal?"

"Girl that found him. Looks like she's spent her last dime and got no place to go. Dirty, strung out." Gardner laughed. "She might have screamed bloody murder if she saw that"—he pointed at Pete—"coming at her."

"Maybe," Whit said. Gardner had all the appeal of head lice, but he had a point. Whit remembered a tidbit he'd read in a forensics book about bodily fluid residue. He carefully inspected the dead man's genitals with his latexed fingers; the penis appeared dry. There hadn't been immediate predeath sex, he bet, but the medical examiner in Corpus Christi could properly make that determination.

Gardner watched him probe the organ. "If it gets hard, yell."

"Don't worry. I will." Whit felt uneasy embarrassment again. No doubt Gardner would gossip back in the police station: *Mosley felt up the dead guy, can you believe it?*

Whit noticed a frame turned down on the bedside dresser, and he righted it. It was a photo of a young boy, on the verge of the teenage years, with a scattering of freckles and mischievous brown eyes. Hints of Pete Hubble lay in his face: the square jaw, the crinkled smile, the brown hair. Signs of Faith Hubble were the small ears, the slink of the raised eyebrow. It was an old photo of Sam Hubble, Pete and Faith's son. Sam was now sixteen, a bright kid Whit had always liked. He wondered how on earth the boy would take this news.

"The only suicide I've worked," Whit said, "the fellow turned every family picture to the wall before taking the big gulp."

"Another vote for suicide." Gardner loaded another roll of film. More flashes filled the room.

Still wearing his gloves, Whit flipped open the video camera's housing. No tape inside.

"Was there a videotape in here Claudia took?" he asked.

"Don't believe so."

"Did you take it?"

Gardner frowned. "Nope."

Whit shut the case. Discarded clothing lay piled in the corner of the room. Still wearing the gloves, Whit picked through the mound. In the pile were faded men's jeans, a cowboy belt still threaded through the loops; a white T-shirt; and men's black briefs that must have clinched the family jewels in a vise grip. Nestled with the shirt were a pair of cotton women's panties, decorated with little intertwining violets. Whit hooked the panties with one gloved finger and raised them toward Gardner.

Gardner glanced behind him to make sure Claudia Salazar hadn't returned to the room. "Ought to check to see if the girl's got her delicates. I'll volunteer."

"A hero in her darkest hour," Whit said. "What has the witness told you?"

"Her name's Heather Farrell. Got that scared-goat look of a runaway. We're running a check on her to see if she's got a record. She said she met Hubble on the beach over the course of the last week, and he asked her to come over tonight."

Whit studied Pete Hubble's face. Little of the boy he had known remained in the dead man's looks. A memory bubbled up: Whit, barely twelve, hanging at the edges of one of Whit's brothers' birthday parties, full of raucous teenagers, and Pete sneaking Whit—youngest of the six Mosley boys—slugs of prime bourbon. He'd thrown up at the party's end, on the shoes of his oldest brother's date, and gotten the last whipping he'd ever received from his father. Pete. Mr. Fun. At least before his brother vanished.

"I wonder how many dirty movies he made," Gardner said.

"Don't go broadcasting details of that career around town just yet."

"Not a chance in hell that's gonna be kept quiet," Gardner said. "Think of all the women he must've had doing the movies."

"Think of all the venereal disease."

Gardner pondered this. "Might suck the wind out of your sails."

Whit opened the small closet that faced the bed. A small collection of men's clothes hung loosely on hangers: pants, sweatshirts, a stacked collection of baseball caps, captioned with ADULT ENTERTAINMENT AWARDS and HOT AND BOTHERED PRODUCTIONS and, oddly, UCLA FILM SCHOOL. On the opposite side of the closet blouses, women's T-shirts, sweatshirts, and jeans were neatly folded across hangers. Below was a box of loosely stuffed papers. On the floor a leather bustier, designed to rein in a majestic-size bosom, and a collection of hot-pink thong underwear lay in an untidy heap.

"A woman's been staying here."

Eddie Gardner shrugged. "Imagine. A guy who has sex for a living keeps a lady handy."

Whit returned to the combined galley/sitting area. He heard Claudia and another officer detailing and bagging the evidence out on the deck, which was most in danger of being affected by the threatening weather.

Opposite the couch was a brand-new television, and videotapes were wedged into an open cabinet. Whit pulled up a tape from one stack. *Cleopatra's Love Slaves* featured an elfin-faced platinum blonde in a golden, vaguely Egyptian costume. She was about to lick a rubber asp caught in her cleavage. Behind her loomed an oiled, chesty fellow in a toga with a lusty stare: Pete. A list of performers covered the left side of the tape cover: Dixxie St. Cupps and Rachel Pleasure and Love Ramsey. After several female names were listed "Big Pete Majors" and another man; the casting wasn't split evenly by gender. But then, men generally weren't the main attractions. Velvet Mojo was credited as the producer and director.

Whit pawed through the rest of the cassettes: *Mixin' Vixens, More Lovin' Spoonfuls, Oral Arguments XI.* "Big Pete Majors" was listed as a performer on every tape. Velvet Mojo was listed on all of them as producer and director, all under the Hot and Bothered label. Whit counted twelve tapes and noticed they were all done in the past year. Pete and his harem believed in hard work.

Whit sat in shock. He wondered if Pete's mother, the senator, knew of her son's career. Or Faith, who never mentioned her ex. Two extraordinarily bright, accomplished women—the shame would burn them both like acid. Personally. Politically.

He noticed books piled on the sofa. There were several books on screenwriting basics, dialogue, technique. Porn didn't require much in the way of story structure, Whit thought, but the books looked well worn.

The other collection of tapes—twice the size of the porn collection—was a world away from the adult tapes, and Whit recognized some titles only because he'd taken film appreciation years ago at Tulane for an easy A. *City Lights,* one of Charlie Chaplin's masterpieces. *The Battle-*

ship Potemkin, a long-ago classic of Russian cinema. Abel Gance's *Napoléon,* D. W. Griffith's *Birth of a Nation. Gone with the Wind.* Films by Alfred Hitchcock, by John Ford, by Stanley Kubrick. And a bevy of obscure foreign cinema, films from Australia and Sweden and Italy that Whit had never heard of. Combine the two stacks and you would have the world's most bizarre film festival.

Whit peeked into the VCR and found a tape already in the drive. Still wearing his gloves, Whit powered up the television and the VCR.

4

THE TAPE SNAPPED into sudden focus. Pete Hubble walked along a curve of rural road, sauntering backward, talking into the handheld camera with the earnest patter of a tour guide. The time stamp in the corner of the screen indicated the footage had been shot ten days ago.

"Here's where my brother's car was discovered," Pete said in his rumbling baritone. The camera panned over a clutch of small white frame houses with a private, ratchety pier jutting into the water. "Before this was just beach and field, and kids parked here."

"I'm sure you never did," a woman's smoky voice commented, off-camera. She apparently was operating the camcorder.

Pete smiled. "I was too shy."

"You triumphed over your phobia." A pause. "Were the keys in his car?"

"No. Never found."

"Any sign of foul play?"

"No. Mom made Corey work for the car. I couldn't believe he'd just abandon it."

"They find *anything* in it?"

"A gas receipt, from Port Lavaca, was under the seat.

So we know he or someone had been driving the car and had been up the coast." Pete shaded his eyes against the sun. "No prints in the car that weren't Corey's. Everyone thought at first that somebody kidnapped Corey. But never a note, never a call."

"So start theorizing. Then we'll go slam some coffee."

"Corey dumped his own car because it would have been traced too easily and he wanted to disappear," Pete said.

"Why?"

"To make my mother suffer." Pete shrugged into the camera lens. "I don't know how to make that part work in the screenplay without Corey looking like a jerk."

"Don't make him a saint if he wasn't one, Pete," the woman said.

Pete shook his head and the tape fuzzed to blue, then resumed with Pete standing in front of a sign. JABEZ JONES MINISTRIES.

"Visual notebook, part two, still scouting locations for the shoot." Pete pointed up at the sign. "Here's where muscle-bound morons come to wrestle with their sins."

"I remind you," the woman's voice said, "my daddy was a preacher. Be nice."

"Jabez declined to be interviewed for my movie. It makes you wonder," Pete said. "I have a feeling he's just waiting to see the movie and sue big-time."

"Let him sue," the woman counseled. "Free publicity."

Pete grinned. "Like I'm gonna have to worry about publicity. I'm gonna be front page on every paper in the country."

"Yeah. Right. Whatever," the woman said. Annoyance dripped from her words, as though there was a secret she wasn't privy to and wanted to be.

The tape jumped again. Pete stood on a stretch of jumbled heavy granite blocks, a fishing jetty near Port Leo Park. The surf surged in and the waves slammed hard against the pink and gray stones, spraying droplets into the air. Wind whipped Pete's hair; the time stamp said this was filmed a week ago.

"Hand me the flowers," Pete ordered. From out of the frame came a woman's hand, covered with jangling bracelets, offering a large bouquet of daisies and carnations, the kind found in the grocery checkout lines, wrapped in green paper. Pete tossed the bouquet into the waves; the flowers churned in the tide, bounced, vanished, churned again. The camera panned up to Pete's face.

"There's no grave for my brother, but we used to fish off this jetty. It's the best I can do." He began to cry, softly.

A few moments of silence. "I think I'm gonna bring Sam here," Pete said, and the woman said, "Oh, you got to listen to reason," and the film went black.

He looked over his shoulder, ejected the tape, and stuck in one of the adult offerings—*Johnny Ampleseed*. The new tape had only been rewound midway. It took less than twenty seconds watching Pete and two bleached blondes kneeling in an orchard to confirm Pete Hubble was indeed a celluloid sleaze. His timeless lines consisted of "Oh, yeah," "Do it, baby," and "Now it's your turn."

Whit felt sick. For Faith, for Lucinda, for Sam. Another part of him wondered: so what was living *that* life like?

Whit put the first tape back in the machine and powered off the television. Pete had been making a film project about his brother's disappearance. Going legit with a film career after working in porn.

Whit went up to the deck. He spotted Claudia Salazar

talking to a sheriff's deputy along the gangplank. Another deputy carefully packed a few bagged and tagged items into a large cardboard box. The ambulance had departed, replaced by a mortuary service hearse, ready to transport the body when Whit gave the go-ahead.

Whit waited for Claudia to head back to the boat. "I'm pronouncing him dead as of 10:45 P.M.," he said. "I'm authorizing the autopsy and ordering an inquest. It's all right to transport the body now." He scribbled details on an authorization of autopsy form, signed it, then Claudia witnessed his signature. "Is it you or Prince Charming that's in charge of the investigation?"

"Delford's given me the case. You thinking suicide?"

"Before we get to that question...he's a porn star."

Claudia blinked, her face paling in the marina lights. "Your shirt's funny, but you're not."

He explained what he'd found, both the adult and legit tapes. Claudia rubbed her face. "This will be a mess," she mumbled.

"Back to your question," Whit said. "Suicide's certainly suggested. There's no sign of a note, but he turned down a picture of his son. I saw the same in a suicide down in Darius a few weeks back. But...considering this guy's livelihood, I'm wondering why that camera—with no tape—is pointed at the bed. And there's a pair of women's panties mixed in with his own clothes. Is our young witness missing any underwear?"

"Oddly enough, I haven't checked."

"There's women's clothing in the closet, including some stuff you ain't gonna see the Junior League sporting during the Buccaneer Ball. If this girl isn't staying with him, it belongs to someone else."

"You think...he was filming a movie and got snuffed?"

Whit shrugged. "I really don't know."

"This is turning nastier by the second."

"Where is your witness?"

"Down at the station. Gardner and the deputies can finish the scene work, I'm going to question her and get a statement." She jabbed a finger at him. "Not a word, Whit, not a word to anyone."

He jabbed a finger back at her but smiled. "Gardner says this girl is a runaway. If you're not going to detain her I don't want her taking off before the inquest."

Claudia nodded. "I'll make sure she sticks close."

"I wonder if the person taping Pete talking about his brother was our runaway."

"Let's talk to her," Claudia said. "We'll compare her voice to the tape."

They walked back to *Real Shame*. Claudia quickly inspected the tape collection and retrieved Pete's homemade tape, and they went back on the dock, toward the marina office. An angry voice boomed along the docks, and they saw a woman arguing with Patrolman Fox at the police tape boundary.

"Lady says she lives on the boat," Fox called to Claudia. "Her name's Velvet."

"Velvet Mojo," Whit whispered, "is the director of Pete's movies."

"Velvet Mojo sounds like a real bad wine," Claudia said. "It's okay," she called back to Fox.

The woman was in her late twenties, with streaky blond hair combed back to her shoulders. She wore a dark long-sleeve T-shirt that read MEAN PEOPLE SUCK and baggy blue-jean shorts with scuffed sneakers.

"Velvet?" Claudia asked as they came to the tape.

The woman stared, and Whit saw fear in her eyes, fueled by the police, the crowd, the hearse.

"What's going on here? Is Pete in trouble?" the woman asked.

Whit immediately recognized the woman's voice from the videotape. Smoky, hinting of hazy bars and purred invitations.

"Maybe we could go inside and talk." Claudia nodded toward the marina office.

Velvet shook her head. "I want to know what's happened. Right freaking now."

"And I want to tell you. But inside," Claudia said.

Velvet allowed herself to be led to the marina office. The wind gusted against them once, smelling of rain.

Inside the office, Claudia gently steered Velvet to a couch and sat down with her. "Velvet—pardon, but is that your real name?"

"Yeah, it's what I go by. But Mojo's made up," Velvet said, as if that could be a revelation.

"So what's your real name?"

"Velvet Lynn Hollister." Her gaze darted back and forth between Whit and Claudia.

"I'm Claudia Salazar with the Port Leo Police Department, and this is Judge Whit Mosley. He's our justice of the peace."

"Is Pete in trouble? Did he—" She stopped.

"Pete has died," Claudia said. "He was found shot to death this evening. I'm terribly sorry."

Velvet accepted this news without screams or tears. Her throat worked in the dim light of the office for a few moments. "Dead? On the boat?" She held herself very still, hands fixed in her lap, eyes dry.

"Yes," Whit said. "He had been shot in the mouth. The gun was in his hand."

They let Velvet digest that bit of news for a moment. She didn't move.

"Did he own a gun?" Claudia asked.

"No. He hated guns. Didn't want them around."

Claudia glanced at Whit. "Would one of his family perhaps have lent him a gun?"

"I avoided his family," Velvet said. "I wasn't up to their high standards. His mother's an A-1 bitch and his ex-wife's her understudy. They didn't want us around."

So Faith knew Pete was in town. Why didn't she tell me? Whit touched Velvet's shoulder; she didn't flinch away. "Where would Pete have gotten the gun from?"

"The boat belongs to a friend of Pete's. He might have gotten the gun from him. I don't know." Velvet began to shiver.

"Who's this friend?" Claudia asked.

"A guy named Deloache. Junior Deloache. He lives in Houston, but he's got a weekend condo here." Velvet grabbed Whit's arm. "Did a doctor look at Pete? Are you sure he's dead?"

"I'm quite sure. I'm sorry."

"Did you see any sign of depression in Mr. Hubble?" Claudia asked.

"You think he killed himself?" Velvet sounded incredulous. "No way. No way, no way, no way." She stood, pacing away from the couch, shaking her head.

Claudia stood. "I know this is hard..."

"You never knew him, Miss Thing, and you're gonna pretend to know him better than me? He...didn't...kill... himself."

Whit asked the obvious question. "How can you be so sure?"

Her glare would have savaged a tank. "Because. He liked himself way too much. He wasn't depressed. If he's dead, someone killed him."

"Fine," Claudia said. "Who would want him dead?"

Velvet's tongue dabbed her lips. "Well, first of all, not me. I know how cops work and I didn't have any reason to want Pete dead."

"What's your relationship with him?" Whit asked.

"We've been friends for a long time. We've worked together on a bunch of art films. Dozens of them."

"So was he your boyfriend?" Claudia asked.

"Boyfriend. How milk-and-cookies. No." Velvet frowned. "Look, go talk to Jabez Jones. He used to be a famous wrestler, now he's a preacher on cable TV. You know him?"

"We know him," Whit said.

Velvet nodded. "Pete's working on a new film project and he wanted some cooperation from Jabez, but Jabez told us no way. But yesterday, I came home from the grocery and Jabez is here and he and Pete are talking on the boat and I can tell Pete's upset—his face was lipstick-red, like his head was about to burst. Jabez was smirking like he'd just popped a good money shot."

Her choice of metaphors, Whit decided, was clearly influenced by her career.

"We'll talk to Jabez," Claudia said. "Anyone else?"

Velvet pinched her lip between finger and thumb. "His ex-wife, Faith Hubble. They'd been bickering over Pete getting to see his son...Faith didn't want Pete to have anything to do with Sam. Pete wanted joint custody, which I knew he wouldn't get, but he and Faith argued about Sam. A lot."

Great, great, great. Whit cleared his throat.

"Where were you tonight, Velvet?" Claudia asked.

"Screw you," Velvet said. "There's no way you're gonna suspect a senator's flunky or a minister, right, so start barking up my butt."

"I'm just asking where you were tonight, when you last saw him, what you last spoke about," Claudia said easily. "No one's accusing you, so just calm down and help us."

Velvet shivered again and sat back on the couch. "Pete had work to do on his screenplay."

"About his brother?" Whit asked.

"Yeah," Velvet said slowly. "How did you know?"

"I saw the tape he had in the machine, scouting out locations, talking about his brother's car."

"Pete wanted to be alone—he writes better—but didn't want to write down at the beach, which is where he usually goes. Said maybe I could go entertain myself. So I went and did some shopping, ate a burger down at a café by Port Leo Beach, and went to see a movie." She stared at Claudia. "I got my ticket stub, and the geek behind the snack counter flirted with me. Alibi enough for you?"

"I'd like to get a statement from you down at the station," Claudia said evenly.

"Am I gonna need a lawyer?" Velvet grabbed Whit's arm. "You're a judge, right? Do I need a lawyer?"

"You're not under arrest, ma'am," Claudia said. "If you want a lawyer, you can get one. We just want to get a statement from you."

"Do you have someplace you can stay, Velvet?" Whit asked. "Y'all's boat is a crime scene, and you can't stay there, at least for now."

Velvet's shoulders sagged, the enormity of the situation

settling upon her. "You mean like friends? No, I don't have any friends here. I don't fit in with all you decent folk."

Whit said, "I'll be sure you have a place to stay."

Claudia gave him a raised eyebrow that seemed to say, *Aren't you the little white knight?*

"Thanks, but I don't need your help." Velvet stood. "Can I see Pete? Maybe I should be the one to tell his mother."

"The police chief will do that," Claudia said. "He's known Pete's mother for a long time. Let's get you down to the station, get your statement, and then we can go from there. Okay?"

Velvet crossed her arms. "Take all the statements you need. Tell me how I can help. Because there is no freaking way that Pete killed himself. None." Her mouth hardened. "And if you people don't find who killed him, I'll make more trouble than you can imagine. I assume you both can spell lawsuit?"

5

THE SMALL CROWD of marina dwellers was a mix of boat bums, Gulf wanderers, and snowbirds. They had little in common except a desire for quiet and the sun-driven crinkle around the flesh of their eyes. They'd been hurried off their boats and they stood clustered in the parking lot, bathed by the glow of the police lights. One could hear mutterings about life being too short and the wrong class of people booking at the Golden Gulf. An overeager Officer Fox had used the word *suicide* in an ill-advised sentence, and the rumor rippled through the small crowd.

The Blade listened to the murmured gossip. His heart jolted like he'd dosed himself with a tickly bit of electroshock. No one paid him much heed, only a couple of the boat bums saying hello. He kept his hands tucked inside his light windbreaker.

He watched a police officer forage in the trunk of a patrol car. The Blade wondered how the officer would react if he leaned close and whispered: *I have a passion I'd like to share with you. Come see my graves.* But he wouldn't. The city would decorate the officer. The news pretties would hail the cop as hero while labeling the Blade as crazy. The boat snobs right here would jockey for camera position and gasp, *Oh, yes, we're terribly shocked. He seemed like the nicest man.* And he probably wouldn't even get to tell his side of the story on TV.

Life was blatantly unfair unless you were willing to take it by the balls and squeeze hard. He watched as one older lady stopped and chatted with the whistling officer. He spoke and she hurried back to the crowd, where she whispered eagerly.

He stood and waited. The elderly lady panted with excitement, ferrying the sad news to each knot of people.

"It's the man who lived on *Real Shame* that's dead," she said to the Blade and two other men. "They think he might've shot himself. Isn't that terrible?"

Shot himself. Shot himself. What wonderful delicious morsels of words. If they were candy he would have eaten them and then licked his fingers.

He wanted to see his new Darling, to touch her, to feel the heavy weight of her hair, lick her skin, and exult in the warmth of her breath against his neck. She would need comfort, poor baby.

"I bet you that trashy girlfriend of his cheated on him and he killed himself." The old woman lowered her voice. "Wearing those thong swimsuits. A piece of trash."

Like Pete Hubble hadn't been a piece of trash, too, thought the Blade. He wondered what interesting pops and creaks the old woman's jaw would make if he broke it.

"She probably won't stay in town," the Blade heard himself say in his thin, wispy voice he so loathed. "Not from here, is she?" *Stupid, dummy!* he berated himself. *Shut up, shut up!*

The old woman nodded at him. She had wrapped her fluffy hairdo in a protective cocoon of toilet paper, and the Blade thought she looked ridiculous. "You're so right. Ought to go back to whatever cesspool she's from."

He nodded politely. Yes, if everyone thought Velvet had left town, then wouldn't it all be easier for him? Perfect.

Three people emerged from the marina office. Lovely, one was his Darling. Why, she wore grief well, as cute as could be in her jean shorts. Pretty is as pretty does, Mama used to say. His mouth went dry with want. The three walked back to Pete's boat, went aboard, and came out perhaps two minutes later. Velvet was sobbing. He could see her bent shoulders in the dim light of the marina.

A man walked with her, steering her toward the police cars.

Panic flamed in him. Oh, no. They were arresting her. That would not do at all, not at all . . .

But they—and now he could see in the dim light the other was a tall man, not a cop—went past the parked police cars, past the quiet ambulance. And he could hear his Darling sob, and—oh, this would *not do*—the man put his hand on her arm, tenderly. The Blade's heart boiled. The man opened the door of a Ford Explorer and she got in, the man helping her like they were on a date.

The man turned toward the crowd. The Blade, seeing his face, grimaced. Heat tickled the backs of his hands.

The Explorer pulled out into the street, and the small crowd of onlookers parted to make way for it. One of those magnetic signs was affixed to the door, white letters bold against a stylized red-and-blue background: KEEP WHIT MOSLEY JUSTICE OF THE PEACE. The Explorer passed within three feet of the Blade, and he saw his Darling's face, leaning against the passenger window. She had her fists pressed to her eyes. He heard the storm of her voice over the car's motor as it shot past.

The Blade hurried away. If they were arresting her, a cop would have taken her away. Not a judge. And she hadn't had a bag. She wasn't leaving town. That thought steadied him as he jumped into his beat-up Volkswagen. He didn't like her running around with that judge when she belonged to him.

That judge. That judge had seen her upset and wanted to help her... wanted to take her to his house and undress her and...

No. No. He knew he was letting his imagination run wild and imagination was his enemy until his Darling was safely in his arms. Judge Mosley was part of law-and-order, after all, so he must be taking her to give a police statement. Or to fill out forms.

Yeah, you know what all those Mosley boys are like. You know.

The Blade revved his engine and headed toward town. He wanted her with him. Forget waiting. Maybe he could catch them before they got into Port Leo's downtown, on the dark bay highway. Flash his headlights, pull them over onto the shoulder or a dark parking lot. Get Mosley out of the car, gut him with one swift move, then cut his throat. He wondered if a judge's blood would reek of musty courtrooms and old thick books. Then he could whisk his Darling to his cabin and make her his, comfort her, take her away from the world's sadness.

He floored the accelerator.

6

—◦《◉》◦—

Do you think he suffered?" Velvet mopped her eyes.

"It was probably over in an instant." Whit believed in mercy, and it was the likely truth.

She rolled down the window a couple of inches, and the cool of the wind slammed into her face. "That little cop. Salazar. She any good?"

"She has an excellent reputation."

"Here in Mayberry-by-the-Bay? How many murders do you have here a year? One?"

"None last year. I think one the year before that."

Velvet wadded up her tissue. "Oh, great, so she lives and breathes homicide. I feel so much better now." She stared at him. "So exactly what role do you play in this aside from chauffeur?"

"When there's a suspicious death, I examine the scene, meet with the people who knew the deceased, talk with the investigators, decide to order an autopsy or not, conduct the inquest, work with the ME in Nueces County if needed, rule on cause of death."

Velvet's eyes widened. "So never mind the cop. All you gotta do is rule it's murder and she *has* to investigate."

"I have to make decisions based on the evidence. I got to be judicial," he said.

She regarded his tropical shirt and ratty shorts. "Yeah, when I picture judicial, I'm seeing you. What are you, twelve?"

He didn't know what to say to her; his inexperience gnawed at him. He cleared his throat. "I promise you I'll be fair, and I'll listen to what you have to say about Pete's... state of mind."

"When will the autopsy be done?"

"In the next couple of days. I'll get a verbal report from the ME first, but we won't have a complete report for a few weeks. And before you keep casting aspersions against me and Claudia, you ought to know that I grew up with Pete. I knew him and his brother." *And I sleep with his ex-wife, so clearly I'm an interested party.*

"Pete never mentioned you."

"He was more friends with my older brothers. But if someone killed Pete, we're not gonna let him or her get away with it."

"I suppose it wouldn't be politically sound to let a Hubble be murdered and let the killer slip free," she said bitterly. "No, I guess you have to investigate fully when it's a state senator's son."

"I know you're upset," Whit said, "and I'm real sorry for your loss, but is there some reason you're cranking on me?"

"I thought judges were all supposed to be big poker players. You don't got a poker face. I can tell by the way you look at me you think Pete and I are trash."

"I don't have a negative opinion of you." He paused. "I want to help you."

She unfolded and refolded her tissue. "Who found the body?"

"A young woman. We think she's a runaway, although she's apparently a few days past eighteen, so I guess you turn into a vagrant then. Um, I saw a video camera set up in the bedroom." She could draw her own conclusions, Whit supposed.

"That's not how you make a movie," she snapped. "You got at least two cameras, not just one, you got better lights than you'd have on that boat, you got a makeup girl. No way was Pete making a movie with that little camera. He was professional."

"But moving on to a new career?"

"Porn had worn him out. It's hard work, you know. He wanted to come home to research and write this script. And he wanted me to direct it once it was done."

"So he gave you a chance to make a real movie?"

Her stare was acidic. "Excuse me. Have you *seen* my movies? They *are* real movies, butthead. I'm the Spielberg of porn. I have plots and characterization and depth and everything."

Whit suspected it was the everything part that raked in the profits. "But this film about his brother had no adult-movie elements," he said. "Right?"

"Of course not. I wanted to try a different kind of project. You know, that's allowed if you're creative. Shakespeare wrote comedies and tragedies. It's only small minds that jam you into one freaking hole forever." She turned back to the window. "So where are you dumping me after I give this statement?"

"I suppose Pete's mother isn't an option," Whit ventured.

"She'd cut my throat in my sleep and bathe in the blood."

"You're sure you don't have any friends in town?" Whit asked.

"I don't want any friends here, thank you kindly."

"Then I guess we'll get you to a motel. You got several choices: the Excellent, which isn't, the Port Leo Inn, the Gulf Breeze. A bunch of B and Bs. There's also a Best Western and a Marriott Suites, too."

"I can't believe Pete is dead and I have to stay at a Best Western." She managed a sniffle and a slight smile, friendlier than just a moment ago. "Any room at your inn? I'm awful quiet and I don't take up much space."

"You don't want to stay with me. I'm a dork who lives with his dad," he said.

"But at the Best Western I'll be alone. I don't do alone real well. I need a Plan B."

"I'm sorry."

"You got a phone in here?"

"Yeah, a cell phone. Here." Whit dug among the tapes and CDs in the storage unit between the seats and handed her the phone. He clicked on the interior light so she could see to dial. Another bit of brightness caught his eye. He glanced in the rearview mirror and saw a pair of headlights jouncing, rapidly gaining on them.

Velvet dialed and waited. "Anson? Oh, good, you're in town. Huh? Oh, okay. This is Velvet. Let me talk to Junior." A pause. "Junior, listen. I got real bad news. Pete's dead." A longer pause. "I'm not kidding. He was shot. I'm okay. I'm holding up. I cried for a bit and now I am getting ready to cry some more. They keep saying he killed himself."

Whit ran through his mental Rolodex of Port Leo, trying to place an Anson or a Junior. Velvet had mentioned a Junior Deloache as the boat's owner.

"I'm not leaving town till we know what happened. Judge Mosley says there's gonna be an inquest. What? I gotta go to the police station. Pete was on your boat and it's a crime scene and I'm booted. So I need a place to crash. Can I stay at your condo?" She listened and hung her head slightly. "No, I don't know when you get your stupid boat back. Yeah. Yeah. Okay, sure, I understand. Sure. I'll just grab me a hotel room. Yeah, thanks for the generosity." She clicked off the phone. "Those jerks."

Whit glanced in the rearview mirror. The headlights behind grew larger.

"No luck?" he asked.

"I hate that greasy little Junior Deloache. He's this piggy-eyed stain, thinks he's a stud. Yeah, with a case of Viagra, maybe." She shrugged. "I can't get into their condo. They're in Houston but are coming down tomorrow, so I guess I'll hotel it."

"I thought you called a local number."

"It's call-forwarding." She blinked at the bright headlights that dazzled behind them. The lights began to flash from dim to bright and dim again. "Somebody's in a hurry."

Whit glanced back in the mirror. "He can go around me if he wants." The car stayed uncomfortably close. Then the lights flashed, dim, bright, dim.

"He wants you to pull over." Velvet handed Whit the phone in the headlights' glare.

"No, thanks." Whit floored the accelerator. He pulled away from the car, and the pursuer dropped back dramatically to a more reasonable speed.

"Jerk," Velvet commented. Whit checked the rearview mirror several seconds later and found the car was nearly gone.

"My office is right across from the police station," Whit said. "I can give you a ride to the hotel after you give your statement."

Velvet misunderstood his charity. "Look, I don't do thank-you sex just because someone shows common human decency."

"I can promise you I wasn't asking for that."

"Why? You think I stink? Do you know how many guys have hit on me since I got here?"

"Probably lots," Whit said.

Velvet hunkered down in her seat. "Lots is half right," she finally pronounced. "Tons is closer."

Whit turned onto Main Street and pulled up in front of the Encina County courthouse. It was a sprawling, grand oddity, shaped by the Moorish architecture popular on the coast a century ago, three stories of heavy Texas granite, designed to survive storm surge and hurricane. The Port Leo Police Department stood across the street, a cracker-box of boring plain brick. They crossed the empty street together. The wind rustled in the drooping palms, and the clouds had dipped low, pregnant with rain.

"They aren't going to arrest me, are they?" Velvet asked suddenly, stopping halfway across the street.

"Did you kill him?" Whit asked.

"No. No."

"Then don't worry. Tell them what they need to know. These are good people. They're not going to hang you out to dry. I promise you that."

She crossed her arms, bowed her head, and the tears came in shudders, and she bleated Pete Hubble's name. Whit didn't dwell on niceties or politics. He took her into his arms and let her cry against his shoulder, like old friends consoling each other in the terrible reality of sudden grief. He couldn't stand there like a wooden post while a woman sobbed. She got his tropical-print shoulder wet and snotty, and when the shaking stopped Whit steered her into the brightly lit doorway of the police station.

7

THE BLADE WATCHED his Darling and that good-for-nothing lecher of a judge embracing in the street. He tried to slow his breathing. He had drawn close to Whit Mosley's Explorer and retreated when his headlights, and the Explorer's interior lights, showed Velvet holding a cell phone. That wouldn't do to have them announce they were being chased or to have a stranger on a cellular connection overhear the Blade doing his best work. He followed them into Port Leo's town square and slowly parked, a block away in front of the black glass of the Gulfstream Bookstore, his headlights cut.

Watching them touch—watching Whit Mosley touch a woman that belonged to *him*—sickened the Blade. He cupped the knife against the round fleshiness of his palm, feeling the bite of its edge. He took calming breaths and tried not to cry in frustration. Patience was beyond a virtue. It was the most basic rule of survival, and to bend patience meant mistakes. Mistakes were not affordable. He had read, in the literature of his own kind, of the most abominable errors: John Wayne Gacy inviting the police keeping him under surveillance to join him for breakfast right when the odd smell floated from the crawlway; Dennis Nilsen showing the first policeman who knocked on his door the grisly plastic bags in his London closet. The Blade decided long ago that he would not lie down and die. So he fell back, and he watched, and he turned on the tape player, and the reedy Beach Boys tape that had been the player's sole occupant for the last three years sputtered into life and the Boys, volume turned low, demanded he be true to his school. He prayed that his Darling would be true to him, singing along under his breath, taking the harmony line.

Mosley and Velvet went into the police station, and the Blade waited. A few minutes later, Mosley sauntered across the street to the courthouse.

You dirty little freak. You're nothing, not worthy to touch her, know her tears. I'm not the nothing. You're the nothing.

Mosley fiddled with the courthouse door and ducked inside the darkened building. A light flickered on a few minutes later in a first-floor office behind lowered blinds.

Perhaps Judge Mosley didn't lock up after himself.

He ran to the courthouse steps and tried the door: locked.

But no, he told himself. Not now. He shivered. One death by violence in Port Leo tonight was remarkable. Another the same night would bring the police out in droves. He walked away from the courthouse. Let Whit Mosley continue to breathe—for now—and let him rule that Pete Hubble died a suicide. He congratulated himself on his self-restraint.

The momentary pride evaporated when he saw the flyer hanging in the bookstore window. Only the dim shimmer from the streetlight illuminated the girl's face, printed on light blue paper taped to the inside of the window. The Blade blinked, his guts coiling like a frightened snake.

The eyes of his last Darling watched him from the flyer. She was smiling broadly. He had not seen her smile, from the time he had abducted her from a faraway parking lot to when he'd laid her in the shallow dirt behind his house.

HAVE YOU SEEN HER? the flyer asked, with MARCY ANN BALLEW written below the question. It gave the young woman's statistics of age, description, height, and weight, and when she was last seen: leaving work at the Memorial Oaks Nursing Home in Deshay, Louisiana, September 30. Her car had been recovered from a nearby Walmart.

He read on, his throat feeling coated with sand. Her wallet had been found two miles outside Port Leo, along FM Road 1223, a week ago. Anyone with information as to her whereabouts was requested to call the Encina County Sheriff's Department or the Port Leo police. A reward was mentioned.

The Blade mentally replayed his time with his most troublesome Darling. When could her wallet have gotten out on the road? he wondered, and with a sick wrench he remembered. As he approached his enclave hidden away from the eyes of other men, she roused from the stupor he'd forced on her with the Valiums and she kicked open a window. He'd veered off the road, whirled to grab her, and belted her hard four times in the face, breaking her cheekbone and nose and knocking her unconscious. He was furious, having to hurt her before his fun; and the broken bones meant he'd never gotten to see her smile. He traced her smile on the paper with his finger: lovely. He missed her.

She must have thrown her wallet out the window before he punched her, trying to leave some clue of her passage. Now the police in Louisiana—and here—must know that she had come through off-the-path Port Leo, Texas.

He swallowed the swell of panic. The police would no doubt be questioning everyone who lived along FM 1223, between here to the county line. How hard would they look, and how hard would they look at him? Capture always lingered in the back of his mind, an unwelcome companion but one as steady as his shadow. Now it loomed as a distinct possibility, and he had not claimed his most precious Darling yet.

He could not take her now. The police would be watching her. But in a few days, especially if Pete was judged a suicide...then she would be ripe, a plum oozing with juice, to be plucked from the tree. Tonight was Monday. He could take her, he believed, by the end of the week. Friday or Saturday.

They could have a deliciously lost weekend together: movies if she were good, dinner, death. Then back to work on Monday.

The Blade began the somewhat arduous process of hatching a plan. What had he overheard Velvet call such contingencies in the grocery store? He remembered and smiled: Plan B.

8

⸺◦◦◉◦◦⸺

THE INTERVIEW ROOM at the Port Leo Police Department resembled a supply closet more than an interrogation facility. In one corner tottered a stack of old computer monitors. The department had upgraded their seven-year-old systems recently and no one wanted the old standbys. A box of shredded documents, ready to be recycled, was shoved against the wall. Two plastic containers of office supplies filled another corner. An old wooden table occupied the center of the room, marred with circles from water cups and soda cans.

Heather Farrell, the young woman who'd found Pete's body, watched Claudia Salazar with mulish eyes. Police Chief Delford Spires sat next to Heather, quiet, letting Claudia take the lead in getting the statement. Claudia noticed, with affection, that there was a crumb of cake caught in his mustache, but she didn't want to point that out with the tape rolling. He had just returned from telling the senator her son was dead. She turned to the witness.

"Okay, Heather, this won't take long," Claudia said. "For the record, do you have some identification?"

Heather Farrell dug in her dirty jeans and produced a tattered driver's license, one that had expired. The birth date indicated that she was two weeks past eighteen. The address on the card indicated she was from Lubbock, in West Texas, far more than spitting distance from Port Leo. Claudia read the information off the driver's license into the tape, then handed the laminated card back to Heather, who proceeded to tidy her nails with the edge of the plastic.

"Your family still in Lubbock, Heather?" Claudia asked.

"Yeah."

"Why did you leave Lubbock?"

"Dirt sucks," Heather said.

"That's a good reason," Claudia said pleasantly. "Any others?"

"I'm an artist. Lots of artists here." Heather shrugged. "I thought for sure those galleries would want to give me a big, fancy show. Strange it hasn't happened yet."

"You haven't updated your driver's license," Spires said.

"Don't drive much these days." Heather gave Delford a caustic look. "Gunk's in your mustache, mister."

Delford groomed out the offending morsel. "Thank you, Heather."

"Where are you living now, Heather?" Claudia asked.

The girl shrugged with a lazy roll of shoulders. A willfulness—either born of stupidity or of hard use—tugged her face into a constant, wary frown.

"Here and there. I camp out at the park down by Little Mischief Beach sometimes."

"Do you have a permit to camp?" Claudia already suspected the answer.

Heather shifted in her seat. "Darn, I lost it yesterday. I haven't found a friendly ranger to give me a new one."

Claudia nodded toward the backpack in the corner. "Those pretty much all your belongings?"

"Yep. Travel light. I don't believe in U-Hauls."

"So you brought everything you had in the world along with you to meet this guy on the boat."

"I guess," Heather said with no energy in her voice.

"You moving in with him?"

"No. I just don't like leaving my stuff lying around."

"Did he tell you his name?"

"Yeah. Pete Majors." Heather took a swig of the tepid cocoa Officer Fox had fetched for her. "He said he was from Los Angeles."

Majors, not Hubble. Big Pete Majors was his *nom de cinéma,* gleaned from the videotapes on the boat. Claudia saw a thin sheen of sweat on Delford's brow, despite the cool of the room.

"Did Mr. Majors tell you why he was in Port Leo?" Claudia asked.

"He was writing a movie about his brother's death. But he was awful depressed about it. I think that's why he killed himself."

"Where did you meet Mr. Majors?" Claudia asked.

"At Little Mischief Beach," Heather answered. Claudia jotted a note on the pad in front of her. Little Mischief was an aptly named, scrabbly beach north of Port Leo, a few miles from the Golden Gulf Marina, known as a kids' hangout, with a small park attached, dense with live oaks and red bays. A good necking spot, but there were better around the county.

Heather brushed fingers through her hair. "The light's good at Little Mischief. I like to sketch the birds, the waves, the old folks walking on the shore."

"Dopers love Little Mischief," Delford interjected. "Am I gonna find some weed in your knapsack, young lady?"

"No," she said, rolling her eyes. "I don't do drugs."

Claudia steered them back on track. "What was Pete doing down at Little Mischief?"

"He'd come down there with a notebook computer, to write or just chill out and throw pebbles in the surf." She wiped a hand across her lips. "Quiet but nice. He gave me money for food."

Claudia made a note. "This money he gave you. Any strings attached?"

A flash of resentment crossed Heather's face. "Of course not. What do you take me for?"

More to the point was what Pete Hubble had taken Heather for. Claudia remained silent for a full thirty seconds, and Heather began to fidget. "I'm not a whore, okay? He was just being nice." She paused. "Maybe he didn't need the money, since he was gonna kill himself."

"So he gave you a loan. What happened next between you?" Claudia asked.

Heather Farrell finished her cocoa and began to tear the rim of the foam cup into strips. Specks of wet, powdery chocolate smeared onto her fingertips, but she didn't notice. "Nothing happened. He seemed real sad. Lonely. Like he'd gotten bad news."

"When did he invite you to his boat?" Claudia asked.

"He said he wanted to talk," Heather said. "He wasn't sure why he would go on living."

"He barely knew you and yet he suggested to you he was suicidal?" Claudia said.

"Sometimes it's easier to talk with a stranger than a friend."

"I suppose. What was this crushing sadness?"

"Pete said his brother...was the source of all the sadness in his life. I gathered his brother died young. And he made mention of some preacher that had screwed his brother over. Somebody Jones." She glanced at Delford. "He made it sound like maybe this preacher was responsible for his brother's death."

Delford cut in. "Pete tell you what proof he had?"

"No. But Pete complained that he couldn't make a case stick." She looked up from her lap, her eyes wide, like a child watching a parent for approval.

"You've got to be more specific," Claudia said. "What exactly did he say about this preacher and his brother?"

Heather scrunched her face. "I didn't take a transcript, and he didn't make a ton of sense. I've told you what I know."

Claudia let silence fill the room and began to tap her pen against the notepad. "He ever suggest you come to his boat and take off your clothes for a movie?"

Heather gave a sharp bark of laughter. "No! I'm not some street whore. I haven't had any problems with the police since I got here a month ago."

"How'd you get over to the marina?"

"I hitched a ride into town from Little Mischief. I got to the marina a little after ten." She tore a long strip of Styrofoam away from her cup and shredded it into confetti. "So I go to his boat—he'd told me it's the big one at the very end of the dock—and I went aboard. I called for him, but there was no answer. The door was open. I went downstairs." Her throat worked. "And there was no one in the kitchen and the living room, so I knocked on the bedroom door."

"It was closed?" Claudia asked.

"Yeah." Heather dabbed at her lips with her tongue. "I yelled out for Pete and pushed hard on the door. I saw him on the bed, right away, and the blood spotting his face." She was quiet for a moment, a youngster staring at implacable death and realizing she would someday feel its grasp.

"I think I screamed. I think I would. I got off that boat like it was on fire. I screamed running down the docks, and people came."

"See anyone suspicious around the boat? Or around the marina?" This from Delford.

"No." Heather tented her cocoa-daubed hands. Claudia yanked a tissue from a box and offered it to Heather. The girl wiped her hands carefully and repeatedly. "I was so worried about Pete, how depressed he was, I wouldn't have noticed anyone."

Delford nodded solemnly.

Claudia thought: *You just don't strike me as the Girl Scout type, sweetie.*

"Do you have your panties on?" she asked Heather.

Heather's mouth twitched. "Excuse me?"

"I'd like to know if you have on a pair of panties."

"Why?"

"Just answer me, please."

"Yeah, I got on panties. You think I'm running around without underwear on?"

"Show me, please. I need you to lower your pants enough where I can see you've got a pair on. Chief, would you step outside for a moment?" Delford blinked at this turn of questioning.

"He can stay. I don't care." Heather stood and yanked down on her beltless jeans with a gentle tug. Claudia could see a slice of panties below the girl's waist, plain white, grimy.

"Thank you," Claudia said.

Heather rearranged her jeans and sat. "Let me guess. You found panties on the boat and wanted to be sure they weren't mine?" She was smarter than she acted. "Those panties probably belonged to his lady friend."

"You knew he had a girlfriend?" Delford asked.

"He mentioned a lady that lived with him on the boat once. But I got the impression he'd had his fill of her. He said she'd made a lot of money off of him, and he was tired of her."

"We'll need you to stay in town, Heather, until our investigation is done."

Her eyes widened. "What, under house arrest?"

"No, but don't leave town."

Heather leaned back in her chair. "I think my statement is done, and I want one of them pro bono lawyers like on TV if you're going to ask me any more questions."

"Two more simple questions," Claudia said. "Woman camping a lot, you carry a gun?"

Heather picked at the table with a dirty fingernail. "No. I have some pepper spray, and I know how to kick a guy's balls all the way up to his throat."

"You ever see this young woman around, maybe down at Little Mischief?" Claudia pulled a flyer from her note-book and pushed it toward Heather. Delford watched without expression.

"Marcy Ann Ballew," Heather read. She scrutinized the photo, as if looking for some vestige of herself in the printed face. "Sorry. Don't know her."

"Where you staying tonight?" Delford asked.

Heather looked discomfited. "Back at the park, I guess."

"If you're still shook up, spending the night alone out

in the dark's no fun." Claudia softened her tone. "You can crash here."

"Oh, great, a jail cell," Heather said. "Thanks but no."

"We'd leave the door open. You're not locked up. It's clean and warm." Claudia ventured a grin. "Real cute guy working the night shift."

The face of Marcy Ann Ballew smiled up at both of them.

Heather shook her head. "I am not staying in any jail cell."

"Then let me call Social Services. They'll find a place for you."

"You just want to keep a tab on me."

"A tab to be sure you're okay," Claudia said.

"I don't need a tab." Heather stood. "We done? I got to go." As if she had errands to run, close to midnight.

Claudia clicked off the tape. "I'll get this typed up and you can sign it."

"Can I come back tomorrow and sign? I'm beat."

"Sure," Claudia said.

"Thanks for answering our questions." Delford stood. "And like Detective Salazar said, don't leave town, miss. There may be a death inquest and you may have to give testimony."

"I'll stick like glue. Later." She gathered up her knapsack and left without a backward glance.

Delford Spires shut the door. "And they say charm school don't make a difference no more."

"She seems awfully sure, on the basis of little detail and thin acquaintance with the man, that he committed suicide. Would a man really kill himself over something that happened to his brother long ago?"

"I worked the Corey Hubble case." Delford sat back

down. "A heartbreaker. Here one day, gone the next, and never a sign of him again. I wonder what this connection is to a preacher. Corey sure wasn't religious—he was a little hell-raiser."

Claudia told him about Pete's tape and the mention of Jabez Jones.

Delford clicked his tongue. "Jabez Jones was just a kid then, too, and was never a suspect. There was never a sign of foul play in that case, period. Corey just ran off and landed himself into real hot water and never resurfaced."

"Pete clearly thought otherwise," Claudia said. "I think I'll talk to Jabez Jones." She watched Delford slump in his seat. She was fond of him, like one might be of an old-fashioned uncle.

"How are the Hubbles?" she asked.

"Devastated. I think they felt they'd just gotten Pete back in their lives. He's stayed his distance. Lucinda's a real strong woman, but this might undo her. They gave me preliminary statements."

A twinge of irritation nipped at her. He'd assigned her the case yet taken statements from the immediate family. Perhaps it had been best, she reasoned, giving him the benefit of a doubt, but she decided to explode the land mine.

"So do they know Pete was a porn star?" She explained the tapes.

"Holy hell, no. At least she didn't mention it to me. Why does a son hurt a mother so?"

"Maybe she hurt him. Parents can be rotten."

Delford snorted. "Lucinda gave Pete the world. It ain't her fault he didn't want it." He sighed, a long, arduous wheeze, and stood. He regarded her with critical affection. "You up for this big a case?"

"Of course." She labeled the tape of Heather's statement and dropped it in an accordion folder.

"You okay about David?"

She closed the folder. "I'm fine, Delford, really."

"I noticed today that you weren't wearing your ring no more."

Claudia's thumb rubbed along the bare ring finger. A band where the skin, shielded by metal that supposedly meant forever, stayed pale. "Yeah, well, the divorce was final yesterday. I sent David back the ring."

"I know it's a tough time, Claud, and maybe I ought to let Gardner handle this one."

"There's no need," Claudia said. "Really, Delford, I appreciate the concern, but I'm fine and work is heaven for me right now."

He coughed.

"I can smell the advice baking," she said.

"I'd treat this like a suicide."

"I don't think Whit and the ME have talked cause of death yet."

Delford ran a finger along a curve of his mustache. "Whit Mosley couldn't find his rear end in the dark with three flashlights. After the election he'll probably be running a snow-cone stand."

"No. He'll be a housepainter," Claudia said.

"You ain't one bit funny," Delford shot back. It was a Port Leo legend: fifteen years ago Whit and his five brothers had, in four masterful hours when Delford was away at a football game, painted Delford's house pink. Violent, electric, Pepto-Bismol pink. Delford, unwilling to be the butt of a joke, had viewed the Mosley boys like crazed terrorists, even after they repainted his house back to its original white. The rest of the town hid its laughter behind their hands and shook their heads in mock scorn at those wild Mosleys.

"You're still not over that prank," Claudia said. "That's why you don't like any Mosley." She herself liked Whit Mosley fine. He'd palled around with her brother Jimmy as kids, fishing, gigging for frogs, swimming in the bay, and Whit never made her—the tagalong tomboy—feel unwelcome. He had kind eyes, gray as the bay when the clouds hung low. And he was easy to work with. The last JP, God rest her soul, puked at every single death scene and guilted Claudia into taking macramé and quilting classes with her. Whit kept his lunch and hobbies to himself.

"I don't like Mosley period. He's running the bench like a beach attraction," Delford fretted. "I'm just saying Pete smells like suicide to me."

"Are you jumping or driving to that conclusion?"

"When I told Lucinda that Pete was dead, she asked straightaway if he'd killed himself. She told me in detail about the mental problems he's been suffering from over the past several years. It's in her statement."

"She knew he was nuts but didn't know he was doing porn?" Claudia asked.

Delford frowned. "Well, maybe she did know. But I wouldn't blame her for not mentioning it."

"His friend Velvet insists he would never commit suicide."

"Let's talk about Pete's friends. This boat he was staying on, *Real Shame*. It's registered in Houston. It's owned by a fellow named Tommy Deloache. In Houston, he's known as Tommy the Roach. Suspected drug ties, suspected money launderer."

"And Pete hanging with criminals bolsters your suicide theory how?"

"From what Houston PD says, if the Deloaches wanted Pete dead, he'd be in the Gulf, sixty feet down wired to blocks. They tidy up after themselves. They don't leave bodies around to be autopsied."

She stood. "I'll keep you apprised of what I find."

"Claud, don't get bent. I'm just asking you to be sensitive to a mother's grief. Remember Lucinda's got an election in less than a month, and this could derail it."

"The senator wouldn't get more sympathy votes if he was murdered as opposed to suicide?" Claudia asked bluntly. "Suicide sounds like maybe she was a bad mother."

"Damn it, Claudia, you've never handled a death this high-profile. And my gut, which is both bigger and older than yours, tells me Pete killed himself. If you chase the wrong path and embarrass yourself, not to mention Senator Hubble, with all this unrelated garbage about porn and Corey Hubble and what not, that's going to be remembered."

He shoved his chair hard against the table.

"Well, Delford, if you don't have confidence in me, don't give me the case."

"I'm just trying to help you. The case is yours. Just mind how you run it."

She nodded, and he turned and left. Claudia stared at the door he slammed behind him.

9

"WHY DIDN'T YOU tell me Pete was back in town?" Whit asked.

He heard the sharp rasp of Faith Hubble's breath. "Oh, Whit. I didn't think it mattered. He said...he wasn't going to stay long. A couple of weeks, no more."

"If I had an ex-wife, wouldn't you have wanted to know if she showed up in Port Leo?" he asked.

"We're not...dating, Whit. We're just...I mean...oh, I can't have this conversation now. Sam's out of his mind with grief, and Lucinda's a zombie."

Whit hated having to press, but he did. "Pete was writing a screenplay, Faith. I don't think he was just waltzing in and out of Port Leo on a quick jaunt."

She couldn't hide the shock in her voice. "Movie?"

"Did you know he was in the movie business, Faith?"

"I can't...discuss this right now. Sam's real upset. He needs me."

"Fine. But I need to talk to you all tomorrow."

"I want that. I want to see you."

"Fine, I'll call you tomorrow. Please give my sympathies to the senator and Sam."

"I will. And thank you, in advance, Whit, for your help. We appreciate it."

They said their good-byes and hung up. Whit wondered exactly what kind of help he was supposed to provide, unasked.

Whit transferred his field notes to an inquest report and assigned the death a case number. He had called the ME's office in Corpus Christi as soon as he got into his office to report Pete's death and the body's expected arrival at their facility. The on-call ME had phoned back and Whit gave her a brief summation of the case. He asked her to be sure and check the corpse for any signs of foul play, although from the body's condition suicide was indicated. He hung up and watched the clouds begin to pour a thin, steady rain on the sleeping town.

He gathered up a notebook from the JP Training Center that offered details on conducting a formal death inquest, locked up his office, and headed down the darkened hall-ways of the courthouse.

Grief, in whatever variety, reminded Whit of his mother. When he was two, she had packed up and walked away from her husband and six sons and vanished into the great blue of the world, and in odd moments he ached for her touch as he might ache for a missing limb. For the first time in weeks he wondered where his mother was, if she were dead or alive. He imagined her buried under an assumed name, or her unmourned bones bleached by the sun, a victim of terrible evil. But not always. He also imagined her munching a peanut butter sandwich, licking stray dabs of plum jelly from her fingers, watching *The Tonight Show,* curled on a bed with green sheets. Green had been her favorite color, she often wore a thin green ribbon in her blond hair, at least in pictures. He could not remember if he ever played with the ribbon.

He wondered if she ever thought of him. Perhaps five sons had seemed manageable and six was just one son too many.

His mother. Corey Hubble. Both gone into the maw of the world.

The difference between Whit and Pete, Whit mused, was that Pete acted. Or at least attempted to peel back the layers of years toward truth and document what had happened to Corey.

Whit admired his guts.

So what had Pete found?

The police station's night dispatcher, a she-grizzly named Nelda, buzzed him into the building. Whit freeloaded a cup of high-voltage, road-tar coffee from her and collapsed on a rough old bench. Velvet was giving a statement to Claudia Salazar, he was told, and Nelda peered at him strangely when he said he'd wait.

Being a shoulder for Velvet was fine. A moron's level of political astuteness demanded that he do nothing more. But he knew she was alone, and he knew the shock of sudden, paralyzing loss. No harm in being friendly. Bitter pills were harder to swallow alone.

Delford Spires ambled toward him while he sipped his coffee.

"Hello, partner," Delford said. "You're not usually such a dedicated public servant."

"Just waiting for Claudia to finish up with Velvet."

"Claud can give the lady a ride to her hotel. Maybe you and I can chat for a second."

Whit followed Delford to the station's back entrance,

where the smokers were exiled under a metal canopy. The rain fell steadily and lightning webbed the sky over the Gulf.

Delford dug in his pocket for a pack of Marlboros and waited until he had one lit and two puffs down before he spoke. "So you were gonna wait on Velvet?"

"I told her I'd give her a ride and talk to her about Pete."

"A ride. I'll bet." Delford blew out a calculated plume of smoke, edging Whit's face.

"I'm just being a nice guy."

"You know what nice gets you with a loose woman?" Delford rubbed the smooth dome of his balding head. "A burning need for penicillin."

Whit waited for the next nugget of wisdom to fall from Delford's lips.

Delford exhaled another stream of smoke. "This is a hell of a mess, Whit. Hell of a mess."

"Yes. I feel bad for Lucinda Hubble." Whit tossed out a verbal card to see if Delford would trump.

Delford did. "Oh, Lord, yes. I hated to be the bearer of bad news, but she had to know. Suicide is so selfish. And this so close to the election."

Whit sipped his coffee, letting Delford believe silence signaled agreement, then said, "We don't know that it's suicide, Delford."

To their right, a blue-light bug zapper sounded a long, fuzzy trill as it dispatched some flying insect to creeper heaven. "Of course not. But I been in law enforcement thirty years, partner. Pete Hubble clearly looks like a suicide to me. No sign of struggle, big old boy like him. He put that gun in his own mouth."

Whit shrugged. "I think I'll wait for the autopsy to make

a ruling. But I sure don't see why he'd come home after all these years just to kill himself. Especially after he was starting a new film project."

"I get it. You're just interested in the media circus, get your name in the paper for the voters to see. I think you owe some common sense and courtesy to Lucinda Hubble that this be handled quickly and quietly."

"Since Dear Abby's not available," Whit said, "how does ramming a ruling through quickly get classified as common sense and courtesy?"

Delford stubbed out his smoke. "It's called decency. Try to add it to your vocabulary, partner. Lucinda's done more for this county than most people have, and she's suffered a lot of tragedy in her life. So show her some compassion."

"The woman has lost her son. I don't plan on being anything but compassionate. Especially if it turns out her son's been murdered."

"And you wouldn't change your mind because you and the senator are in different political parties?" Whit had had to make a party affiliation to get the appointment from the county commissioners, but he felt no allegiance to any political party.

"Party lines bore me, Delford."

"I imagine. The only party line you're interested in is the one leading to the keg."

Whit patted his pockets. "I like that one. I better write it down and note the time and date you actually attempted a joke."

"Listen, Whit." Delford lowered his voice but kept his amiable smile firmly fixed. "We all know you're sort of learning as you go, but you sure don't want the voters to realize that you're, shall we say, still climbing the learning curve."

"For all your preaching about compassion," Whit said, "I haven't heard you show one bit of sympathy for Pete Hubble."

"Lucinda doesn't deserve for that good-for-nothing son of hers to muddy her name from the grave. You're gonna be out there alone, Whit, looking like a fool when the police and the family—who know the truth—all say it's suicide and you're chasing shadows."

"What is this, a good-old-boy plea to stay in step?" Whit said.

Delford shook his head. "You must've sniffed some of that pink paint, son. I'm not pressuring you to do diddly. My judgment is based on years of police experience. This is your first big death case, Whit. You screw it up and it's real public, and it's right before the election." He laughed and crushed his cigarette under his boot heel. "And just a tip: voters don't vote for candidates who consort with porno queens."

Delford went back into the police station. Whit watched the rain and finished his coffee. When he went back inside, Nelda told him Claudia and Velvet had left not three minutes before. He drove home, devoured a ham sandwich and a bag of corn chips while watching a *Monty Python* rerun on cable, and went to bed with his JP training materials. He read every detail on death inquest procedures.

He wondered how the voters would react if he and his brothers painted Delford's house again.

Reading the procedures, written in law's natively ornate style, made him drowse. His thoughts drifted to the last time he had been with Faith, making hurried love in a

Laurel Point motel last week. She had seemed distracted, going through the motions of lovemaking without her usual ardor, kissing him as though she were tasting a sour peach. He had wondered if she was growing tired of him or preoccupied with Lucinda's reelection campaign. Now he wondered if it was because Pete had reentered her life.

He doused the lights. When he fell asleep he dreamed not of Faith or Irina or Velvet but of his mother, calling his name like a siren from the surf-churned rocks.

10

———◄◦►———

"THAT JUDGE," VELVET said to Claudia as they pulled into the Port Leo Best Western's half-full parking lot. "Tell me about him."

"What exactly do you want to know?"

"He said there might be an inquest. He gonna be fair?"

"Extremely fair," Claudia said.

"He looks like a beach bum not tidied up all the way," Velvet said. "I directed a movie called *Here Comes the Judge*. I know, bad title, but schlock's part of the game. I worried that Flip Wilson's estate would sue. Did great on video. I had a guy who wore nothing under his judge's robes in one scene, and he did the court reporter and half the jury."

"Wow, you really are a film visionary," Claudia said, not wanting to hear a synopsis of adult movies. "A real Scorsese."

"Aren't you the meow kitty? I guess I shock you," Velvet said.

"You're trying too hard to shock me."

"And why would I do that?"

"If you don't think what you do is wrong, and you beat people over the head with it, they'll probably keep their opinions to themselves."

"And what do you know about my profession? You know, most of the people in the adult film business are married. They work it just like a nine-to-fiver, then go home to their families."

"I'm sure there are hired killers who have white picket fences. It doesn't make it respectable." Claudia turned to her. "I don't believe in exploiting people."

"You ever use an informant in your line of work, Ms. High-and-Mighty? Maybe someone who's fallen on hard times, gotten himself in a little lick of trouble, and wants to stay out of jail? And they can, if they give you names and numbers and know who's fencing what or where the marijuana's stashed?"

Claudia stopped the car in front of the lobby doors. Rain slid down the windshield, blurring the world. "That's different. I'm enforcing the law."

"You're taking advantage of their weakness to get what you want. Don't lecture me about using people, baby. I launch careers, I let lonely guys have some fun in the privacy of their own home, I show shy ladies how to make a man their love slave forever. It's a public service, if that resonates with you."

"I have less than zero interest in debating you, Velvet. But I don't know of many women who could do what you do and not feel degraded. Tart it up however you like."

Velvet regarded her with interest. "I bet Whit wouldn't wear anything under his robe, if I asked him."

Your old one's barely cold yet. David wasn't even dead, only her spanking-new ex, but she couldn't imagine touching another man right now. "Ask him and see what happens."

"Well, hello, raw nerve," Velvet said. "Didn't mean to trespass."

"I'm not in the market, and I'm especially not in the market for Whit Mosley. I'm just being a realist. I know Whit. You're not his type, and you're involved in a case he's adjudicating."

"Men are the simplest maps, honey, and no one can unfold one better than me. I just go for the thing pointing true north, and I learn all I need to know. Whit's no different." She paused. "He up for reelection, like Lucinda?"

"Yes."

"I'm sure the Hubbles will be riding you like the Pony Express to run the investigation the way they want."

"They don't have any influence over me," Claudia said.

Velvet watched the rain splatter against the windshield. "Whit defended you to me, said you were a good investigator. I just hope he's right. I'm sure in a little town sucking up to the right people makes all the difference in promotions."

"You've suffered a really nasty shock tonight, and I'm real sorry about your friend. So I'm just going to ignore what you just said, because you don't know the first thing about me."

"You're the one who got out the label maker, sweetie." Velvet opened the car door and ran through the rain. Claudia, peeved, followed her.

They went inside the motel lobby and got Velvet checked in. Claudia asked, "You're gonna be okay here alone?"

"I'd be better if there was a wet bar. I'll settle for a shower and a bed. Thanks for the ride."

"We'll talk tomorrow," Claudia said. "I'll have a patrol officer bring you by some clothes and toiletries." Let her see actual, respectable small-town nice. Maybe she would unleash a squad of church ladies on Velvet. No one could be nicer than church ladies on a mission.

"Thank you. Now go work hard and get the person who did this," Velvet said. She turned off and went down the hall toward her room.

Claudia drove back to Golden Gulf Marina. The crowd had returned to their boats, although several craft showed lamps' glimmers from behind the curtains. People still awake, shocked at death's close amble, watching television or drinking decaf to lull themselves to sleep. In the gentle downpour she walked to *Real Shame,* watching the yellow crime scene ribbons flap in the breeze. She boarded and heard a low voice talking inside the cabin.

"Yeah, it's all taken care of. Not a problem."

She opened the door and Eddie Gardner smiled, clicking off his cell phone.

"What's going on?" she asked.

"Not much, just finishing up." He gestured to a stack of bagged items and rolls of film, neatly tagged. "How did the statements go? You squeeze a confession?"

"Hardly. The girlfriend is sure he didn't off himself, and the young woman who found the body is sure he did. I'd like to send both to Credible Witness School." Claudia thumbed through the stack of bagged items: bedding, individual items of clothing, including the pair of women's panties (Velvet had said forcefully that she owned no pair with violets on them), wineglass, wine bottles, the videotape that Whit had found.

"Find anything interesting?" she asked.

"Not counting the dirty movies, no. No contraband."

She smiled. Gardner could be a toad but he wasn't a bad guy, just overimpressed with himself. Both the other single women at the police station pined to date him, although the attraction eluded Claudia. She ought to shove Velvet toward Gardner and away from a decent guy like Whit. She'd make Gardner's day.

"Delford—with all the tact of a fart in church—told me to treat this like a suicide."

Gardner stopped piling the evidence into a case. "It looks like one."

"I know. But considering who this guy is, to automatically assume..."

"Well, Delford's a man of strong opinions, but he's solved practically every major case he's ever had. He knows police work."

"He's old friends with Lucinda Hubble. She won't want her son's movie career brought to light, and I frankly don't blame her."

Gardner shrugged again. "Look, Claudia. Delford clearly has confidence in you. If he didn't trust you, you wouldn't be here."

A sudden pang of embarrassment at having shown her doubt hit her. Gardner went back to his work, not looking at her.

"I know. Thanks. Can I give you a hand with the evidence case?"

"Naw, I got it." He hoisted a box to his shoulder. "You coming?"

"In a minute. I want another look around."

Gardner headed out the door, grunting as he carried the box. "They've got Fox sitting out on the dock all night to watch the boat, make sure no one comes aboard."

"Great. Thanks, Eddie," she said.

In Pete's bedroom, Claudia carefully flicked on a light,

using the edge of her hand. Black fingerprint dust marked the most obvious spots: the light switch, the door handle, the metal nightstand table, where Gardner and the deputies helping out from the sheriff's office had dusted and lifted prints. *I'm glad David wasn't on duty.* She didn't want to see him up close and personal quite yet, and it would be impossible to avoid with her in the police department and him in the sheriff's office.

The body and the bedding were gone. She opened the closet door. She pulled some of the files out of the box. The minutiae of everyday life: phone bills, store receipts, credit card slips, bank records, all haphazardly clumped together. Pete wasn't rich, but he wasn't destitute. He had a balance slightly over ten thousand dollars in his Van Nuys, California, account according to his most recent statement, and he'd opened a new account last week at the Texas Coastal Bank, Port Leo branch, with an opening balance of four thousand. She jotted down the Van Nuys address; she wanted to check with the police there about both Pete and Velvet. It bothered her that he was staying on a boat with ties to a criminal family. Such affiliations did not appear overnight with a snap of the fingers.

She was searching the main cabin when Gardner came back aboard.

"Hey, Eddie, did you see a laptop computer?" she asked.

Gardner inspected a handwritten inventory pulled from his pocket. "There was a small portable printer in the other room, but I didn't see a computer."

"Help me look."

Nothing turned up except some dust bunnies beneath a couch and a box of shotgun ammunition hidden in a back drawer.

"Two people have told us Pete had a laptop and now he doesn't," Claudia said.

They searched again, behind furniture, in closets, in cabinets, for another half hour.

"I don't think it's here, Claudia."

Claudia crossed her arms. "So where is it?"

11

———◆◎◆———

Early Tuesday morning Whit awoke to his father prodding at him with a thick finger.

"Get up, little bit," Babe Mosley rumbled, and Whit was lost in a childhood moment, his father between wives, Whit being ordered to rise before dawn and fix Daddy a coffee with bourbon. Breakfast at the Mosleys' had never been like in the cereal commercials.

Whit blinked at his father's frown. "Did my alarm not go off?" Hopefully he was still dreaming, if he was going to suffer being referred to as "little bit."

"Why didn't you tell us last night?" Babe demanded. Despite his childish nickname he was a big barrel of a man, close to six-five and two hundred fifty pounds. He boasted a full head of grayish blond hair and clear blue eyes, but the cherubic face had softened like a souring cheese, moldered more by the dozen-plus years he'd spent drunk. The vodka aged him more than the weight of raising six boys and marrying four wives. Years of sobriety, combined with an addiction to various fitness programs, had restored his vitality, but no medicine had erased the drunkard's veins.

"My son's the judge—a job I got you, thank you kindly— and I have to hear that Pete Hubble is dead on the radio."

Whit stumbled to the bathroom. Babe followed him to the doorway.

"Daddy, I can't talk about cases." Whit started the shower.

"This is your golden opportunity, Whitman."

Whit doffed his boxers and stepped into the hot spray. "Say what?"

"Lucinda Hubble rules this county like Queen Bee Victoria. This story's gonna be huge. It's your chance to show the voters what you can do, boy."

"I thought that's what I was doing for the past six months." Whit squirted shampoo into his hand and soaped his hair.

"Yes, but this gets your name in the papers. Front page. You got to milk this, son. When you gonna do the inquest? You'll want to do a formal one, not just issue a cause of death. Make sure the Corpus paper's there. Get your photo taken a bunch, maybe at the crime scene. In your robe, and wear proper shoes for once. Issue press releases, all that." Babe rubbed his hands together. "That Buddy Beere must be passing bricks with all this terrific publicity you're gonna get."

"You get this morning's merit badge for good taste," Whit said. "A man is dead, you know."

"I'm sorry for Pete and the Hubbles—you know that. What was Pete doing back anyway? Where's he been?"

"Working for the CIA," Whit answered above the roar of the shower, to give Babe a meaty morsel. "Something about nuclear release codes in Ukraine. Perhaps we shouldn't tell Irina."

"You're not amusing to your daddy."

"Oddly enough, making you laugh about a death case

wasn't on my to-do list today. I got breakfast at the Shell Inn with Patsy and Tim."

Babe frowned. "You tell Georgie to quit slinging mud all over town about poor helpless Irina."

"News flash. You not only remarry again but you fund a competing café. Of course she's mad at you." Whit rinsed shampoo from his head and soap from his body. Babe handed him a towel.

"Georgie'll forgive me—she always does. Women are far better at forgiving than men could ever be," Babe said.

Whit thought of Faith Hubble and wondered if that was really true.

The Shell Inn was an establishment one might generously term a *hybrid*. The front of the restaurant offered serviceable meals, catering to the fishing crowd and the retirees who refused to slap down more than five bucks for a meat-and-two-vegetable plate. The back contained a funky, dark bar that boasted its own atmosphere—breezes of bourbon, mists of beer, warm fronts of tobacco smoke. For the old guard of Port Leo the Shell Inn, which had been in continuous business since 1907 except the five times it was nearly destroyed by hurricanes, was a basic requirement of life in town, up there with a newspaper and water service.

Georgie O'Connor Mosley perched by the cash register, sipping milky coffee and contemplating the *Corpus Christi Caller-Times* financial section. She had been Whit's first stepmother, his mother's oldest and dearest friend. Georgie and Babe had married more out of friendship and a mutual hope to provide six devastated boys a mother, but those reasons shriveled under the never-setting sun of reality.

Georgie, relentlessly practical and blunt, and Babe, a roaring drunk still in love with an absent first wife, only lasted three stormy, legendary years. The six Mosley boys all loved Georgie without reserve. They knew the bullet she had taken for them. Babe had bought the Shell Inn for her the Christmas after their divorce, a parting gift, and Georgie kept the Mosley name to irritate him.

"Tell your daddy he should've listened to me about those overseas stock funds," Georgie said as Whit entered. "I'm making a killing. I could buy and sell Babe right now."

"He's more conservative with his money," Whit said.

"I would think anyone who imports firm young former Communist flesh into his bed would be receptive to new ideas." Georgie kissed his cheek—she smelled of lip balm and oranges—and steered him to his corner table where Patsy Duchamp and Tim O'Leary sat.

"No coffee for Whit, Georgie, until he gives me a quote," Patsy Duchamp said as Whit sat down. Patsy was the editor of the *Port Leo Mariner,* a biweekly paper, and like Whit she had trudged home carting an English degree from a prestigious college. Patsy's hair was as dark as a crow's feathers; she had sharp, penetrating eyes; and she rationed her smiles.

"No comment, Patsy," Whit said as Georgie sloshed steaming coffee into Whit's cup.

"Quote, please." Patsy's breakfast had already arrived, and she stirred a pat of butter into her grits.

"It looks like he died of a gunshot wound, but I'm not saying anything official until we get an autopsy report from Corpus."

"I heard it looked self-inflicted," Patsy said.

"I for sure have no comment now."

"Then you'll call me the moment you know what the ME says, anyway. Or you better," Patsy said. "Pretty please."

"When did you take a Pollyanna pill?" Pete Hubble's death might be the biggest story of the year, of the past five years, especially if it was murder, and Patsy lived for news to cover beyond city council and navigation district meetings, fishing tournaments, and high school football.

"You talk to the senator yet?" asked Tim O'Leary, the county attorney. Tim looked worn this morning.

"No. Late night?" Whit asked.

"Yeah."

"Too much merlot or too much Graham Greene last night?" Whit asked. Tim only had two vices.

"It was an Australian cabernet, and too much Greene is impossible," Tim said.

"You two aren't gonna start talking literature and ignore all this juicy news," Patsy said. "So let's talk Pete Hubble."

"Actually, let's not," Whit said. "Let's talk about Corey Hubble."

Patsy lowered her eggy fork. "Oh, I smell me an ongoing series of stories."

"Patsy, if I farted, would it be off the record?" Whit asked.

Patsy looked stung. "Fine, we're miles off the record."

Whit glanced around. No one was seated close to their table, an orchestration of Georgie's. "Tell me what you remember about Corey Hubble."

"Annoying," Tim said.

"A rotten little punk," Patsy said.

"Never got over his daddy's death," Tim agreed.

"Mad at the world," Patsy added.

"Pissed at his own shadow," Tim said.

"A pothead," Patsy said. "He hung around with dopers, you know."

"I always thought he was gay. He hated sports." Tim might relish his thick Tolstoys and full-bodied syrahs, but he also worshiped football and fishing, preferences iron-cast in most male Coastal Bend genes.

"Not gay," Patsy said. "Corey dated my cousin Marian. In a way that should have gotten them on *Jerry Springer*. They beat each other up a couple of times. If memory serves, Marian told me Corey would diddle her for exactly one minute with a look of incredible gratitude on his face and then slap her around." She lowered her voice. "And I heard once he used to torture cats and Lucinda sent him to a therapist in Corpus, but that might have been political mudslinging. Cats are big with the retiree vote."

"Do you remember anything about when Corey vanished?" Whit asked. His regular order of scrambled eggs, garlic cheese grits, bacon, and biscuits arrived, and Patsy and Tim waited until the waitress had refilled their coffee cups and retreated.

"People said he'd run away to embarrass his mother." Tim gave a hangover frown to Whit's food. "When he never came back, then I think everyone imagined he'd been murdered while hitchhiking or some other unpleasant end."

Patsy nodded. "It was common knowledge Corey resented Lucinda's career in politics. He'd already lost a father, and now here was his mother throwing herself into the most time-consuming career possible. Probably he got involved with the wrong people somewhere, South Padre or Galveston or Mexico, and ended up dead."

Whit made a leap of faith that Patsy would stick to her

word about being off the record. "Do you remember Corey and Jabez Jones being particular friends?"

Tim faked puking. "It annoys me no end that what Port Leo is going to be known for on television is an ex-wrestler who performs ab crunches while quoting Scripture."

"You know, if my memory's not fading with age, Jabez was the last person to talk to Corey," Patsy said. "I covered it in the high school paper."

"Could you do me a huge favor and dig up the clippings from when Corey vanished?" Whit asked.

"Nothing more you can say?" Patsy asked.

"No. Can I still have the clippings?"

"Lucky for you there are little retired ladies bored enough to do schlepp work at the *Mariner*. Sure, but what will you do for me?" Patsy asked.

"I'll call you as soon as I have prelim autopsy results," Whit promised.

Patsy smiled. Like the Aztec goddesses, blood placated her.

Claudia had just finished showering after four hours of fidgety sleep when the knock came at her door. She pulled on her robe, wrapped her heavy black hair in a towel, and peered through the door's security hole.

David.

She had not seen him since he walked alongside her down the county courthouse hallway, saying quietly, *Listen, I'm sorry you did this, Claud. You know I still love you*. Her attorney had tucked a hand on her elbow and steered her away, past the flyers and the benches and the secretary puzzling over a soda choice at the Coke machine and out to the bright fall light, the morning haze burning to wisps over the bay. She had walked in married and walked out free and clear. She had gotten in her car, suddenly flustered and near weeping, and driven halfway across Port Leo toward the home they shared before she remembered she didn't live there anymore.

But she did still live in Port Leo, and both she and David were peace officers. Why not grab the inevitable by the throat and give it a good shake? She opened the door.

"Morning," David Power said. He'd gotten his auburn hair cropped shorter than usual. He wore his Encina County deputy's uniform, and she noticed the creases were flattened. She had tended his uniform for him, since he'd burn his hand if he got within ten feet of an iron. Dark circles daubed the fleshiness beneath his eyes, and he'd missed a patch of reddish bristle on his jaw during his shave.

"Good morning. What's up?" *Keep it brief, keep it polite.*

"Just wanted to see if you were okay. I heard about the Hubble case."

"Short on sleep, but fine."

David shifted his beige Stetson from one hand to another. "You know, if y'all need help, the sheriff's department, we're glad to assist."

"Thanks. It's under control." She didn't say anything further, and he massaged the brim of his hat, drumming his fingertips against the band.

"Everything okay in your new place?" he asked.

"Yeah, sure." She knew he wanted to be invited in, but she didn't want him in the little space she had staked out for her own. She drew the robe a little tighter around her front in atypical modesty.

His voice lowered. "Claud, I've seen your skin before. Remember Padre?"

They had honeymooned on South Padre, the mightiest and most beautiful of the long chain of Texas barrier islands, and unfortunately it had been the best time in the marriage, a week away from both their cloying families, a week away from car wrecks and burglaries and speeding tickets. David loved to invoke Padre, as if teeth-chilling margaritas, orange-bright sunsets, and spine-rattling sex could serve as the basis for the rest of their lives.

"David..."

His blue eyes narrowed and his fleshy mouth thinned. "You're alone, right?"

"I told you there's no one."

"Right. I never hit you. Took wonderful care of you. Never cheated on you. You just don't love me anymore. Same old, same old."

"Are you coming to check up on me, spy on me, or belittle me?" She kept her voice neutral.

David Power's jaw worked. "Check on you. Sorry. I crossed a line. It still hurts. It's gonna hurt for...an indeterminate period of time. I don't want to hurt you back, Claudia."

"I'm sorry for your hurt. I am. But we've had this discussion a hundred times before, and there's no point in rehashing."

Her phone rang and she said, "Look, I've got to get going..." and he said, "I need to ask you about something else..." so she shrugged and said, "Wait a sec..." and hurried to the telephone.

"Hello?"

"Claudia Salazar?" A throaty woman's voice but brisk as a Marine.

"Yes, who's calling?"

"Hold please," ordered Captain Brisk. Instead of Muzak there was a recorded, sleek baritone, with soft strains of "America the Beautiful" playing in the background. The voice intoned: "Proven leadership for the Texas Coastal Bend...Senator Lucinda Hubble. Protecting our children. Protecting our elderly. Protecting our precious coastal ecology and protecting our health care while protecting our economy." Lots of protection. Claudia wondered if the faithful automatically wore condoms during rallies. "A former nurse, Senator Hubble especially understands the needs and concerns of our retiree population. Vote November seventh to reelect Senator Lucinda Hub—"

The verbal pabulum broke off. "Ms. Salazar?" Not Miss Brisk, but instead a confident, bright voice.

"Yes, this is Detective Salazar." Claudia had a sudden feeling she was going to need the title. She turned and saw David had stepped inside the apartment, shutting the door behind him, and he blanched as she used her maiden name. She had been Claudia Power for the twenty-two months of the marriage, but no more, and David in particular seemed to take her revived surname as a hard slap.

The voice on the phone honeyed slightly. "Detective. Good morning. This is Faith Hubble. I'm Senator Hubble's chief of staff."

"I'm sorry about your ex-husband, Ms. Hubble."

"Thank you. It's a terrible tragedy. My mother-in-law and my son are having a difficult time with Pete's death."

And you're not? Claudia wondered. "That's understandable."

"I'd like to meet with you and find out where we are in the investigation."

We, Claudia noticed, as though Faith Hubble were busily lifting prints and completing paperwork into the wee hours. "We've collected a certain amount of evidence, but we don't as yet have autopsy results. I would like to talk with you and your family as soon as possible."

"Talking with Lucinda—is that absolutely necessary? She's absolutely grief-stricken. And we already gave our statements to Delford Spires."

"Yes, ma'am, and I'm sure this is a difficult time for you all but, yes, I do need to speak with her, as will Judge Mosley."

"Perhaps you and I could meet first. To discuss how to deal with the media."

Claudia watched David inspecting her bare apartment, his face emotionless. "We already have policies in place, ma'am."

"Yes, I'm sure you do, but this is far more high-profile than a drunken tourist drowning, and there's already been serious news leaks," Faith said. "Let's meet in an hour, shall we, at your office?"

"Fine." Let them meet to discuss the press, but Claudia would seize the opportunity for a frank discussion with the dead man's former wife.

"See you in an hour." Faith Hubble hung up.

Claudia clicked off the phone. David stood at the apartment's large window, looking at the parking lot. "You should have gotten a bay view, Claudia."

"I've seen the bay every day of my life," she said. She didn't want to mention she couldn't afford a bay view on her single-woman salary. "Thanks for stopping by, but duty calls."

"Speaking of duty…Poppy's birthday is this coming weekend, and I was hoping you could go to his party with me." Poppy was David's grandfather, Patrick Power, closing in on ninety, now relegated to the care of a Port Leo nursing home but still the patriarch of the old-coast Irish clan. "If you're not there, Poppy will wonder why."

"Oh, David, that's not a good idea."

"Um, well"—he gave her a half-apologetic smile—"Poppy doesn't know about the divorce, Claud. He doesn't believe in divorce and we haven't wanted to upset him. His heart's weak, you know."

Claudia believed Poppy's heart could serve as a rich source of granite. "Tell him, David. I'm not going to play along in a charade."

"Thanks a bunch, Claudia. Please. One favor. You know how Poppy loves you."

"Yes, he's never missed a chance to pat my fanny."

"You want to hurt me, fine, whatever. Just don't hurt my family."

"I don't want to hurt anybody! I just want to have my own life!" Now she was yelling, doing exactly what she had promised herself not to do.

"This life is what you want?" David gestured at the drab apartment. She had hardly unpacked any belongings in the month she had been here. A few Salazar family pictures stood on a dusty coffee table, dishes stacked in the sink, a futon unfolded in the den and sloppy with sheets. She'd let David keep most of the furniture just to spare herself the whining. "You don't seem to be relishing your singleness."

"I'm busy with work," she said. "Aren't you?" Anything to change the topic.

"Yeah. I'm working this missing-person case. Girl from Louisiana they think ended up here."

"Marcy Ballew? You got that one?"

"Yeah."

"I briefly met the girl's mother when she stopped by the station," Claudia said. "Terrible, not knowing what happened."

David, that master of the wounded glance and gesture, took full advantage. "Yeah. Not knowing what went wrong. I know exactly how the lady feels."

12

SIX BERTHS DOWN from *Real Shame,* where Pete Hubble breathed his last, was a fifty-three-foot workhorse Hatteras sports fishing boat christened *Don't Ask.* This was a craft used to take serious fishermen out into the deeper bowl of the Gulf, where the marlin and shark (hopefully) provided thrills at an exorbitant hourly rate. *Don't Ask* belonged to an oddball friend of Whit's, a man known to most people simply as Gooch. Gooch did not socialize overmuch. He was unfailingly polite and ethical in his dealings with other guides, the marina, and his clients, and admired for making small loans to guides who frequently needed a cash boost at the end of the month. Most of Port Leo was happy to give him his privacy, because Gooch was ugly and big and had a hard, no-tolerance light in his glare that explained his boat's name. Whit had only found him to be generous, loyal, and slightly east of sane.

For twenty minutes Whit had been mired in quicksand conversation with the marina manager, who could tell him nothing new about Pete and Velvet. The manager, who smelled slightly of soured baby formula and had an unnoticed glob of infant burp on his shoulder, explained that *Real Shame* had begun docking at Golden Gulf only five weeks ago and its bills were paid by check mailed from a company in Houston, TDD Holdings. The arrangement had been handled by an elderly man in a wheelchair who apparently worked for TDD, name of Anson Todd, and the manager had not seen Mr. Todd again since the *Shame* docked. As for Pete and Velvet, they had not mingled much with the other marina residents, nor had they caused any trouble. Whit left the office, spotted Gooch on his boat, and headed down the T-head.

"An honest man would be at work by now," Whit said as he came aboard.

"I chose to use this day for reflection and self-improvement." Gooch grinned, showing slightly uneven teeth. "I gave myself the day off. I figured you'd be back down here soon enough."

Kindness demanded one say Gooch was simply not handsome. His face was too gaunt for his body and married a too-prominent, bumpy nose with small, muddy brown eyes. He kept his sun-streaked hair cut short in a military burr. But he was powerfully built, stone-carved arms and legs, the kind of physique that encouraged burly bar patrons to keep observations about Gooch's unfortunate face private.

"Coffee, Y'Honor?" Gooch asked.

"Please, with milk and sugar."

Gooch pointed toward the galley.

"You're the embodiment of the service economy, Gooch." Whit fixed his own cup and went back up to the deck, where Gooch gobbled his way through a leviathan bowl of Cap'n Crunch.

"You want some?" he asked through a milk-dripping mouth.

"No, thanks."

"Screw your stepmom yet?"

"My father and Irina are very happy, thanks for asking."

"And you're very miserable," Gooch said.

"You've got to make some more room on this wall for your diplomacy awards," Whit said. "I didn't see you docked here last night when duty called."

"I spent the evening over in Port Aransas playing poker. I didn't sail home until this morning."

"Were the gossips awake?" No hen yard could compare to marina liveaboards for rapid-fire rumormongering.

"All I've heard is that the guy on *Real Shame* shot himself in the mouth. Now it'd be a real shame indeed if that hot little number living with him on the boat really did it and got herself sent to girly prison, where she could never experience the joys of Gooch."

"You've met Velvet?"

"Her name is Velvet?"

"Velvet Mojo."

"Stripper or actress?"

"An adult-film director."

Gooch set down his cereal bowl. "No, we haven't met. Cute but rough. Like a mare that's been rode hard and put up wet, like my dad used to say."

"Who would know about them here?"

Gooch shrugged. "They kept to themselves. Not much for fishing and not much for boating. I saw them docking once. They needed about five people to help them dock properly." He considered. "Probably they talked with Ernesto." Gooch went to his radio and spoke briefly. He left the radio on to hear the chatter of the working fishermen and guides across St. Leo Bay and beyond. Whit could hear three or four male voices, joking, chattering, one complaining about a dearth of redfish, someone asking that a poker game be rescheduled for tomorrow, someone else hailing Captain Bill. "Ernesto's the marina handyman. He sees the cops coming, he hides, so I bet no authority figure has taken a statement. He'll be down in a second. So spill details."

Whit told Gooch, who he would trust with the launch keys for America's nuclear arsenal, what he knew thus far about Pete Hubble.

Gooch laughed. "Lucinda Hubble walks around town like she's got a coal lump up her tush and none of us are good enough to sniff the diamond. Her boy's off making adult films. I love it."

"You've got to quit being overly sympathetic to people, Gooch."

"I wonder if this Velvet was planning to ply her trade here."

"Please don't tell me you want to audition."

Gooch tapped his unshaven chin. "It's an interesting moral dilemma. Most men pretend to have fantasies straight out of a porn movie, but how many would actually walk the walk and show their worth in front of rolling cameras?"

"Not me. I'm too shy."

Gooch watched Ernesto Gomez hurry down the T-head. "I, on the other hand, have a decided lack of inhibitions. I would be a natural, strutting among the starlets. But I wouldn't do a porn film either."

"Why not?"

"Any time you see a blue movie, remember this: those women were once somebody's baby girls. Do you think a single one of them thought in kindergarten: Gosh, when I grow up, please, please let me be smart and talented enough to be a porn star? No way. They're Barbie dolls who got bent along the way."

Whit sipped his coffee. "Pete Hubble was a kid once, too."

"So he had some deep-seated shortcoming, and he was proving he was a so-called real man. Or maybe he wanted to piss off Mommy. Or maybe he wanted to just lose himself and forget some nastiness. This concludes our Psych 101 lecture." Gooch shrugged. "I feel as sorry for him as I do for the women."

"Even though he got to sleep with more women than you or I ever will? Combined?"

"So he screwed hundreds of women. You think he got to *sleep* with them? No, Whit. No real kissing, holding, enjoying each woman for her unique sparkle in her eyes, the taste of her skin, the shape of her lips when you bring her pleasure. No. It was assembly-line sex. No, thanks."

Gooch stood and invited Ernesto Gomez in rapid-fire Spanish to come aboard. Ernesto was in his fifties, with a moon-wide face centered by a nervous smile. His left eye wandered slightly, and he kept that side of his face turned a bare angle away. In Spanish, Gooch offered him coffee and asked if they could converse in English as Whit's Spanish was execrable. Ernesto nodded and kept his tight grin locked in place.

"Judge Mosley grew up with the man who died," Gooch added.

Ernesto frowned in sympathy. "Very sad, yes."

"Did you notice many visitors to his boat?" Whit asked.

Ernesto glanced at Gooch, who murmured in Spanish and nodded reassuringly.

"Pete had a few visits. A rich-looking lady. A teenage boy. The dirtbag."

The rich-looking lady was probably either Lucinda or Faith. The boy was no doubt Pete's son Sam. "The dirtbag?" Whit asked.

Ernesto's face wrinkled in distaste. "*Sí*. Bossy, no respect, young, too good for everyone else. Has Porsche but keep it dirty, don't take care of it."

"You know this guy's name?" Gooch asked.

Ernesto shook his head. "Sorry, Gooch. He come here once, twice a week, over the past month or so. Take the boat out for all the day, come back at night. Fishing I suppose. One time they argue, I'm fixing rot two boats down, I hear them. Laughing, yelling. Much drinking."

"What did they argue about?"

Ernesto murmured to Gooch in a low torrent of Spanish. Gooch patted him on the knee. Ernesto glanced back at Whit.

"Money," the old man said. "Money to be paid to Pete."

"This man owed Pete money?"

Ernesto considered and scratched his lip. "I think that how it was."

"Yet you said they were partying together."

"Not yesterday, not after arguing."

"Can you tell me what they said?" Whit asked.

Ernesto grimaced. "They talk too fast for my English. But dirtbag all red in the face. I hear them yelling, I come over to the boat, want to be sure all is okay. I see through the windows. Dirtbag took swing at Pete, but Pete, he strong and big. Dirtbag just heavy, has hands of man who never works. Pete pushed him down. Dirtbag left, very angry."

Ernesto, pressed, gave a more detailed description of Dirtbag: heavyset, around five-ten, blondish, late twenties or early thirties, thinning hair, bright clothing, always loud.

"The teenage boy you saw—do you know a young man named Sam Hubble?"

"No. I saw the boy once, yesterday at lunch. I guess skipping school."

"Any others you can remember?"

"Yeah, short guy last week. Handed me a piece of paper on his way to Pete's boat, blue and red and white, talked plenty. Smelled like mints, too much mints, you know?"

"That sounds like your esteemed opponent Buddy Beere," Gooch said. "Isn't he an unrepentant Altoid sucker?"

"This paper, what did it say?" Whit asked.

Ernesto waved hands. "Wanting folks to vote. You see all those signs around now."

"Campaign flyers from Buddy," Gooch said. "That savvy bastard, courting the illegal immigrant vote."

"Did you hear anything last night?" Whit asked.

"No, nothing until the cops came. I was asleep."

"You ever see any young women coming around to his boat?" Whit asked.

Ernesto nodded. "Yeah, I forgot, with that preacher. The one on TV with the big muscles. He brought lady with him. But she big and scary, big muscles." Ernesto glanced back toward the marina office. "Mike be mad I not working."

"Don't worry about Mike," Whit said. "Have the police talked to you about this?"

Ernesto appeared stricken. "No, please, mister, no *policía*. I don't know nothing about nothing."

"It's okay. Don't worry," Whit soothed. "One other question. The woman named Velvet. You see her around much?"

Ernesto smiled. "Velvet. Yes. She bakes good chocolate cookies. Every few days give some to me."

Velvet baking cookies. Whit tried to summon the image and pictured a hausfrau in a leather apron and stiletto heels.

"You ever see her bake an éclair?" Gooch asked with a leer. Ernesto looked confused, so Whit asked: "Did she and Pete get along okay?"

"Sure, yeah."

"She mess around with any of the guys around the marina?" Gooch asked.

"No. She nice." Ernesto put the bright smile back on. End of commentary.

"*Gracias*. I appreciate it, Ernesto." Whit shook his hand. Ernesto hurried back toward the marina office.

"I'm guessing the rich lady was Lucinda," Gooch said. "Unless there's a bored matron around here in need of sexual servicing. Your stepmother, for instance."

"Funny, with a hint of vicious."

"You could outdo Pete Hubble on the annoying-your-relatives scale if you do your Oedipus impersonation, Whitman."

"Gooch, you're a crank. I'm finding a place to live right after the campaign…"

"Ah, yes. The campaign. Waging a fierce one, aren't you? I particularly enjoyed your interview on *Face the Nation*."

"Are you done?"

"Whit, please campaign today. The thought of Buddy Beere at the bench makes me want to move to a judicially sound country. Like Cuba."

Whit's cell phone buzzed. "Hello?"

"Whit? It's Faith." She sounded crisper this morning, less frayed with shock.

"How are you?"

"We're holding up. Lucinda finally slept last night; Sam slept with me. To just get his dad back and then...it's a hard thing for a kid."

"I need to talk to y'all. For the inquest."

"Would this afternoon work for you?"

"Yeah. How about four?"

"Fine." Her voice lowered. "I wish I could see you...just us. I could use a hug. Or something stronger."

He didn't flirt back, watching a gull alight on the bow of *Real Shame*. "How's Sam handling this?"

"My son is a tightly controlled mass of nerves. He's upset but he doesn't want to show that he is. His father did matter to him, even a lousy SOB like Pete." Her tone turned bitter. "A father always would."

"What can I do to help?"

He meant to help Sam, but Faith took the inches and made them miles. "Please just...hurry us through all this legal rigmarole. Don't drag it out with a public inquest hearing. Help me protect Lucinda and Sam from what is sure to be unpleasantness, Whit. You'll do that for me, won't you?" Her tone, usually cool, even in wriggles of heat, took on a slightly cajoling tone.

"I'll do what I can."

The quiet stretched. But she finally said, "I appreciate it. I'll see you at the house later."

Whit clicked off his phone. Gooch studied a tidal chart and yawned.

"I must have a gift certificate for unwanted advice. Do this, do that. Rule it's suicide. Don't hold a formal inquest."

Gooch raised a crooked brown eyebrow. "Rule how you please, Judge, and screw 'em if they can't take a joke."

13

VELVET CAME AWAKE suddenly, in the bright haze from the motel windows. She rubbed her eyes and thought: *So now starts the rest of your life. What are you going to do?*

Sleep remained impossible after that prissy cop dropped her off at the motel. She lay awake, listening to the hum of the air conditioner as it chilled the room, and the gentle bump of her heart as she hugged a goose-feather pillow close to her body.

Pete dead. And only yesterday he'd said to her: *I'm not gonna do another flick with you until all this with my brother is settled, understand? You can help me or you can fly back to California, but I'm not leaving now.*

She'd pouted, furious. *Well, if you loved me you would.*

He'd set his lips tight and turned away from her. *I guess I don't love you, then, Velvet.*

And now, even though she was sure Pete hadn't meant it—the words could not be undone now, loved away, erased, made into meaningless wisps.

Velvet thought about Lucinda Hubble and Faith Hubble, and a hot cinder formed in her heart. *Hatred* was too polite a word for what she felt. She thought of young Sam Hubble and her throat tightened, for Sam and Pete and what could never be. If God were merciful, Pete strutted in heaven now, and her own mother might be meeting him at the pearly gates, smiling at him with all the love she'd once lavished on Velvet, taking him by the hand, introducing him to the other souls flitting from cloud to cloud.

That image made her cry. *Like you believe in that anymore, girl.* Pete was probably frying in hell and scooting over in the bubbling oil to make room for her.

The cry did her good. Velvet dried her tears on the pillowcase. Enough weepiness, it was time for action. She needed a Plan B. The Hubbles clearly wielded influence here. The local powers-that-be, she suspected, would treat her as Pete's embarrassing girlfriend if it was suicide and a possible suspect if it was murder.

And she had zero intention of sitting like a lump and letting herself be moved around the political chessboard.

She decided Claudia Salazar would be useless, but Whit Mosley wouldn't. She reviewed the mental picture she'd formed of him: nicely tall, trim, full blondish hair, tan but not from idling on a beach, face a little too boyish for his years, kindness in the smile. Smart but not snotty, a beach bum grown up, perhaps only recently. Average teeth, firm legs and butt, terrific hands—the checklist of how she typically evaluated the rookie male talent for her movies on initial meeting, before the pants dropped. She liked a man with strong hands. The hands were seen more in the movies than you would think—cupping breasts, running fingers through hair, holding faces for a kiss. And Whit might be putty to a woman with her talent and charms and persuasive skills.

At nine in the morning she called her production company's lawyers in Van Nuys and a few friends, ignoring the time difference between the Texas coast and California, breaking the sad news about Pete. She left a voice mail for the lawyers to find her some legal representation in Corpus Christi, a big-city attorney hardened enough to deal with state senators and provincial police.

Then she took a bath, relaxing herself in the soapy hot water, and only when a stray thought crossed her mind did she sit upright in a panic.

What if whoever killed Pete thought she knew what Pete knew?

She didn't. He'd kept his research about Corey tight to his chest, just telling her all was going well. He had discussed none of the screenplay with her.

The killer might not believe that. She dried off, combed her hair, and sat naked as she leafed through the Coastal Bend yellow pages, researching pawnshops and gun dealers.

The images played across the television, the screen the only light in the cabin, and the Blade sat and watched as Big Pete Majors took Velvet Mojo from behind, both of them grunting like animals, she tilting her head to keep her wraparound sunglasses on during the pounding encounter. They moaned so much it sounded like they had intestinal disorders. Pete did not offer a range of theatrical nuance. He just knelt behind her, ramming with his hips while Velvet pleaded with him to go stronger and faster, more like a testy coach than a lover. Pete's face was as blank as the boys the Blade remembered from the mental home. He watched the tape twice before he finally fell asleep in his recliner.

He awoke in a sour mood because he had dreamed not

of Velvet but of Whit Mosley, laughing at him. *You? She's gonna pick you over me? What reality does that happen in, loser?* The Blade had watched Whit in public and women smiled at him, whereas women suddenly recalled other appointments and hurried on their way when the Blade tried long conversations. Hating Whit was easy. The Blade imagined Whit dead, hollowed out, and himself stepping into Whit's skin, pulling the pallid skull-less face over his own like a mask, fitting his fingers into Whit's fingers like gory gloves.

Why not kill Mosley as well as take Velvet? He considered. Dismemberment held a certain appeal, as did evisceration, although they certainly cut short the fun. He considered decapitation overrated; heads seemed mocking without bodies attached. The Blade had learned that truth the hard way.

He'd never wanted to kill a man particularly before, but it promised an interesting difference—like fries after a solid week of potato chips. He daydreamed about Whit dying from a slow, careful series of cuts, and a slow whisper filtered into his ears. He stared at the ceiling and its whirring fan. The fan, spinning, resembled a dark eye. Mama's eyes. He stared, barely breathing, only hearing Mama's voice telling him what he must do.

He awoke and knew he had slipped to that inky world that Mama had shaped. She used to say, with her sure smile, right before she warmed the wrench on the stove or clicked the clothespin shut on his little privates: *We're together forever, honeybunch, and don't you ever forget it.*

It was a good thing, he would think, that he had managed to become the hero of his own story. Mama had not won. He had. He would still.

His phone rang; he picked up and chatted through morning niceties, then listened.

"This young woman who found Pete's body," the familiar voice murmured into his ear. "Do me a favor. Give her some money. Get her out of town."

"Sure," said the Blade. "I can do that for you."

"Santa Fe is lovely this time of year, and I bet there's a nice, affordable youth hostel. Or perhaps Florida, if she's still set on a beach." He listened to detailed instructions and hung up the phone.

His thumb began to itch for the keen sharpness of his knife. If Heather Farrell needed to leave town...well, many were the avenues. A hefty bribe paled compared to other options. He'd gotten away with this every time. (Well, except that one time, so very long ago.) Why not again? He was already in the mood.

He considered how best to approach the problem and how to avoid any messy ramifications. A lure, simple, would do. Nothing could interfere, after all, with his plan for Velvet. He ducked under the sagging bed he slept on and reached for his Bowie knife. It was lovely, stout, and sharp enough to cut hopes and dreams. He rummaged in a box with MAMA'S STUFF written on the side in thick Magic Marker and found a worn sharpening stone. The Blade dragged the knife back and forth across the stone, a rhythmic caress that whispered: *Heath-er, Heath-er, Heath-er.*

The Blade flicked on his stereo. The Beach Boys sang in perfect harmony about their 409, and the knife moved to the beat.

14

CLAUDIA WROTE A terse report on the investigation's status and left it on Delford's empty desk. She grabbed a cup of thin coffee from the kitchen. When she got back to her desk, the dispatcher was buzzing her. She had a visitor in the lobby, Faith Hubble.

"I get the feeling," the dispatcher whispered, "she don't like waiting."

The lobby was barely ten feet by ten feet, cramped with a chair, a side table of old magazines, and a rack of flyers on safety and community policing. The woman sat in the chair, pulling a loose string from the tattered upholstery and snapping it with her fingernail.

"Mrs. Hubble? I'm Claudia Salazar."

Faith stood and offered a hand. They shook hands quickly, and Faith followed Claudia back to her office.

From their phone conversation, Claudia had pictured a different woman. She'd imagined one of those no-nonsense Austin politicos, health-club firm and sorority-girl petite, blond-helmet hair, with a crisp suit and jump-when-I-say demeanor. Faith Hubble was a big-boned woman, approaching six feet tall, generously chested and thighed, with a creamy complexion and thick brown hair arranged in a hurried French braid. Pretty but loosely put together. Her Italian suit was tailored, black with a white silk blouse, but the jacket was already rumpled and a smear of jam soiled the cuff. Claudia imagined Faith more at home on a honky-tonk bar stool than a campaign trail.

"Have a seat, Mrs. Hubble."

"Thanks for seeing me on such short notice, hon. I assume we're both pressed for time, so I won't dillydally with you—what's the status of the investigation?" Faith kept her eyes—bright hazel beauties—firmly fixed on Claudia's face, like a drill sergeant surveying a sweating recruit.

"Mostly we're waiting for lab reports." Claudia was uneasy with the idea of snapping to and giving this woman a complete rundown, but she suspected Delford would provide the Hubbles all the information. There was little point in being evasive.

"And when will the lab geeks deliver?"

"Tomorrow. Or the next day."

"Any way to rush them?" Faith asked. "Obviously the family wants to know what happened as soon as possible." Her voice was low and throaty, as though corroded by cigarettes or whiskey.

"Science can't be rushed. Certain tests take a certain amount of time." Claudia paused. "I'm sure you and the senator wouldn't want the tests to be inaccurate."

"Honey, I'm dealing with a devastated mother and a heartbroken son. They need some sort of closure."

No grief of your own? Claudia thought. Faith Hubble carried herself more like a woman inconvenienced than bereaved. *How would you feel now if David died, though?* A sense of loss would be inescapable. David had not been a bad husband, just not the right one for her. Their life had not been all misery. She hoped her heart would be big enough to mourn his passing.

Faith straightened her sleeve, noticed the jam, and muttered in anger. Her fingernails were painted cranberry red, and she clicked them together impatiently.

"I'm also dealing with a press corps with a decided lack of scandal or news in this campaign, and they're gonna be on Pete's death like dogs on ribs. They got deadlines and imaginations, hon, and they're gonna write. I'd like to be sure your department doesn't feed them newsy tidbits that are inappropriate."

"We've told the press nothing but the bare essentials. That a man was found dead on a boat at the marina and we're investigating."

"Pete's death was all over the radio this morning, Detective. They knew his name, that he was Lucinda's son."

"I'm sure the press spoke to people at the marina. People could see which boat we swarmed over, I guess they knew his name. I'm afraid we can't stifle the public. Or Pete's friend Velvet."

Faith rubbed her forehead. "Do you know what it's like to have your life be tabloid fodder? It's like showering in a glass bathroom." She shook her head. "I know...that y'all know what Pete did for a living. Delford told us. And I can't let Aaron Crawford use this to defeat Lucinda. He could use Pete's suicide as an unfair disparagement on Lucinda's abilities as a mother."

He was your husband. Father of your child. Do you even care one bit about him? Claudia wondered. "Such a tactic might backfire. Voters might see it as a rotten attempt to gain from Mrs. Hubble's personal loss."

"Never overestimate the voters," Faith said.

"No confidential information will leak from this department. I'll be sure all press inquiries are routed to me or Delford."

"I'm thinking of my son. Not the political damage to Lucinda," Faith said. "Sam…doesn't know. You understand."

"Sure."

"And I would like to review any announcements that your department makes on the investigation."

Claudia stiffened. "That's not going to be possible."

Faith set her chin in her palm and kept her tone relaxed. "Let me clarify, hon. I said review. Not approve or edit or block. If you're going to release damaging information about Pete, I'd like the opportunity to prepare a statement on the senator's behalf. Surely that's reasonable."

Claudia suddenly felt dumb in the face of this woman's impenetrable confidence. "We'll try not to blindside you."

"Thank you, Detective. I sure do appreciate it." Faith stood to go.

"I need you to answer a few questions first," Claudia said pleasantly.

"Delford took our statements. Surely you've taken the time to review them."

"It's best if I can hear it from you. Please." Claudia gestured at the chair. Faith sat, folding her small Italian purse in her lap. It, too, was black. *All the trappings of widowhood without the teary inconvenience of grief.*

"Were you in regular contact with him?" Claudia asked.

"Not until he returned to Port Leo. Before that—perhaps a couple of times a year. Sam's birthday, if he remembered, and at Christmas. I imagine Christmas is his slow season."

"With so little contact, you can't make a reasonable judgment as to whether he was suicidal, I suppose," Claudia ventured. Faith had already mentioned suicide twice, as though it were a given.

Faith frowned. "I think someone in porn has serious self-esteem issues. Don't you?"

"Perhaps. He didn't send you child support?"

Nails clicked. "Why is that relevant, pray tell?"

"I'm trying to determine if his son was part of the reason to come home."

"Making me and his mama squirm was the reason. When Pete announced his intention to leave me and our infant son and go to California for this folly of being in movies, I knew he'd fail. He had lofty goals but no real talent and the self-discipline of a drug addict. When I found out he'd ended up doing…adult films, I wanted to be sure he could never hurt Sam. Or Lucinda." She rubbed her tired eyes. "I'll give him a smidge of credit that he did send support for Sam every now and then, but he sent it to his mother. She would then turn the money over to me. I in turn would donate it to charity. Starving children in Ethiopia, monsoon relief in Bangladesh. Always a good cause far removed from us."

"Why give away the money if it was intended for your son?"

"That money was earned on Pete's back. Or other body parts," she said dismissively. "I didn't want Pete's smut translating into food in my son's stomach."

"When was the last time you spoke to Pete?"

Faith shifted in her seat. "Yesterday morning. He phoned the house, wanting to talk to Sam."

"How did he seem?"

"Depressed. Unhappy. If you had ended up like him—utterly failed, utterly cheapened—wouldn't you be depressed? He'd seen the lives that Sam and I have built. Sam and I have a good life. I think Pete regretted the choices he'd made. If our lives are the candy store, he definitely had his face pressed against the glass."

"Do you know if he'd sought professional help?"

"Pete on a shrink's couch? Never. He thought couches were good for one thing and one thing only."

"You didn't like the way he made his money or lived his life, but you didn't object to him seeing your son?"

Faith tented her fingers beneath her chin. Her hands were like ivory. "No, I didn't like it. But Sam's like the rest of the Hubbles, he has a mind of his own. He wanted to see his father when his father came back, so I permitted limited visits. Better that than Sam sneaking around to see Pete."

"How would you characterize their relationship?"

"Relationship?" Real anger tinged her voice. "Sam spent most of his childhood wondering what was so wrong with him that his father shunned him—as though the child were the damaged goods, not the man. But when he got to know his father, Sam finally realized Pete counts as little more than a sperm donor."

"You mentioned Pete was depressed when he called you. Can you be more specific?"

Faith fingered a wrinkle in her tailored slacks. "He asked if he could speak to Sam. I told him Sam had already left for school. He begged me to let Sam know he'd called and I agreed. We said good-bye and hung up. That was the last time I spoke to him."

"Do you know if Sam returned his father's call?"

"I gave him the message, but Sam didn't seem particularly interested in phoning his father back."

"Let me get this straight, ma'am. He didn't mention to you, after y'all found out Pete was dead, whether or not he'd talked to his father that day?"

Faith shifted in her seat again. "Sam probably talked to him, yes. I don't remember. It was a very long, upsetting evening."

"How badly will it hurt his mother's campaign if voters learn Pete was a porn star?" Claudia asked.

Her throat worked. "I have no idea."

"Surely when he showed up, you had to calculate what the possible damage might be."

"Lucinda has been an outstanding senator for the past sixteen years. She's easily won reelection and her approval ratings are high. There's no reason to think she wouldn't have the voters' support."

"You sound like a press release given breath," Claudia said, and Faith stiffened. "No one in her office was eager to advertise about Pete, were you?"

"I have no intention of being harangued by you."

Claudia suspected the damage, from Faith and Lucinda's viewpoint, would be considered catastrophic. Nuclear. Career-ending.

"Do you know if he kept a gun?" Claudia asked.

"I have no idea."

"Do you know if he was having financial problems of any sort?"

"No."

"Do you know if he was involved with drugs, anything illicit?"

Faith's mouth tightened, as though a stench had drifted

into the cramped room. "If I'd suspected for a moment he was a drug user, I wouldn't let Sam within a mile of him."

"Do you know if he was still involved in porn?"

"He told me he wanted to leave that business." Faith rubbed her lip. Perhaps it was more politic, Claudia considered, for Faith to paint Pete as on the road to reforming. A bad guy who'd come home to Senator Mommy and seen the error of his ways before his unfortunate demise. "If there is anything suspicious about Pete's death—if it's not suicide—then I suggest you take a long, hard look at that Velvet woman. She's entirely unstable."

"How so?"

"How mentally stable could she be, sleeping with hundreds of men? It would warp a soul. Warp a heart."

"Do you know she's done that? I thought she directed, not acted."

"As if that matters." Faith dismissed the difference with a flutter of fingers. "You're a woman who works in a male-dominated profession, right, Detective?"

"Yes."

"So do I. And a woman like Velvet is a traitor to all women. We fight and bust our butts to be considered equals, and she traps women as carnal playthings. Made-up dolls that exist only to pleasure men." Faith leaned closer. "She was obsessed with Pete. She didn't want him to come back to Texas, but she followed him. Pete might have been making the best effort to shed that world, and here she is, blocking his every move." She leaned back. "I think Pete probably killed himself. But if your tests argue otherwise, I think she killed him."

"Funny. She says the same thing about you. At least that's what she told Judge Mosley."

Faith's smile tensed, then relaxed. "Thanks for letting me know, Detective. I'll sue her for slander."

Claudia had waited to see if Faith would broach the subject of custody. "Speaking of legal proceedings . . . I understand Pete was considering fighting for custody of Sam."

Faith blinked, then laughed. "Surely you jest. He wouldn't have a prayer in family court."

"He never mentioned a desire for custody of Sam?"

"No. Never. Not once. Who says so?"

"Velvet."

"Consider the rather polluted source."

Claudia shifted focus. "Do you know anyone named Deloache?"

"No."

"Did Pete ever talk about his brother Corey to you?"

A surprised blink. "Corey? No. He's a forbidden subject."

"With Pete? Or with the senator?"

"With Pete. It was too painful for him. They were real close."

"He didn't tell you he was making a film about Corey?"

"No. He didn't—but Judge Mosley told me last night. Pete never mentioned a movie to any of us. You can imagine how awful it would be for the senator, ripping open terrible old wounds." She raised her palms up in mock surrender. "Another perfect example of how unthinking Pete could be."

"Pete had a laptop computer that's missing. Do you know where this laptop or a copy of his notes or script might be?"

"Goodness, no," Faith said. Claudia saw the faintest tremble of the woman's bottom lip. "I assume . . . on the boat."

"Did you ever visit him on the boat?"

"Yes. Once, when I went there with Sam. I wanted to be sure Pete was creating a suitable environment for visits. That whore Velvet wasn't around. That helped."

"If you were on the boat, then I'll need to get your prints," Claudia said sweetly. "We want to identify everyone who's been aboard and see if there are prints not accounted for."

"You must be joking."

"I'm not. It's painless."

Claudia took Faith's prints herself there in her office, quickly and efficiently. Faith spoke not a word during the procedure and wiped her hands clean with a cloth Claudia handed her.

"Senator Hubble and I will cooperate in every way," Faith said. "I just hope you'll cooperate as well and remember that the senator's done a great deal for this region." She dropped the cloth back on Claudia's desk. "Your family's been in Port Leo for many years, haven't they?" Her voice, asking, was shiny as a knife.

"Yeah."

"Your dad's a shrimper?" Asking when it sounded like she already knew.

"Yeah."

"That's a very honorable profession." She gave Claudia a half smile, shaped like the cruel crescent Claudia remembered from high school: the popular girl grinning, closing in for the kill on some mouse of a geek. "He ever have trouble holding on to his shrimping license?"

"No. Never. Not a bit of trouble."

"That's good. You know, licenses are much harder to come by these days. The senator's trying to make sure we get the right balance between preventing overharvesting of the bays and protecting our economic interests." Faith wadded up the ink-smeared cloth. "I suppose some shrimpers will lose their livelihoods because their licenses will get bought out by the state. Or won't be available at all."

Claudia said nothing.

"I certainly appreciate the information you gave me." Faith's smile was as warm as summer honey. "May I call you Claudia from now on?"

Claudia nodded. Faith Hubble shook hands and lumbered to her feet, tucking her too-little purse under her arm. Claudia walked her to the front door, Faith saying hello to every person they passed, and then headed back to her office alone, her stomach twisting.

She went to the quiet of the ladies' room and washed her face in icy water. She stared at her dripping face in the mirror. *That mouthy witch just threatened your father, didn't she?*

Maybe the woman was just making conversation. Or not. Maybe Faith Hubble was rattled after having to give her prints, feeling a little cornered.

She thought of her father, Cipriano, waving at her as his little shrimp boat chugged toward the Gulf for a day's work, empty nets hanging behind him like ancient tattered flags, rope and nylon to cull a precarious living, him telling her to be a good girl.

One simple step would set her course aright. Take Delford's blunt but good advice and treat Hubble as a suicide. Pete Hubble was a moody loser, outcast from a respected family. He'd earned a debased living, and it wouldn't surprise her in the least if the toxicology tests revealed drugs in his system. He probably had killed himself and spared both his family and Velvet the shock of finding him by inviting Heather Farrell to the boat.

You're some cop. Quiver like a little kid and let those two tell you how to do your job. She fumed—she should have confronted Faith Hubble right then and there. She called Whit Mosley at the courthouse.

"Hey, Honorable, it's Claudia."

"What's the matter? You sound deflated."

"No, just tired." Suddenly she didn't feel like embarrassing herself with private revelations to Whit. "I wanted to update you on where we are." She told him about her questioning of Velvet, the missing laptop, and her discussion with Faith, sticking to the facts. "What do you think of suicide as an explanation?"

"Your boss came down hard on me last night to push for suicide," Whit said. "I didn't appreciate it."

"He…" Claudia stopped herself. Delford Spires had been her ardent supporter, her mentor on the force. "I know he's never been your favorite, but he is a smart man. I'm sure he meant well."

Whit updated her about his discussion with Ernesto Gomez and the information he had gleaned. "I'd like to know who this dirtbag is that Pete argued with on the boat. We should ask Velvet."

"I'm going to have a background check made on Pete Hubble, see if he has a record in California. I'm going to check Velvet, too," Claudia said. "I'd like to visit Jabez Jones. His name keeps cropping up."

"Take me with you, but I'm booked up until this evening with the joys of court," Whit said.

Claudia said, "I'll call and see when we can meet with him."

"Fine. I'll call you as soon as I know details that are forensic and meaningful," he said.

"Fine. Bye," she said, still feeling peevish. She had a lot of phone calls to make, computer searches to do. She picked up the sheaf of pink messages left for her by the dispatcher. Two from Patsy Duchamp at the *Port Leo Mariner,* no doubt looking for a quote. One from her mother, no doubt to berate her for divorcing Deputy Wonderful. And one, surprisingly, from the Reverend Jabez Jones.

She reached for her phone.

15

———◦◦◦◦———

Heather Farrell spent a damp night in a grove of bent live oaks near Little Mischief Beach, surrounded by bluestems that stood tall and thin and kept her hidden. Lying on her back, the limbs of the oaks were fingers of a gnarled claw pointing away from the bay, shaped by the ceaseless wind. At night the trees looked frightening, transplanted from the forest where Hansel and Gretel roamed. When she awoke she peeled a scrawny orange and ate, watching the few pleasure boats plying the waters on a brisk autumn morning. She got out her notebook and began to sketch the boats: the prows cutting the water, the foaming curl of wake left in their path, the hard angles of stern and bow and flying bridge.

She hummed as she drew.

She hoped Sam would come. His father was dead, and Heather knew propriety demanded Sam be at home. He was no doubt upset. But she hoped he might prefer the solace of the beach rather than his frostbitten mother and egocentric grandmother. He might prefer her.

Heather wished for a shower; she had settled for a quick sponge bath at the police station. She rubbed toothpaste on her teeth and gums with her finger and rinsed and spat with a gulp of water from her oversize water bottle she kept in her knapsack. She emerged from the oak motte and headed down to the shores of Little Mischief Beach, and found Sam there, watching the waves inch against the sand.

Heather came up behind him, wanting to touch the cool skin at the nape of his neck and feel his hair, the same color as his father's. Instead she gently touched his back.

Sam Hubble turned. The wind had reddened his smooth cheeks. Red lines webbed his eyes. A dribble of snot clung to one nostril.

"Hi you," he said.

"Hi yourself." She kissed him shyly on the cheek. She dug a tissue from her jeans pocket and dabbed his nose. "It's okay. It's all okay."

"We shouldn't be seen together," he said softly. "And one of my grandmother's jerks will probably be out looking for me. I'm supposed to be at home, inconsolable with grief."

Heather loved that Sam used big words like *inconsolable*— he sounded so smart. Smart guys were sexier to her, but she didn't know many. She'd get him a little tattoo, maybe of heather in bloom, when they eventually got to New Orleans, and then he'd just be to die for. "So we sit tight?" she asked.

Sam shrugged and sniffed. "Probably for the next week or so."

"And then we can go? We can get out of here?"

"Yeah," he said.

"But you'll be a runaway. No way is your grandmother going to let you go."

"I got that covered. There won't be a stink—she and

Mom won't come looking for me. That's a guarantee. They can tell people I've gone off to boarding school in Houston." He wiped his nose with the back of his hand. "If they don't let us go, then I start talking."

Heather heard the resolve in his voice, but it didn't ease the churn in her guts. She leaned away from him and with her fingernail drew a heart in the soft sand. Their plan seemed utterly impossible, but she wanted in her heart to believe it would work. That they could be together, free of Pete and Lucinda and Faith. *Me, the smiley-girl optimist. There's a switch.*

"I want to believe this will work…that we'll be safe from them," Heather said.

He didn't respond, staring out at the bullet-gray bay.

"Are you okay?" she asked.

Sam shrugged. "He was a two-week dad. What's that, two weeks out of my whole life, Heather? I don't even want to figure out the percentage. I've been to summer camps that lasted longer."

He fell silent. Heather ached to take his hand, but instead she kept her palm pressed against the damp cool of the sand.

He cried. Heavy, big tears for his father, and she hugged him close. He surrendered to hard, racking sobs, and Heather thought: *He couldn't cry like this in front of his mother or grandmother. Not allowed.*

"I'm sorry," he gasped. He was sixteen, two years younger than her, and their being together was utterly insane. But the world was insane, so why couldn't they succeed? He leaned toward her as she wiped his cheek clean of tears and he kissed her, hard, and they leaned back in the sand, smearing the heart she had drawn.

*   *   *

Whit's day typified the joys of the justice court. He first magistrated into the county jail a sobbing carpenter from Darius, a small fishing community on Encina County's northern tip, who had blackened his wife's eye and broken her nose during a morning argument over burnt toast.

"Don't put me in jail, please," the man pleaded. He was not much older than Whit, but he mewled and cried like an ashamed child. His wife's blood still splattered his T-shirt. "I'm claustrophobic. I'll go flat crazy, Judge. Please, please."

"Listen, Mr. Reynolds." Whit wished he could refer to him in open court as *you sniveling little dick*. "I don't want to hear one bit of whining, complaining, or bitching from you. Are you listening to me, sir?"

Big sniffle from the oversize baby. "Yes, Judge, sure am."

Whit informed the accused of the charges against him, his right to retain counsel, his right to remain silent, his right to request appointment of counsel if indigent—all the Miranda warnings the man had heard when he was arrested by the Encina sheriff's deputies. Big Baby blinked a lot, as though his brain were clogged, so Whit—carefully and calmly—walked him again, in plainest English possible, through his rights. It was his first arrest for family violence assault. Whit set bond at ten thousand dollars, the maximum.

"That's more money than Mama's got," Big Baby wailed, forgetting Mama would have to pony up a percentage, not the whole amount.

"Such concern for a lady," Whit said, "is very touching.

But wrong lady." He stared at Big Baby. "I'm also serving you with an Emergency Protective Order, Mr. Reynolds, at your wife's application. That means, after you make bail, you can't go near her for sixty days."

"But I love her," Big Baby sniffed.

"Then you got sixty days to let your heart grow fonder. You go near her, you're gonna be right back in front of me and I will get medieval on you, Mr. Reynolds."

Big Baby was led out of the courtroom, bawling afresh, saying he sure hadn't meant to hurt his sweetie pie. Whit silently wished castration were back in judicial fashion. But he put his smile on and turned to the next case.

That morning, Pete Hubble tucked in the back of his mind, Whit signed arrest warrants for four hot-check writers (two of whom were sisters who had apparently gone on their overdrawn jaunt together, which made him a little sad); set a forty-thousand-dollar bond for a chronic burglar who had been captured driving away from his just-burgled ex-girlfriend's house with cash, electronic equipment, and all his sugar's lingerie; and heard guilty pleas from and sentenced six minty-breathed minors in possession of tobacco to twelve hours of community service each and a tobacco awareness class. Whit thought the class sounded worse than the public service, which usually consisted of tidying the beaches. The puffers' parents grimaced at him as though he were sentencing their little darlings to rock splitting, and he thought, *There's a dozen votes lost*. He saw Buddy Beere, his opponent, sitting in the back row of the courtroom, watching him with all the warmth of a spider approaching the squirming fly.

Grabbing a quick lunch at his desk, he ignored three

phone messages from his father. He returned four phone messages from the newspapers in Corpus Christi and Houston, telling them that Pete Hubble had apparently died from a gunshot to the head and he was awaiting autopsy results before releasing cause of death. He'd never rated a phone call from the Houston paper before, and the rising prominence of the case made him nervous.

After lunch, Whit interviewed from the bench a Port Leo woman who had told her sisters and neighbors over the past week that President Kennedy was living in their attic, hiding from the Cuban missiles, and dallying with an aged Marilyn Monroe. The assassination in Dallas and overdose in Hollywood never happened and Kennedy, now with a shaved head and a beard, had been fishing along the bays of the Texas coast ever since with his blond companion. The woman claimed she employed them as a gardener and maid on occasion. For their protection and hers, she had taken to carting around a loaded pistol that was a family heirloom.

Whit nodded solemnly through her recitation of her reality. She'd shaved her eyebrows and she often ran a finger along the hairless, ghostly arches, as though twisting the reels that played for her mind's eye.

The woman said, "Mr. President adores the water, but he just couldn't show his face on the East Coast again. And the rest of the Gulf Coast is closer to Cuba." She lowered her voice. "West Coast, too many cameras. And they shot Bobby there. That's why Jack stayed here. And that's why I keep the gun handy. Protection."

"That's considerate of you," Whit said. Her two sisters stood to one side, crying quietly. The woman smiled serenely as Whit signed the warrant to detain and transport

her to a medical facility for a psychiatric review. Whit—as
gentle as a summer breeze—explained to the woman that
she would go to see some doctors at Port Leo Memorial.
She smiled, determined to indulge him in this silliness.
The constable led the woman and her sisters away. Traffic
court didn't seem so bad then.

Court concluded, he walked down the private hall back
to his small office, shrugged out of his robe (wearing a
polo shirt, jeans, and Birkenstock sandals underneath), and
hung it carefully on its hanger. He'd made three phone calls
to the Nueces County medical examiner this afternoon,
quick breaks between cases, and they hadn't cut into Pete
yet. To make matters worse, a downtown drug deal had
soured last night in Corpus Christi and three twenty-year-
olds had shotgunned each other into oblivion. A woman
had been found strangled over in Ingleside, and apparently
Pete Hubble, senator's son, warranted no special rank to
break ahead in the line of corpses. The deputy medical
examiner, Liz Contreras, promised she would call him as
soon as she had some details.

A musical, double-knuckled knock rapped at his door.
"Hey there, Whit!" Buddy Beere stuck his head in, with
miles of smiles for his esteemed opponent.

"Hello, Buddy. How can I help you?"

*You could vacate this office for me in a couple of
weeks* was the answer Whit imagined flitting across
Buddy's mind, but instead Buddy offered Whit a friendly
hand. "I wanted to invite you. To a debate. Between you
and me."

Whit shook the proffered hand and Buddy sat down,
uninvited. He reminded Whit of a teddy bear gone to
seed. He was more stocky than pudgy, in his early for-

ties, with brown hair straggling across his head. In campaigning he smiled a lot, as though grinning were as expected as breathing, crowing an ill-defined platform he termed "real judicial fairness," as though Whit managed the justice court with all the probity of a Salem witch trial.

"What exactly would we debate, Buddy?" Whit asked. "Would you sign arrest warrants differently than me?" *Probably would. With a little happy face drawn next to his signature.*

Buddy shook his head. "No. I mean on the critical issues facing voters. No offense, Whit, but your daddy, bless him, sort of waltzed you onto the bench and the voters don't know much about you." As if that was Buddy's responsibility to fix, and as soon as he did Whit's unrobed butt would hit pavement. "Other than your fondness for too-casual apparel."

"Don't know me? I've lived here most of my life, and my family's been here since Texas was part of Mexico. What's to know?"

"Well, I was sitting in the back of the courtroom earlier. Observing. You sentenced those teenage smokers to community service. You could have given them a two-hundred-dollar fine."

"Those kids are all from families living out at Port Leo Country Club, and community service will make a bigger impression than scribbling a check. They ought to get their hands slapped *and* a little dirty."

"Well, we could debate the rightness of that real easy," Buddy said with satisfaction.

Whit watched Buddy eyeing the black robe hanging

in the corner. "Buddy, don't you already have a good job down at the nursing home?"

"Sure do." Buddy was an administrator at Port Leo's one nursing home, down in a crook of St. Leo Bay.

"Well, then why do you want my job? It can't possibly pay you as well as the nursing home does."

Buddy's florid mouth worked. "I want to make a difference in people's lives."

"Buddy, I frankly don't know what we would debate about. I sentence to community service—you'd do a fine. Big effing deal."

Buddy's smile tightened at the brush with profanity. "How about debating moral fiber?"

"Moral fiber? I'm opposed to it. Unless it fights colon cancer."

"I've heard you've been keeping company with a woman of less-than-sterling repute."

"Are we talking about Pete Hubble's friend?" *Not Faith,* he thought.

"Yes."

"Well, I heard," Whit said, "that you were keeping company with Pete and his friend Velvet as well." A junior high refrain: *I heard she heard you said they said.*

Buddy's smile died a natural death. "You better not be spying on me."

"Is it true?"

"Why not just have me testify at the inquest?" Buddy asked, and Whit smelled a stinky political ploy.

"Buddy, I'm not subpoenaing you when we're running against each other."

Buddy tugged at his lower lip, like a reluctant tattletale. "Well...I was out campaigning and Pete stopped me. He wanted to know how he could get close to his family again. He had been a disappointment to them and he wanted to make amends."

"And what did you tell him?"

"To leave town. No one wanted him here at all."

16

STATE SENATOR LUCINDA Hubble kept a collection of heads on the top shelf in her study. Johnson, Nixon, Carter, Reagan, Bush, and Clinton represented the presidents; for the governors of Texas she had George W. Bush, Ann Richards, Mark White, Bill Clements, and Dolph Briscoe. All grinned like decapitated clowns, rubbery skin sagging without bones. Their false-lipped mouths gaped, caught between mirthful smile and slackened grimace. Lucinda also had one of herself, complete with trademark puffy red hair and big azure-framed eyeglasses.

Whit had arrived ten minutes ago, a little past four. The housekeeper, a dour Vietnamese sparrow of a woman, told him Faith was out, Lucinda was on the phone, and would he mind waiting in the senator's study? Anything to eat or drink? she offered. The kitchen and dining room tables creaked under the weight of the collected casseroles and salads and pies brought by neighbors and churchwomen and by the county power elite. But only a few mourners stood gathered, nodding with awkward sympathy.

He wondered if the truth about Pete was leaking, like a slow hiss from a balloon. Faith had stood him up, perhaps off conducting damage control. What would people say to

Lucinda? Sorry your son's dead or sorry he turned out so badly? The visitors in the living room looked fretful. He followed the housekeeper and sat alone, studying the study.

Underneath the political gallery of plastic masks stood an old pinball machine themed BIG SPENDER, with a fat cat tossing bills to an admiring crowd of 1920s zoot suiters and flappers. Prominently behind her desk were her framed nursing certificates, yellowing with age. On the wall hung an array of photos: Lucinda Hubble with President Bush, with President Clinton, with Willie Nelson and Ann Richards, with a steady parade of Texas celebrities. In each picture Lucinda gave a thumbs-up, as though marking another successful conquest. Lucinda's office was almost too relaxed for a politician.

Warm, friendly. Where the senator could meet with the common folk, show she was just a good old gal.

There were no pictures of her sons. A couple of Faith and Sam, both formal portraits, the kind given as Christmas gifts in gold frames. Faith smiled, but only like she'd just passed a CPA exam. Sam looked like he'd wandered out of a National Honor Society meeting, serious and bespectacled and boring. The perfect political grandson. Certainly the two sons had been failures in that regard.

A small stereo sat in the corner, playing soft solo piano music. Whit wandered over to the stereo, picked up the CD's jewel box. Bach's *Goldberg Variations,* played by Glenn Gould.

"I find Bach a great comfort," Lucinda Hubble said from the doorway. She looked sunken and diminished. She wore a faded olive-green cardigan and a pair of old khakis, as though she might be loafing in a library or tending winter pansies in her flowerbeds.

"Hello, Senator," Whit said. "I'm so very sorry about Pete."

"Thank you, honey." She cleared her throat and dabbed her eyes with a monogrammed handkerchief. "These wells have just about run dry. I'm sorry to keep you waiting, but that was the governor and his wife on the phone." She said this with only the slightest hint of superiority.

She came and stood by Whit, her fingers playing air piano. "Do you hear Gould? He hums and breathes along as he plays. All that careful structure Gould builds, note by note, each one a key brick in a musical house, each note, each rest, played to his own exactitude, but still he can't contain the passion he feels for the music." She switched the music off.

"It's beautiful," Whit said.

"Pete hated classical music," she said. "He hated anything touched by beauty."

Lucinda Hubble gestured at the chair on the other side of the desk, and he sat. She eased herself down into a heavy leather armchair.

"Your daddy's already called, and he and Irina have brought us a lovely casserole. It's something Russian and quite unpronounceable, but I'm sure it's delicious. So thoughtful. You thank them again for me, honey."

"Yes, ma'am, I will. And I won't keep you long now. I just need to ask you some questions so I can make a determination on cause of death."

"Of course." She placed her hands, palms down, on the expansive smooth teak of the desk.

He wondered if she knew about him and Faith. She had given no sign—no sly smile, no slight frown of disapproval.

He led with a suggestion for suicide. "How would you describe Pete's state of mind in the past few weeks?"

"Depressed," Lucinda said. "He felt he had wasted his life because of the . . . particular career he had chosen."

"You knew about the porn?"

Lucinda flinched at the word but nodded. "I found out a couple of years ago. I called Pete at his home. He was apparently in the middle of shooting a film." She crumpled the handkerchief. "I could hear the women in the background. Laughing at me. Hollering about which one would get to appear in a scene with my son first." She touched at her blue eyeglasses. "Not what a mother ever wants to hear. I hung up. I told Faith. She already knew, she'd been shielding my so-delicate feelings. I was devastated, of course. I didn't speak to him again until he came back to town."

"I think the press will find out," Whit said quietly.

"Not from me, they won't. And if they find out from you or from Detective Salazar, or any member of either of your offices, I will hath more fury than hell," Lucinda flared. "I can't have Sam knowing about this. I just can't."

Not to mention the voters. "Do you think Velvet is going to stay quiet?"

"I can't control her."

"Did Pete say why he was coming home?" Whit asked.

"He said he no longer wished to pursue his acting career." Whit believed the words *adult films* or *dirty movies* or *skin flicks* were never going to pass her lips.

"How did he plan on supporting himself?"

"He didn't say. I assumed he had savings, or could find legitimate work. He does know—knew—film production. Perhaps at a television studio in Corpus Christi or with Jabez Jones's outfit."

"How much contact did you have with Pete after he returned to Port Leo?"

"An hour, here and there," Lucinda said. "The chill had gone deep for years." She sank slightly into the bulk of the cardigan. "And selfishly, I did not want to be disappointed by him again. Pete thrives on disappointing others. I was happy to see him, but I wanted him to rehaul his life. I wasn't willing to get too close until I thought he was sincere." Lucinda perceived the reaction in Whit's face. "Perhaps I sound harsh, but mothers are mortal, too."

"No, I know it must have been tough for you. He told you nothing of this Corey film he planned?"

"I didn't know one word until Faith told me this morning. But I doubt Pete would have completed any real film. Bless his heart, he didn't have the talent. The drive."

"I'm wondering why Pete chose Corey as a subject, after all these years."

"Penance, I suppose. He blamed himself for what happened to Corey."

"Why?"

"Aren't you the youngest of a whole passel of boys? Didn't your brothers take care of you?" She offered a wan smile.

"Yeah, when they weren't bossing me around or beating me up."

Her smile faded. "Corey disappeared on a weekend when I was out of town on business. He vanished while he was on Pete's watch, so to speak. Pete never forgave himself." She shrugged. "I think he's been killing himself, slowly, for a long time. When certain people do wrong, they turn away from the world. Isolate themselves, slip on the hair shirt and self-destruct. It's why he went into porn, and I think it eroded every bit of self-respect he had." She looked at Whit hard. "I've always believed you have to put your troubles behind you and soldier on."

"Maybe he came across new information about Corey's disappearance. Like that Corey was still alive." It was a balloon to float.

The silence hung for nearly ten seconds. "I am certain Corey is dead."

"Why?" Whit asked.

"Because Corey would have contacted us if he was alive. He wouldn't have let me suffer for all these years."

"Why did Corey run away from home?"

"Don't resurrect the other worst day of my life." For the first time she showed raw emotion, anger flaring her nostrils, her cheeks reddening.

Whit waited. Lucinda dragged her fingernails through her mop of red hair and gave a pained sigh.

"I will never be able to author a book on good mothering, Judge. Taxpayers are easier to corral than willful children. Corey got involved with drinkers. Dopeheads. All to punish me for the time I was spending in Austin and the higher standards of behavior I expected from my boys. After their daddy died I let them run wild, do what they wanted, but once I was elected, they had to toe the line. It was not too much to ask of them. Pete tried, at least, but Corey slipped the leash like a wild dog."

"I know. I remember him, you know."

"Yes. He would have been about your age, now, wouldn't he?" She pondered Whit's face wistfully.

"You don't think he's living happily on a commune in Montana or a farm in Virginia?"

"Does that really happen with most missing teenagers, Judge?" Lucinda asked with a touch of frost. "I'd be overwhelmed to know Corey was in some idyllic retreat. Let me assure you the uncertainty of not knowing what happened to Corey is an ongoing thorn in my heart."

"When was the last time you spoke to Pete, Senator?" Whit asked.

"A couple of days ago. I wanted him to come to dinner alone, but he wouldn't come without Velvet. He declined the invitation, told me he'd talk to me soon."

"I'm curious. How had you and Faith explained Pete's absence to Sam?"

Lucinda smiled thinly. "We told him Pete worked in industrial films—you know, training tapes, corporate tapes for business conventions. Sam accepted it. Pete never told him any different—it was part of the agreement for him to see Sam."

"Did Pete ever talk about a change in the custodial arrangement?" Whit watched Lucinda's face turn pale.

"I don't understand."

"Pete was contemplating suing for custody of Sam."

The silence filled the study until Lucinda leaned forward and her chair squeaked. "Judge, have you lost your mind? Be realistic. How on earth would Pete stand a chance in a custody hearing?"

"I don't know," Whit said. "You tell me."

"He couldn't have been serious. No family court would give Sam to Pete."

"Did he ever ask about joint custody, now that he was back?"

"That would be an issue between him and Faith," she said sternly, and Whit thought, *Yeah, right, like you wouldn't be all in the middle of that.*

"Last point," Whit said. "The boat Pete was staying on,

it's owned by a family suspected of being involved in a drug ring. Y'all know anything about them?"

He could almost hear a political future boiling away in the room.

"Most certainly not," Lucinda managed to say. "Pete's friends were his friends, and his associates have nothing to do with us. I would expect you would not leak that news to the press as well." A vein throbbed in the hollow of her throat.

"So you didn't try to find out who was giving him room and board when he came back?"

"I don't like what you're implying, Judge." For the first time he saw anger storm in her eyes, her jaw set, her mouth narrow.

"Sorry, but I find it hard to believe you just let him waltz back in the middle of an election and didn't research his friends, his benefactors, his purpose in being here."

"I can't control what you believe. But I would be very careful as to what you imply to the world." He saw her scrutinize him with new eyes. He was not being, he supposed, the easygoing Whit Mosley who liked to wander the beach and never put two shakes into a job.

"I'd like to speak to Sam."

Her shoulders stiffened. "Of course. Assuming that his mother is present. He is a minor, after all."

"Of course. Thank you. You've been very helpful."

"But"—she raised a finger—"I ask that you not discuss this custody idiocy with Sam."

"I can't promise that. I'm sorry. I need to talk to him about any subject relevant to his father's death."

"I won't have you subjecting him to Velvet's foolish notions. I'm assuming she's the one claiming Pete wanted custody?"

"Yes."

"A pathetic attempt to hurt us and I won't permit it."

Whit kept his voice mild, out of respect for her loss. "This is how it works. I interview him, and you or Faith can be there, and if there's nothing he can add, fine. Or I can call him as a witness at the inquest. Put him on the stand."

Her fingertips worked along her palms, awkwardly kneading the flesh. "Why don't you let me discuss it with his mother?"

"That would be fine." Whit stood and offered his hand. She shook it, but the cozy neighborliness had evaporated.

He saw himself to the door, but before he left the Bach CD suddenly roared in the study, the icy cleanness of the notes as loud as hammers.

In the late afternoon the teenagers—aimless, tans not faded from summer gold—were out in meager force. Two girls sat cross-legged on an arc of crushed shells at one end of the beach. A boy waded in the gentle surf, black jeans neatly rolled up past thick calves, dragging a bamboo stick in the water, watching it cut a wake through the waves.

Claudia parked in the small, sand-smeared asphalt lot that fed off the old Bay Highway. From the lot she could see the whole, nearly straight line of the beach that terminated on the south with several acres of wind-bent oaks, and the private fishing pier on the north for Port Leo's nursing home. The pier, she remembered, didn't get much use, but two healthy-looking old ladies, their faces shadowed by big, neon-colored sun hats (one magenta, one turquoise), stood on the pier, trolling simple rigs with slack lines.

The elderly women reminded her of David, begging her

to attend his Poppy's party. David was looping a hook back into her flesh, securing it into her jaw, making sure she could not dash from whatever shadow he might cast across the water of her life.

She saw Heather Farrell easing herself down the mangy slope of grass to the flat of the hard-packed beach, a notebook under her arm, a sandwich in her hand, the girl chewing and tossing a scrap of crust to a hovering gull. Other gulls swooped near, pleading with cries, waiting for the generosity to be extended. Heather popped another two morsels upward and then ran, leaving the gulls to sort out the buffet. She sat, kicked off her shoes and ate, keeping her feet just beyond the encroaching tide.

Claudia sat down next to her.

"You wolfed that down," Claudia said. "You hungry? I'll buy you dinner."

Heather dusted the crumbs from her fingers with a quick slap. She tucked a fleck of mayonnaise from the corner of her mouth onto her thumb, then wiped her thumb on her jeans. "Do you always criticize other people's table manners?"

"We're not at a table."

"Slap me. You really are a detective." Heather watched the Gulf inch toward her feet, then retreat. She kept the notebook close to her, on the other side from Claudia.

"Brought this for you to sign." Claudia produced a statement. "Read it first and make sure it's correct."

Heather scanned the document and signed her name at the bottom. "There. Perfect. Satisfied?"

"You sleep okay last night?"

"Sure."

"Amazingly unrattled by finding a dead body."

Heather dragged a hand through her hair. "What am I gonna do, run home to Lubbock?"

"I can help you find a real place to stay."

"Aren't you out of your jurisdiction, Officer?" Heather asked. No insolence laced her voice. "Little Mischief's not in Port Leo proper."

"The sheriff's department might consider you a vagrant, Heather. Camping out here." She could call David, ask him to check on this beach later this evening.

Heather shrugged. "I moved."

"Where to?"

"A friend's house." She wiggled toes at the froth of the surf as it kissed her heels. "Since you're gonna ask me for all the details, her name's Judy Cameron. She lives on the west side of Port Leo. I'm crashing there. So you don't need to follow me around. I'm perfectly safe."

"Judy have a phone number?"

"She didn't pay the bill and got disconnected, but her address is still in the phone book. 414 Paris Street. Beige brick house with a motorcycle out front."

"Why don't I give you a ride back there now?"

"Why don't you quit hassling me?" Heather asked. "Look, I'm all warm and gooey inside from your concern, but I'm fine. I'm a grown woman."

"If there's anything you haven't told us about Pete's death, you're going to be hip-deep in trouble. I won't be able to protect you then."

"Shouldn't you have another cop here to play bad, if you're good?" Heather laughed. "You ought to watch more TV and get your shtick down."

"Why'd you buy bus tickets this week? Two of them?" Claudia asked.

Heather turned her gaze back out across the bay to the hump of Santa Margarita Island. "You're a busy bee."

"It was easy to check."

"Judy and I thought we'd go to see friends in Houston. That okay with the local Nazi regime?"

"I don't want you leaving town before this inquest."

"You can't expect me to wait around forever."

Claudia fished a card out of her pocket. "In case Judy kicks you out." She jotted numbers on the card and handed it to Heather. "That's got my home and my office number. And my ex-husband's number—he's a deputy with the sheriff's department."

"He cute?" Heather asked.

"Very," Claudia said. "Call. I'm around twenty-four/ seven."

"I'll program you on my speed dial. Thanks."

Claudia dusted the sand from her rump and walked away. When she reached her car, she watched Heather sitting, notebook open, sketching with a pencil, the sunset painting the low clouds orange and purple, the light beginning to fade.

Two pelicans glided across St. Leo Bay with graceful swoops, the tips of their wings barely brushing the water. Claudia watched them fly, and then she drove back to town.

The two old women lumbered inside the nursing home, their cackles of laughter drifting down the beach to Heather. A Caspian tern, squeaking its nasally call, dove down into the darkening water, its bill bloodred but not from prey. The tern shot back into the sky, wet, dinnerless. Heather watched it. *You don't always get what you want, babycakes.* The tern tried again, farther out into the bay. Heather watched the surf-walking boy and the two chatting girls leave the beach. When she looked back out, the tern was gone. Shame. She opened to a blank page and began to sketch out the muscled wings, the probing beak, the egg-shaped head.

She stopped as the sun set behind her. She wished Sam were here, to drink red wine, cuddle up close to her, run his tongue along the backside of her ear. But he wasn't coming. No escape from the Hubble guardians. No escape at all—

A hand grabbed her shoulder.

17

---◦◦◦---

WHIT MOSLEY AND Faith Hubble had first made love—an altogether too kind term, considering the bourbon and muscle cramps involved—in July. They met at a wind-down party after three days of ShellFest, Port Leo's annual salute to all things crustacean and culinary. Over ten thousand fairgoers, both locals and tourists, jammed the St. Leo Bay area to guzzle beer, buy crafts, stomp to forgettable jazz and blues and country-western acts, and to deplete the shrimp and oyster populations through structured gluttony. Lucinda judged a shrimp recipe cook-off, glad-handed voters, and raced back to her Austin condo with Sam in tow to hear a classical piano concert at UT.

Faith didn't. She lingered in town, hanging out at the Shell Inn, drinking bourbon in a back booth with a clutch of old high school girlfriends. The women's group slowly merged with two more groups, which is what happens in a small bar where nearly everyone knows everyone else and has been drinking for three days. Tables were pushed together, drinks ordered again, and Faith sat next to Judge Whit Mosley. She vaguely remembered his brothers from her school days, knew he was the youngest of the wild and handsome pack of Mosley boys. Even though now a judge he dressed like a townie bum without two dimes, in his frayed, sun-faded orange polo shirt and weathered khaki shorts and Birkenstock sandals. But the legs leading to the sandals were nicely formed, and she liked his odd gray eyes and the direct and knowing way he smiled, not at all put off by her height or weight. She grinned at the quiet way he indulged the drunken boasts of his friends when the topic turned to fishing, not joining in but not deflating his buddies' hackneyed tales, and although his polo shirt was old and the neon orange a color out of style, the chest and arms beneath the fabric were tanned and firm.

He didn't look like any judge she ever knew.

She had been lonely for a long time, plowing all her time into Lucinda's career, and no one had given her jokes a sincere laugh in a long while. He offered her a ride home; she was drunk. She asked him to come inside and have a cup of coffee and a couple of aspirin to help sober themselves up (although she had watched him nurse a single Corona for two hours and knew the only drunk one was herself), and while they stood chatting in the kitchen and the coffee brewed, she surprised herself by reaching out for him and saying, "Is that a gavel or you just happy to see me?" Her jokes got worse with more bourbon.

It wasn't a gavel and he amply liked her, too. They spent the next several hours in bed, half of the time sleeping, the other half making strenuous love. She was left gasping but energized, freeing some long-buried shadow of herself to face the world. She watched Whit nap and traced his lips with a fingernail while he softly snored. Since Pete had left her, the few men she'd allowed intimacy with her tended to be older and snagged in the intricate web of state politics. They talked of little else. Here was a man lying beside her who was younger with a flat stomach and long legs and probably not overly bright but he knew how to make her feel shivery good. She brushed his light fuzz of whiskers grown in the course of the day, wondering how quickly he would bolt in the morning.

He didn't. He made love to her again, and she almost wept with pleasure and an odd relief. She didn't want a romance, but she did want him, warm and kissing her throat and giving his halfway smile as he filled her. They began to see each other discreetly. She didn't want Sam or Lucinda to know—he was the only private part of her life—and Whit didn't argue.

They saw each other perhaps twice a month. Faith and Whit learned about the constellation of small motels along the Coastal Bend, little way stations in Rockport and Aransas Pass and Laurel Point and Copano. They would meet, share a bottle of Shiner Bock while kissing and slowly unburdening each other of their clothes, soap their skin in the shower, make love on the bed, and then talk—about her work, about his struggle to learn enough law to be an effective JP, about books they'd both read. He was smarter than she thought. A love of reading was, other than sex, the only thing they had in common. All perfectly friendly.

But now he had failed her, and the memory of the taste of his skin soured in her mouth. Faith backed her BMW out of the Hubble driveway and gunned the engine toward Whit's house.

Faith rocketed over to the Mosleys', ready to carve Whit's guts into ribbons of flesh, but instead the storm turned to shower. She cried as soon as she saw him.

Babe and Irina were dining with friends in Rockport and would not be back for quite a while.

Faith and Whit sat in the cramped living room in the guesthouse, the Corpus Christi news turned on but muted. Pete's death—as the son of a prominent state senator, not as a porn star, which had not yet been mentioned by any news source—had been the second story, after the gunshot war that had slowed down the Nueces County coroner's office.

Faith's hard, heavy weeping slowly eased. Whit handed her a wad of tissues to replace the ones she'd rendered sopping, and he poured them each a hefty glass of an inexpensive merlot. She gulped down a third of the glass in a long swallow.

"You don't think you can cry for someone you ceased to love a long while back." Faith sniffed, tamped her nostrils with the tissues. "I keep thinking of the boy I knew and married, not the sleaze he turned out to be...but he came home, and all I saw was the sleaze. Nothing more." She drank again. "This is good, Whit. Thanks. You know how he proposed to me? On Port Leo Beach, at midnight. The beach was closed, but we snuck in and sat on the sand and counted stars. He told me I had missed one, and then he dangled this beautiful diamond on a string before my eyes." She studied the red depths of the wineglass. "I loved him then—sure I did. But he married me only because his mother wanted it. I found out later she'd bought the ring for him and told him just how to propose. She knew what would light my fire." She set the wineglass down, folded her fingers together in her lap. "Whit, you've got to believe me...We didn't have anything to do with Pete's death. Nothing. And Lucinda, she shouldn't have come across so tough with you."

"Why didn't you tell me Pete was back in town?" Whit kept his voice gentle, quiet, and unaccusing.

"Because...we didn't want anyone to know he even existed anymore. But he cooperated with us. He kept a very low profile. I mean, I guess a couple of people commented to me he was back, but no production was made of it." Her mouth twisted. "Did you want to waste away our motel time chatting about my ex?"

"You didn't want people—or me—to know he was back because he had starred in blue movies?"

"Yes." She took another bolstering slug of wine and shuddered.

"Not because he could derail Lucinda's campaign. And your career. Not because he was going to sue you for custody of Sam."

"Look, as far as I'm concerned, Whit, this custody crap is a complete fiction Velvet dreamed up in her screwed-stupid little mind."

"You asked me to help y'all get through this, to not make a big production of the inquest. But I'm not doing you any such favors until I know what's going on here."

"I clearly don't mean diddly-squat to you, do I?"

"This has nothing to do with us, Faith. But I don't believe a man who wants to get his child back just kills himself."

"I don't suppose it's occurred to you the source of his depression was he knew he'd never, ever get Sam."

"Yes, it occurred to me. It also occurred to me to wonder exactly why he'd even think he had a chance in court. Did he have something on you, Faith?"

"There's nothing that could trump porn!" she barked at him. "For heaven's sakes!"

"There are worse crimes than dirty movies."

"Not to a family court." She stood. "I came over here to talk, not to be grilled by you."

"You came over to presume on our relationship," Whit said. "You're asking me to not make a public spectacle of the inquest for Sam's sake. But I'm asking you for an explanation of what was going on with Pete. This cuts both ways, sweetie."

"I told you what I know." She sat again.

"Perhaps I should excuse myself from the case."

"No. Don't." Panic flashed in her eyes. "You do that, you'll have to explain why, and I don't want Sam to know about us."

"Don't lock Sam in a glass bubble forever."

"Look, it hasn't been easy for him…no father…his grandmother and I so busy. And now, with Pete dead, I can't rub salt in his wounds, please, Whit. Not now." She covered her face with her hands.

"The boat Pete was staying on. It's owned by a family suspected of heavy drug activity up the coast."

"Lucinda mentioned that." She leaned back against the thick pillows of the couch and dropped her hands. "He chose well, didn't he? One little explosive charge after another to sink his mother's ship."

"He's the one who's dead, not Lucinda." He sat next to her. "Where were you last night?"

"Am I not supposed to be insulted at the question?"

"That's up to you, Faith."

"I was at home last night, with Sam. I haven't spent enough time with him lately. We had dinner, watched TV, went to sleep early. It's all in my bland little police statement."

"Okay," he said. "Thanks."

She took his hand. "I've been nothing but honest with you. I'm sure he killed himself, okay? All these other diversions—this Corey movie, this custody idea, him staying on a drug hound's boat—I'm begging, Whit. Keep it all out of the inquest, can't you? It has no place. If you don't you're letting a nobody like Pete win. Over me. Over us."

"I can't promise that, Faith. I can't."

She rose, her face contorting as though slapped. "The problem with you, Whit, is that everyone has low expectations of you and you never disappoint."

A rap sounded at the door. Faith fell silent. Whit stood, wondering if she might go hide in the bathroom or closet, but she stayed put and he went to his door.

It was Claudia. "Hi," she said, and she glanced past his shoulder to see Faith Hubble standing by the couch, the empty wineglass on the coffee table, the half full one next to it.

"I'm sorry," she said. "I didn't realize you had company."

"Come in," Whit said. "Mrs. Hubble and I were just discussing her ex-husband. You want something to drink?"

"I'd love a Coke." Claudia sat down while Whit busied himself dumping ice cubes in a glass and cracking open a liter bottle of cola. He brought Claudia her soda. The silence between the two women hung thick as fog on a cool winter morning.

Claudia broke the quiet. "I'm glad you're here, Mrs. Hubble. I just confirmed with Anders Sorenson that he was hired to represent Pete in suing for custody of your son. I thought you might be able to help us understand why."

"As I was just telling the judge," Faith said slowly,

"Pete's legal concerns were his own matter. He'd ignored Sam for most of his years, and he was no parent. He had zero grounds for a serious bid for custody."

"So why hire Sorenson?" Whit asked. Anders Sorenson was from an old Port Leo family, one of the best-regarded attorneys in the area, almost seventy, a scrappy, dapper little man feared in the courtroom.

"Because Sorenson's backing Lucinda's opponent?" Faith flared. "*I don't know what Pete was doing.* I can't repeat that too many more times without thinking the two of you are brain-damaged."

Neither Whit nor Claudia spoke.

"I have to go, unless you have further questions," Faith said. "Sam is expecting me for dinner."

"I would like to speak with Sam," Whit said. "Briefly."

"Call me tomorrow and we'll set up a time." She picked up her purse and didn't give Claudia another glance as she walked out the door. Whit followed her out of the guesthouse, past the pool. She didn't break stride and she didn't look back, and he didn't call out to her. He went back to the guesthouse.

Claudia stared at him. "I heard her yelling at you before I knocked on the door."

"I've known her for a while. She's upset."

"And?"

"Her kid's the most important thing in the world to her," Whit said. "But she's right. Pete wouldn't have a prayer in family court."

"Unless she's done something far worse than adult films," Claudia said.

Whit sipped his wine.

"I thought you and I could talk to Jabez Jones together

tomorrow morning," she said. "Your clerk said it'd work with your schedule."

"That's fine," he said.

She touched his arm. "Anything else you want to tell me, Honorable?"

"No," he said. "Nothing else at all."

18

Velvet eased the magazine out of her Sig Sauer 9mm automatic pistol. She tucked the Sig far down into her purse. Then she yanked it out of concealment, past tissues and car keys and compact. Four seconds. Too long, but stacking the gun atop her billfold and cosmetics made her nervous; she had no concealed weapons permit. She supposed she could always just fire through the thin leather of the purse.

Finding the gun had been easier than she imagined. She'd hired a cab to take her to Corpus Christi, rented a Chevy Caprice at the airport, and driven to a ragtag collection of pawnshops. She found that cash and a quick but ardent display of her professional skills spoke volumes to one particular dealer. She'd never seen a registration form.

She'd picked up a small tape recorder as well, the kind used by reporters. Voice-activated in case someone said something interesting she wanted to keep. This she stuck down in the depths of her purse.

Velvet practiced pulling the automatic from her purse for ten more minutes until the motion felt fluid and natural and the gun didn't feel so alien in her grip. If Junior Deloache became a problem, she thought, she'd have to fire without flinching. She imagined shooting him in the stomach—clearly the biggest target on him—and tried not to think about how much blood might explode from his guts.

Him or you. Just think of it as him or you if it comes to that. Junior was, she thought, most likely full of bluff, and he might even be useful to her.

Her fantasies shifted from gunning down a hot-breathed Junior Deloache to placing the cool barrel of the Sig against Faith Hubble's head and forcing that awful woman to sing the truth. *Yes, I killed him, I killed him, please don't hurt me…*

A gentle knock rapped on the door. She went and peered through the peephole. Faith Hubble stared back at her through the security hole, arms crossed, frowning like she wanted to bite the world in half.

"Velvet? You there?" Faith called. She knocked again.

Velvet hurried back to her purse. She clicked on the recorder and found the ammunition in the bottom of the bag.

"You're stupider than I thought," Gooch said.

Whit nursed his beer. He and Gooch sat in a deserted corner at Georgie's bar at the Shell Inn. Being a Tuesday night, the bar was mostly empty, only a few figures quaffing down liquid forgetfulness in the shallow light. The tarpons on the wall, mounted over draped netting, caught the glow of the television along their preserved curves. Georgie sat at the bar, smoking a cigarette and working the *New York Times* crossword puzzle with a bloodred pen.

He had just confessed to Gooch about his affair with Faith and was now receiving a quota of due lashings.

"What do you think Buddy Beere might make of this,

Whitman?" Gooch rattled the ice in his near-empty glass of bourbon. "He'll fry you into political hash."

"Buddy doesn't have to know. And Pete's her *longtime* ex. I don't think there's a professional conflict in me handling the case."

"Buddy will. And no secret in this county gets kept forever," Gooch said. "There's too many big mouths and prying eyes and booze." He finished his drink with a toss and signaled to the barkeep for a refill. She didn't see him, giggling with Eddie Gardner at the bar. Whit watched Gardner, who had pointedly ignored him. If Claudia was slaving over the Hubble case tonight, Gardner wasn't.

"I've discovered the silver lining. You blow the election, you can work for me," Gooch mused. "I'm thinking of buying a much bigger boat, you know, a serious party barge. If I do it, you can wriggle out from under Babe's wing and grab a real life."

"Yeah. Scrubbing decks, gutting fish, keeping drunks from going overboard. And best of all, taking orders from you. My life's dream."

"You ain't got room for snooty." Gooch finally got the bartender's attention when she turned from laughing at a joke of Gardner's. She nodded and brought Gooch his drink. Whit watched the young woman hurry back to Gardner, intent on not leaving him shifted in neutral too long.

"Why do cute girls like a greaseball like Gardner?" Whit wondered.

Gooch shrugged. "You ask this while diddling Faith Hubble."

Whit considered. "She's fun."

"And willing. Is that all you require?"

"No."

"What else? Breathing?" Gooch put a hand over his heart in mock horror. "You're not in love with her, are you?"

"Of course not," Whit said.

"So she's just someone you sleep with?"

"She's . . ." Whit stopped. *Lover* implied more emotional depth than either he or Faith had yet brought to the bed. *One-night stand* was logistically incorrect. *Sexual release* carried all the warmth of freezer burn. He just liked her; he still liked her. "We're in a shadowy area."

His map of Faith's heart consisted of the roughest sketch. He knew Sam was her north star, her everything, with perhaps Lucinda and her political career a near second. But when they were together—from the first time—she had shown an openness toward him that he suspected few others saw. He didn't believe her capable of sticking a gun in a man's mouth and pulling the trigger.

He was pretty sure. Fairly sure.

He finished his beer. Crap. Not sure at all, even though he'd tasted her skin, felt the broad warmth of her back pressed up against his chest, explored the shape of her mouth, smelled chamomile in her hair, knew which ribs produced ticklish laughter. He didn't know the shape and size of her heart.

And Claudia. She'd greeted Faith with all the friendliness of a mongoose eyeing a swaying cobra. Claudia sure hadn't believed it was a simple interview. Miss By-the-Book would blow a mighty shrill whistle on him in two seconds flat if she smelled a conflict of interest. And he couldn't blame her.

Just then Whit noticed a chunky blond man lumber up from a darkened corner of the bar, wearing a gaudy-awful tropical shirt, and head out the door. He bumped into an older man entering the bar and said, "Watch it, old fart." The old man, already drunk, ignored him.

Whit said, "Come on," to Gooch, tossed dollars on the bar to settle the tab, and followed.

As they went out, the man clambered into a red Porsche. Grit and bird-guano splatters dusted the car. The Porsche jerked out of its slot and revved onto Main Street.

Whit ran to his Explorer, Gooch following.

"Explaining soon?" Gooch said.

"Heavy. Blond. Loud. He looks like the dirtbag Ernesto described. And he's driving a messy Porsche, just like Ernesto said."

Whit tailed the filthy Porsche down Main Street, past the shopping district where seasonally challenged store owners had already hung Christmas decorations and dangled sprays of light in the palm and red bay trees. On his left was the bay, with rental condo developments lining the shore. Most had been built in the 1970s during a last-gasp oil boom and retained the unfortunate, granola-esque architecture of the time—boxy, with diagonally layered strips of wood for siding and balconies ringed with thick oak beams.

They drove past the Port Leo city limits for a half mile and the Porsche wheeled into a condo resort called Sea Haven. Its name was written in cursive rope for that authentic nautical air. Missing windows and sawhorses suggested renovations were under way.

The Porsche parked next to a flooring company's van, and the driver unfolded himself from the car. Big, with terminally moussed hair and pimp-bright clothes: a crimson tropical shirt adorned with purple parrots, bright yellow golfing pants, snow-white high-top sneakers. He straightened his britches with a decisive yank as he ambled toward the building.

Whit drove past, U-turned, and circled back. The man still stood in the yard, talking to an elderly man in a motorized wheelchair.

"Stop and talk to them or go on?" Gooch asked.

"Carpe diem and all that crap," Whit said. "Let's stop."

The old man watched them park and raised a hand to silence the young man. Whit was suddenly conscious of the KEEP JUDGE MOSLEY megasize magnetic sign on the side of his Explorer. He and Gooch walked toward them. The steely scowl on the old man's face deepened.

"Hello," Whit said. "I'm Whit Mosley and I'm the justice of the peace here in Encina County."

"I see." The old man nodded toward the garishly patriotic vote-mobile, bright under the streetlights. "I'm Anson Todd."

Whit recognized the name from the marina manager; Todd was the man who'd made the docking arrangements for *Real Shame*. "This is Leonard Guchinski," Whit said.

"Charmed," Gooch said.

Whit kept his eyes on the hefty guy. "I understand you're acquainted with Pete Hubble."

"Why do you ask or care?" the younger man challenged.

"Junior," the older man said with a bored note of caution.

Ah, young Mr. Deloache. "I'll take that as a yes. I'm conducting the inquest into Pete's death and I'd like to talk to you about him."

"We have nothing to say," Junior said in a petulant voice. "Nothing."

"Come in for a minute," the old man invited, as though

he'd not heard Junior's pronouncement. His voice, scratchy, reminded Whit of a dusty, worn record. "Junior, do me a favor. We're out of cereal and I'm not facing the morning without my raisin bran. Run down to the store." He pivoted the wheelchair sharply and zoomed for the condo's lobby.

"Anson, we got cereal," Junior called to the old man's back.

"Not the kind I like," Anson said, not giving Junior another glance. "Go."

Junior, abandoned, stood slack-jawed and then loped to his Porsche and roared off. Whit and Gooch followed Anson into the condo's lobby. Wood shavings, tattered wallpaper, and a half-dismantled reception desk, cluttered with a forest of empty soda cans, decorated the half-done vestibule. A couple of construction workers, begrimed with sawdust but getting excellent overtime, inspected unfurled blueprints with lukewarm interest.

"Late night to be working construction," Gooch said.

"Late night to be bothering people," Anson said.

They followed Anson into a cramped, rackety elevator. Anson punched eight, the top button.

"So you own this building?" Whit asked.

"No." Anson declined further explanation. Anson Todd looked to be edging seventy. He wore a black turtleneck, gray sweatpants covering withered legs, and wire-rimmed glasses over cat-green eyes. An ugly, welted scar scored his temple, and his overlong gray hair was combed over to hide the mark.

"Let me guess. You work for Mr. Deloache, Senior," Whit said.

The elevator stopped, and Whit held the door for Anson to wheel himself out. Anson motored out of the elevator into a garishly appointed suite. It looked to Whit like an animal lover's nightmare: zebra prints on the wall, a leopard sofa, a tiger skin on the floor. The monotony of hides was broken by the neon-kissed furniture that had likely been purchased at the House of Lime. A thick-necked youth glanced up from the television; his overinflated physique made him look like he had been gulping steroids with his mother's milk.

"Hey," the young man greeted Anson, a wary glance going to Gooch and Whit.

"Go watch TV in the master bedroom," Anson ordered. "Come if I call you."

"Sure," the monosyllabic hulk agreed. He lurched up from the couch and stomped into another room, slamming the door behind him.

Anson Todd said, "I love chaperoning the mentally deficient. Have a seat, Judge. Mr. Guchinski." He gestured toward an expansive leather sofa the color of a frozen margarita. Instead Whit wandered to the wall of windows that showed a panoramic view of St. Leo Bay and the Gulf. To the north, the huge piers jutting out into the bay dazzled with light, and house lights along Santa Margarita Island glittered like a broken bracelet of diamonds.

"I see why you stay here instead of aboard *Real Shame*," Whit said.

"Actually, the *Shame*'s not wheelchair-friendly. I stay off except for an infrequent fishing trip. Coffee? Beer?"

Gooch leaned against the window, thick arms linked behind his back. Whit eased onto the plush leather couch.

"No, thank you," Whit said. "We won't take up much of your time."

"You won't need much, Judge. We don't know a thing

about Pete's death. Yes, Mr. Deloache Senior owns *Real Shame* and has for five years. But Pete was an acquaintance of Junior's. Mr. Deloache never met him."

"The gun that was found in Mr. Hubble's hand wasn't registered."

"If there was an unregistered gun aboard, then Mr. Hubble or his lady friend brought it. Not ours."

"She denies that."

Anson smiled. "Once she's over her grief, maybe her memory improves."

Whit wondered if memory enhancements came in the form of fists or threats. "I've spoken with witnesses who say Junior visited Pete pretty regularly at the marina. Argued with him about money. Behaved badly yesterday."

"Define *badly*."

"Tried to rough up Pete."

"Junior? He's a teddy bear. He couldn't bruise fruit. Look, from where I sit, you got hearsay. You got anyone who's positively ID'd Junior as being there?"

"Don't," Whit said. "His father owns the boat."

"Okay, yeah, but you got anyone who will ID Junior as being the argumentative type you're looking for?"

"Yes."

"Really? 'Cause Junior wasn't here yesterday. Neither was I. We been in Houston the past few days, we just drove in this morning. Got a whole bunch of people who will confirm that."

"Why are y'all down here? Because someone died on your property?"

"Junior's in charge of getting this resort project completed for his dad. You could call him a project manager. You should. He loves it."

Whit raised an eyebrow. "Let me guess. Junior manages the project and you manage Junior."

Anson grinned. His teeth were yellowed from cigarette smoke.

"How well did you know Pete?" Whit asked.

"I met him just once. Let me tell you, Judge, I find porn boring. I find porn stars even more boring. Especially when they're male. Pete had all the brains of dandruff."

"What about this money Pete and Junior supposedly bickered over?"

Anson cleared his throat. His voice took on a soft volume that had no softness in the tone. "Look, Judge, I agreed to tell you what we know, not undergo interrogation. We knew the guy, we didn't have anything to do with his death, and Mr. Deloache is gonna want his boat back pronto."

"Mr. Deloache is going to have to wait for the investigation to be over," Whit answered pleasantly. "Mr. Deloache, both the senior and the junior, need to answer questions."

"Let me ask you one. How many times was Pete shot?"

"Once."

"Where?"

"The head."

Anson crinkled his nose. "Gee. Once in the head. Can I have suicide for four hundred dollars, Alex?"

"Or maybe it was an execution," Whit said. "Gangland style."

"Gangland? I haven't heard that term since cable showed the James Cagney movie marathon." Anson leaned back in his chair. "Look, Judge, you want to explore slander, keep talking. We got a whole flock of lawyers up in Houston that wouldn't consider you a light hors d'oeuvre."

"I can call you and Junior as witnesses at the inquest. Mr. Deloache, too."

"I've told you we know nothing. And I got nothing to give you, Judge, except the pleasure of my company and a good cup of coffee." He smiled. "I bet you know the good fishing spots in St. Leo Bay. We ought to get our lines tight some time."

Whit imagined more of Anson's boating expeditions involved concrete mixes and pleas for mercy rather than suntan lotion and cheap bait. "Thanks for your time. I'll see you in court." He headed for the elevator, Gooch silently following, and pressed the button.

The fishing bonhomie vanished. "It's not a good idea to waste Mr. Deloache's time."

"It's not a good idea to waste mine, either," Whit said. The doors slid open, and Whit and Gooch stepped on the elevator. Anson Todd stared at them until the doors slid shut.

"You're such a tough guy," Gooch said. "I released a vast flood of urine into my pants, out of sheer terror."

"You do smell funny," Whit said. "Watch me. I'll subpoena both of them so fast their beady little eyes'll pop."

The elevator doors slid open with a creaky fanfare. Junior Deloache stood there with a box of raisin bran crushed under his arm and a six-pack of beer. He looked like a delivery boy gone to seed but a cold light of calculation touched his eyes.

"Hi, Junior," Whit said. "Could we talk for a second? Just outside?"

Junior shook his head. "I gotta make sure Anson gets his high fiber."

"I'd like to see what all you're doing with Sea Haven. I only have a couple of questions for you."

Junior shrugged and Whit and Gooch followed him through the dismantled lobby to a large patio, aglow with fuzzy security lights, bare of furniture, with an emptied, cracked pool. A decaying cabana-cum-bar with a graying palm-thatched roof stood nearby, lopsided with neglect.

"Welcome to Groo-vin' Central," Junior said. "Once we get it cleaned up and lure all the young chickies here."

Gooch said, "Oh, yes, I just see chickies flocking here by the dozens."

"You gonna have the money to finish?" Whit asked.

Junior gave him a scornful sideways glance. "Why wouldn't I?"

"Didn't you owe Pete Hubble serious money?"

"Most certainly did not."

"People at the marina heard the two of you bickering about money. Saw you shoving him around on your boat."

Junior frowned, but Whit saw he had to think about it first. "Your sources are faulty, man. I didn't owe him money."

Gooch asked, "So what did Pete owe you?"

"And you would be who?" Junior asked. "You the bailiff for the judge or something?"

"Gooch is just a friend along for the ride." Whit wished Gooch would shut up.

"There was no owing of any sort, man. There's a real difference between friends goofing around and arguing. I just got a big voice."

"When did you last see Pete?" Whit asked.

"A few days ago, last week. He and I took the boat out."

"Do you want to talk about whatever this money issue was at an inquest hearing? Because I'll call you to testify if

I think it's relevant. Or if you're not cooperating. I'm sure the police would be interested."

Not testifying, Whit suspected, might be a family virtue long drummed into Junior, probably since he broke the legs of his first G.I. Joe in the nursery.

"I had no reason to want Pete dead. See, Pete promised me I could be in a movie."

"The one he was making about his brother?"

"Tragedy is not my style. A, you know, different kind of movie." Junior swiveled his hips with a not-so-subtle grind.

"I see. Pete was going to let you be in a groo-vin' movie," Whit said in an understanding tone.

"Yeah, you're on board now."

"Anson and your dad must've loved that idea."

The smile faded.

"I got the impression whatever Anson said, you did." Whit gently poked the box of raisin bran.

"Yeah, well, that's me being nice to an old fart. Anson's already got one wheel in the grave."

"So with Pete gone I guess your movie career is on hold. Unless you can convince Velvet to cast you in her next opus."

He grinned. "That's no problem."

"Why is that?"

Junior set the cereal and beer down, gently, stood, and rubbed his palms against each other, warming his fists for use. "You know, you're grilling me like chicken, dude, and I don't got to give you the time of day."

"Oh, yes, please let's get physical," Gooch interrupted. "I haven't had a workout today, and you got punching bag written all over your gut."

Junior started a retort, then seemed to reconsider as he

noted the size of Gooch's biceps. "I sure as hell ain't gonna answer any more questions."

"Fine. I'll see you in my courtroom." Whit had found his weapon—Anson's and Junior's loathing of court—and wasn't about to surrender it.

A cold rage lit Junior's eyes. "My daddy's attorneys will eat you alive."

"What's with these attorneys and the food metaphors? Eat us alive and grilling you like chicken and consider Whit an appetizer? No wonder you're chunky," Gooch said.

"Gooch. Don't," Whit said. He shrugged at Junior. "So start working your cell phone and get all of your daddy's attorneys down here. The bill the lawyers charge to your dad for all that travel time should be substantial."

Junior considered this—calling his father to gather a bevy of lawyers in Port Leo—and suddenly cooperated. "Look, Judge, you want to chase down the right fox, you need to look at the X-Bitch."

"Who?"

"Pete's ex. He called her the X-Bitch, you know, like *The X-Files*? Freaking alien weirdo. She was about to drive him crazy."

"How so?"

"Man, how didn't Faith? Over at his boat all the time, trying to sweeten him up. I caught Pete and Faith once, I swear, inches from screwing. Velvet would've had a coronary."

"Velvet says Pete was just a friend."

"Yeah, right, they're just friends after he's screwed her a couple of hundred times. You know women don't think that way, not even porn stars." Junior laughed, relaxing now that the topic was back on treasured ground. "But the X-Bitch, hell, I think she kinda had a split personality going as far as Pete was concerned. She wanted him but she wanted him gone. She works for that nightmare of a mother of his, and you know they were soiling their panties when he moved back. He told me his mother offered him money to go away. He didn't want to do it and I'm all like, dude! Are you nuts? Take the money, ditch Port Lame here and go back to L.A., where life is real." Junior shook his head. "He should've taken that money. He really should've."

Anson wheeled into view in the open doorway. "Junior!" he bawled. "Get in here."

Junior picked up his groceries. "I had every reason to want Pete alive, and his family sure as hell didn't. Later." He turned and went back to Anson, walking past him without a word. Whit followed him back through the lobby. Anson wasn't in a mood to parry further.

"Good night, Judge," he said with solemnity, and motored himself back into the elevator after Junior.

Whit and Gooch walked out of the lobby. Junior hardly appeared credible on paper, but his words gave Whit pause. If Velvet was right, and Pete was going to sue for custody, had Faith tried to disarm him with sex? And if Lucinda had truly offered her son cash to fade away... what had she done when he refused?

It suggested they knew damn well Pete might be suing for custody, and had more than a prayer of winning. But Junior would be hard to present as a credible witness.

"I must get the name of the reform school he attended," Gooch said. "I want to sponsor a scholarship."

Whit walked past Junior's Porsche and noticed the rear left corner looked like it had suffered a minor accident. The left taillight was smashed. Whit remembered the one-eyed Porsche he'd passed last night heading away from the marina, trash disco blaring into the night—hours before Anson claimed they'd arrived in Port Leo.

The Blade was tired.

Midnight had come to Port Leo, his favorite time, and he stood beneath a canopy of live oaks and listened to the wind—the wind that had caressed, in its time, every inch of the world, every woman—whisper through the oak limbs.

It was a good day, he supposed. He knew where Velvet was, a toy just waiting to be opened. His plan for Heather Farrell had been put in motion. He could sleep and dream up a store of delights that, in the days ahead, he could make real.

Not every man, he knew, was so blessed and rich. He went into the garage to prepare his boat for its chores.

19

Mom?"

Faith Hubble was jolted out of sleep. She had been dreaming: dreaming that Port Leo was gone, left far behind her on a boat arrowing deep into the bowl of the Gulf, and Pete stood to one side of her, Whit on the other. As the spray from the prow cooled her face against a blistering sun, the two of them seized her shoulders, upended her over the railing, and she plummeted toward a canyon of water, falling for miles. She had glanced up and Pete and Whit were gone, Lucinda and Sam standing in their places, watching her die.

She pulled her head from the pillow. Sweat touched her shoulders, her back, between her legs.

"Mom?" Sam said again. Purpling shadows marred the skin under his eyes. He looked as though he hadn't slept in a week. "You okay?"

She smiled. She certainly was. "Yes, honey, I'm fine." She patted his hand. "It's all gonna be okay. I promise you that."

Velvet munched on a cold Pop-Tart and counted the money again, the bills new and stiff and feeling like revenge under her fingernails. She made the edges of the bills flush with a smack against the bedside table. As down payments went, it wasn't half bad. And since her production company wasn't being at all helpful on the legal front ("Sorry, Velvet. Don't know a lawyer in Texas and we just can't get involved"—the bastards), the money was more necessary than ever. Money from Faith to stab Faith, eventually. She liked the idea.

She finished her Pop-Tart then studied the pastry's box to see if the phrase was trademarked—not a bad name for a movie. Pop-Tarts. Could play up pop music, could play up oversweet breakfast treats. Trademarked. Oh, well. She folded the money—twenty thousand—into the bottom of her suitcase, hiding it inside a light windbreaker.

She showered, considering her next move. Shooting Faith would have been a bad idea and she doubted that she could have pulled the trigger. But she had loaded the gun and stuck it in the bottom of her purse as Faith knocked on the door, just in case.

Just in case the crazy ex-wife tried to kill her.

But Faith had not had murder on her mind. *Listen, Velvet, you know and I know that Pete killed himself. You saying anything else is just a ploy for publicity.*

You mean a ploy for justice.

No. Publicity. I did a little checking, sweetie. Pete tried to kill himself four years ago, swallowing pills. I got the hospital records from Van Nuys. I'm giving them to the police and to Whit Mosley.

It doesn't mean anything.

You know what else I found out, sweetie? Your last five movies have bombed. You tried to get all artsy instead of just delivering the smut, and no one cares what you're doing now. You're broke, Velvet.

Get the hell out of here.

And Faith, instead of getting mad, gave her that superior little smirk. *So mature. Don't you know I can help you? Get you back on your feet so you can*—the smirk again— *get back off them right away. And you and I can both be happy.*

Velvet rinsed her hair clean of lather, turned off the shower, reached for a towel. She felt better than she had yesterday, when the knots and rocks in her gut shifted with every breath. She stepped out of the shower, wondering if Pete was looking down or up at her, and whether he hated her now.

Don't hate me, Pete. I promise you I'm not done with them yet, and Faith Hubble's going to fry, fry, fry. She would have to launder the money the Hubbles would be steering toward her, polish it with a veneer of respectability, before she called the papers in Dallas and Houston and Austin. It shouldn't, she figured, take very long.

She got dressed and checked the gun again, at the bottom of her purse. It fit in perfectly next to the handheld tape recorder. Faith's voice on that tape—cajoling, begging, offering bribes for silence over Pete's still secret career— was better than any bullet. A bullet meant only a moment's suffering.

Suffering. She thought of Sam, Faith's pleas that he be protected from all the pain about Pete's career, and she remembered Sam and Pete sitting on the prow of *Real Shame,* Pete drinking a bottled beer, Sam sipping a Coke, awkwardly talking, settling finally on a discussion of baseball. Pete liked the Padres, Sam the Rangers, and she shamelessly eavesdropped, hearing them warm to each other, talking about trades and homers and a mutual loathing of the Yankees. Sam had finally laughed at one point. Warm tears had welled in her eyes and she thought, *Who the hell are you, June Cleaver?* Maybe she should say nothing forever, let Sam think his father just made industrial films. Pete wouldn't want Sam to be ashamed, to bear the brunt of his sins. Or she could take the money, throw it at Sam, say, *Here's what your mama wanted to pay me for silence, hon. Know who you're living with.*

She dug the creased business card out of her purse, smoothed it out, then dialed Whit's number.

At ten after nine Wednesday morning, Claudia drove past an elaborately painted sign that read JABEZ JONES MINISTRIES. Above the logo was a gold cross etched over a pair of gargantuan biceps.

"Did you know that the disciples did not work out on a regular basis?" Whit slurped a cup of hot coffee he'd snagged at Irina's café.

"Judas was flabby, too," Claudia said. The road leading to the compound was surrounded by a dense growth of bent oaks and lined by hardy palm trees. They drove past another sign that read SALVATION AHEAD—FEEL THE BURN.

"So what happens if you go to hell? Don't you still feel the burn?" Claudia asked. She didn't feel the burn, but she felt the tension in the car. She and Whit hadn't talked since she'd seen Faith at Whit's place. Whit had seemed tired when she picked him up at the courthouse. He updated her about his talk with Junior Deloache and Anson Todd. Another angle for her to present to Delford, although she fretted her boss would welcome news of Pete's friendship with hoods no more than theories of murder. "Do you think he's this corny on purpose?"

"Absolutely. It's sort of like asking if pro wrestlers consider themselves athletes," Whit said. "Do you remember Jabez Jones from school?"

"Vaguely. Geeky, glasses, the kind of preacher's kid you felt bad for because you just knew he never got to have one lick of fun," Claudia said.

"I remember seeing him wrestling on TV. Joltin' Jabez Jones. I nearly didn't recognize him. Especially in gold tights."

"My father considers pro wrestling a religion."

"Religion doesn't have much to do with his appeal," Whit said. "He's just like those TV specials on pets that attack or cops' greatest chases or us all watching a president get caught with his pants down. Everything is entertainment now. He's just making lo-cal evangelism another genre."

They turned into an asphalt parking lot. Jabez's compound was the original odd folly of a Fort Worth oil baron who had built a television studio outside Port Leo, part of an ill-conceived plan for a fishing network. The few shows he produced bombed and the compound stayed shuttered for a few years until Jabez Jones defected from the pro wrestling ring to start his church and show, *Holy Cross-Training*. It had found a shaky home on stations serving rural markets with low-powered religious programming.

The squat cabins were painted a glossy white. A game of women's volleyball, played in modest shorts and T-shirts adorned with gold crosses, was under way in a sand pit. A couple of men stood by, watching, attempting unsuccessfully to look pious while ogling the bouncing breasts.

"He's Hugh Hefner with a Bible," Whit said.

Whit and Claudia were barely out of the car when the welcoming committee arrived. She was six feet tall, well muscled, and wore her platinum-blond hair closely cropped. She wore a tight white T-shirt with a gold cross emblazoned on the chest and cargo pants bulky enough to conceal an armory. Whit remembered what Ernesto had told him about one of Pete's visitors: she big and scary, big muscles. "Hi. I'm Judge Whit Mosley and this is Detective Claudia Salazar from the Port Leo police. We have an appointment with Jabez," Whit said.

"Regarding?"

"He wanted to share some information with us regarding a case," Claudia said.

"Follow me. But if he's not done with his taping, you'll just have to wait."

Claudia and Whit followed the Amazon along a crushed-oyster-shell path that led down from the main complex toward a finger of the bay.

"I'm sorry, I didn't catch your name," Whit said.

"Mary Magdalene."

Whit shot Claudia a look. If Mary Magdalene was this tough, Whit thought, heaven only knew how deadly Esther and Ruth were. Eve could probably kick major butt, too.

"This is an impressive setup." Claudia gave Whit a frown that said, *Don't you dare laugh.*

Mary Magdalene nodded. "Oh, yes, the Lord has smiled on Jabez."

"He's smiling on that volleyball court," Whit said.

"Jabez says exercise is a way of paying homage to what the Lord has created, in making man and woman. Building muscles is worship." She flexed her own thickened arms.

"I've always believed our bodies are temples," Whit offered. Mary Magdalene gave him a quick scrutiny, then apparently dismissed his temple as one devoted to a lesser god.

The volleyball bounced into the grass near them. One of the comely disciples chased it. She scooped the ball up, and Whit thought: *Do I know her?* But the young woman turned and sashayed back to the game.

"Jabez doesn't have much trouble getting a date, does he?" Whit observed in what he considered to be a completely friendly tone. Claudia withered him with a glare.

"Jabez doesn't *date*." Mary Magdalene spat out the last word. "He doesn't care a whit for the temptations of this physical world." Her voice hardened. "The temptations of the flesh are the seed of all evil."

Whit surveyed the immaculately kept buildings, the sand-rumped girls playing volleyball, the new Cadillac parked right by the administration building door with JABEZ on the plate. "He's a real Francis of Assisi," Whit said to Claudia, his voice lowered.

"Sissy?" Mary Magdalene had misheard.

"No, sassy," Whit answered. "He sasses that old devil, don't he?"

Mary Magdalene raised one platinum eyebrow. "Jabez could kick the devil down to hell, and don't you forget it."

Whit and Claudia reflected on this platitude in silence. Claudia pinched Whit on the meaty part of his arm to ensure he wouldn't comment.

Mary Magdalene escorted them to a small stretch of beach full of cameras, portable sound booms, and spandex-clad missionaries. Sparkling white sand, cleaner-looking than the grayish beige grit on most Texas beaches, had been spread over the native soil.

Whit and Claudia stood back to watch the spectacle. Jabez Jones, well over six feet tall, two hundred thirty pounds of muscle with less body fat than a moth, lay on his side, scissoring his tree-trunk legs into the air, counting off reps while providing a little insight into the Book of Luke. Behind him two women (one svelte, one heavy for the dieting viewers to bond with) and a less beefy man mirrored his exercises, all beaming like angels.

"Now, hold the lift until the Scripture is done," Jabez boomed. " 'I tell thee, thou shalt not depart thence till thou hast paid the very...last...mite.'...There! Amen! Bless us all, did you feel the Holy Spirit invigorating your limbs? I know I did. I'm just coursing with the Holy Spirit right now. You keep doing those leg lifts and the devil himself won't be able to catch you. Now let's start our cool-down, and our Scripture for that is one of the more relaxing Psalms, a personal favorite of mine, number sixty-one."

Whit resisted the urge to lead a cheer.

Cool-down completed, Jabez jumped to his feet, did a hand clap, reminded viewers about his 1-888 number and website to place requests with Jabez's Prayer Workout Chain or to order his fitness-theology tapes. "Remember, your donations make all the difference in fighting flab... and sin! Praise God! Call now!"

God—who, in Whit's mind, represented the infinite beauty of the universe—as a weight-loss shuckster.

Finally a nasal-voiced director called, "That's a wrap. Beautiful, Jabez." Jabez gave a weary sigh and wiped the sand off his oiled legs. The crew began their cleanup.

"I'm curious, Mary Magdalene," Whit said. "Where does all the money come from to pay for this wonderful spread? Jabez's wrestling career must've been lucrative in that worldly goods way."

"The Lord provides," Mary Magdalene intoned.

"The Lord must provide on a real regular basis," Whit

said. Claudia shot him a look: *Quit antagonizing this woman*. Whit moved to the left a couple of feet to avoid another pinch.

Jabez Jones trotted over, smiling. "Hello, Detective Salazar. Judge Mosley. Bless you."

"Hello, Reverend." Claudia nodded. "We had an appointment?"

"Of course. Thank you for escorting them here, Mary. We can talk here along the beach, it's quiet and peaceful." He gestured with his oak-tree arm down a stretch of beach away from the camera crew.

"Jabez?" Mary Magdalene clearly didn't want to leave his presence. "I can stay—"

"Go. It's fine," Jabez said.

"If you'll excuse me," Mary Magdalene said, "I have the Lord's work to do." She uttered this with a mysterious air, as though this activity involved Navy SEALs, Russian microfilm, and Jimmy Hoffa.

They followed Jabez. The morning had turned shiny, the sky cloudless. A wheel of gulls cawed above their heads, swerved as one, and dived for food in the lapping surf. Shriveled husks of two dead Portuguese man-of-war jellyfish lay on the sand.

"Mary Magdalene seems real sweet," Whit said.

"She's very devoted. I rescued Mary Magdalene from the streets of Houston. She was homeless, hopeless, strung out on dope, not strong. I made her strong," Jabez said.

"You and your faith," Whit said.

"Absolutely," Jabez agreed, as though he and the Lord made an awesome tag team. "So, Whit. You're a JP now. How very...rewarding for you."

"I like it," Whit said.

"I surely hope you're reelected," Jabez said. "I mean, running that restaurant and that delivery service just didn't seem to be your calling." The comment was topped with such a dollop of theocratic sugar that it might not be an insult. Jabez smiled in the light of his expensive muscles and his expensive compound and his expensive television crew.

"Gosh, Jabez, thanks. And I pray on a near-constant basis that you get picked up by a TV station that actually serves a metropolitan area."

Jabez's smile never dimmed, but one of the balloon-shaped muscles in his arm tensed. The preacher turned to Claudia. "I called because I thought I might be able to help you with your inquiries."

"We understand you'd been to see Pete recently."

"Yes. I offered him spiritual counsel. He and I have known each other for a long time. He was going through some difficult times." He paused and dropped his little bomb. "He wanted custody of his son."

"That we knew," Whit said.

Jabez crossed his bulky arms. Small gold crosses were tattooed on his knuckles. "Oh. Well, perhaps I'm not being helpful. The Hubbles were, of course, opposed to him filing. Trying to settle with him. I guess you knew that as well."

Whit and Claudia exchanged a quick glance. The Hubbles had consistently claimed no knowledge of Pete wanting custody. If Jabez was being truthful, then they were lying.

"What did he have on them that would have made them even negotiate with him? You only go out-of-court if you're not sure you can win, and Faith and Lucinda should have been as sure as saints," Whit said. "What leverage did Pete have?"

Jabez shook his head. "Don't know...Your Honor. Pete kept that private." But there was a flicker of an amused smile behind his solemnity, and Whit wondered.

"I understand you and he fought. Argued," Whit said.

"Ah. Velvet?"

"Yes."

"She misunderstood. Pete wanted me to be a character witness for him. I was willing, because I do think everyone can change, and Pete seemed sincere in wanting to improve his lot. But I told him he would need to accept God in his life, and he got mad at me then. There were no other arguments."

"So did Pete discuss any other aspects of his life with you?" Claudia asked.

A pained look crossed Jabez's gladiator-handsome face. "When I was in wrestling...well, some of my colleagues were attracted to women of dubious morality. Some of them worked in adult films, and I heard, through them, about Pete. I actually saw him at a dinner party a few years ago, hosted by a wrestling promoter. He looked terrible. He asked me not to tell anyone back here about his...career. I've kept my word. Gossip is the devil's venom poured in an ear. So do you suspect the Hubbles?"

So much for the evils of gossip, Whit thought.

"We have no suspects at the moment. We're not even sure it's a homicide," Claudia said. "Judge Mosley will be conducting the inquest in the next couple of days."

"Would suicide surprise you?" Whit asked.

"I don't quite understand why he would come home and work on getting close to his son, then kill himself."

Whit changed topics. "Did he mention that he was work-ing on a film?"

Jabez's mouth gave a cautious twitch. "I prayed he would not resume his career."

"No. A documentary about his brother Corey. He says on a tape we found that you refused to cooperate with him."

The mouth twitched again and a muscle flexed under the cross-laden T-shirt. "That's not so. I just couldn't be of much help to him. He had called me . . . when he came back to town. That's how we got to talking. He did ask me to tell him about the day Corey vanished."

"And you said what?" Claudia asked.

Jabez paled under the store-bought tan. "Well, I was one of the last to see Corey before he was reported missing. Pete asked me to restate what I remembered. I'm afraid I wasn't much help to him." He stared out at the flat plane of the bay, stretching away like green glass.

"You and Corey strike me as unlikely friends," Whit said.

Jabez shrugged. "I wanted to help Corey. He was in trouble at school, at home, and sinking further. I thought I could help him reshape his life."

"So he was like a project," Whit said. "You could get your Samaritan merit badge by turning him around."

"That's a crude way to put it, but yes. If I didn't think the Lord could turn around lives, I would never bother with a ministry."

"And Corey was willing to be preached at?"

"You have an admirable ability for oversimplification, Whit," Jabez said. "It must serve you well in traffic court. No, he wasn't willing to be preached at. But he was willing to have a friend he could talk to, who didn't smoke dope, who didn't want to drag him down. I was a refuge."

"You were a goody-goody. He was a punk. I'm frankly surprised Corey Hubble would give you the time of day," Whit said.

"You just never know about people, do you?" Jabez said.

"So what happened the day Corey vanished?" Claudia interrupted.

"Corey had planned to spend the night with me. We were going to watch movies at my house. I'd gotten a tape of *Godspell,* thought he might like the music and it'd give me a way to witness to him. He called and canceled at the last minute, saying he was sick. I never heard from or saw him again."

"Did Pete share any theories about Corey with you?" Claudia asked. "Any information he had found about his brother?"

Jabez Jones considered for a moment, and the pause reminded Whit of a talented preacher waiting for the congregation to lean forward, eager for the next word. "It makes no sense to me. Pete mentioned a possibility that Corey was still alive. And in some kind of trouble."

20

———◦◦◉◦◦———

Y OU KNOW THAT motto, What Would Jesus Do? I look
at Jabez and wonder, What Would Jesus Think?" Claudia
said.

"He's lying," Whit said.

"Prove it."

"Oh, proof. My gut tells me. He's a publicity hound. If
he can link himself to a high-profile death, he will."

"Listen, Honorable, you can't prove he's lying any more
than you could prove Faith Hubble has lied. Or anyone
else," she added quickly.

"You think Faith's lying?"

"Faith Hubble is running scared."

"Don't pull a punch here."

"She threatened my family, Whit. Very subtly. She
implied my father might lose his shrimping license."

"You must have misunderstood."

"You don't misunderstand a threat to your father's livelihood. I felt like belting her in the face." Claudia turned
onto Highway 35 that threaded back to Port Leo. "I sensed
a weird vibe between you and Faith Hubble last night."

"No. I've just known her for a long while. She's worried
about her kid."

"Don't let your friendship warp your judgment."

"I'm going to get tired, very quickly, of you and Delford telling me how to do my job."

"Don't get all huffy."

Whit was silent for a moment. "So say what you think, Claudia."

"You have a political future at stake, Whit. I know you want to win the election, even if you act like campaigning is pimping. And I don't relish examining bodies with that grease-wad Buddy Beere. So all I'm saying is, you show the Hubbles a hint of favoritism, you're gonna get cooked. I don't believe for one second they can contain Velvet from leaking news of Pete's career. The news is going to hit big, and you better handle the inquest with every i dotted and t crossed."

"As opposed to gunning for them. Like you," Whit said dryly.

They passed the WELCOME TO PORT LEO—SWEET SPOT OF THE GULF sign, surrounded by smaller signs from city churches, the Chamber of Commerce, the Kiwanis and Rotary Club. "As long as they don't gun for me. She guns for me, my family, I don't tolerate that."

"I still think you're mistaken about Faith," Whit said.

"I'm not getting into a fight with you, Honorable." Claudia turned into the town square, parking in front of the police station. "But why did Heather Farrell say Pete blamed Jabez for Corey's death? Jabez sure isn't going to tell us. How would Heather even know about a connection between Jabez and Pete?"

"Maybe she's got a different connection to Jabez. Other than Pete."

Claudia shrugged. "I'll track Ms. Farrell down and ask her."

Whit turned to her. "Let's say Jabez is telling the truth. Pete thought Corey was alive...so where's Corey been all these years?"

Claudia's office was cramped. Delford sat in the creaky wooden chair next to her desk, eyes bleary red. Even his wax-perked mustache drooped, its tapered corners sagging. Whit slumped in the chair at Eddie Gardner's desk, his feet propped on a stack of papers.

Whit watched as Delford and Claudia brainstormed.

"The most obvious answer is usually the right one," Delford said. "Suicide."

Claudia shook her head. "Pete lived on a boat owned by established criminals. He wanted his wife's kid. He could derail his mother's political campaign. He was digging into a brother's disappearance that could have been murder and made accusations against a wannabe television star. Are you and I looking at the same picture?"

"Yeah, well you can look at inkblots and come up with different interpretations, Claud," Delford said. "He was a pervert and he didn't have squat of a future. We've had more than one person say, and folks that knew him better than you and I, that he was depressed and maybe suicidal."

"Your stubbornness," Claudia groaned, "is about to make me suicidal."

"He tried to kill himself a few years ago. Faith Hubble got the police report from Van Nuys. He downed a bunch of pills and vodka." Delford clicked his tongue. "I'd have thought, Claud, you would have unearthed that little nugget."

A slow creep of color bloomed along Claudia's cheeks. "I'd like to see that report, if you don't mind."

"Suicide once doesn't mean suicide again," Whit said.

Delford growled low in his throat. "No. Let's never grab hold of the obvious, shall we?"

Claudia turned referee. "Let me tell you what else I've found before you two start debating. Pete's been arrested twice out in California: once for public intox, once for disturbing the peace and public nudity. Apparently while filming one of his little epics in the great outdoors. He didn't serve time. Both were over five years ago." She flipped a page. "Velvet has no record. She told me in her statement that Pete rented that laptop on a monthly basis from Baywater Computers. I called the store owner, and Pete hadn't returned the system. We still haven't located it. I'm going to get a diver down into the marina to look for it. Maybe it went overboard."

Delford said nothing.

"Phone records I've got Fox checking out. Mostly calls back to California, although he has several calls to Missatuck, Texas, over the past week. Up in deep East Texas. Know it?"

"Never heard of it," Delford said. "So let's say it's murder, just to indulge you, Claudia. Who do you like?"

"Faith Hubble," Claudia said instantly.

"Right. A respected leader and mother," Delford said. "Same for you, Whit?"

Whit felt like he was walking on quicksand in leaded boots. "I don't know. Certainly Pete was a threat to the campaign. And Pete was serious about fighting for custody, although no one believes he had a prayer."

"Given what we know," Claudia interrupted. "But it works if Faith's closet was dirtier than his."

Delford snorted. "That's hard to imagine."

"Junior Deloache or someone working for him would be my guess," Whit said. "If you have a crime, look for criminals."

"You're deep," Delford said.

"Since you think I ignore the obvious, don't ignore the Deloaches," Whit said carefully. "I've got to go. Court and duty call." He left.

Delford waited until Whit shut the door. "Sloppy work, Claudia. Not learning about that suicide attempt. Doesn't make us look good." His voice, usually a cajoling drawl, rang hard and steely.

"I'm sorry. I'll call the Van Nuys police right now and confirm."

"See that you do," Delford said. "I got a meeting with the mayor. Let me know what you find out. And don't screw up again, Claud." He slammed the door behind him.

Who the hell are you turning into, Delford? she wondered. She reached for the phone and asked Nelda to get her the Van Nuys, California, police department.

21

———◦◉◦———

AT LUNCHTIME, WHIT grabbed a booth in the back of Café Caspian, surveying the small crowd in his new stepmother's restaurant. Babe had cautioned Irina that the Coastal Bend population included many military retirees who might blanch at patronizing a Russian café. Whit privately thought most of the retired military males would rush (in well-organized step) to slurp Irina's coffee once they spotted her in her black miniskirt and white T-shirt.

Café Caspian was perhaps a quarter full, mostly retirees with a smattering of real estate agents, secretaries, and artists gossiping over Russian specialties like *piroshki* (meat-filled dumplings), *golubtsi* (cabbage rolls), *borscht* topped with sour cream, honey breads, and *blinis*. Whit wished he had invested in sour cream futures before Irina opened the café; he would have made a killing. She also served more mainstream foods, such as thick ham sandwiches; fish, shrimp, and oysters fresh from the bay; and what she called *bitokes à la Russe*—hamburgers dolled up with sour cream (of course), onion, and nutmeg. These had been an unexpected hit.

Tributes to both Irina's motherland and her adopted

land decorated the walls: a beautiful color photograph of the Statue of Liberty; a portrait of Peter the Great. Reproductions of elegant Fabergé eggs and peasant Russian dolls lined a shelf; on another was a framed collection of miniature American and Texan flags. In the window hung several KEEP WHIT MOSLEY JUSTICE OF THE PEACE signs. Irina, the Soviet-born fiend for democracy.

Irina slid into the seat across from him, holding a steaming cup of tea and pushing her chestnut-brown hair back over her ears. Her face was elfin; he had always pictured Russian women as either kerchief-headed grannies, sun-and-nutrient-starved model waifs, or steroid-gulping swimmers. But Irina looked fresh and healthy, not tall but not frail, eyes of watery blue, and a generous mouth.

"Go campaign today." She took her stepmother role seriously. "Buddy Beere has a van covered with campaign signs patrolling Main Street."

"He offered to debate me."

"Of course you accepted."

"No. I'm too busy doing the actual job. But I need two favors."

"Tell me."

"I need to borrow your computer."

"Sure. You need the computer now?" she asked.

"I'd prefer to use it after hours, if you don't mind."

"No problem."

Why does a Russian accent nail you right in the crotch? Perhaps he had fixated on Natasha on the old *Bullwinkle* cartoons in a freaky erotic manner.

She jangled a set of keys from her pocket, pried a silver key off the ring, and slid it across the table.

"Extra key. Lock up when you're done. Second favor is?"

"I want you to befriend someone but you cannot gossip about it."

"Who?"

"Her name is Velvet."

"That sounds like a horse's name."

"She's not. She's a friend of the man who died. She's a little unconventional, but she could use a friendly face. She's meeting me here for lunch. I'll introduce you."

"You always find the strays that need help, yes?"

"Don't tell Dad. He'll just say that I'm not being focused on the campaign."

Irina made a dismissive noise. "Forget him. You know, I think I am the only one who knows the real you some-times. Isn't that silly?" She leaned over and gave him an irreproachable peck on the cheek. "You are a thoughtful boy, Whit."

A boy, and he was older than she.

Velvet stepped inside the café. Whit waved her over, introduced Irina to her.

"You're Judge Mosley's stepmother?" Velvet, dressed modestly in tourist-trap Bermuda shorts and a pale yellow T-shirt, shook hands and sat, not taking her eyes off Irina. "Maybe I should go recruit in Russia. I do training films. Corporate stuff."

Irina smiled politely and excused herself. She returned with tall glasses of iced tea, took their order for salads and *bitokes,* and scurried to the kitchen.

"So now you're making training films?" Whit said.

"I cut a little deal with Faith Hubble. Mouth zippered shut for now. For Sam's sake. Pete wouldn't have wanted him hurt by, well, by the truth."

"So you and Faith are bosom buddies?"

"I loathe her with all my heart. But Sam's a good kid. I don't want him hurt. But I don't want them to just sweep Pete under a rug, either."

"So how are you doing?"

She shrugged. "I'm cried out. When do you have autopsy results?"

"Probably today. At the latest tomorrow." He stirred his tea. "Pete tried to kill himself once before. You neglected to mention that to us."

"Oh, that. He took the wrong pills."

"A dozen of them?"

"He took the pills because I didn't cast him in a quickie movie I was making. We had a fight the week before, and I was fed up with him. Pete could be a prima donna. So he downed some tranqs and called me on his cell phone to drive him to the hospital. I didn't believe him, and by the time I got to his place he was tanked out. Otherwise I wouldn't have bothered with the hospital. I just would have made him puke. I've jammed fingers down throats before."

"A lot of suicide among your coworkers, isn't there?"

Velvet shrugged. "Shrinks kill themselves more than any other group. So don't be thinking my colleagues are all mental cases. We're not."

"No, like me, you're all well-adjusted models of society." He meant it lightly, as a joke on them both, but he'd punched a well-pummeled bruise.

"Yeah. Just like the well-adjusted models of society that buy all our movies."

Their salads arrived, blanketed with blue-cheese dressing. Velvet waited until the server left before speaking.

"You probably don't know the names I've been called by your well-adjusted types when I've bothered to go on radio shows or done web interviews. Whore. Slut. They cease to mean much after a while." She offered a smile. "I prefer to think of myself as a pleasure engineer."

He laughed because he could tell she needed him to.

"At least this way I get to choose what I'm called, Whit. *Whore*'s a term coined by men to trample any woman with sexual vitality." Velvet licked the blue cheese from her fork with a slow, baroque flourish of her tongue. Whit waited for the chain reaction of heart attacks to decimate the retired men in the restaurant, but no one keeled over.

"That makes you uncomfortable," Velvet said. "You're all squirmy boy now."

"I am not."

"What a squirmy man needs is a kiss gone bad," Velvet said.

"A what?"

"In regular movies, ninety percent of the time, you get the kiss and that's it. Maybe they wriggle, real fakey, in bed. But it's antiseptic sexuality. In adult movies you get the kiss and two seconds later the cast is getting way down and dirty. I just call it a kiss gone bad. But it's really good. You know, you're my ideal audience. Single, a little bored, too respectable to ever solicit a prostitute but probably in need of sweet relief."

"I'm not bored," Whit said. He felt color creeping up past his collar.

"Have you ever seen one of my movies, Whit?"

"No."

"Have you ever seen any porn movie? Be honest."

"Yes," he admitted. "When one of my brothers got married, we had a bachelor party with an X-rated tape rolling on the VCR."

"If you watched it, and it made your little soldier stand at attention, honey, you can't look down your nose at me. I'm giving you and every other man what greases your wheels." She lowered her voice even further. "I bet my tapes are under more beds and hidden away in more closets here in your sweet little small town than you would ever imagine."

"What do you want me to say, Velvet? Good for you?"

"I just don't want you to act like what I do is so terribly wrong. I'm not filled with angst over what I do."

"All this angst Pete supposedly felt about his brother's disappearance, is that really why he ended up in porn?"

"He did it because it's fun," she said in a flat voice, fork poised above the messy salad.

"Fun. And that's why you did the movies, too?"

She began to eat her salad, not answering him, shoveling drenched chunks of lettuce in her mouth, staring at her plate. "Drop the armchair psychology."

"It's just that . . . you seem too smart for this."

She glanced at him quickly. "Oh, and so the blue movies are full of morons, huh? Judgie boy, I've worked with computer programmers, accountants, lawyers. People who want to make one flick, just for laughs, use a horny-corny name, get in, get out. You think they're better than me 'cause they do drive-by porn?"

"No," Whit said. "But I want to know why you and Pete did these movies."

"Why? Want me to make you a star?" she asked.

"I'm quite sure I'd be a disappointment on film."

"You got a good jawline. That's important. The camera likes you better."

"So why? I just would like to know."

"There's no soap opera answer. My folks didn't beat me, my dad didn't abuse me, none of that tabloid talk-show stuff." She set her fork down. "I'm the worst-case scenario of a preacher's kid. My dad was a Methodist minister in Omaha. I wouldn't mind going back there one day, live life a little slower."

"Your mom?"

"Died when I was four. Lupus."

"I'm sorry."

"I don't remember much about her, except she made the best lemon pie you ever ate. I'd sit on the kitchen floor while she baked, waiting to lick the spoon. And she liked gardenias. The house always smelled of them before she died." She leaned back against the booth's seat. "My dad married his church secretary just to give me a mama. She was a mean old cow who'd gone to the Hitler Secretarial School, and when I turned sixteen Dad was dying of cancer. He told me they'd slept together exactly one time. That was it. She cut him off right after because she had all the sensuality of a stale raisin. That's what's wrong with this world: there's not nearly enough love or happiness or orgasms."

"About your mom...my mother took off when I was two. Never saw her again," Whit said. "And my dad was a drunk until I was seventeen."

"Geez, you should've ended up on the other side of the camera with me," Velvet said. "Since nothing is our own fault and everything is the fault of our family's, right? Wrong. I don't blame my mom or my dad for any of my choices, Whit. I wanted to make a lot of money, I wanted to make movies, and I liked the sex."

Whit pictured a little girl, sitting in a kitchen smelling

of lemon peel and gardenias, the soft camouflage for a sickbed.

"I wanted to go to film school. Be the female Coppola. But that costs money, Whit, and I wasn't filling the bank waiting tables or mopping up spilled beer or tutoring kids in algebra. I met a guy. He said I could make a lot of fast cash, use a fake name, no one would ever know." She paused. "So I stayed in it. We build these little worlds for ourselves and then we never get to move out."

"Meaning no one was gonna hire you for legit film work once you went down Porn Street?"

"The judge's robe does a nice job of covering your vicious streak."

"It's vicious of me to point out the obvious?"

She said nothing.

"What you gonna do after Pete is buried?" Whit asked softly.

"Go back to California. Find the next guy who can perform when there's a camera three inches away and a crew of five standing around picking their noses."

"Don't," he said. "Don't do that."

She smiled but not the kind of smile that said aren't you sweet. "Gee willikers, Whit, you gonna sweep me off my feet and save me from myself?"

"I just think you could . . . not do these movies anymore."

"Why are you a judge?" she asked suddenly. "You don't fit the type at all. Too free-spirited to be comfortable judging other people."

"My dad got me the job," he said, and she laughed.

"But you're sticking with it, right? You want to be elected. You're like a small-town Gerald Ford, wanting everyone to vote for you and really give you the job you got handed. Why?"

"I never wanted to be a politician. I hate that part of the job. But I think truth matters, even the little truths of small-claims and traffic court."

"And death inquests."

"Yes."

"Bull," she said. "You like the power, Whit. I can see it in your eyes, that quick flash of *yes, I'm the judge, don't mess with me.* I like the power, too. When some lonely, horny guy slides one of my tapes into his machine, I have power over his pleasure. I can make him tingle all over or I can make him as limp as string. Never had much power as a kid, I bet." She smiled, a cat warming up for a good purr. "Littlest of six boys, you probably didn't get to pick when you took a pee. I'm not inclined to surrender my power any more than you are, Whit."

Their *bitokes* arrived, and Irina plopped in the booth, chatting up Velvet, asking her if she'd walked through the shopping district and seen the Arts Center and the Maritime Museum. Velvet, steeped in sudden courtesy, spoke with complete assurance and sounded like an aspirant to the Junior League. Irina left them, patting Velvet on the hand, telling her how nice it was to meet her.

Velvet toyed with the prescription-pad–size dessert menu clamped above the salt and pepper. "What if... you decide suicide, and more evidence comes later that says not suicide?"

"I can reopen the case, conduct a new inquest. But considering Pete tried to kill himself before, if the autopsy remotely suggests suicide..."

"I knew you'd cop out. You're not going to risk your own political neck to help me."

"Give me something, then. Do you know anything

he knew that could have gotten him killed? Anything specific?"

She shook her head. "You don't think that's keeping me up at night? That maybe whoever shot him thinks I know what Pete knew? I don't. I don't."

And he saw fear, a naked cancer, in her eyes.

22

—◦◦⊙◦◦—

IT HAD BEEN a bad afternoon for Claudia.

She got confirmation that Pete Hubble had once attempted—albeit clumsily—suicide. She hated that Faith Hubble was right. About anything.

There was a Judy Cameron in the Port Leo phone book, at the Paris Street address mentioned by Heather. Ms. Cameron was a math teacher at Port Leo High School, but she had never heard of Heather Farrell and had no transients lounging at her house.

So Claudia gobbled a messy lunch of barbecue shrimp and cole slaw downtown, then headed for Little Mischief Beach. No Heather Farrell. The two scruffy girls on the beach she'd seen yesterday claimed not to know Heather or to have seen her.

She'd then stopped by the Hubbles, an exercise in futility. Lucinda, Faith, and Sam all stuck by their statements. Lucinda gave yes and no answers. Faith Hubble was polite but clearly irked at going through her statement again. Claudia remained friendly, crisp, and polite with them but feeling out of sorts and frustrated.

You don't like Faith Hubble, fine. Look at every suspect. Don't be blindsided, she told herself.

So she tromped back to the station to engage in a Deloache hunt. She spoke with the Houston and Galveston police departments and did simple queries against a statewide criminal database. Thomas Deloache Sr., age fifty, had a quilted history: twice dragged before a grand jury, but never indicted. He had started most likely as an enforcer for the Montoya crime ring and took over when Montoya and his son both died, ignobly, crushed by a beer-laden semitrailer on the Houston stretch of I-10. Thomas Deloache Sr. kept a low profile, but he was suspected of handling about five percent of the drugs funneled through the Houston-Galveston area.

Five percent was worth millions.

The successive generation of Deloaches offered mixed hope for a criminal dynasty. Two sons, Tommy Jr. and Joe. Joe was the bright one, attended a Catholic prep school in Miami, went to college at Texas but didn't finish, opting to enter the family business early. Galveston police suspected him in two murders, but the lack of bodies and evidence stymied investigations. Junior marched to a different, perhaps palsied drummer. He had been arrested a few times on very minor charges, never anything worth more than a slap on the wrist. One hot check, swimming in very public Mecom Fountain in Houston when drunk, attending an illegal dogfight in Galveston. Barely finished high school, never attempted college. She went to go find her boss.

To her surprise Delford seemed more willing to listen to the potentials of a Junior Deloache being involved in Pete's death.

"Why would Junior Deloache be in Port Leo?" he asked.

"One of his dad's legit business concerns is a couple

of small motels in Galveston. They're clean as a whistle, which is driving the Galveston cops nuts. Papa might be turning over that side of the business to Junior; it's less risky. He and his associate, a guy named Anson Todd, both told Judge Mosley they were renovating the old Sea Haven. And Judge Mosley thinks they've lied about their whereabouts the night Pete died."

"I bet the Deloaches launder dirty money through the so-called legit businesses like these condos." Delford tapped his finger against his lip. "Do they know how the Deloaches run in the Houston drugs?"

"Probably different channels. Some from other parts of Texas, some up from Mexico, some in from the Gulf."

"So why's he here? There wouldn't be near the market in Port Leo for drugs, unless shrimpers and retirees suddenly go coke-happy," Delford said.

"But we've got navigable bays. Quiet beaches. Only a few hours from the south side of Houston, closer to Padre and all those tourists. And a lot fewer officers."

Delford frowned. "So Junior's here to smuggle drugs?"

"Junior may be exiled where he can do the least amount of damage. The Houston detectives told me he's famous for being an overgrown brat."

"Even if Pete turns out to be a suicide we need to know about these people. Sit down for a minute."

She sat, smelling a lecture in the air.

Delford flattened his palms on the table. "Claudia, I have faith in you. But one area where you could stand definite improvement is in dealing with people."

"Pardon?"

"Why are you grilling the Hubbles on their statements?"

"I didn't grill anybody. I hadn't even talked to them

before today. I just wanted to review their statements with them, see if there was anything else they wanted to add."

"There wasn't. I won't have the senator and her family treated like criminals."

"I did no such thing."

He rubbed his stubby-fingered hand across his eyes. He looked ten years older, she realized, than he had last week. There'd been a bad cancer scare with him last year, and a sudden tremble of worry took her. He was not a young man anymore.

"Are you okay?" she asked.

"Fine. Just tired." He leaned back in his chair and a new hardness tensed his jaw. "I'm pulling you off as the lead investigator in the case."

Her face felt frozen. "Why?"

"Because one thing we're going to be in this department is professional, and you haven't been."

"How?" *Don't get mad, stay calm,* she thought. A finger of sweat trickled down her back.

"You clearly don't like Faith Hubble, and it's coloring your view of this case. And given all the likely publicity, it's best Gardner takes the lead. You can still work on the case, just under his direction. I already sent him to Corpus this afternoon for the autopsy."

Claudia heard her voice go ragged. "This is unwarranted, Delford. You've never treated me this way before."

"Defensive don't suit you. I've made my decision."

She sat stunned.

Delford's phone buzzed. He scooped up the receiver and listened. "Yeah, oh, yeah. I forgot. I'll send up Claudia." He hung up and gestured toward the blue flyer on his wall of

Marcy Kay Ballew. "That missing girl's mother from Louisiana's here. Can you talk to her?"

"That was the sheriff's case." David's case, to be exact.

"Technically, yes, but she's been wanting to know what we're doing in the city to help." Delford shrugged. "Maybe this'd be good for you to focus on now."

"I'll talk with her." Anything was preferable to sitting through an undeserved rebuke.

Not quite. "By the way," Delford said, "your ex is with her."

David sat, ramrod straight, his deputy's Stetson resting on his knee. His stare drifted to Claudia as Mrs. Ballew talked; Claudia forced herself to concentrate on the woman's words.

"Marcy is a really good girl. The rose tattoo, that was simple foolishness. I'd already started saving for when she wanted to remove it. She is really quite sweet." Mrs. Ballew perched at her chair's edge.

"I'm sure she is," Claudia said.

"And it would be easy for me to say I have no intention of being a pest, but I have every intention of being a pest."

"You're certainly not a pest, and I want to assure you we're doing everything we can to search for your daughter here in the county." David nodded at Claudia. "Detective Salazar and I are used to working together, and I'm sure we can find your daughter."

Gosh, you hardly ever spoke so gently to me. Claudia opened her copy of the Ballew file that David had brought; the same picture from the flyers was on top. A photo, probably taken at a chain department store, based on the cheesy fake background of an autumn-kissed farm and barn.

Marcy had reddish hair, cropped short, slightly crooked teeth, thin lips, skin supple as a peach.

"No leads from the flyers yet, right?" Claudia asked David. He nodded and foisted his extrasympathetic gaze toward her.

Mrs. Ballew swallowed. She was a spare, florid-cheeked woman, with a red frizz of hair and too-long nails painted a bright lavender. She wore khakis and a denim blouse, dressed for a day shopping at an outlet mall instead of beating the pavement for her missing child. "Well, everyone back in Deshay said that Marcy ran off, you know, but I didn't believe it. Yeah, she had once before, but that was after a huge fight and she told me she was running off and I dared her to and she went to New Orleans for two nights and then ran out of money and came home, crying for her mama." Mrs. Ballew blinked, worn out by her monologue. "Marcy don't have a boyfriend right now, so I don't think she took off with a boy."

"And no one in your family, your circle of friends, knew Port Leo?" David asked. He kept glancing at Claudia and she thought, *Don't use this woman's grief just to get within two feet of me.*

"No, none."

Claudia wondered if the Ballew girl had traipsed to the Coastal Bend for an unannounced vacation, lost her wallet, maybe turned to hitchhiking or hooked up with some of the party-minded sail bums that trolled from Galveston to South Padre Island. She hoped that was the answer.

"Will they drag the bay again?"

"Probably not, ma'am," David said, "unless we have new reason to."

"Will they search again?"

"Until there's more evidence to point she actually stopped in the county, probably not," Claudia said.

Mrs. Ballew sagged.

"And you're absolutely sure that your daughter knew no one in Port Leo?" Claudia asked.

"She hung out with boys, sometimes, at the bars, and sometimes they weren't from Deshay. She never mentioned Port Leo to me."

Claudia debated. No clues, no witnesses, no reason for the girl to be here. But she couldn't just turn this woman away. "Tell me about Marcy."

Mrs. Ballew pointed toward the file. "But you have the information…"

"I know. But it would be more helpful coming from you. You live in Deshay. How long have you been there?"

"Three years. We used to live in Shreveport. But in Deshay I got a job working for a cousin of mine at his shrimp restaurant, and he's promised to make me a full partner in a couple of years."

Shrimping was big along the Louisiana coast, and it was a lifeblood in Port Leo. Was that coincidence? But she'd consulted a map: Deshay was a fair ways north of the Louisiana coastline and huddled up close to the Texas border. "Did Marcy work?"

"As little as possible," Mrs. Ballew said, as if by rote, and she burst into tears, long, heaving sobs that carried the force of long suppression. Claudia hurried around her desk and squatted next to Mrs. Ballew, put an arm around her, and placed a tissue in the woman's hands. David fiddled with the brim of his Stetson, paling under his freckles.

"Sorry," Mrs. Ballew gasped as her crying subsided. "I'm sorry. I'm sorry."

"You're doing great," Claudia assured her.

"I always said she didn't work hard enough, and now I'm so afraid she's dead, and I make fun of her for being lazy. But that was the thorn between us, you know. Not a joke but the one thing I got mad at her for, the not working hard enough." Mrs. Ballew exhaled a long *whooosh* and wiped her face and nose.

"Tell me about her job." Claudia pulled her chair close to Mrs. Ballew's.

"She worked as a nursing home aide in Deshay. She'd change the patients' beds, mop up the floor, spoon lunch into their mouths. It was either that or road crew for the parish, out in the heat and wet. But she liked the clients, especially the old ladies. She'd tell me when a new widower arrived and all those old women would just start a-prissing." Mrs. Ballew mopped at her eyes. "Marcy said she could make their last days happy if she snuck Viagra into the food."

"What's the name of the nursing home?"

"Memorial Oaks."

Claudia wondered why it wasn't a crime to use the term *memorial* in a facility designed to house the still-living. "Tell me about the day she went missing."

"September thirtieth, she worked her regular shift, from noon to ten at night. Usually she came right home, showered to get the Lysol smell out of her hair, got ready if she was going barhopping. She didn't come home."

"The staff at Memorial Oaks were the last to see her?"

"Yeah. Her supervisor said she left about ten after ten. She stayed to help with a patient who'd puked all over himself." As Mrs. Ballew's lip trembled, she wondered the inevitable: *If Marcy had been her usual lazy self and not stayed that extra ten minutes, would she have escaped the boogeyman?*

"And none of her things were missing?"

"No, all her stuff was at home. Her car was found about ten miles away, at a shopping center parking lot. But she hated that center. She never went there, so I don't know why she would go that night."

Bad with a capital *B*. The girl was, in Claudia's opinion, an abductee and probably dead. But how and why would her ID surface in Port Leo, hundreds of miles away?

David cleared his throat importantly but said nothing.

Claudia glanced at the file. The wallet, when found on the road outside Port Leo, had had a credit card and thirty-three dollars in cash in it. The most likely scenario was that the Ballew girl had been killed close to Deshay, although the Louisiana police had not turned up a trace of her. Assuming she was dead, someone—either the killer or an associate—had come to Port Leo, where they chose to throw Marcy Ballew's wallet—still containing cash—onto the road.

"We traced the movements of the registered sex offenders in Encina County, seeing if any of them had gone to Louisiana recently, if any had a connection to Deshay. So far nothing," David said.

The words *sex offender* made Mrs. Ballew go white.

"Deshay is a long way for someone to go to commit a crime against a stranger," Claudia said. "There must be some other connection."

"I can't think of one," Mrs. Ballew said mournfully. So for the next forty minutes Claudia worked through Marcy's life: old boyfriends, old high school friends, former coworkers, any hobbies or interests. David hardly asked a question.

Mrs. Ballew enumerated her daughter's interests. "She did like watching cable TV, the movies, and she liked wrestling on TV a lot, and figure skating, what with the fancy costumes."

"Wrestling? She ever watch Joltin' Jabez Jones?" Claudia asked.

Mrs. Ballew brightened. "Oh, yeah, the guy who became the preacher? Sure, she watched his show. She was a big fan of his."

23

---•◦◉◦•---

THE HONORABLE WHIT Mosley curbed the impulse to put the small-claims hearings on a kitchen timer. Watching the Augustine brothers bicker was like rewinding a moment from his own rowdy family's past, where the six brothers routinely waged war over who scarfed down the nacho chips and who erased the Super Bowl tape and who spread lard across a brother's bedsheets.

The division between the Augustines—who seemed to be sharing IQ points—was a homemade barbecue grill. Each side had laid out the facts of their case in a style that would have won them admirers on the tabloid talk-show circuit.

"Let me get this straight," Whit said. "Tony, you built the grill using your own labor, correct?"

"Damn straight. Sir." Tony Augustine nodded. He was a year older than Whit and had been a minor bully in junior high, and now realized he might pay for past transgressions. "Sweat of my own brow, Judge."

"But you used Cliff's materials, correct?"

"That's right, Your Honor," said Cliff Augustine. He had never pushed anyone out of the lunch line and suspected he had the moral high ground. "I spent all the money on the materials: the bricks, the racks, the wiring, all of it."

"And, Tony, because there would be no grill without your high level of craftsmanship"—the sarcasm was not lost on Judge Mosley's clerk, the constable, the Augustines, or the few spectators waiting to argue their own cases—"you now want it back."

"Well, yeah." Tony gulped. "I mean, we were gonna share it, but now our wives ain't getting along. It's a real sweet grill, makes the best ribs you've ever put in your mouth." A hint of bribery honeyed Tony's voice. Whit believed a plate of the heavenly meats might anonymously arrive at his doorstop, if all went Tony's way.

"It's ridiculous that two grown brothers can't resolve this," Whit said. "You're wasting this court's time, boys. So call me Solomon. I'm ordering that the grill be divided equally. Right down the middle. You get the right half, Cliff, and you get the left half, Tony."

"That'll destroy it!" Tony exploded.

"Are you nuts?" Cliff demanded.

"Watch it," Constable Lloyd Brundrett, who served as bailiff in Whit's court, rumbled.

"Sorry, Your Honor," Cliff said in sudden meekness. "I'm sorry. I'm very sorry."

"Or option B is you two resolve this peaceably right now," Whit said. Neither Augustine spoke.

"Fine, that's my judgment. The sheriff's deputies will execute this order at their earliest..."

"Wait!" Cliff yelled. "Please. Please, Judge. Wait. All right, Tony built it. He can have the grill. I don't want to see it ruined."

Tony pumped his fist in the air in a redneck jig.

Whit rapped the gavel and pointed it at Tony. "Stop that celebrating. Right. This. Minute."

The hand dropped; the hips ceased their victory sway.

"Tony, if your brother is letting you have the grill, I strongly suggest you work out a plan to reimburse him for the cost of his materials, over time and either with cash or barter. Maybe you could feed him and his family some of that barbecue you bragged about. You need to be a good brother. Understood?"

Tony finally nodded, surprised and still pleased.

"Fine. Case dismissed."

His clerk handed him the file for the next case. Neighbors bickering over ownership of a lawn mower. In the next hour he adjudicated four more cases. Patsy Duchamp slipped in and sat in the back row of the courtroom. When he completed the last case and the courtroom emptied, Patsy approached the bench and slid him a folder.

"The news clippings on Corey Hubble you wanted, Whit," she said.

"Thanks. The margaritas are on me."

"Sure could use a good quote for the Hubble story."

"I'm sorry, Patsy, not yet. I should hear from the ME's office real soon." He tucked the file under his arm and promised to call her as soon as there was news.

Whit ducked down the hall into his office, relieved to have the day's docket done. Five cases in justice court resolved in barely an hour. The voters could not say justice wasn't swift in Encina County. Maybe he ought to make that a mainstay of his campaign.

Whit opened his office door and found Sam Hubble sitting in front of his desk, head bowed, hands in lap.

The boy stood slowly. "Hi, Judge Mosley. You got a minute?"

"Sure, Sam. How are you?"

"Holding up. I'm kind of freaked about my dad."

"That's understandable." Whit's tongue felt thick and oily. He sat behind his desk, smoothing the black robe. Trying not to let the thought *I've been sleeping with your mother* play across his face. "I know this is a tough time for your whole family."

Wow, what next can I pull out from the bag of clichéd platitudes?

"I wanted to talk to you about my father. Stuff...I couldn't say with Gram and Mom around. If you want, we can call them after I've said what I got to say." His tone was resolute. He looked like Pete: broad-shouldered, tall, lanky, with a shock of brown hair. He'd inherited Faith's eyes, hazel and direct, and a thin slice of a mouth that reminded Whit of Lucinda.

"Then let's talk."

"I'm sorry for what I did," Sam said, and Whit's stomach dropped. "My dad killed himself. I know because...I found the body. First. Not that girl."

Thin light slanted through the half-shut blinds, and in the bars of shadow Sam reminded Whit not of the other Hubbles, but of lost Corey, hunched, beaten down.

"I didn't want anyone to know," Sam said. "But I can't do this to Gram, let her think...maybe Dad was murdered." He swallowed. "I went back to the boat Monday night. To see my father."

"Did he know you were coming?"

"No. I just wanted to talk with him. It felt weird sometimes, knowing he had been gone most of my life and yet he was now just a few miles away."

"Did you get along with him?"

Sam shrugged. "He wasn't as bad as I thought he would be. But he abandoned Mom and me. I wasn't ever going to forgive him. Yeah, I could get along with him okay, but forgive, never. I think he knew that."

Sam pulled a folded paper from his pocket and laid it on Whit's desk. "I went to go see him about eight-thirty. The boat was dead quiet. So I went aboard and I found him." The boy's voice quavered. "I freaked. I tried to wake him, but he was clearly dead. His skin...it was still warm." He wiped at his mouth with the back of his hand. "I, like, froze, I didn't know what to do. Then I saw the note. It was on the nightstand table."

"So you weren't at home with your mom, like you said in your statement?"

"No. I snuck out; there's a trellis by my window. It's a quiet climb. Mom didn't know I was gone. I'm sorry I lied on the statement. I didn't know what to do." Sam's voice broke. "Because of what my father wrote."

Whit took a tissue from a box and carefully unfolded the note. It was written in typeface, from a computer printer:

I came home thinking I could fix what was broke in me and I can't. Mama, I'm sorry for the pain I've caused you and what I did to Corey. I killed him. I didn't mean to, but I did. We argued over his drug use all those years ago, and I hit him and he fell and hit his neck funny against the stair banister. He was dead in less than a minute and I panicked. Before you came back to town I took his body out past Santa Margarita Island and weighed it down good and dumped it. I didn't know what else to do. I have tried to deaden the pain of this for years with all the wrong things in life and I just can't go on. This way is better. Sam and Faith, please forgive me. I love you both. Velvet—I don't have the words. Be good. Mama—

good luck in the election and I hope me ending my pain
doesn't mess up things for you. You haven't had an influence on me in years so no one should blame you. I am
just really unhappy about the person I am. Sam this has
nothing to do with you at all. You are aces and I love you.
I am so so sorry and please forgive me. Pete.

Whit set the letter down on his desk. A tremble of nau-
sea touched his stomach.

"You're going to have to give the police a revised statement, Sam."

"I know. But I came to you first...My mom said you
decided whether or not it was suicide. Will you go with me
to talk to the police?"

"Sure. But I'd like to know why you kept the note, why
you didn't say anything right away. There was a marina full
of people there you could have told."

"I know. I just...I didn't want everyone to know he'd
done what he said to his brother. I didn't—I was worried
about Gram's election, what this would mean. My grandmother...she's gonna kill me for this. Not helping out right
away. Telling a lie."

"What happened after you found the"—Whit nearly said
body and managed to edit midstream—"after you found
the note?"

"I stayed with him, for a few minutes." Sam lowered his
eyes. "I know, it sounds weird, but I didn't want him to be
alone. It seemed wrong to leave him. I thought of calling
the police, but I thought maybe, what with Gram's election
coming up, maybe I shouldn't be in the news. So I just left,
left the boat and left the marina." He wiped his dripping
nose. "Pretty awful, huh? Am I in big trouble?"

"Let's call the police and call your mother." Whit picked up the phone and dialed the station. Claudia wasn't in, but he was transferred to Delford.

Delford blew out a long sigh. "Now, here I was telling y'all it was suicide, and you and Claudia bickered with me the whole way."

"Sam is here, but his mother needs to be present if he's going to give a statement."

"Of course. I'll give Lucinda and Faith a call right now."

"Thanks. We'll walk across the street in a minute," Whit said and hung up.

"I'm sorry," Sam said.

Whit placed the suicide note into a manila folder. Outside the sky was a sweet blue smear and the Gulf wind whipped Whit's robe around his legs. Sam shaded his eyes against the unclouded sky.

Two questions occurred to Whit. "Did you notice whether your dad's laptop was on the boat?"

Sam shook his head. "I didn't notice a computer around."

"And did your father ever discuss a new film project with you?"

Sam shook his head. "He didn't talk about his work to me. Did you know he made movies for driver's ed?"

"Yeah," Whit said, "I knew."

They crossed the street and went inside to the police station.

"Quite the development," Whit said after Sam had gotten settled in the chief's office. The Hubble women had not yet arrived but were on their way over. He and Delford had retired to the kitchen.

Delford filled a coffee cup with a shaking hand. "Relief. I'll sleep better tonight."

Whit folded his arms. "You'll have that note tested for Pete's fingerprints, right?"

"Showboating is over, Whit."

"It's typed, not handwritten. And his computer is still missing. Am I supposed to believe he typed a suicide note, then tossed his laptop into the marina?"

Delford started to argue, then shrugged. "Damn, you're difficult. Fine. I'll tell Gardner."

"Why not Claudia?"

"The case is Gardner's now," Delford said through tight lips. "Not that there's much of a case now, partner."

Delford was right. Whit left. He didn't want to see Faith right now. He walked to his car, shrugging out of his robe. He tossed it in the backseat and drove a half block to the ice cream store he once managed. He was halfway through a chocolate-almond double scoop when his pager beeped. The Nueces County medical examiner's office calling.

24

THIS DOESN'T HAVE to be awkward," David said. He smoothed his damp hair with the flat of his palm.

Claudia's fingers tapped against the computer keyboard. "Of course not. But it is." She finished her report and saved copies to the hard drive and a diskette.

"I don't want to make you uncomfortable," he said.

She popped the diskette from the computer. "You're not."

"So what's bothering you?" He palmed his hair again. "When you get mad, you don't vent. You keep it all locked inside. But I know you're steamed."

He's not your husband anymore, and you don't have to skirt an issue to keep the peace. "I felt like you were using that interview with that poor woman as a reason to see me."

He laughed. "Well, don't we think well of ourselves?"

"Am I wrong?"

"I didn't steer her to you. She wanted to talk with PLPD, and Delford said you. But I'm not sorry to see you."

"David, aren't you hurt? Doesn't it bother you I didn't want to be married to you anymore?"

"Did you want to hurt me?"

"Of course not."

His mouth thinned. "Sure. Yeah. It hurts bad. I miss you

awful fierce when I get home and it's just me and the TV. But, like you said, we're still gonna run into each other."

The casual sweetness of his tone prickled her skin. "Well, I think it's just best we don't overdo our time together. The point of a divorce was to be apart."

"Was it all bad? Did you just hate me, or what?" He blinked. "I would really like to know. I want to fix ... whatever's wrong with me."

She touched the back of his hand. "Oh, David. No, it wasn't all bad, and no, I don't hate you," she said. "I feel like we got married because everyone said we were such a cute couple. It's not enough. I know some woman's going to scoop you right up, because you're a great guy, and I'll still be a moping loner. But I wasn't right for you."

He carefully put his hat back on his head. She saw wetness glimmer in his eyes—he had never cried in front of her—and he said, "Okay, thanks. I really did just want to know."

David bumped into a smiling Eddie Gardner as he left, the two men exchanged friendly hellos, and Eddie dumped a photocopied piece of paper on Claudia's desk.

"Suicide note. With prints from Hubble and his son," he said. "And it clears up the Corey Hubble case, too."

Claudia read. "Are they going to look for Corey's body?"

Eddie shrugged. "The Hubbles asked we not release the note to the press. I suppose the Coast Guard or maybe the parks department will look for remains, but that's gonna be a waste of time. Mosley's inquest is gonna be just a formality now." He smiled and sat. "Man, I love clearing cases."

"Congratulations." Claudia turned back to her paperwork on two burglaries she had cleared on Friday, wishing she could slap the smirk off his gaunt, ten-dollar-tan face.

An hour later, Eddie left for drinks at the Shell Inn with

most of the day shift. He invited her to go, but she declined with a polite smile.

"Hey, no hard feelings, right?"

"Of course not," she said. He grinned, slapped an Astros cap on his head, and sauntered out, whistling "Cheeseburger in Paradise."

She waited until he was gone for ten minutes and headed down the hall.

The old files of the Port Leo Police Department moldered in a locked back office. It was quiet now at 6 P.M. None of the other detectives were here, most of the clerks had headed out, and the patrol shift was out cruising Port Leo.

Unlocking the ink-black storeroom, she pulled on a chain to click on a naked lightbulb. The room smelled of old paper, damp brick, and, oddly, garlic. She went to a wall of cabinets. The files were organized by year, and then in turn by case number. Only a few major cases had not been cleared. She wondered what murderers still walked free, with the warm sun of Port Leo aglow on their faces, full of easy confidence that they would never pay.

Claudia pulled Corey Hubble's file. It was thinner than she expected. The disappearance of a state senator's son surely would mean a thick, bulging file. This file was starved for data.

She scribbled her name in the sign-out book along with the file number and returned to her office.

An old file was simply a snapshot of a tragedy. No papers in here could capture the boy that Corey Hubble had been: what was his favorite TV show, did he like chicken or beef wedged in his enchiladas, which local jetty did he think had the best fishing? All these fading papers represented was bureaucratic eulogy.

Delford Spires had been the detective on the case, one of his last before being promoted to police chief. She noted the year of Corey's disappearance and did some quick math: Delford had been with the Port Leo police for fifteen years at that point. She began to read.

Senator Hubble had reported Corey missing on July 21. She had gone to a political meeting in Houston, leaving sixteen-year-old Corey and twenty-one-year-old Pete at home. Pete and Faith were recently married, Faith finishing college at Texas A&M in College Station, a few hours distant. Faith had not been home that weekend. She had been at summer school, completing her degree.

Someone had typed out a rough chronology, based on Delford's interviews. Thursday, July 19, Lucinda had left for Houston. The boys spent time at their jobs: Pete working for a video store, Corey for a florist as a delivery boy. Friday, July 20, Corey planned to spend the night at a friend's house, the friend being Jabez Jones, the son of the minister at the Lord's Coast Evangelical Church.

Pete claimed that he had last seen his brother on Friday, shortly after lunch. Corey acted upset but would not discuss what the problem was. Claudia looked through the papers for Pete's statement and found the corroborating quote: *Corey came back from being at his job and he was furious. I asked what about and he wouldn't tell me. But he said that he was going to go fix what was wrong. I asked him what he meant and he just said he'd teach her.* No hint that Pete might have beaten his brother to death at that point.

The chronology went on. Pete worked that afternoon at the video store, then went out for hamburgers and barhopping with three male friends. He got home shortly after midnight. Corey was not there, having planned an overnight stay with Jabez Jones. The next morning Pete worked all Saturday at the video store, starting at nine, and he did not get home until after five that afternoon. His brother was not at home, but Pete did not consider that unusual—his brother was often out. Pete fixed himself dinner and his mother arrived home unexpectedly, a day early from her conference. She wanted to know where Corey was, and when Pete didn't know, she started calling friends. They were unable to find him. She then reported him missing to the police at nine o'clock at night.

Claudia dug down for a statement from Jabez Jones. It was there, but added nothing to what Delford had already noted. Corey had called and canceled the sleepover. And then apparently vanished.

The rest of the reports and interviews painted an increasingly grim picture. School counselors called Corey manipulative, unstable, and attributed his behavior to his father's painful cancer death five years earlier. The boy seemed to have few friends willing to talk to the police. One of Corey's teachers described him as "talented but erratic" and mentioned he had gotten into trouble twice for fighting in school. The teacher said that *Corey has a somewhat twisted view of the world being in place to primarily serve his needs. His dad died, so the world owes him. Clearly this idea is not sustainable. With change in life being inevitable Corey will face some real challenges. I worry that he has a not well-developed regard for the rights of others to have lives separate from his.*

Another note in Delford's scribble: *Some rumors that he is sexually active but only when he can be rough with the girl. Cannot yet get anyone to confirm this. He might have left if he roughed up some girl but have not been able to*

find anyone who would admit to sleeping with him. Pete
said Corey dated Marian Duchamp, will check.

Whit had mentioned that Patsy Duchamp claimed her
cousin had slept with Corey and gotten slapped around for
the trouble. There'd also been the rumor of animal torture
Whit had mentioned to her, but she found no notes regarding that subject.

Corey Hubble stood out in her own mind as a kid who
lounged in the smoking area at the high school, always
slightly apart, not quite fitting in with the roughnecks, not
hanging in with the populars (where she remembered Pete
dwelling in splendor), not clustering with the geeks for col-
lective security. She remembered he had blue eyes, wide,
sad-looking. Several pictures of Corey Hubble lay stashed
in the file, a school photo where he glared dourly at the
camera, and several family photos. In them, Lucinda and
Pete always smiled, Corey always frowned. There was only
one picture of him smiling, sitting with his wasting father
in a lawn chair, touching his father's pasty arm. Mr. Hubble
smiled with the thin certainty of the dying.

She paged through the rest of the file. An immediate
search of the county turned up nothing except the boy's
car, parked in a grove of windswept oaks not far from
Big Cat Beach, found the day after he was reported missing. A detailed report on the car and its condition indicated
no sign of foul play. An interview with one of Corey's
friends indicated the vintage Mustang was Corey's pride
and joy. He couldn't imagine that Corey would leave it
behind if he was cutting out from town. St. Leo Bay, Aransas Bay, Copano Bay, and St. Charles Bay were searched
for his body; nothing. The investigation widened, to San
Patricio and Matagorda counties, to Corpus Christi, to

South Padre Island, to Houston, to Austin, all places a
runaway teen might find attractive. Nothing. The task
force disbanded five months after Corey Hubble vanished,
although the file stayed open and assigned to one detective:
Delford Spires.

Periodic updates followed: a possible sighting in Houston, one from Dallas, one from San Antonio. Nothing
resulted in a real lead. He was banished to the limbo of
milk-carton photos, pictured on direct mail pieces as a
public service. Nothing.

There was little indication in the notes that the FBI or
Texas Rangers had proffered much help, although with
Lucinda being a state senator one would think every
agency in the state would be hunting Corey Hubble. Apparently not, or they had no more success than Delford.

Not a single thing to suggest that Pete Hubble had done
away with his brother in the heat of an argument. No physical evidence in the house. No physical evidence in the Hubbles' small fishing skiff. Nothing.

She stuffed the file in her heavy purse and headed out
the door. On the way she talked to Nelda, the dispatcher
and main Guardian of the Files. Being a Baptist, Nelda
hadn't gone to happy hour with the others. "Do you remember any citizens phoning or asking for information about
this case recently? The Corey Hubble file?"

Nelda nodded. "Yeah, a guy stopped by. Big guy, late
thirties, tall, kind of muscled up some. I remember he wore
a lion's-head chain around his neck, not so classy-looking. I
told him to talk to Delford."

Claudia thanked her. So Pete Hubble, murderer of his
own brother, wanted to see the file on Corey.

Why would he need it if he already knew the truth?

25

DON'T EVER SEND me a famous body again." Dr. Liz Contreras, deputy medical examiner for Nueces County, had a voice that reminded Whit of crumpled foil—raspy, bright, a little grating.

"You finally get some pressure to hurry Pete Hubble along?"

"I got a call from the governor's office. Some aide to an aide with a degree in snotitude. I explained to said flunky I don't have powers over time and space to hurry up blood tests."

"Then let me be the first to thank you for your quick work."

"Don't thank me too quick. You need to chew out your evidence people. I've already had a chat with your delightful Mr. Gardner." She cleared her throat. "Hubble's hands weren't properly bagged. The GSR readings are not going to be particularly accurate."

Whit had counted on the gunshot residue tests to help him determine if Pete had been holding the gun when it fired. A high level of residue implied suicide.

"How was the bagging screwed up?"

"The bag on the victim's right hand wasn't fastened

properly, and the bag itself has defects—holes, as if torn by rough handling. Now, that said, I found gunshot residue on the right hand, but the amount could have come from Hubble pulling the trigger and then the residue getting worn off with crappy bagging, or because someone stuck the gun in Hubble's mouth and Hubble's hand went to the gun or was by his mouth or jaw. It's not definitive that he pulled the trigger or that he didn't."

Crap. If Liz said outright suicide, his ruling became simple. "So what can you tell me?"

"Time of death was between seven and nine o'clock. He'd eaten shortly before he died, most of a pepperoni-and-mushroom pizza, a number of tostada chips, and several glasses of red wine. Death was instantaneous. Bullet entry wound through the mouth—the angle is consistent with a gun placed in a mouth with little or no struggle. So he wasn't lurching or fighting when the gun fired. That could indicate self-inflicted." She made a humming sound, and he pictured her scanning her report. "The bullet didn't exit the skull. I've retrieved it and sent it to the crime lab here. Dried blood around the mouth, specks of blood on face and hands. The specks on his face are blowback—blood and tissue bursting forward from the bullet's pressure moving through the head." She paused.

"What?"

"Well, this amount of blowback, we ought to have seen it on Hubble's right hand as well. There's very little there."

"Would the bad bagging of the hands account for that?"

"Maybe. But I would still expect to see as much blowback on his trigger hand as on his face. The amount of blowback on the gun itself is consistent with what I would expect with a self-inflicted shot. Hubble's prints are readable on the gun, according to the lab. They said there were a couple of partials but not readable enough for an ID."

He thought of Eddie Gardner, easing the gun out of Pete's mouth and thumbing the safety.

"Could that have happened if an officer handled the gun improperly?" Whit asked.

"Possibly."

"Did he have sex before he died?" Whit asked.

"No."

"We did find a pair of panties by the bed, mixed in with his clothes."

"Then have Gardner check those panties for seminal traces or pubics. We will comb the deceased down for hairs and fibers not his," Contreras said.

"What's your considered opinion as to homicide versus suicide? A lot of folks are watching me on this one."

Liz Contreras's voice softened. "That he is lying in the bed, with this bullet angle, is a big suicide supporter. There's just no sign of struggle. The lack of blowback and gunpowder residue could be attributed to the poor handling. But I can't say with certainty. If there's much reason to believe he was depressed or suicidal, you'll probably be safe in ruling for suicide." She paused. "He'd had a lot to drink, too. His blood alcohol count was point two—that's a lot of hooch, might supercharge any depression. Toxicology on narcotics will take a while longer. I've sent fingernail scrapings, hairs from up and down, and the bullet to the crime lab, along with hand swabs. They can do a double check on my work there. That's about it." She paused. "If your inquest is showing he was suicidal, you're probably safe in ruling that way, Whit."

"Thank you, Liz. If I decide to do a formal inquest, you'll come testify?"

"Sure," Liz said. "Especially if you'll treat me to one of those Russian hamburgers at your stepmom's place."

He chatted with her for a minute more, hearing all about her young daughter's dominance of the Pee Wee soccer leagues in Corpus Christi, then clicked off.

He called Delford, left a message asking him to call, and then nearly dialed Patsy Duchamp at the *Mariner* to give a statement. But he felt tired, and oddly disappointed. There was no case here to be solved, really, after all. And Patsy didn't have a paper hitting the streets again until Saturday. He could talk to her in the morning.

He went home, ate a quiet dinner with Babe and Irina, and was getting into his car to go to Irina's café to borrow her computer when Velvet pulled up. He stood in the yard and waited for her to get out of the car.

"You got a minute for me?" she asked.

"Yeah. I have some news for you," Whit said. "We have a suicide note." He explained to her Sam's revised account.

She leaned against her car. "No way, Whit. I sure don't believe he killed himself, and I sure don't believe he killed his own brother."

"The note said Corey's death was an accident."

"I still don't believe it." She stalked around the yard in a circle, burning nervous energy. "I don't believe it."

"Why? Why not?"

"Because he was a genuinely sweet guy. He was. I can look at him the same way I look at you and know you couldn't kill someone."

"We never, ever know people exactly the way they are."

Velvet shook her head. "I want to see this note."

"The police and the Hubbles haven't released it to the

press yet." He watched her fidget. "I don't think I can get you a copy. I'm sorry, Velvet."

"His damned family. They'll say Pete was a murderer and a suicide. I mean, why not kick him when he's dead?" She crossed her arms. "Don't you have autopsy results yet, anything to contradict that stupid note?"

He wasn't about to disclose Liz Contreras's findings, not yet. "Nothing yet." He paused. "Tell me about Junior Deloache."

She crossed her arms. "Junior? What's to tell?"

"I understand he wants to be in movies."

To his surprise she laughed. "Honey, I couldn't sell tickets to Junior. The biscuit, shall we say, lacks yeast."

"He says Pete promised him."

"Only if Junior bought his way in."

"You mean, an actor pays you?"

"Not exactly. I've known investors who've wanted to come watch the shoots or take some photos of their own. Or screw a starlet, if she didn't mind. But never while the camera was rolling."

Whit studied her. "Pimping for investors. What does that have to do with love and happiness and all that stuff you whacked me with at lunch, pray tell? Doesn't that make you just a glorified madam?"

"Life is a tough business."

"And you're running right back into the sleaze."

"What am I supposed to do, Whit? Put down roots here in Pleasantville?"

"Why not make this film about Corey that you and Pete planned?"

She stared. "Without Pete? I don't think so. Plus, the purse is empty. He hadn't gotten the financing."

"Any excuse will do, right, as long as you can make more porno crap."

"This crap is what I do, and I tend to be quite good at it." She stepped closer to him. "Would you like to experience how good? We could do a tape together, never release it in the U.S. Distribute it in Asia only. No one here would ever know."

He didn't say anything for ten seconds, and she laughed. "No smart answer? Whit, under all that assurance you're such a white-bread boy. If I took you on, you'd be toast."

"And if I took you on, maybe I could help you get out of the pit you're in. Deep in your heart you know porn's wrong. You know. I can tell you do."

"I don't. I'm not one bit debased. I'm superior to any man who pays money for my tapes. And the last thing I need or want is a white knight to bring me a new set of morals. Mine are just fine," she said. "I don't tell you what you do is wrong. Let me guess why you're still living at home at your advanced age. Your stepmother's charms?"

"No."

"Whit, you're a sweet man. But you look at me like a street whore maybe your church could sponsor. I like my life as it is."

"I like you, period, and I don't want to see you ruin your life."

"It's mine to ruin, as you put it."

"If I rule for suicide, what are you gonna do?" he asked.

"I don't know. Does that note mention his career?"

"Not directly."

"If it wasn't for Sam... I'd blast Lucinda Hubble with Pete's career in every paper I could."

"Why do you hate her so?"

"Because, Whit, she hated her own kids. Pete told me once his mother treated him and Corey like stagehands in her great play of life. Faith should have been Lucinda's kid. She seems to relish the role of Little Miss Macbeth. If Lucinda won't stand by Pete when he's dead, I ought to hit her exactly where it hurts. With the voters."

"Vendettas don't get you far."

"They get you far enough." She got in her car.

Whit stood in the yard, in the twilight, and watched her go.

"Excitable thing, isn't she?" a voice called to him, coming across the yard. Whit turned and saw Buddy Beere, dressed in a suit the color of a stale brownie and thick-knotted polyester tie, clutching a sheaf of campaign flyers.

"Hi," Whit said.

"Hi, Whit. Hope you don't mind me canvassing your neighborhood. Just out meeting the voters."

"Well, I suppose if you haven't grown up here and known most of the voters all your life, you need to campaign." He felt extraordinarily peevish, and the sight of Buddy, in his lumpy suit and sweaty brow and dork's tie, only irritated him.

Buddy didn't rise to the bait. "If it makes you feel better, two houses on the street already said they were voting for you." Considering there were at least fifteen houses, Whit saw the jab.

"Thanks."

"That was Pete Hubble's girlfriend, right?" Buddy asked. "You still chasing her?"

"Part of the inquest is gathering information on the deceased. To do that you have to talk to the bereaved. You'll have to learn that if you win." Suddenly he was tired

of arguing and jousting with this little man so determined
to take his job away.

"Good night, Buddy."

Buddy rolled his remaining flyers into a cylinder.
"Whit? One question. Did you have to buy your robe, or
did the county buy it for you? I just want to be sure I get the
right size."

26

CLAUDIA CALLED WHIT on his cell phone before she collapsed in bed, giving him an update on what she'd found in the Corey Hubble case file. He told her about the autopsy results and the bad bagging.

"You'll really have to discuss this with Delford," she said. "Out of my hands now."

"I'm sorry," Whit said. "Delford's being unfair."

"Well, let Gardner handle it," she said. "Apparently the lesson learned here is that the Hubbles warrant special treatment." She paused. "Gardner did do the tests on the note. There were two sets of prints. Pete's and Sam's."

"I guess that settles that," Whit said.

Driving to the Café Caspian, Whit watched gleaming lights dot the harbor: fishing boats, pleasure boats, the restaurants by the piers that jutted into the bay. His cell phone buzzed as he pulled up in front of the darkened café.

"I understand you are Sam's confessor." Faith sounded hoarse and worn. "He says you were very good to him. Thank you, Whit." Less frosty than when she'd stormed from the guesthouse.

"You're welcome. How are y'all doing?"

"Sam is still upset, and of course Lucinda is having to deal with Pete's confession."

"You talk to me like you're talking to the press."

"Do I? I guess so. I've got spin doctors from Austin circling and offering advice. Forgive me. Sam is devastated. Lucinda is in shock. If Pete had just told her then what happened with Corey...how their lives would have been different. The suffering we would have been spared. Needless, so needless." She paused. "I'm sorry I've been so testy. Frankly I could use about seven hours in bed with you."

"Faith...do you believe the note?"

A silence. "Of course I do. I feel horrible for Pete now, imagining what he must have gone through. Why he decided to steep himself in what passed for pleasure. Why he couldn't tell me..." Her voice broke for a moment and then she laughed, one of those soft laughs, not funny, made at the sadness of the world. "I always considered him a failure as a husband. I must have been an equal failure as a wife."

"After Corey vanished, did Pete seem different? Troubled?"

He could hear Lucinda's voice in the background, apparently talking on another line, soft and mournful. "Pete was never the same. But all I can worry about is Sam, okay?"

"I'm sorry, Faith." Condolences never counted for much with him. They always seemed designed to coddle the giver in the face of mortality. But he tried. "I'm so sorry."

"At least it's over. Thank you, Whit. Bye."

He unlocked the café doors and headed back to Irina's office. An untidy whirl of papers covered her desk. A calendar from the local branch of the Texas Coastal Bank was pinned to one wall. Framed on her desk was a selection of photos of family in faraway Russia. A dour mother, a sunny brother who needed orthodontic work and wore his hair in an unstylish chop. Irina rarely spoke of them, as though they were from a chapter of life best forgotten.

He powered up her iMac, accessed the Internet, and found himself on the Yahoo! web portal. He began with a search for "Big Pete Majors," the film name Pete Hubble had used for his career.

A number of websites popped into view, along with brief descriptions. Most of the sites appeared to be online businesses selling pornographic videos. The site with the highest relevance in the search proclaimed itself as "THE Big Pete Majors site for the Truly Devoted Fan." Whit clicked on it.

The site belonged to a Truly Devoted Male Fan of Pete's. It offered reviews of Pete's cornucopia of movies, a message board where Pete's fans could post deep thoughts, and a gallery of downloadable pictures of Pete, both by himself and in action with his co-stars.

No banner proclaimed on the site's front page that Pete was gone. The copy below the BIG PETE MAJORS UNOFFI-CIAL TEMPLE OF APPRECIATION read: *If you're a Big Pete Majors fan, you've come to the right place! This is a labor of love for me (I'm Kevin). ALL Pete's fans are welcome here str8, gay, bi, whatever! Enjoy!!!!!!!!*

str8? Whit studied the code a moment before realizing it meant "straight."

Kevin certainly had scads of free time. Whit explored the message board: there were a few dozen messages, some months old. Several messages were titled PETE LEAVING PORN?

It was a hot rumor, and Pete's devotees promulgated reason after reason: AIDS, erectile dysfunction, drying out in Betty Ford, conversion to fundamentalism, an ongoing bicker with porn directors. The final message was posted by Kevin: *It is my privilege (as you know) to know Pete slightly, because he's appreciated my efforts online, and I just talked with him via phone and he said NO WAY is he cutting out from porn!!!! He said to tell you all he really appreciates our concern, but he is due back in L.A. in a few months. He is doing some so-called legit work (hush hush) back in Texas (where one MAY surmise that everything is indeed bigger!). Don't know if he'll still be exclusive with director Velvet Mojo, but some Pete is better than no Pete. So stop the rumors, he's not sick and he's not dead and he should be back in front of cameras soon.*

The message was dated last Monday, early afternoon. Hours before Pete died.

Whit found nothing of interest in the rest of the messages—mostly discussions of which films showed Big Pete Majors to advantage, comments on his acting skills, discussions of which starlets he had the hottest sex scenes with. All from participants with odd code names such as *lovergrrl* and *madforpete* and *boyslut69*. Consumers of sex—as opposed to those actually having sex—needed reviews before plunking down their hard-earned money, Whit supposed.

He scooted back to the Temple of Appreciation's main web page. He found a link to send e-mail to web master Kevin. Whit clicked on the link and typed in: *Hi Kevin, I'd like to talk to you about your recent conversation with Pete. I know Pete here in Texas, and I'm afraid I have some unsettling news and would prefer to talk rather than e-mail you. Would you please call me—my phone will pay the bill if you call my cell phone. 361-555-6788. Thank you. Judge*

Whit Mosley, Justice of the Peace, Encina County, Texas.
He hoped his title might induce a more rapid response.

Curiosity got the better of Whit, and he clicked on
the gallery's front link. The pictures were organized by
action. Pete alone. Pete receiving oral sex. Pete mastur-
bating. Pete doing it doggy style. Pete doing it with Asian
girls. With black girls. With bottle blondes. With two girls
at once. A wide menu, to appeal to the widest possible lack
of taste.

Whit remembered the boy that Pete had been: fun,
carefree, quick to tease, helping to toilet-paper the oaks in
front of Delford's house, high-fiving the Mosleys after the
infamous Pepto-pink paint incident. That boy was gone.
Maybe all this sex, all this pleasure, was a dam against the
grief over what he had done to his brother.

Whit returned to the search engine and typed a search
on "Velvet Mojo." The list returned a number of sites selling videos and one site entirely devoted to Velvet herself.

This site proclaimed itself to be *VelvetRocks! the only
site for America's preeminent female director of porn.* A
picture of Velvet that was at least five years old, dressed in
leather biker garb with carefully moussed platinum hair.
She sat astride a gleaming motorcycle. A sternness hardened her face instead of the wanton pucker of the rising
starlet. The site included a listing of the movies she had
directed (over sixty), links to purchase her videos, a listing
of awards she had garnered from the adult film industry
(seven), and a whole bevy of reviews by the pornorati, as
Whit mentally termed the more slavish fans. She had performed on the other side of the camera at the beginning of
her career for ten films, two of which were described on the
site as "classics."

There were pictures from her appearances, available for download.

A guiltiness Whit hadn't known since he'd stolen peeks at his older brothers' carefully stashed *Playboy*s when he was young rumbled along his bones. He had never seen naked photos of a woman he knew socially. But curiosity won the advantage over refinement, and he clicked on a thumbnail-size photo.

What slowly filled the browser's screen was a color still from a movie that portrayed postal workers breeding at will. Velvet was in a badly buttoned clone of a mail deliverer's uniform, her breasts about to break out from the confines of the cloth. Her blond hair was combed huge, her lips painted crimson, her cheeks rouged. One hand crept down from the flat plane of her stomach to the too-tight serge of her uniform's skirt.

Whit swallowed. Velvet looked far prettier in person, in her sweats and jeans and her hair not a cumulus cloud. In the picture she was a doll maddened with lust. She didn't look like any real woman he knew. The true woman lay buried beneath the trying-too-hard stance and the stage paint. He selected a second picture for download. As the picture slowly built, Whit could see that Pete lay atop her, her oversize breasts jabbing into his overpumped chest, both of them grinning with ecstasy so faked it looked like pain.

A kiss gone bad, she had called it.

He clicked off the downloading picture before the whole bonanza presented itself. He knew these people. He couldn't watch them this way.

On a whim, he did a web search on Pete Hubble instead of Pete Majors. He slowly paged through the results. Zip that was relevant: only a cluster of genealogy sites that listed various Peter Hubbles from the past three hundred years in their databases. He did a similar search for Corey Hubble and got one result back other than the regular cluster of genealogy sites. The enthusiastic Kevin's Pete-tribute site. Odd.

He moved the mouse toward the link at the same time the office lights went black and a force shrieked past his ear. The iMac's screen burst with a bright, blinding nova. Whit fell behind the desk, clutching his head.

"Hello, Judge," a voice rumbled from the doorway. Low, throaty, a man's voice, hoarse, neutral of accent or drawl. "Stay down on the floor and you won't be hurt."

Whit stayed exactly where he was, his heart pounding hard against the thin carpet. The desk shielded him, but in the pitch-dark he couldn't see his assailant. A faint electric crackle served as the dying gasp of the ruined computer. Whit heard his own ragged breathing, far too loud.

"Listen, Your Honor," the polite voice said. "I could have blown your head off now and I didn't. That's because I want you to listen. Are you listening?"

"Yes," Whit croaked. He tried to think of any weapon there might be in the office: nothing.

"Good. You rule that Pete Hubble committed suicide. If you don't, you die. And so does your father. And so does his wife. And so do Claudia Salazar and Delford Spires. You will all be killed at the same time, by, uh, multiple operatives. Understand?"

"I understand," he whispered.

"And should you go to other authorities with this threat, not only will you be killed, but also your five brothers and their families. In Houston and in Atlanta and in Austin and in New York and in Miami. We know where all our little Mosleys flock. Do you understand?"

"Yes," Whit answered. His voice sounded raw.

"Say it with conviction. I think judges need conviction." A small, sickening laugh. "Pick one of your brothers. I'll kill him to prove I mean business."

Horror flooded Whit.

"Pick a brother," the voice said genially, "or I order them all killed."

Whit gasped. "Please don't. I'll do what you want."

"Which one?" The voice oozed enjoyment. "Teddy in Houston? It'd make Father's Day rough for his three little delectable girls. Or Joe in Atlanta? That software company probably pays him big, his widow should live large on insurance. How about Mark in Austin, who so wants to be a writer? Isn't he your favorite brother? Let's spare the world another awful poet."

"Please don't hurt them. Please!"

"Pick one," the shooter snapped.

"Me. I pick me!" he screamed. "Just leave them alone!"

A slight laugh. "Said with conviction. So how will you rule?"

"Suicide, suicide, suicide."

"Fine. I'm generous tonight so all your brothers get to wake up tomorrow and screw their wives and breathe the air." A pause. "Sorry about Irina's computer, but better it than the back of her head." In the darkness he sensed the shooter leaning over the desk, toward him. To look up would mean death.

"Now here's what we're going to do, Your Honor. You're going to stay kissing the floor here for the next thirty minutes. Because a buddy of mine is watching this café, and if a light comes on, or you move, I come back and shoot you. Do you understand me?"

"Yes," Whit answered. "I completely understand."

"Don't let me down, Judge."

Whit heard the door shut. He heard only the harsh labor of his own breathing. He fingered his neck, face, and ear; there was no wound. He lay perfectly still on the floor.

The guy sounded like—what? A polite psychopath? A government agent? Or like a tough guy who'd seen a lot of bad movies. *Multiple operatives.* Who the hell was this?

You willing to take a chance? With your life and your family's?

He let the thirty minutes pass, not moving in the darkness. His cell phone rang, and rang, and rang, but he did not answer it.

27

From the bay Port Leo appeared as a luminous stitch against the black fabric of the night. The always open Port Leo State Pier glowed along its long thrust into St. Leo Bay, and even from this distance Whit saw stick figures moving, eclipsing the lights, and he imagined he could see the lines the fishermen cast out into the bay, as thin as spider's silk. Whit sat in the bow of *Don't Ask* and sipped at a jelly jar full of bourbon.

He had left the café, hauling Irina's ruined computer after him and cleaning up the debris. He'd phoned Babe, said he wouldn't be home that night and that he'd dropped Irina's computer while moving it. He promised to replace the computer.

Babe sounded unconvinced. "You're not with this girl-friend of Hubble's, are you? You better not be blowing this election thinking with something other than your brain."

"I'm not, and thanks for the vote of confidence. Be sure all your doors are locked, Daddy. And keep your gun at your bedside."

"Whit, what is it? What's wrong?"

"Just do it," Whit said. "I got to go."

Whit felt safe in one place, and that place was now settled in the calm of the bay, a moat between him and the world.

Gooch poured the right bourbon and was the consummate listener. When Whit finished, outlining the investigation, the attack, and the threats against him and his family, Gooch said, "Of course we have to destroy these people."

Whit said nothing.

"It's an insult to the rule of law. Even when the rule of law is The Not-Always-Respectable-but-Ever-Honorable Whit." Gooch sipped his spring water and stared out over the empty dark of the water.

"I should warn Dad and Irina and my brothers."

"If this jerk wanted them dead right now, he wouldn't have bothered telling you. Listen to me. Whoever did this is scum and he deserves a quick ending."

Whit listened to the water slap against the sides of the *Don't Ask*. "If they're following me, they might figure out that I've told you."

"I'm hardly the authorities. I'm simply a grizzled fishing guide." Gooch finished his drink. "I'm curious as to who could field this army of darkness, devoted to nothing but eliminating a legion of Mosleys."

"Junior Deloache."

Gooch shrugged. "Junior doesn't strike me as the forceful type on his own."

"So he sends one of his goons in his place."

"But this person knew details about you, your family. Junior is not oriented toward homework. Who else's cage have you and Claudia rattled?"

"Well, Delford took her off the case and she's steamed about it."

"But Delford was threatened as well."

Whit shrugged. "Could be a cover so I don't suspect him. But there's a huge stretch between Delford yanking Claudia off this case and then Delford ordering me to be shot at and my whole family threatened. I've known Delford Spires for years. No way."

"What about our senator?"

"Not Lucinda's style. You may not like her, but she's not the kind to use thugs."

"Lucinda Hubble is exactly the type to use hired muscle. I am not fooled like our fair electorate. I do not find her amusing or colorful or even particularly bright. There is something missing in that woman's eyes, some common trace of humanity. I don't doubt she lets Faith's hands get dirty while she keeps her own gloves white."

"But this guy clearly didn't know about the suicide note Sam found. The note makes it much more likely I'll rule for suicide, even without a threat. If the shooter knew about that... why threaten me? I think it puts the Hubbles in the clear."

"Indulge me, Whit. What if it was a Hubble? Say your fair Faith."

"I'm indulging." Whit kept his voice steady.

"At the least Lucinda is Pete's mother. There's a bond there that should survive just about anything, and you say she was clearly torn about him coming home. But Faith, this is nothing but nightmare for her. If Pete comes home and sours the election for his mother, Faith loses her job. Pete wants her kid and thought he had enough leverage against her that he hired a lawyer. If he did have dirt, it had to be radioactive for him to be considered the superior parent. She's down two strikes. And she's fiercely protective of Lucinda. Her I could see."

Whit took a hard swallow of the bourbon, let it burn his throat. "She'd be capable of killing Pete. I have no illusions there. But they consider the case closed now because of the note. She doesn't benefit from this threat against me."

"Unless she doubts you buy the note and wants insurance." Gooch showed compassion the only way he knew how, by shifting subjects. "And Jabez Jones? His name keeps popping up here."

"I think not," Whit said.

"Why?"

"Gunplay doesn't seem his style."

"There's a lot of testosterone in his ministry. You know, the Bible is deplorably violent." Gooch smiled. "You're neglecting one other possibility."

"Who?"

"Velvet."

"You're joking."

"Am not."

"She's the one clamoring hardest for me to rule homicide. It makes no sense."

"Look, Whit, she could be working a carefully constructed sham. She looks like Pete's advocate, but she retires from town quietly when you rule suicide. She nicely puts herself out of suspicion."

"I just don't see her as a killer."

"Whit, are you sleeping with her, too?"

"No."

"You never know about people, Whit."

The statement and Gooch's even tone made Whit stop. "No, I suppose not."

Another blanket of clouds unfurled over the western Gulf after the fall of evening; Whit longed to see the long swath of stars that scored the autumn sky over the coast. He heard a soft whispering, and he looked over the bow. Barely discernible in the darkness, several dark shapes surfaced into the gentle cups of waves, puffed misty air, then slowly submerged again. A small herd of porpoises, sleeping. He listened to them rise and fall in their total calm.

"So how are you going to rule?" Gooch finally asked.

Whit set down his drink. The shakiness had passed, but the liquor hadn't calmed him—just made him scared and drunk, all at once. "Ruling for suicide makes everyone safe. For now. But what does that say about me? You think people here would vote for me or respect me if they knew I caved in to a threat?"

"I've known cowards, Whit. You ain't one."

"I lay on that floor for the instructed thirty minutes. I didn't even answer my cell phone when it rang."

"Not cowardice. Prudence. Learn the difference." In the dark, Gooch cracked his knuckles. "I still vote we find out who's behind this and destroy them."

"And by destroy you mean call the papers and the cops and put them away forever."

"I mean making sure they can never threaten anyone again. By means fair or foul."

"I can't support anything illegal. I'm a judge."

"Whitman. Please. The court of Gooch is eminently fair. These people put themselves at risk when they threatened you. You would have been entirely within your rights if you'd had a gun and shot the bastard. Self-defense. Think of this as extended, ongoing self-defense."

"No."

"I remind you that you could have chosen to run to the police. You did not. You came to me. Do you expect me to sit idly while my friend is threatened? You knew I would take action."

"I just don't want anyone killed, Gooch."

"You sell me short every time, Whitman. I never said I would kill anyone."

"You never said you wouldn't."

"You can hardly open up a can of certified, high-octane whoop-ass on these people and then start setting boundaries." Gooch stood and stretched. "I'll sleep under the stars, even if they're playing hide-and-seek tonight."

"I have my own ideas on how to move forward," Whit said. "But I want to think them through."

"Then we'll talk in the morning." Gooch pulled a sleeping bag from a kit on deck and unrolled it, stretched out his big body on it without getting inside. "Good night, Your Honor."

"Good night." A pause. "Thanks, Gooch. I mean, really, thanks."

Gooch turned his face in the direction of the sleeping porpoises. "You're welcome."

Whit went below to the guest stateroom and climbed into a berth. The draining of adrenaline throughout his body hit him hard. His head dropped onto the pillow, and his last waking thought was he had come as close to death tonight as he ever had and did he even want this stupid justice of the peace job anymore?

Or did he even deserve the job?

The Honorable Whit Mosley fell asleep before he could decide.

Heather Farrell stood in the dark curve of Little Mischief Beach. She knew Sam hated surprises—he was such a careful thinker—but money was money and they could use another five thousand. New Orleans was expensive. Sam never worried two seconds over cash, but Heather had searched in trash bins for half-eaten sandwiches, burgers doubling as housefly helipads, and fries cold and clotted with grease. Only she had the money sense. No amount of money lasted forever, and five thousand bucks was worth waiting on the cold dark beach in the middle of the night.

Heather eased down on the sand, holding her flashlight. In the dark of the beach she would be hard to find. Just like she and Sam would be. Once they got to Houston and then bought tickets to go on to New Orleans, they could rent a cheap room near the Quarter under invented names and nab some weed and lay in bed and smoke, spend whole days making love, stopping only to wander among the tourists, devour crawfish and boudin, and drink icy Jax beer.

It was funny. She wouldn't have touched a younger guy back in Lubbock, but travel broadened a girl. Sam was different than the pimpled boys. Confident, and funny, and making love he did not act or feel like a kid but a full-grown man. Sweet and kind. And smart, he had it all worked out where his mother and grandmother would have to let him go and have his life. He had convinced Heather his outlandish plan would work just fine.

Shoes crunched against the crushed shells along the lip of the beach. Her thumb moved to the toggle on the flashlight. Hand over the money, she nearly growled, as a joke, like she was robbing the guy. But then she thought he might not appreciate humor. He didn't smile much.

Funny the way people were, the way you could never guess about them, what lay under a skin—

"Heather?" a voice called softly behind her. She wasn't

afraid, she knew he was coming, and she stood and dusted damp sand off her jeans. She clicked on her flashlight, the cone of light illuminating her worn sneakers.

"Hey." A soft hiss of a laugh. "You can turn that off."

"Let's get out of here. I could use some coffee."

"No, this won't take long."

"All right," she said. "Do you have the money?"

"Yes. Five thousand dollars, as we agreed, and you and Sam Hubble leave town."

The guy was so stupid. He had no idea she and Sam were planning on leaving town anyway, and here he was bribing her to do exactly what she wanted.

"It's going to screw over his grandmother in the middle of this election," Heather said in her tough-chick voice. "You sure that's what you want?"

"I want," the man said. "I'll miss *you,* though."

"And I'll miss you, too. You never looked down on me."

"Of course not." A pause, the only sound her breathing and the soft swish of the waves. "I like you, Heather."

A coyness tinged his voice, and she wondered if numerous unsavory strings were attached to this sum of money. On the road a car passed, loud jazz blasting from the windows, and the man held himself perfectly still until the car was gone.

"The police," he said. "They questioned you pretty thoroughly about finding Pete Hubble's body."

"Yeah. But they didn't bug me too bad. I could handle them."

"Did you really not see anything? Hear anything when you went on Pete's boat?"

Suddenly her stomach roiled and a prickle rose along her arms, her legs, the small of her back. She just wanted the money, and she wanted off this dark beach. A whirl of what was going to be—a narrow little room in New Orleans, street curbs reeking of beer, blowing sugar off a hot beignet onto Sam's face for fun, zydeco drifting from a hundred open bar doors, her pockets heavy with money, Sam's breath cool against her ear after loving—flashed through her mind. Her throat ached.

"There was nothing to hear. I mean, Pete was already dead. He killed himself."

"Yes. But the police doubt you."

She blinked. "No, they don't."

"They know you lied to them."

"I didn't lie. He was dead when I got there."

"And you saw nothing suspicious? Heard nothing suspicious?"

"Nothing to see, nothing to hear," she said, more annoyed than afraid.

"Just between you and me, were you going to make a movie for him?" She heard a creeping breathlessness in his tone.

"What?" she said. "No."

"Too bad. I would've liked to have seen him nailing you."

Heather blanched. "Just give me my money."

"Yes, Darling," he said, and the knife swung up hard, burying itself in her stomach, deep. His hand slammed over her mouth. Heather's eyes widened in agony and disbelief, and blood bubbled out of her, from the wound and surging past her lips.

Sam, Sam help me, and then she tried to scream for her mother and then the knife was gone and she didn't even feel the flick across her throat but she slid into a strange darkness quite different from night.

The Blade held her close against him, smelling peanut butter crackers on her breath, feeling her death shuddering through him, then ended the embrace. Heather Farrell fell bonelessly onto the sand. Blood soaked his clothes, but after all, that was very easily remedied.

He wiped the knife on Heather's jeans. He pulled a large folded square of plastic from the back of his pants. It was warm from resting against his butt, like the knife had been. Carefully he rolled the body onto the plastic sheet and wrapped her in the shower-curtain shroud. He carried her toward the far end of the beach.

The fishing skiff bobbed in the shallow waves. He dumped the body into the boat, grabbed a small shovel and a plastic bucket, and dug up the blood-sodden sand. He motored the skiff into deeper water and aimed the prow across the heart of St. Leo Bay.

He trembled. He really had nothing against her, didn't really want her the way he desired his Darlings, but now it was done and a shaky rush of triumph dried his mouth. Again, he was okay. Again, no one had seen. Again. For all the times he felt dumb as a stump, lost among other people, this he could do and do it okay.

The Blade steered the skiff out into the night, deep into the bay. He spotted a rather grand fishing trawler anchored in the middle, halfway between Port Leo and Santa Margarita Island, but its lights were down and he gave it a wide berth. The clouds lay heavy and low over the sky, like a second shroud, blocking out the clear stars, and he moved unseen on the waters.

28

❧

At nine Thursday morning Claudia, supercharged by a large chocolate croissant from an art district bakery and a double espresso stronger than Gulf crude, waited to interview Jabez Jones about the Marcy Ballew case. David stood in the small bare study, hands on trim hips, inspecting the photos of Jabez body-slamming a thick-barreled antagonist during his pro wrestling days. David's uniform needed pressing, and she wondered if he wore it as a silent you-fled-domestic-bliss rebuke.

"I'm pretty sure all this wrestling's faked," David said.

Delford had called her last night, asking her to work with David, per his request.

Are you mad at me or what? she had asked. *Why are you putting me through the wringer? First you cut me from the Hubble case. Now you're inflicting my ex on me.*

"I'm just expecting you to work with the man. It's a whole hour out of your day, Claudia. Just do it.

She wondered if the pay was better in Rockport or Port Aransas than Port Leo.

Jabez Jones entered, filling khaki shorts and a crisp T-shirt that read BE STRONG—I SAMUEL 4:9. His thighs looked like wooden blocks and a light sheen of sweat coated his face. Morning workout or morning prayer? she wondered. He mopped at his face with a hand towel.

"Hello, Deputy Power." He shook David's hand warmly and nodded toward Claudia. "Detective Salazar, we're blessed again with your presence. Carrot juice? Smoothie? We probably even have coffee, although I'm not fond of polluting my temple with stimulants."

His temple. But Jabez's expression remained perfectly serious.

"No, thanks," Claudia said. David shook his head.

"Well, I could use a protein shake," Jabez said. "Why don't y'all come with me and we can talk in the kitchen?"

They followed him to a kitchen where a young woman sliced cantaloupe with the precision of a jeweler. She gave Jabez a come-hither grin, but her smile froze when she saw Claudia and David.

Claudia thought: *Where do I know you from?* The girl's slender, doe-eyed face looked vaguely familiar. She moved with a complete awareness of her small body, setting down the knife with a shrug of short-snug hip, turning from the counter and leaning against it slightly to bring her breasts to full tilt against her shirt.

"Good morning," she said.

"Rachel, would you mind excusing us?" Jabez said.

"Just a moment." Claudia sidestepped around Jabez. She held up the picture of Marcy Ballew. "Have you seen this young woman?"

Rachel glanced at Jabez, who shrugged. She studied the flyer. Claudia remembered her then, the girl from the volleyball game when she and Whit had interviewed Jabez before.

"No. I've never seen her," Rachel said.

"Thanks," Claudia said. Jabez nodded, so Rachel left. Claudia noticed David watching her exit. It was probably inspiring to a newly single guy, and she thought, *Quit it, quit looking at her.*

Jabez startled her. "May I see the picture of who you're looking for?"

"Yes." She handed it to Jabez.

"Her name is Marcy. We think she was in this area recently," David said.

Jabez handed Claudia back the photo after a blink's worth of looking. "I don't know her."

"Her mother told us that she was a big fan of your wrestling career and your new show," Claudia said.

The Adam's apple rose slightly in his oak of a throat. "A fan? Well, I'm sorry I don't know her, then, and sorry I can't be of further help to you."

Claudia smiled. "I don't know about Deputy Power, but I think I will take one of those shakes you offered, if you don't mind. I'm afraid I skipped breakfast. Then we can ask you a few other quick questions."

Jabez's smile was as tight as his shirt. "Certainly. Melon or strawberry? I load them with vitamin mix and wheat germ as well."

It would nullify the chocolate and the espresso. "I'll have whatever you're having."

"Nothing for me, thanks," David said. "Fruit tears up my stomach real bad."

Jabez turned to fix the beverages.

"Do you take in runaways here?" she asked.

Jabez pushed aside the cantaloupe that Rachel had been slicing and began to peel a banana. He peeled a second one and upended both in a blender. Then he began to wash and slice several strawberries. "People come to our camp for succor, for comfort. I believe they are safer with us than on the road, don't you?"

"I don't know much about what all you do here."

"We pray, we minister." He dumped the cut berries in with the bananas, poured in some milk and ice, and thumbed on the blender. Claudia waited until the pureeing stopped.

"This girl's ID turned up alongside a road two miles outside Port Leo."

"She didn't come here." He sprinkled wheat germ and shaved carrots and some other powder Claudia hoped wasn't strychnine into frosted glasses and poured the blended froth over them. He rummaged in the industrial-size fridge and held up an egg to her with a raised eyebrow. She shook her head and he cracked the raw egg into his frosted glass. She heard David gulp. Jabez garnished her glass with a slice of cantaloupe and handed it to her.

"Thank you." The drink tasted sweet on her tongue but had the texture of cement mix. Jabez gestured for them to follow him.

They went into an adjoining living room–cum–training center. If Jesus preached poverty, Jabez wasn't listening. A state-of-the-art Nautilus machine towered in the corner. Expensive contemporary furniture—Danish, and out of character with the Victorian exterior of the home— adorned the room. A wide-screen television dominated one corner. Photos of Jabez's glory days in the wrestling ring covered the wall. In one he held aloft a weighted championship belt and snarled at the screaming audience of modern-day gladiator junkies.

One small cross hung on the wall, fitted in between a

pair of ringside wrestling photos. No pictures of Jesus the gentle shepherd.

"We'd like to show her picture to your followers," David said.

"They don't follow me. They follow the Lord. *Followers* makes it sound like a cult."

"Well," David said pleasantly. "No offense meant."

"You start a new church, offer seekers new answers to old questions, find success with it, and then people question you."

"You glorify the body, though," Claudia said.

He flexed the muscles in one arm. "We consider our bodies temples to the Lord, since we are sculpted in His image. Our own bodies are reflected in the Body of Christ that the church forms." He ran a hand over the muscle in his arm like it was sacred velvet, a priest admiring his vestments.

"You certainly have a lot of young women here," she said.

"I'm sure there are many young women at your own church."

Claudia smiled. "But they don't live with Father O'Hearn or Father Aguilar."

"I don't sleep with these young women, if that's what you're implying."

"You just focus on having female disciples? That it?" David asked.

His gaze hardened. "The way I bring the Lord to them appeals to them, just as a prayer book appeals to an Episcopalian or bowing toward Mecca appeals to a Muslim."

"You're sure the Ballew girl didn't make her way here?" David asked.

"I will happily swear on a stack of Bibles that I've never laid eyes on her face before."

"You are the only connection we've yet found between this girl and Port Leo," David said bluntly.

Jabez drained his shake in such a pronounced swallow it reminded Claudia of a python downing a rat. "You have no cause to bother us."

"This girl had no reason to be in Encina County that we know of except for you." Claudia set down her drink on a glass-topped table. "I'm sorry, but I feel like you're not being completely honest with us."

"I've given you no reason for doubt."

"I wonder," she said, hoping to shake the tree. "You have this missing girl who might have come here to see you. You're seen arguing with Pete Hubble on his boat, and he is now dead. I suppose it might be coincidence. I suppose it might not."

David shot her a questioning look with the barest shrug of his shoulders.

Jabez crossed his buffed arms. "I don't get easily intimidated. Jesus is on my side, in my heart, in my brain. I can withstand Satan. Comparatively, you're not that frightening."

"Satan can't get a search warrant, Reverend. And Satan can't put every aspect of your operation under a microscope. How do you think your television flock would react to news of you being investigated?" Claudia asked.

"On what charge? I've cooperated fully." He laughed. "I might expect this of a provincial buffoon like Delford Spires, but I always marked you as fairer and more intelligent, Ms. Salazar."

Claudia shook her head. "So why do I believe I'm going to have to lean on you very hard to get the truth?"

He smiled beatifically. "Lean away. I have a great PR

firm in Austin. They've already laid out a plan for any crisis. Arrest, investigation, scandal—not that it's likely."

She let the silence hang. "Fine. Anything else, Deputy Power?"

David shook his head, a numb look on his face.

"Loved the shake," Claudia said.

"Go in peace," Jabez said. She wanted to slap the sure smirk off his face.

They got into David's cruiser and shut the doors. David didn't start the car.

"You know, Claud, I miss that little spark of tough you got," he said.

"You said you wouldn't do this. Talk about us."

"Sorry. I just admired the way you wouldn't let him walk all over you."

A group of Jabez disciples jogged past the parking lot, legs lifting into perfect beat, mouths moving to a chant of prayer.

"I knew I should've joined a gym," David said. "I saw the lustful stare you gave those arms of his."

"You saw nothing," Claudia said. Great. David was teasing her now, bantering.

As David drove down the palm-lined road leading to the encampment and halfway down to the highway, the girl Rachel stepped out of the growth, waving her arms. David stopped the cruiser, and Claudia lowered her window.

"Cops, right? Can we talk a minute?" the girl asked. Her voice shook.

"Sure," Claudia said.

"Not here. Someplace else."

David let the girl into the back of the car. Rachel ducked

in and pointed at a side road, curving off to the right. "Pull in down there so no one sees us. He's gonna be looking for me soon enough."

David obeyed. Claudia turned to Rachel. "Do you know that girl in the picture?"

"No, never seen her. But I know Pete Hubble."

"What?"

"Pete's a friend from California. I did a couple of movies with him this year, and he lent me some cash." Claudia studied the young woman's face, and saw anew the vixen clinging to Pete on the cover of one of the tapes. *Cleopatra's Love Slaves.* Done up as a horny Queen of the Nile, pulling a rubber asp through her cleavage and kissing the snake's head. Hadn't one of the stars had the silly name of Rachel Pleasure? Different hair, but the same girl, the same wide blue eyes, the same elfin face.

Rachel hunkered down in the seat. "Just listen, okay? If I'm gone long, Mary Magdalene will smack me. She already hates me."

"We're listening," Claudia said.

"Pete wanted dirt on Jabez Jones, and he asked me to help him, said he'd pay me what I make in a month's work doing flicks. I said sure. He flew me out here and I checked into the camp." Her voice wavered. "We don't get to watch television—except for Jabez's show—or listen to radio or read papers, but last night I was in Jabez's room and heard them say on the TV news Pete was dead."

"He shot himself," Claudia said.

"But Pete was supposed to get me out. They watch us like hawks."

"Didn't Velvet know you were here?" Claudia asked.

Rachel shook her head. "He didn't want Velvet to know

about his business. Plus she doesn't like me too well. I'm a way better actress than she is."

"Um, we'll get you out," David said. "You want to go now?"

"Look, if Jabez knows Pete planted me here, no way am I staying. But I don't have the evidence Pete wanted."

"What were you looking for?" Claudia asked.

Rachel bit her lip. "Pete thought Jabez knew who killed his brother, years ago. He thought maybe Jabez had made all his money by keeping his mouth shut or maybe was in on his brother's death. I couldn't find anything about that, though, but I did find something else. Dope."

"Do tell," David said.

"I made sure I got close to him once I got here." Rachel peered out the back windshield, as though the hounds had been released. "That's why Mary Magdalene hates my guts. I'm the new favorite."

"He says he doesn't sleep with his ... followers," Claudia said.

"Right. He was screwing me last night while the news was on. I had to keep lying there while he huffed and puffed and watched himself in the mirror. I thought I was going to die when I heard them talk about Pete. He's rough about sex, too. Something's not right with him, let me tell you. He likes to snort a little coke, especially when he and I are about to get busy. He keeps it in his bedroom."

David revved the engine. "If we get you out right now, will he flush the cocaine?"

"I don't know. I'm due for phone duty for the prayer line in thirty minutes. They'll look for me."

Claudia frowned. "Can you sit it out so he doesn't suspect and let us get a search warrant?"

Rachel nodded. "If you think it will help." She got out of the car. "But hurry. And you got to get me out of here when you get back."

"We will, I promise," Claudia said. "I promise."

David backed out onto the road, floored the accelerator, and peeled down the road toward the highway. "Claudia, this is huge!" he roared. "Holy hell!"

Claudia thought: *Oh, no way was Pete gonna kill himself with that girl stuck at the camp. No way now Whit can rule for suicide.*

29

LYING ON THE bunk in the thin morning light, Whit opened the file of clippings Patsy Duchamp had given him yesterday. He heard Gooch clopping about on the deck. They had already scarfed a quick breakfast of yesterday's doughnuts and were chugging back to shore, where Whit would begin his great judicial charade and try not to get himself or anyone else killed.

A note from Patsy was stuck on the thick file of clips: *Whit, sorry if it's overkill, but the lady who did this is a retired military librarian, and let's just say she is a COMPLETIST. Hope this is helpful. You owe me a pitcher of Shiner Bock. Patsy.*

Completist was right. The woman had found practically every mention of Corey Hubble. Whit skipped the first clippings, looking for the ones specifically related to Corey's disappearance.

The first articles were entirely straightforward, except for the inherent lurid appeal of headlines like SENATOR'S SON MISSING or HUBBLE SUSPECTED RUNAWAY, and it was the same information Claudia had shared with him from the police report. The tone of the quotes—most of which were from Delford and only a couple from Lucinda—went

from fear of Corey being a victim of foul play to a seem-
ing certainty that he had run away. No indication Pete, or
anyone else, was suspected of killing Corey. The story garnered fewer inches as time passed. No new developments
emerged.

He set the clippings from, during, and after Corey's
disappearance aside and went back through the rest.
One was Lucinda's husband's obituary, with Corey simply listed as a survivor. Many were articles about Lucinda's original campaign for the Texas Senate, picturing
her stumping for votes with her two sons. Pete beamed,
happy and proud; Corey wore the smile his mother told
him to.

In a photo showing his mother on election night, when
she narrowly won, Corey smiled in stunned amazement, as
though victory was an unexpected pleasure. A few more
clippings offered coverage of legislation Lucinda Hubble
sponsored. He had stopped to read one article, dated a
month before Corey's disappearance, about Lucinda's fiery
stand on nursing home reform when his gaze drifted to a
picture on the far side of the page.

It was a common photo for the *Port Leo Mariner*: proud
fisherman hoisting aloft a sizable catch. The paper actively
courted show-offs to promote Port Leo as an angler's paradise. Four goofily grinning teenagers held high a trio of
big bullet-shaped fish. The caption read: *Tight Lines for
Teens—Corey Hubble and friends caught a trio of beautiful red boogers, 22", 25", and 26", while out on St. Leo
Bay on Nov 22. Not pictured are the many biggies that
got away. The kids used dead shrimp. Pictured (l to r):
Corey Hubble and Marian Duchamp of Port Leo, Thomas
Deloache Jr. and Eddie Gardner of Houston.*

Whit stared at the photo. He tucked the clippings back into the envelope. Then he went up on the deck to help Gooch dock at the Golden Gulf Marina.

After Gooch gave him sound advice on how to avoid assassination throughout the day ("watch your back something constant and scream fire if attacked"), Whit headed for his car. The T-head—and the docked boats—smelled of sharp diesel fuel, brewing coffee, and the sugary-piss tang of spilled white zinfandel. He watched terns arcing over the gently rocking boats, scouring for generous breakfast scraps. His cell phone chirped. "Whit Mosley here."

"Hi. My name is Kevin McKinnon. You had sent me an e-mail about Pete Hubble?" A low baritone, calm, an accountant's voice.

Kevin, creator of the online Temple of Appreciation website, dedicated to Pete.

"Yes, Kevin, hello, thank you for calling back."

"Yeah, well, what did you want?"

No point in hemming and hawing. "I'm sorry to be the bearer of bad news. Pete has passed away."

Silence. "You're not funny."

"I'm afraid I'm quite serious. I'm the justice of the peace here in Port Leo, Texas, Pete's hometown. He died Monday night. I'm supervising the inquest into his death."

More silence. "Oh, no, no, no." The pain in his voice, the raw loss, stopped Whit.

Whit waited a moment, letting the man regain composure. "I saw a posting on your site that you had talked with him this week."

"Yes. How did he die?"

Whit told him briefly, without mentioning the suicide

note. Kevin's low baritone became a breathy, agonized mewl. "If this is a joke, it's in really bad taste."

Under other circumstances an amateur pornographer chiding him on taste might have been good for a laugh over drinks with Georgie and Gooch. Deep grief colored Kevin's voice, sounding as true as the grief of the Hubbles.

"I'm so terribly sorry. But it would be helpful if you could tell me what you talked about."

"I want some confirmation of this, mister. You fax me a death certificate."

"How about if you call me at my office at the Encina County courthouse? I'll give you the switchboard number, you can talk to the operator and know you're really talking to a judge."

The offer disarmed him. "This is real?"

"You talked to him in the hours before he died. Did he sound suicidal?"

"Hardly. He sounded elated. He'd gotten the funding for his movie. His regular movie."

"Did he mention where this money was coming from?"

"No. I guess he couldn't get the producers who regularly funded his porn work to back this movie. He said he needed a half million and he'd gotten it."

Whit kept his voice under control. "He had landed a half-million dollars?"

Kevin coughed. "Why would he kill himself if he had gotten the money? That makes no sense."

"He didn't mention who his investor was?"

"I'm sure. I can't believe he's gone."

Whit wondered: *What was Pete to you, just a picture on a computer? Or more?*

"Forgive me, Kevin, but can you tell me what your relationship was with Pete?"

"Just a friend. Yeah, I dug his movies, I dug watching him, he was hotter than hell, man. But he was straight as an arrow. There was nothing between us. He liked that I had done a website about him. He was cool, thought it helped sell more videos for him, and it didn't cost him a cent."

"Did he ever mention his brother Corey to you?" Whit remembered that the one Internet search he'd done on Corey Hubble pointed him toward Kevin's site, oddly enough.

"Yeah, he told me the whole sad story once. I posted a page about his brother on the site a few months ago, you know, thinking to help. A picture of Corey, details about when he vanished, a number you could call if you had information. Pete's answering service."

"Did he ever mention any of these names to you: Junior Deloache? Or Eddie Gardner? Or Jabez Jones?"

"No. Sorry," Kevin said. "I can't believe now I got to write an obituary. Where do I start?"

"Kevin, thanks. If there's anything else you remember…"

"Yeah, wait. The money. He joked about it. I figured his financier had just given him a check, but he joked about how heavy the bag was. Maybe he got the money in cash."

"Thank you, Kevin. Thanks so much." Condolence seemed even more awkward now than it had with Faith, but he tried. "Please know how sorry I am for you losing your friend."

"Thanks. Thanks. I got to go."

Kevin hung up. Whit hurried to his car, made sure

no mobsters hunked behind his tires, and fired up the engine. The car didn't explode. The day was off to a positive start.

Why would anyone give a no-talent porn hack a half million in cash to make a movie? Another hack, Whit thought. Junior Deloache.

His phone buzzed again.

"Where are you?" Claudia demanded. "I need a search warrant and I need it fast."

"You aren't going to get away with this," Mary Magdalene screamed. Claudia ignored her and watched two county deputies search the back closet of Jabez's master suite.

"It would be helpful if you would just tell us where Jabez is," David said. His eyes shone brightly in excitement.

Mary Magdalene flinched. "He was called away on the Lord's business."

One of David's fellow deputies came in the room, shook his head. "No sign of Jones on the grounds. Car's gone."

"So where is he, Mary?" Claudia asked.

"I don't know."

"You're his right-hand woman and you don't know." Claudia crossed her arms, suspecting that Jabez leaving Mary behind to feel the heat was an increasingly tender subject. "So I guess he just figured you could take whatever rap was coming. That's really Christian of him. What a guy."

Mary Magdalene trembled, but not from fear.

A deputy, a lanky young Vietnamese man, carried an old, worn maple box from the closet. Inside was a thick Bible. Inside the Bible, in neatly hollowed-out trenches of Scripture, lay three vials of white powder. David daubed a bit on his tongue, tasted, and nodded at Claudia. "The pause that refreshes. Cocaine, boys and girls."

Claudia turned to Mary Magdalene. "Help us, Mary, or we can't help you when the judge starts throwing books your way. Where is Jabez?"

Mary Magdalene fell to one knee, her mouth twisting in silent prayer.

"Start searching the other barracks," David ordered, "and let's call the DEA in Corpus. And we need to get an APB out on Jones."

"She knows where he is," Claudia insisted, pointing at the prayerful Mary. "She knows and she's—"

Mary Magdalene exploded from the floor and pile-drove into Claudia, sending them both sprawling out into the small hallway. Thick fingers with sharp nails, like pikes, dug into Claudia's windpipe, and a fist slammed against her left eye. Claudia rammed upward with her knee, finding the softness between Mary's legs, and she grabbed Mary's thumb and bent back hard. A scream, and then the hands were yanked away, the other officers pinning Mary on her stomach, cuffing her in an instant.

Claudia climbed to her feet, David helping her. Her shoulder ached and the skin around her eye was numbed. Mary screamed imprecations, not the sweet language of theology but the salty poetry from her days on the street.

"I'm fine," Claudia said before David could start fawning over her hurts. She knelt by Mary. "You just complicated your life about a hundred times. I'm starting to think you're not particularly bright. Here's a chance to get smart, Mary. Where is Jabez?"

"'His enemies shall lick the dust,'" she hollered, her face purpling in rage. "You'll die just like the trash does!"

"Y'all the ones licking dust. Or snorting it," David said.

"Die like the trash does?" Claudia asked. "Or die like the trash did?"

Delford Spires shook his head. "I hope everything's nice and clean about how y'all got that warrant and did that search." He pointed at Claudia's eye. "That's gonna go shiner."

"It's not like I was having my photo done soon for employee of the month."

Stiff silence.

"So that leaves us, Delford, with an awful interesting situation," Claudia said. "Pete Hubble placed this girl in Jabez's camp. I can't imagine he would go to all that trouble, then blithely kill himself."

Delford sipped a cold coffee. "I can't explain away a suicide note, Claudia. Especially one that has just Pete's and Sam's prints on it." His tone was final, dismissive, and he fixed her with a glower designed to make her crumple. She fired a salvo back, tired and achy and sick of being railroaded.

"I assume you've spoken with Judge Mosley about the coroner's findings and the problems with the bagging of the hands."

"Yes, I have," Delford said.

Eddie Gardner reddened. "Claudia, you saw the body with me," Gardner said. "I didn't screw up the bagging."

"I didn't say you did," she said evenly. "I'm just telling you what the ME and Judge Mosley said."

Delford tweezed a mustache end into sharp perfection. "Eddie, review the chain of custody for the body. Make sure we can account for the bag damage. Probably the mortuary crew tore 'em."

"Yes, sir," Gardner said. "One other thing on Hubble. Since we have a time of death, we can locate the boats that came in and out of Golden Gulf during the period, since *Real Shame* was at the end of the T-head. Claudia and I already have accounted for five of the six boats that departed and all the boats that arrived. No one saw anything helpful."

"And this last boat?"

"A cruiser called *Miss Folly*. Owner lives up near New Orleans and treks all over the Gulf coast. He didn't file a float plan." A float plan was the maritime equivalent of a flight plan, required of commercial vessels, optional for personal craft.

"Let's get that boat found," Delford said to Eddie. "I don't want the press suggesting we're not being thorough. Claudia, let's talk."

After Gardner had shut the door behind him, Delford folded his hands on his desk. "I noticed you checked out the Corey Hubble file. Find anything interesting?"

"No, not really."

"You're still pissed about being pulled as the lead."

"No, it's your decision."

"Claud, come on. I know you too well. You're madder than a wet bee. But listen, I want Gardner handling this."

"Like he did the bags?"

"I did bruise your ego. Well, now." A crinkle—a near smile—crossed his face. "Point taken. Hubble's just about over, soon as Whit issues a damned ruling. Focus on the Ballew case."

"It's really the sheriff's case, not ours," Claudia said. "Unless you're scheming with mine and David's parents to stick us back together."

Delford laughed, the low tremble that she knew, and she felt a sudden warmth again toward him, this contrary, whim-ridden old toot who could either advance you fast in the department or mire you down forever. "Your mama scares me, Claudia, and I would be reluctant to cross her. I just want you to provide the sheriff's office with support. Consider yourself loaned to them."

And therefore out of your hair, Claudia thought.

"So you go put some ice on that eye. Or a nice steak," Delford said.

Claudia went back to her office. A whirl of paperwork covered her desk: two new burglary reports to follow up on, a shoplifting case. Gardner came in a few minutes later, swigging a Dr Pepper. He shut the office door and leaned against it.

"Aren't you clever?" he said.

"Pardon me?"

"You screw up, so you start trying to make me look bad."

"You're mistaken."

"You're gunning for me, Claudia. Maybe you damaged those evidence bags without me seeing."

"Oh, get over yourself."

He shot an unexpected missile across her bow. "You think because you're Mexican and a woman you should get all the good cases."

"Just because you're an idiot," she said sweetly, "doesn't mean you should get all the bad ones."

Eddie Gardner leaned toward her and growled, "I bet you scratch when you screw."

She stood. "Get away from me, and don't you ever talk to me like that again."

He stepped back, a wounded look on his face. "I don't

know what you're talking about, Detective Salazar." He opened the door and left.

She sat, bile polluting the back of her throat, wondering why autocracy and viciousness had suddenly fouled this perfectly nice police department. Delford had turned tyrannical; Gardner, who she always suspected was a pig, had gone from mildly amusing to no-tolerance disgusting.

She went down to the kitchen to get a glass of ice water. She found Patrolman Fox snacking on a Butterfinger bar. Chocolate gummed the corners of his mouth.

"What's up, Bill?" she asked, and he swallowed his candy.

"Working hard for Eddie. I wore my fingers to the bone phoning on the Hubble case."

"What's going on with that?" She dumped ice into a glass and filled it from the faucet.

Fox shrugged. "I called all the numbers on Pete Hubble's phone records. He knew some strange people, let me tell you. Most of them seemed to be people that he knew through his, um, film work." The milk-breathed Baptist boy could hardly say the word *pornography*. "I made notes. I haven't typed them up yet."

Claudia picked up his scrawled pieces of paper. In the last days of his life Pete had called a couple of porn directors and a screenwriter in legit film. He'd called his mother, several times, his ex-wife three times. There were a couple of calls to the Placid Harbor Nursing Home—the home David's grandfather lived at, down by Little Mischief Beach, and that reminded her that she wanted to have another talk with Heather Farrell. She wondered who Pete knew there. And still the number in far East Texas, in the little hamlet of Missatuck, the one she'd tried the morning after Pete's death, and Fox had similarly gotten no answer. The phone company said that the number belonged to one Kathy Breaux. Pete had called her four times in the three days before his death.

Claudia went back to her office and picked up the phone. She dialed the Missatuck number. It was now disconnected, and no new number listed.

30

THE AFTERNOON LIGHT slanted through the tilted blinds. Bars of light and dark lay against Whit's desk—for once, cleared of the usual fan of papers and the half-full coffee cup. Whit sat across from Claudia, still in his judge's robe, an askew collar of yellow tropical-print shirt peeking out from the sober black. He had finished with traffic court by two, and she'd given him a quick synopsis of the developments with Jabez Jones.

"I don't care much about that suicide note," Claudia said. "But there's no way I believe Pete put Rachel into Jabez's camp as a spy, then decided to kill himself."

Whit loosened a stray thread from the throat of his robe. "Did Rachel say she'd told Pete about the drugs she'd seen?"

"Actually, no, she hadn't talked to him since she arrived at the camp. It was too risky, they thought. So let's say Pete found out another way Jabez was dealing."

"Dealing?" Whit said.

"He clearly had more than he could personally use. Gives Jabez a motive."

"I suppose." Whit shrugged.

Claudia cocked her head. "You sound like you've

graduated from the Delford Spires School of Low-Key Investigation."

"So Delford's finally made it to your hallowed people-I'm-mad-at list?"

"I've made room for him. Gardner's king." She told him about her confrontation with Eddie Gardner.

"Be careful of him. Very careful," Whit said.

"He's a mouth. I can handle him."

"Seriously, Claudia," Whit said, and she saw he was dead serious. The sharp-eyed glare on his face was the one he usually reserved for magistrating repeat offenders and irksome litigants. His mouth twitched slightly. "He's trouble."

"Why's he on your list, Honorable?"

"Just don't cross him, okay? Trust me."

"What's going on?"

"Nothing. Tired. Inquest is tomorrow at one. I decided to call a full one in the courtroom instead of just issuing a ruling of death."

She supposed the political capital of a high-profile death was too good for him to waste right before an election. "Sure, fine. I've got my notes ready to testify."

He dug into his desk drawer and handed her a phone number. "This is a number Pete used in California with an answering service. It might be interesting to see who in Port Leo, or in Texas, called him."

"Haven't you been the busy bee?" Claudia said. "Thanks, I'll have Fox check this."

"I've got to go. Promise me you'll be careful."

"About what?"

"Just be careful, all right?"

"Sure." She walked back across the street to the police

station, wondering who had wedged the coal lump in Whit's butt.

Whit watched Claudia cross the street, a sudden whip of wind from the bay mussing her dark hair. She tucked the errant strands behind her ear and darted inside the police station.

He let the blinds fall. That morning he had called each of his five brothers. He heard updates on teething nieces and upcoming software releases and the casual cruelties of writer critique groups. But nothing of bullets, of shady characters lurking in darkened driveways, ready to make innocents pay for Whit being the wrong judge in the wrong place at the wrong time. He ended each conversation with a story about random violence he claimed to have seen on TV and begged them all to be extra careful.

He had trudged through the day's duties of signing warrants, a brief truancy court, and a long and maddening traffic court session. Tomorrow was the inquest; he didn't have much time. He picked up the phone.

"Velvet? It's Whit Mosley. I need a favor from you. Do you still have a key to *Real Shame*?"

"I do." She sounded lazy, sleepy, as though just awakening for the day. If she was, he wondered what she'd been up to all night.

"I'd like to stop by and borrow it, if I may."

"The cops have a key."

"I'd like to borrow yours."

She was silent for a moment. "Well, yeah, that's okay."

"I've got an errand to run first, but I'll be over in an hour or so."

"I'll see you then, Judgie."

He hung up, doffed the robe, and in his beachwear shirt
and khaki shorts and sandals headed over to the trashy
west end of Port Leo.

The Blade watched the little waves surge up Little Mischief
Beach, the sand flat, wet, and clean. The damp, fine air—
the ocean exhaling—smelled of salt and freshness. No sign
on the beach Heather Farrell had ever been there, no blood
on the sands, not a gap-toed footprint to mark her passage.

He turned away from the water and the little voice,
tinged with his mother, that whispered and berated in the
curvy hollow of his ear roared: *Do you think she only had
the clothes on her worthless back?*

He stopped. He turned toward the beach. Past the
gentle crescent of sand, into the parkland, was a motte of
live oaks, ringed with high grass. Hadn't he watched her
there once, stretching against the Tower-of-Pisa-bent trees,
scratching her foot?

She had to have camped nearby.

He bolted along the stretch of sand, up through the bluestems and the grasses, panic drumming its rat-a-tat in his
chest, Mama's voice laughing at him, hiding in the wind.

He searched for a half hour among the askew oaks
and the tall grasses. He found only a narrow rectangle of
crushed bluestems, where a woman's sleeping bag might
have lain recently. A discarded peanut butter crackers
wrapper fluttered, caught in the tall grass.

The trailer park was named Rainbow's End. The pot of
gold, however, was nowhere in sight.

He knocked on the wrong door, and a sleepy elderly
woman told him Marian Duchamp made her home in

trailer number six. The woman pointed over to an immaculately maintained trailer, a veritable palace among the weed-choked lots.

Whit wondered why anyone would voluntarily live on the Texas coast in a mobile home. One hurricane—one mild tropical storm—roaring ashore could move the trailer half a county inland. In small fragments.

Whit knocked once on the door. Inside, an afternoon talk show's theme jazzily trilled. The door lurched open. A woman who should have looked younger than she did, wearing frayed cutoffs and a faded Corpus Christi Ice Rays T-shirt, tottered in the doorway.

"Marian Duchamp?"

"Maybe." She blinked against the bright afternoon light.

"I'm Whit Mosley, the justice of the peace for Encina County. I'm conducting a death inquest, and I'd like to ask you a few questions."

"Um, okay. Um, what about?" Lunch had apparently been of the liquid sort.

"Corey Hubble."

She stared.

"A friend of yours who disappeared several years ago?" Whit prompted.

Marian Duchamp digested this request. She was clearly drunk. A wine bottle rested against her hip: French Beaujolais, surprisingly, not your typical trailer-park fare.

Georgie, the walking she-database, had provided him with the local lore on Marian: a good-looking tomboy and jock up until the last year of junior high, when her father drowned in a boating accident. The dead father had reached from the grave to drag his daughter down; Marian Duchamp had raced into a self-destructive spiral of drugs, booze, and petty theft. Dropout from school, lived on her mother's mercy, Georgie had said. Just a shame.

"Corey. Yes." She spoke slowly.

"Can we talk about him?"

"Well, I'm drunk, but you know, I'm not out in public, Judge, so I don't think that I'm in the wrong this time."

"I'm not here to arrest or bug you, okay? As long as you're not planning on driving anywhere today, are you?"

"Don't have a car, so I guess not." She laughed, a rough, unpleasant guffaw, and the wine wafted on her breath. She contemplated him with a half smile. "I remember you. One of the Mosley boys."

"Yeah, the youngest." At once he almost regretted his words. Forever the baby of a certain notorious family. But when five older brothers had already speeded and fished and slept and drunk a path through the town's consciousness, cutting your own distinctive way got progressively harder.

"Yeah, I knew your brother Mark," she said. Her smile warmed, not quite sultry but at least friendlier. "Come on in."

A sober feminine hand clearly maintained this space: gold-trimmed family photos, a small milk bottle holding fresh carnations on the dinner table, a sofa with neatly arranged pillows, embroidered with platitudes like BLOOM WHERE YOU'RE PLANTED and PRINCESS OF QUITE A BIT. Dust would not dare show its unsightly face; the home appeared as pristine as a freshly tended hotel suite. A stand of wine bottles, emptied, stood along the breakfast bar. Whit read the labels: Cakebread, La Crema, Cuvaison. Not a dollar vintage in the bunch.

"You have a nice trailer," Whit said.

"I found quality help," Marian smirked. "And you know,

good help is really hard to find. I'm ever so lucky. Have a seat. You on duty? Do judges do duty? Want a glass of quality red?" Her gaze drifted across his throat, his chest.

"No, thank you." He sat on the couch, and she tumbled into the recliner. He knew she'd once been attractive in a lanky way, but now her skin looked sallow, her belly was a little wine barrel, and patchy shadow, new applied over old, caked her eyelids.

"What's Mark doing these days?" she asked.

"He's living in Austin, still single, getting an MFA in creative writing at UT. He's finished a novel and is working on a collection of poems."

"Well, la-di-da, fancy, fancy, fancy. Po-ems." She paused. "I know some words that rhyme." She confessed this with a tinge of embarrassment, as though she had neglected a gift handed her by the gods.

Whit let silence sit between them for twenty seconds, and Marian fidgeted and half smiled at him. "I understand you knew Corey Hubble when you were kids," Whit said.

"Ancient history now, like Vietnam and the Renaissance."

"His brother Pete died recently, and he was working on a film about Corey's disappearance. We're interested to know who he talked to about Corey."

"We being who? The police?"

"We being me, really." He suspected she had no liking for the police. "The inquest determines if someone is responsible for the death of another. The voters are my boss. I work for the county."

"You don't work for Delford Spires?"

"No," Whit said. Marian, the wild teen, would have no love for a longtime police chief. "I'm not one of his favorite people."

Marian abruptly got up from the recliner and refilled her glass with Beaujolais. Not the gentle arc of a pour— more of a rough slosh, spilling the wine. She licked wine from her hand, then drank half the glass down, then refilled again before she tottered back to the recliner.

"So this is upsetting to you, or you're just thirsty?" Whit said.

"There's nothing to tell about Corey Hubble."

"Pete didn't think so."

"Yeah, and now he's gonna be crammed in a coffin for eternity." She shuddered. "No, thanks."

Whit was silent. Marian Duchamp, in this state, could hardly be considered a credible witness. At least in court. But instead he got up, found a glass, poured in a small trickle, and sat again.

"I remember Corey, you know," he said. "I knew him, but not well."

Watching him sample the wine, she visibly relaxed. She traced the ring of the glass with a fingernail.

"He...was jealous of you," she said with a soft laugh. "Does that surprise you?"

"Sure does. I'm nothing special."

"Well, you had a mess of brothers. You always had family around. Corey didn't have nobody after his daddy died. Pete was the pet, and his mama just wanted to go write laws and mess around in Austin. Serving the people, what a crock."

"Didn't he have you as a friend?"

She laughed. "*Friend*. There's a nice clean word. We screwed now and then." She watched him for a reaction to her crudity.

"He ever hit now and then?"

She giggled. "Hey, I hit him back. He was a mean little punk when he got crossed."

"You ever hear of him roughing up other women?"

She tongued the rim of her glass. "I was the only one stupid enough to date him."

"So what do you think happened to him, Marian?"

"I really don't know." She sipped some wine, not looking at him. "Why should I tell you anything anyway?"

"Well, I need your help, and you're the only one who can help me. No one else will."

"That's a lousy reason."

"You mentioned Delford Spires before."

She shrugged.

"You think Delford did a crappy job of investigating Corey's disappearance?"

She laughed, not a funny or kind laugh. "That was the fox watching the freaking henhouse."

"Why?"

"Corey hated Delford Spires's guts."

"Didn't every teenager in town?" Whit cajoled, laughing, tasting a little more of his wine. "I was in the terrorist crew that painted his house pink. You remember that?"

She brayed laughter, recognizing the widely loved—or at least widely discussed—prank played long ago on the police chief.

"So what was Corey's beef with Delford?"

"I think," she said slowly, "Corey took off because Delford caught wind of what he was planning."

"Which was?"

"Well, Corey was probably kidding—you know loud-mouthed kids, but he told me he was gonna kill Delford Spires." She held her wineglass very still, in both hands.

Whit kept equally still. "How did he plan on doing this?"

She shrugged. "He had his daddy's shotgun."

Whit watched her; she stared at the hem of her cutoffs. "Why do you think he told you this, Marian?"

"Just to impress me. He was ten pounds of crap in a Dixie cup."

"Why did he want to shoot Delford?"

"I don't know. He never told me why...so I never took him seriously. I mean, look, he couldn't have been serious. Delford Spires is still alive."

"But Corey probably isn't," he said, and she burst into tears.

"You think Delford killed Corey?"

She cried, she shrugged. "I shouldn't have said anything."

Delford might be many things—political, pushy, too good-old-boy for a changing world, but Whit didn't believe Delford was a cold-blooded killer. Especially a killer of children.

"Why didn't you tell anyone this?"

"I did. Corey's mama. I was afraid to talk to the police—afraid of Delford, I mean. I didn't know what to think. So I told the senator, I phoned her, and she thanked me and nothing ever came of it. You know, I figured Corey would come home and she didn't want him in trouble with Delford."

Marian Duchamp got up with overdone precision, stumbled to the kitchen, and freshened her glass.

We build these little worlds for ourselves, Whit thought, remembering what Velvet had said, *and then we never get to move out.*

"Do you remember two friends of Corey's? From Houston. A boy named Eddie Gardner, another boy named Junior Deloache."

"Think so. They summered down here sometimes and fished in the fall on weekends. Junior always had lots of cash and dope to share." She remembered too late Whit was a judge and murmured, "Well, I don't do anything illegal anymore, okay?"

"What about Eddie?"

"Just some lame friend of Junior's."

And now he was a detective on the Port Leo police force. A very recent hire.

"You seen either of them around lately?"

She shook her head. "Not in years, not since Corey took off."

The door to the trailer opened, and a tall, fiftyish woman peeked her head inside. Her hair was pulled tight into a proper gray bun, and she wore a cleaning smock, festooned with a brightly colored, grinning cartoon chicken waving a spatula. She carried a grocery sack.

"Oh, excuse me, hon. I didn't know you were entertaining." The lady smiled with maternal grace at Whit, as though about to pat Whit's head and offer him a sugar cookie.

"Oh, come on in, Mama," Marian said. "This is Whit Mosley—he's a judge."

Whit helped Mama Duchamp tote grocery sacks. One bag clinked, full of bottles of wine: merlot, chardonnay, pinot noir, all of it the better stuff. He put the bags on the kitchen counter without comment, and Mama Duchamp murmured that she'd just brought some refreshments for her sweet baby girl and oh, she'd tend to getting those bottles put up.

"Have some red, Mama," Marian called.

"Perhaps later," Mama Duchamp said.

"I was just going," Whit said. He thanked Marian for her

time. She blinked, as if confused as to why she'd been crying, why he was here. With her mother in the room Marian
seemed sunnier, as though reassured, like a puppy, that the
milk dish brimmed full.

Mama Duchamp stepped outside with him, shutting the
door on Marian's hollered, slurred good-byes.

"I know you're a busy man, with a lot of doors to knock
on," Mama Duchamp said. "Good luck in the election. I
hope you win. I don't trust people named Buddy. It's like
they want to be your friend before you even know them."

"Thanks. But I actually wasn't here campaigning. I was
asking Marian about Corey Hubble."

He could smell the wry odor of throat lozenges on her
breath. "Why?"

"She says Corey was planning to commit a murder
before he vanished."

"Oh, my lands. Marian doesn't know what she says. She
doesn't think."

"It's hard to think when you're drinking all day."

Mama Duchamp's smile twitched. "She's nervous. It
soothes her."

"Do you do this all the time? Bring her what she needs
to live?"

Her long, narrow hands smoothed the chicken apron.
"Marian doesn't fend well for herself. She messes up. It's
just easier if I . . . arrange things for her."

"My brothers and I used to do that for my father. He was
a drunk."

"Don't you presume to stand here and lecture me."

"Aren't you tired of helping her along?" Whit asked.

She brought a hand to her lipsticked mouth. "Tired of
it? Marian could be lying out in an alley, scrounging on a

beach, selling herself for loose change. This way...I can keep an eye on her."

In a cage nicely gilded by the glint from wine bottles. "I suppose it's one way to be sure the kids stay in touch." He felt a sudden fury with this woman, letting her daughter drown by inches in scrubbed comfort. "I'll bet her liver's like wet tissue paper. Do you see the yellow tint in her eyes? That's death creeping in. Marian's about my age. She won't have long. Get her some help."

"Get off our property. I'm certainly not going to vote for you now, and I doubt that any member of the Garden Club will either once I make a few phone calls."

"I don't want your vote, Mrs. Duchamp," Whit said. Her face crimsoned, and she fled to the trailer. She shut the door quietly.

Whit roared out of the trailer park. His hands shook.

Get up, l'il bit, make me some bourb'coffee. Now. Babe's voice, slurring from the past. And Whit crawled from bed, being extra quiet, and made the coffee, poured in the extra big dollop of whiskey to ease Daddy's morning nerves. He was eight.

Whit pulled in at the next gas station and filled his tank.

Delford. Corey. What else to that story was there? Say Corey did come after Delford with a shotgun. If Delford killed Corey in self-defense, there was no reason to keep it secret. Marian's testimony about Corey's plans would have made a self-defense plea simple. If Delford or any of the authorities had heard of Corey's threats, Corey would have promptly been arrested, charged, and dealt with in the judicial system. That was Delford's way. He would never play judge and executioner. He had too much at stake to risk it over a punk kid like Corey Hubble.

But if Delford had killed Corey, then Delford could eliminate every iota of bothersome evidence. This theoretical killing might be impossible to prove.

He tried to imagine Corey stalking Delford, a grungy doper rich kid following around a respected officer. Corey would follow Delford, learn his routine, attempt to strike when Delford was most vulnerable—so when was that? What had the boy seen? What had he known? Why was he headed north?

He wondered where Delford was that fateful weekend.

Whit got out of his car, filled his tank, bought a fried apple pie and Dr Pepper at the convenience store, and ate a second lunch, all the while considering what would light the fuse of an angry, self-centered fifteen-year-old.

He didn't think of it until he thought about his own childhood, his own missing parent and what actions lit his own slow rage.

Jealousy. Resentment. The hungry need for a parent, even one who shows no interest.

Whit got on his cell phone and called Georgie.

31

THURSDAY EVENING, AS the sun began its dip below the horizon, Claudia drove down Highway 35, searching for Heather Farrell. No one at Little Mischief Beach had seen Heather, and Claudia suspected that she might have moved on. Whit's constable, Lloyd, had not been able to serve Heather the subpoena to appear in court tomorrow. Lloyd was cruising around the other local parks, hoping to spot her, and was concentrating on the northern half of the county. Claudia decided that Heather might have migrated south.

At least her need to find Heather had taken her away from David's gloating.

"Claudia, we just made our careers. Both of us," he had exulted. The Jabez Jones case was the biggest of his rather staid term in the sheriff's department, and he could hardly contain his excitement.

"You need to find Jabez first," she cautioned. "I wouldn't be counting any promotions until then."

"What do you think I should wear for *Entertainment Tonight,* if they want an interview?" David wondered. "They cover wrestling stories, right?"

"Your uniform." Claudia knew any answer was easier than an argument for sanity. "But pressed, okay?"

She turned off the main highway, at an intersection marked by crumpled, wood-grayed county piers, a reminder of the last big hurricane three years ago. The money to repair them had gone instead to new piers in Port Leo and Laurel Point. The piers were abandoned now except for a flock of pelicans, preening on the rotting posts. She remembered walking along the short piers with David, hand in hand, breathing the smell of buttery popcorn, of salt, of dead mullet, of bait souring in the air, of spilled chocolate ice cream melting between the boards. Her wedding ring had felt newly heavy, a sudden anchor with a chip of diamond.

There was a small park on the south side of St. Leo Bay, and she drove slowly past it. A family of three was strolling along the beach. An elderly woman sketched in the fading light, perched atop a picnic table, squinting at the wind-whipped bay. Claudia stopped and gave a description of Heather to the family and the woman. No one had seen her.

Claudia got back in her unmarked Taurus and headed farther south, the road curving down toward the hamlets of Encina Pass and Copano. She saw a white BMW speeding toward her, the driver intent on a phone. The car bulleted past, and Claudia saw Faith Hubble at the wheel.

Claudia lacked both a radar gun and jurisdiction. She headed down toward Encina Pass, and three minutes later she spotted Whit Mosley, getting into his Ford Explorer, the campaign sign magnets peeled off the sides. In the parking lot of a little puck of a motel, a twenty-dollar-a-night joint that catered to poor hipsters, tourists on bony budgets, and cheating husbands from Corpus Christi.

It didn't cater to justices of the peace and senators' chiefs of staff.

She pulled in beside Whit just as he started his car. She saw him force the smile, the faked-pleased look that suggested *gosh, I'm glad to see you* when it really meant *oh, hell* to the nth degree.

And a deep-inside part of her, never touched by David, twisted.

Claudia got out of her car. Whit powered his window down.

"Hi," she said. "What are you doing in this part of the county?"

He didn't answer right away. "Talking with a friend."

"Faith Hubble, maybe?"

He didn't say anything. "I saw her speeding down the road not three minutes ago. I couldn't imagine why she was gracing a remote part of the county with her divine presence. So what's going on, Honorable?"

"I wanted to ask her," he said mildly, "about a shotgun."

"Shotgun?"

"Corey Hubble owned a shotgun. I asked what happened to it after he vanished."

"And you had to discuss this with her in a backwater motel?" She remembered their faces when she'd arrived at Whit's door—the way they both focused on her, the way they didn't look at each other with her standing there, the wineglasses set close together on the coffee table.

Whit clicked off his engine. "I can't discuss it."

"Can't or won't?"

"Doesn't matter. Either way I'm not talking about it."

Claudia swallowed, aware suddenly of a sheen of sweat on her palms, the back of her legs, her shoulders. "If you're involved with her...you should recuse yourself from the inquest."

"I disagree, Claudia. But I can't discuss this with you. You're going to have to trust me."

"Whit, please..."

"I have to go now. I'll see you tomorrow." And he powered up the window and drove out of the lot. She stood in the oily smear of his parking place, watching him go.

She got back in her Taurus, and looked for Heather Farrell for another hour without success before she headed home.

Whit lay on his back in his bed, watching the ceiling fan rotate above him.

Did you think you were James Bond? A romp in the hay would loosen her tongue—she'd talk about whatever she knew about the day Corey vanished? The meeting had been rushed, the lovemaking awkward. Her kisses wore on his lips like sandpaper, and she had pulled away, frowning, saying, *We doing this or not?* And so he had, but the sex felt more duty than pleasure, and her finishing gasps when she arched against him sounded forced. Perhaps Velvet should have taped them with all the sincerity they had shown.

Faith claimed to know nothing about Corey's disappearance, a shotgun, or a grudge against Delford Spires. The more he talked, the more hastily she rinsed and dressed, and when she left all she said was, "Give me a lead time of a couple of minutes, okay? And you drive back via Old Bay Road, not the highway." Then the door shut, with not a single kiss good-bye.

And Claudia. He wanted to tell her, confide in her, but if he did, she and his family were at enormous risk. What if the man in the dark had been Delford or Eddie Gardner? What if his brothers were being watched right now, as threatened? The risk was too much. He would go on with his plan, conduct the inquest tomorrow, rule, and then worry less about the peace in his job title and more about the justice.

Finally he slept, and he dreamed of himself and Claudia's brother Jimmy, boys gigging for frogs in the murky backwash creeks, Claudia tagging along, the serious pest.

32

⟣⟶●◉●⟵⟢

Aᴛ ᴛᴡᴇɴᴛʏ ᴛɪʟʟ one Friday afternoon the Blade debated whether or not he should take a seat for the inquest. The hearing would start shortly, but he did not wish to be conspicuous by his presence. It was pleasant to sit in the cramped confines of the VW Beetle and watch the few television reporters strutting on the county courthouse lawn. All three of them, from the local Corpus affiliates, primped their doughnut-glaze hair. Again the sudden urge to simply get out of the car, walk over to them, and say, *Do I have a story for you—but you must call me the Blade,* washed over him, and he pumped up his Beach Boys tape, listening to them implore Rhonda for help, and the desire ebbed. To the Boys, Rhonda was a patron saint of love; perhaps he could find a Darling with the same name one day. Encina County was a Rhonda-rich environment. And perhaps one day he would walk up to a reporter and let his infamy begin. But not today.

If that scum-bucket judge did his job and ruled for suicide, then Velvet would have no reason to stay. Her time in Port Leo would end, and her sojourn with him could begin. He would treasure each second with her, each second an eternity to play again in his mind for the rest of his life. His mouth dried with want. Then it would end, as always, and he would be sad for a while, until the next craving rose like a lick of fire.

So don't do this. Don't do this anymore.

The voice in his ear was not Mama's, but a boy's voice perhaps like his own from long ago. *I'm sorry for what I do but it has to be done. I need it to be done.*

He pulled his Bowie knife out of its sheath and slid it beneath the driver's seat. He had cleaned and sharpened it again, after its last use.

The Blade saw Velvet hop out of her rental car and hurry inside the courthouse. She was modestly dressed, in black jeans, a thin, dark sweater, a baseball cap, and the reporters took little notice of her, which pleased him. He switched the Boys off. He could wait for her here. He smiled. Soon his Darling would breathe his same air, know his wanting, share the beginning of a brief forever.

Whit's clerk was a chain-smoking widow named Edith Gregory. She was on the outer edge of her fifties, with a thin, sparrow's body, dieted by years of smoking. She stood in Whit's office as he pulled his judicial robe over an unusually somber blue button-down and khaki combo and eyed him critically.

"Them pants need pressing," she said. "You think that little Russian gal could learn an iron." Edith was friends with Georgie. "Those Communists probably all wore grocery bags."

"I'm responsible for my own laundry, Edith."

Edith worked her empty fingers as if she had a cigarette. "We need to get responsible for keeping you in office. I got to work for Buddy Beere, they gonna have to give me a raise."

Whit straightened his robe and gathered the papers of the inquest record. "Okay, let's go."

Edith stopped him and he glanced at her. An unexpected softness touched her blue eyes, and he thought: *If my mom was alive and here she'd be about your age.*

"You just got this hangdog look on your face that's got me worried," Edith said. "Just remember, you're a judge. Act like one. Make me proud."

Six months and she doesn't give me a pep talk until now. "Thanks."

They walked out of his office and down the hall. He followed her into the small courtroom. Lloyd, the constable, bellowed, "All rise!" and the packed courtroom stood in near unison. The Hubble contingent occupied the front row: Faith, Lucinda, a tired-looking Sam, the rest of the power base for Encina County; to their left, Claudia Salazar, watching him as though he were a leper trying to blow kisses, and Delford Spires and Eddie Gardner, a couple of patrol officers; his father and Irina. In the back sat a large bevy of the curious, Velvet squeezed among them, replete in cap and dark glasses. In the back corner, to his surprise, Junior Deloache lounged, wearing a Houston Astros baseball cap and a Houston Rockets T-shirt. Deloache stared at him, and he wondered if he ruled for homicide if Junior would just go outside, flip open a cell phone, and call in the death orders.

"The Honorable Whitman Mosley presiding!" Lloyd blared. Whit sat and the crowd settled into their seats, wood creaking as butts eased down. He opened his inquest file, carefully prepared by his clerk. He glanced at the court reporter, borrowed from the county court. He wanted a written transcript of the proceedings to file in the inquest report.

Take step one and don't get killed.

"Good morning, everyone. This is a tragic event, this loss of life, and it has received a lot of local publicity. But this is a courtroom, and outbursts will not be tolerated. Anyone who creates a disturbance will be held in contempt and removed from the courtroom by the constable. Is that understood?"

Silence from the gathered. Lucinda Hubble looked pained. Velvet looked tense. Junior Deloache pushed his Astros cap back farther on his head and scratched his forehead with a beefy finger.

"Let me explain, quickly, the point of a death inquest hearing. It is to determine whether or not anyone is responsible for the death of another," Whit said. "I will question the witnesses. There is no jury in this case, and no one stands presently accused of a crime." He glanced at Lloyd. "Constable Brundrett, please call the first witness."

Lloyd said, "I was unable to serve process on Heather Farrell, Your Honor. I have not been able to locate her. I believe she may have left the jurisdiction. She's a known transient, and she lied to the police regarding her whereabouts."

"Did you find any trace of her, Constable?" He already knew the answer but wanted it in the record.

"Yes, sir. We found she had bought two tickets on Greyhound. Her reservation on the bus was for three days from now."

"But she's already gone?"

"Apparently, Your Honor."

"Thank you, Constable. Next witness?"

"Calling Detective Edward Gardner of the Port Leo Police Department."

Gardner came to the stand. Whit swore him in. Gardner gave a precise, rapid account of last Monday night's events.

"Did you find a suicide note?" Whit asked.

"No, Y'Honor. The deceased's son brought one to our attention later."

"Who covered the deceased's hands with protective bagging?"

Gardner stared at him. "I did, Y'Honor."

"I was told by the Nueces County medical examiner's office the hands were improperly bagged."

Gardner turned his gaze out to the crowd. "Yes, sir. I checked the chain of custody. At some point before delivery to the morgue the bag covering the right hand was damaged."

"The end result being the medical examiner's office had difficulty getting an accurate gunpowder-residue reading on Mr. Hubble's hands. I suggest, Detective, before you investigate another crime scene that you refresh yourself on appropriate forensic procedures." Whit knew he sounded like a textbook, but he watched as the borrowed court reporter recorded every word.

Gardner's face soured with anger. "Yes, sir," was all he said, but he did not look at Whit; he stared out into the crowd, as though at attention. Whit dismissed him from the stand. Claudia looked ready to jump out of her seat, notes in hand, but Whit didn't call her as a witness.

Next Dr. Elizabeth Contreras, deputy medical examiner for Nueces County, gave the same summation of autopsy findings she'd given to Whit, stressing that she could not make a definitive call as to whether the gunshot wound was self-inflicted. Whit asked her only a few questions and Liz kept her testimony concise.

"Was there any other indication of violence to Mr. Hubble?" he asked. "Had he been drugged or assaulted in another way?"

"He was intoxicated, and we're awaiting toxicology results, but no, there were no other signs of violence on him."

Whit thanked Liz and she stepped down.

"I'm introducing into the inquest record," Whit said, "a suicide note found at the scene by the deceased's minor son." Whit held up the note, properly bagged. The audience was silent; tears coursed down Lucinda's cheeks. "In fact, I would like to read the note into the transcript of this hearing."

Whit read the note aloud in a slow voice, the final pain of Pete Hubble and his confession for the death of his brother Corey. Lucinda sobbed, noisily, and Faith hugged her. Sam trembled, his eyes locked on Whit. Velvet made some protesting noise; the other attendees shushed her. She glared at Whit as he finished.

Whit let the silence hang before he picked up his gavel. "This court rules that the deceased, Peter James Hubble, committed suicide by self-inflicted gunshot wound on last October 12. I am going to certify a copy of the inquest summary report for delivery to the district court. This court is adjourned." Whit rapped his gavel. It was over quick, and he saw the disappointment in faces that the hearing had been peculiar and short.

Velvet didn't disappoint. "Are you freaking kidding me? What is this? Do I even get a chance to talk?"

"Court is adjourned, ma'am," Lloyd warned in an even tone. "You got a complaint, take it outside."

Velvet yelled, "If I can't get justice here, I will get it somewhere else, Mosley!"

Whit ignored her, gathering his papers. A low chorus of boos erupted around Velvet, and she pulled away from one older woman who tried to console her. She stormed out of the courtroom.

Whit whispered to Lloyd, "Follow that woman, please. I want to know what she does."

Lloyd navigated through the throng leaving the court-room. Claudia pushed past and caught Whit's arm.

"I'd like a word with you, Your Honor. In private," she said. Her voice was low, but her tone was white with rage.

"About what?"

"About why you didn't call me to testify in this hearing."

Whit shrugged. "I really didn't see the need." He stepped down from the bench.

Claudia stared at him, incredulous. "The need? You ignored Pete's connection to Jabez, his dealings with Deloache, the bad blood with the Hubbles, the custody bat-tle that was brewing. What didn't you ignore?"

He walked out of the courtroom by the back entrance, and she followed him down the hallway. The departing crowd buzzed like angry bees. Whit imagined Senator Hubble holding tearful court before the television reporters.

Claudia shut the door behind them.

"I really don't want to tell you what I think of you right now," she said.

"You can. I don't break easy."

"You had acres of room for doubt, Whit. The fact he consorted with known criminals. The fact that everything about this movie project seems to have vanished. The fact he was taking on his mother and wife for custody of his son. The fact that he had a young woman actively digging dirt on Jabez Jones and finding it."

"The fact that evidence was improperly handled by your department. Maybe you should just trust me on this, Claudia."

"Trust you? Trust you when you won't tell me why

you've suddenly dropped a hundred IQ points? Whit, you have a responsibility! Or is your responsibility to make Faith Hubble happy?"

"Now the police don't have to continue the investigation." He didn't look at her, doffing his robe and sliding it onto a hanger.

"I guess not. Delford'll have hard nipples over this."

"Thanks for the image," he said. "You know, if additional information came forward at a later date, I could reopen the inquest."

"I suppose so. But will big Faithie let you?"

"That's enough," he snapped in a hard voice. "You might consider keeping your venom to yourself until you know the whole story."

She ground her teeth together. "Fine, Your Honor." She made the title slightly mocking in tone. "So tell me."

"I certainly left enough room in the inquest record for more information to be brought forward," Whit said slowly. "I didn't call Sam Hubble as a witness, didn't have Heather Farrell testify to what she found, didn't mention the connections between Jabez and Pete, between Deloache and Pete, and I emphasized the sloppy job that Gardner did. Like you said, acres of doubt."

Claudia stared at him. "What are you cooking up, Honorable?"

"I'm going to leave town for a few days."

"Why?"

"It's the smart thing for me to do."

She was silent for several seconds. "Whit. Have you been threatened?"

She surprised him. He liked Claudia, but she had struck him as the plodding sort of investigator who was dogged and determined but not particularly given to flights of imagination. She seemed more given to flights of impatience, irritability, and stubbornness.

He kept his face very still. "Of course not."

Delford Spires opened Whit's door, knocking at the same time, and bestowed a thin smile—the kind used at funerals when you see someone you haven't visited with in a while and you're glad to see them but sick over the reason.

"Whit. Claudia." Delford nodded. "You kept justice swift, Whit. I know this has been hard on everyone."

"Another cleared case," Claudia said.

Delford shook his head. "You're taking this the wrong way, Claudia. I've known Lucinda a real long time and I knew Pete. Just like him to come home and mess this up for his mama. She gave her kids the world and look what it got her." He brushed his mustache with a nervous flicker of his fingers. "Now I want you to focus on helping poor Mrs. Ballew in finding her girl."

"How about finding Heather Farrell?" Whit said.

Delford shrugged. "She's a runaway."

"Who bought two tickets on the bus, didn't use them, and now has vanished," Whit reminded him. "I wonder who that other ticket was for."

Heather being gone was unexpected to him. She might have seen something and been silenced by the same people who had threatened him. A sharp, hot shame crawled through his body. Yeah, Heather might be sitting under a railroad crossing right now, picnicking on fried fish, or she might be facedown in the bluestems, two bullets in her head.

If so, he decided, they would not get away with it. Forget

the election. "I would certainly feel better if y'all would find Heather."

"Fine," Delford said. "We'll put a notice out on the wires for the nearby counties. Claudia, would you excuse the judge and me for a moment?"

Claudia stepped into the hallway and closed the door behind her with a final stabbing glance at Whit.

"You think you're a big deal," Delford said. "Let me give you every assurance you're not."

"Get out of my office."

"I don't like you dressing down Gardner in open court. You talk to me and only me about problems with my officers. You made our whole department look bad."

Whit opened his mouth, full of sharp responses. He remembered the bullet whizzing past his ear, Irina, Babe, his brothers, their wives, his beautiful nieces, his wriggly nephews. *Not yet,* he thought, *not yet but oh, if you threatened my family I'm so going to fry you.* He said: "I'll keep that in mind."

Delford put his Stetson back on his head, as carefully as hanging a picture. "See that you do. At least while you get to wear that robe." He smiled and left, shutting the door behind him.

Whit sat down at his desk and waited. Lloyd returned in a minute, face flushed from exertion.

"What happened? Did she leave?" Whit asked.

"Yeah. With that guy in the Astros cap."

Junior. Velvet had left with Junior, of all people. *If I can't get justice here, I will get it somewhere else.* He wondered what sort of justice Junior might offer.

"Did it look like he forced her to leave with him?"

"No. They talked outside for a few minutes. She was all

in a tizzy and he calmed her down. Then they walked to his Porsche, talked some more, and she followed him in her car."

"Thank you, Lloyd." Lloyd left, and Whit stopped at Edith's desk.

"I'm taking some time off, Edith. Please clear my docket and reschedule my hearings. If Judge Ramirez can take them, that's fine with me. If not, reschedule for late next week."

Edith frowned at him. "Well, that's short notice."

"Sorry. I have to go."

"Shouldn't you be campaigning?"

Whit shrugged. "In an odd way, I am."

He gave her the inquest papers, had her make a copy for him, and then had the originals prepared for filing with the district court. He ran a quick errand to the police station, then drove toward Golden Gulf Marina, Velvet's key to *Real Shame* in his pocket.

33

CLAUDIA RETURNED TO her office; Gardner was talking low on the phone, serious and somber, just saying yes or no. She felt a mix of worry and anger toward Whit. He was in some kind of trouble, she was sure, but he wasn't about to let her help him. Men. Thought they could do everything themselves. Truth be told, he was probably bedding Faith Hubble and that ruling was just a pure favor to her, cleanly sweeping a doubt-riddled case under the rug.

Do you really think so little of him?

Gardner finished his conversation and left without a word. He had barely spoken to her after their exchange. A pink message slip lay on her desk, David pestering her about the party for his grandfather. Perhaps a party would do her good, even if it was full of David's relatives, who seemed to regard her as clinically insane for leaving their darling boy and even being held at a nursing home, the kind of place that inevitably depressed her.

She opened the Ballew file, desperate to take her mind off Whit and Eddie and Pete Hubble. Maybe a reread would prompt her mind to look at the Ballew problem in a new way.

Wait a second. Speaking of nursing homes, Marcy had worked at one. The Encina County deputies had called the home in Louisiana and garnered nothing useful from the staff regarding Marcy's disappearance. Inspiration struck. She and David had concentrated on the flimsy connections between Marcy's wrestling interest and Port Leo, but what if there was a professional connection? She phoned the director of Port Leo's home, Placid Harbor, a snip-voiced woman named Roselle Cross.

"Ms. Cross, have you ever heard of a nursing home in Deshay, Louisiana, called Memorial Oaks?"

"No."

Claudia drummed a pencil. "Y'all ever have much contact with the staff at other nursing homes?"

"Well, the administrators do, if there's a transfer. Buddy Beere usually handles that."

"I'd like to talk to him."

"Sure. He's usually around."

"Thanks." Claudia gathered her notes and the Ballew file and headed for the door.

The boat still smelled of death.

Whit closed the door behind him. *Real Shame* had not had its windows opened to the air since Pete had been found, and the atmosphere felt as oppressive as a wool blanket in summer. The Deloaches would soon take back possession of their boat and scrub away all traces of unpleasantness. He suspected that *Real Shame* would sail within days, away from police scrutiny in Port Leo.

He went down to Pete's stateroom. The air still smelled, slightly, of human waste and blood. The mattress still lay bare. The closets were empty. The diver Claudia recruited had found no trace of Pete's laptop and no sign of discarded diskettes or papers.

Whit figured Pete had not destroyed his research as a sad pre-suicide gesture. He had either shipped it off to someone else for safekeeping or the killer had taken it or destroyed it. Unless Pete had hidden it—and the boat still seemed the most likely place. And where had the supposed half million in cash gone? If Whit had either of those, he might have enough information to protect himself and his family. Or enough to get them all killed.

He rooted around the boat for an hour, finding nothing. No more tapes of Pete exploring scenes for his Corey movie, no computer diskettes squirreled away in couch cushions, no notes outlining the past. He was pawing through the small cabinets in the head when a phone rang. Not his cell phone in his pocket.

Whit followed the ringing to a bedside table. In a drawer was another cell phone. Its readout announced CALLER ID BLOCKED. He clicked the phone on.

"Hello?" he said.

"Hello? Pete?" A woman's voice.

"Yes," Whit said, simultaneously thinking, *What the hell are you doing?*

"Why aren't you answering your other phone?"

"Lost it," Whit improvised.

"Look, some cop in Port Leo's been calling here and leaving messages. I had to disconnect my number. I want to know what's going on."

"Nothing." He made his voice tired, indistinct.

"I'm still waiting on my money, sweetness."

"Your money . . . okay," Whit said. "Let's get that to you."

Silence hung like a blade in the air. "Who is this? Where's Pete?"

"He can't come to the phone right now…" Whit tried lamely. "Who am I speaking with?"

She hung up.

Whit clicked through the menu options on the cell phone. There were no unheard or archived messages, no numbers listed for speed dialing, no numbers listed in his phone book, no numbers listed in his call log. Pete had covered his tracks. Whit cursed.

But it had sounded long-distance, and the woman's voice was a soft, throaty drawl, definitely Southern, not one of Pete's California starlets. And she was expecting money. He pulled out his own phone and called the police station. Claudia was out and he had no intention of talking to Gardner or Delford. But he got Nelda, the dispatcher, to go look in the Hubble file and tell him that the phone number in Missatuck, Texas, the one that Claudia had been unable to get an answer from, was registered to a Kathy Breaux. He tried the number: disconnected, and no new number given in its place. He could force the phone company to give him the number. But chatting on the phone would accomplish nothing.

It was gambling time.

Whit pocketed Pete's phone and left the boat, hurrying to his car. He headed home, a loose plan he'd formed earlier taking solid shape. He called Velvet's hotel room, got no answer, left a message for her to call him on his cell phone. He left a vague note for Babe and Irina, packed a bag, tossed it in the back of his Explorer, and headed out of town. He didn't notice the flooring company van following him from the marina, idling on the other end of Evangeline while he stopped at home, and he didn't notice the van and another car staying a good distance behind him when he roared north onto State Highway 35, aiming toward Houston and the East Texas piney woods beyond.

Claudia hated nursing homes because she suspected she'd slobber her last in one someday. Probably a well-meaning niece or nephew would shuttle her into a Medicare bed, tsk-tsking the whole time about poor old Aunt Claudia.

Placid Harbor wasn't bad as nursing home facilities went. The word *placid* suggested residents in a drug-induced fog. But the view across St. Leo Bay and Little Mischief Park was postcard pretty, and many of the residents were mobile and articulate, and management kept it clean. Not so bad for an iceberg to die on.

Roselle Cross's office was modest, furnished with a Victorian desk, memorabilia from local Port Leo girls' softball teams on the walls, and photos of cheery and plump Roselle hugging residents. The decor in the photos showed these lovefests happened during Thanksgiving, Chanukah, Christmas, St. Patrick's Day. Every day a holiday at Placid Harbor.

Roselle returned to the office. "Buddy called in sick today, but I checked our files. We haven't had any transfers from any homes in Louisiana."

"Where have you had transfers from recently? Say in the past year?" Maybe she could delve further into the Ballew girl's employment history, see if there was another connection through another home.

Roselle Cross kept a patient, holiday-quality smile and vanished into the front office. She returned five minutes later, armed with documents. "Well, in the past year we've had three from Corpus, two from San Antonio, one from Aransas Pass, one from Port Isabel, and one from Austin."

"What about transfers out? People leaving Placid Harbor for someplace else?"

She scanned her papers. "One to Brownsville, one to Laredo, two to Corpus."

"When these people transfer, how do they get here?"

"Well, with the close-by cities, like Aransas Pass or Corpus, usually it's an ambulance service that moves them. Or family members. Depends on the client's condition."

"And what about the more distant towns?"

"Again, the family often brings the client. Or, for a charge, we can take or fetch them ourselves, depending on the client's condition."

"So who would do this?"

"Buddy or more likely someone working for him. And a nurse or nurse's aide, if needed."

"And nothing on Deshay, Louisiana?"

"Absolutely not."

"Okay, thanks." She stood to go. "I understand there's a party here this weekend for my ex-husband's grandfather. Mr. Power?"

"Oh, yes. He's a delight." Roselle Cross managed to say this without the barest hint of sarcasm. Claudia liked her better immediately.

Claudia paid a guilt trip to David's Poppy, ready to shrug off blistering blame for making David unhappy if David had gained a spine and told his grandfather about their divorce. But luckily, Poppy was asleep, snoring in his bed with wild abandon, his mouth slack, lips pale with age. His roommate, watching a Spanish-language soap opera, turned up the volume higher and told Claudia in strident

Spanish, "You live your life for all these years and then you got to worry about roommates. Roommates, like you're in college. And me with a Purple Heart."

Velvet awoke slowly. Clambering toward wakefulness required enormous effort; her limbs weighed like stone. The darkness around her was oceans deep, so dark that it was not an absence of light but light's very opposite.

She breathed and fabric blocked her mouth and throat. Her tongue, dry as sand, wriggled against the plug and felt rough texture of cloth and masking tape.

She strained to move. Cords bound her wrists and ankles. In her confusion she remembered a silly flick she directed two years ago, *Fit to Be Tied,* and mostly, she and the cast laughed and giggled through the scene. They had found nothing enticing and erotic in bondage, lacking few restraints themselves. Pete starred in the movie and groggily she called for him, but the mouth plug turned her plea into an inarticulate moan.

She ached—her head, her jaw, her stomach—and she became aware that thick, dense silk covered her eyes. She could see no light creeping in around the blindfold's edges.

Fear rose in her, sudden and sour as bile. She wrenched hard against the cords. They did not slacken.

She tried to remember where she had been.

Junior Deloache's condo. After that moron Whit ruled for suicide, Junior had invited her over for a drink. To calm down and think over the next move, he said. Like he was suddenly Pete's advocate, the jerk, talking about the army of lawyers his father could command. But she had not wanted to be alone. She would have preferred having a glass of wine with Claudia Salazar, trying to persuade her to keep the case open somehow. A female friend, a tart in arms, would have been nice to have. She wanted to slap Whit; he had said he was on her side and he was a liar. Kangaroo court is what it was. But Junior was there, being kind.

Kindness had always mattered.

She remembered, coming out of the fog, a scream forming in her throat.

They're at Junior's condo, drinking whiskey. Anson's not around. He gives her the shivers, creeping around in that wheelchair. Velvet gets quickly and angrily drunk. Junior paws her breasts and mutters about film speeds and money shots.

"Let's do a movie," he says. "Right now. C'mon."

She shrugs off his hand and pours more bourbon, thinking he'll be too drunk to get hard and too little to notice and suddenly he belts her, harder than she's ever been hit before. She realizes she spoke her thought aloud. The world devolves into a spinning circle of stars, and she fights as Junior yanks down her jeans, rips her thong in half, pulls loose her sweater, snaps off her brassiere. The Sig's still in her purse and she clambers toward it, but he punches her once, twice, and she's lying on the carpet, stunned, bleeding. Through the foggy haze of pain she sees Junior setting up a camera, aiming it toward her, then shucking his Houston sports team clothes.

"Gonna make a movie now, bitch," he says. "The working title is Do Velvet Hard. *Already planning the sequel. Gonna call it* Velvet Tells Me Where the Money Is.*"*

"Stop it. Stop, Junior, this isn't funny."

He is erect and he jabs a button on the camcorder. "I'm not gonna get screwed over anymore. I'm a businessman.

I'm gonna get to be in a film, and I'm gonna get my money back."

She stumbles to her feet, intent on getting that gun and shooting him, where's her purse, but he hammers her again, his fist bouncing off the back of her head, and she falls to the floor. She pukes up the bourbon and . . .

Then what?

She breathed around the mouth plug. This wasn't the movie, was it? Her head ached.

"Junior?" she tried to say.

. . . she hears the doorbell ring. Not the condo elevator door creaking open, not Anson wheeling back, but the other entrance, the stairs, and she hears Junior cuss softly.

A chair creaked, next to her. A finger, callused, ran along her cheek.

"No, darling. Junior's not here."

She held herself very still.

The voice was low, a man's, a little gravelly. "Would you like the gag removed, darling?"

She nodded.

"You should understand—no one can hear you, but I won't tolerate you screaming. At least not for now."

A metal point inched down her leg. It stopped at her knee and pressed, gently.

"Owww," she groaned.

"If you scream, darling, we'll get right down to my fun. I'll dig open those tits and we'll see if they're real."

Velvet held perfectly still, not even daring to breathe.

"Nod once if you understand."

She nodded.

The knife point left her knee. Gently the hands caressed

her face. She heard a lock snap—*he has this thing locked on my face!*—and the mouth plug was pried loose from her lips. A finger, wrapped around a damp cloth, cleaned out her mouth, dribbled welcome water over her tongue. She resisted the urge to bite down and take the finger off.

"There you go, darling," the man said.

She wetted her lips with her tongue. "Who are you?"

"I'm your new lover."

A sick chill goose-pimpled her skin. "Will you take off the blindfold?"

"Not for a while. More fun this way."

Fun. That word again. "Where am I?"

"Heaven."

"Where's Junior?"

"Hell. Where he belongs."

She offered a fake, soft laugh. "No, really."

"Junior isn't going to bother you anymore. I took care of him for my sweet darling."

"Why am I here?"

"I need you," he said.

Her tongue felt dry as dirt again. "Yeah, baby, I can sure understand that. We all need. Perfectly natural." She used her film voice, coy, trying to keep from shaking. "But I can't give you what you need all tied up, baby."

"Quiet now," he said, brushing her hair with his fingertips.

"I have a name, baby. Velvet."

He hummed, low in his throat.

"You untie Velvet, hon, you let me go, I'll give you what you need."

She felt a finger run along her naked breasts, her stomach, the cup of her navel. She suppressed a shudder.

"What's your name, honey?" she asked.

She heard the chair shift. She could smell his breath, reeking of garlic and fried shrimp. He nibbled her ear and ran his tongue along its edge.

"What's your name?" she tried again in a whisper, her voice cracking.

"My name is Corey," he whispered back. "Corey Hubble."

Then he climbed on top of her. She began to scream.

34

WHIT DROVE, FOLLOWING Highway 35 as it snaked up the slow curve of the Texas coast, merging into Highway 288 north of Freeport, then sliding onto Interstate 10's thick rope when he reached the sprawl of Houston. He crept through Houston's never-ending rush-hour traffic and headed up toward the deep pine forests and shallow bayous of far East Texas. He could take I-10 to Beaumont and then 87 North to 1416, a farm-to-market road to the little town of Missatuck, where he suspected Kathy Breaux was waiting for Pete and her unexplained money.

Whit reached Beaumont around eight Friday night. The towers of the refineries glowed like an alien metropolis. With his window cracked he could smell the sour egg odor of natural gas and chemical plants, overpowering the barest hint of pine.

Hungry, he parked in the oil-stained lot next to a cheap diner with a neon fork spearing the window. At the counter he ate a greasy hamburger topped with kill-your-neighbors-strength onions and gulped a jumbo glass of iced tea. As he ate, he studied again the clippings file that Patsy had sent. He reread each article and found himself going back to the first article outlining Corey's disappearance:

"Corey is impulsive," Senator Hubble said in a brief statement to the press. "I don't think Corey wants to be spending much time in Austin. I have no reason to suspect that Corey has run afoul of someone. I hope that if he is reading this he realizes the joke is over and he should please call us soon."

The accompanying photo showed a stolid yet pained Lucinda Hubble leaving the Port Leo police station, brave, head held high but wearing dark glasses. A clearly shocked Pete, old beyond his years, walked next to her, grimacing. Delford stood next to Lucinda, a Rock of Gibraltar.

Of course he had.

The phone call to Georgie Whit had placed yesterday was a simple question of whether there had ever been rumor of a relationship between Lucinda Hubble and Delford Spires. Georgie, the human archive of local lore and gossip, had said, "Well, they've always been friends. I wondered if Delford wanted more at one point. But I guess any chance of romance fizzled after Corey vanished. Lucinda never let another man close to her."

It was circumstantial, it was wispy hearsay, but it made Whit wonder. A boy who felt anger and unending grief over his father's death and acid resentment toward his mother would not welcome a new suitor. Whit had felt the same sting when Babe split with Georgie and began wooing local divorcées. He had cordially hated all his father's girlfriends. Childish, yes, but common. But he still could not envision Delford ruthlessly killing a teenage boy.

He gathered up his papers and walked out of the diner, heading across the dark plain of the parking lot.

"Hey, you," a voice boomed, and a hand borrowed from

Goliath grabbed Whit off his feet, dragged him several feet behind the building, and slammed him into the back brick wall of the diner. The back of his head hit hard and pinwheels filled his vision. Whit lashed out with a fist and grazed a temple. He blinked and cool fingers curled into his throat, making themselves at home, squeezing the life out of him. His head pounded back into the bricks.

"Hey, you," the voice repeated. "Gonna talk." In the dim light Whit could see Mr. Words was a young, rough kid with thick arms, big hair, and a pair of narrow-lensed sunglasses most commonly found on pimps. He'd seen the guy before. The muscled-up kid at Junior's condo. Out of the corner of his eye Whit saw more movement, heard the quiet creak of a wheelchair.

Oh, no.

"I hate a thief worse than anything," Anson Todd said in a hushed voice. "And you an elected official. American democracy is going down the toilet. You corrupt bastard."

"Yeah," Mr. Words agreed.

"What—" Whit attempted to breathe, grabbing at Mr. Words's hand, trying to pry the fingers from his throat.

"I want the money, Judge Smart-Mouth," Anson hissed. He wheeled close to Whit and with an arthritic fist punched Whit in the balls. Hard. Whit gagged. Amazing how slight a punch it takes to savage a pair of testicles. Mr. Words slammed Whit to the oily pavement, yanked his arm straight, spread his fingers against the parking-lot grime.

The throat grip relaxed momentarily so Whit could breathe and speak. "What money?"

Wrong answer. Fist squeezed, blood fled from his throat. The wheelchair—heavy itself and full of old man—rolled over his fingers, backed up, rolled forward again. Whit gritted his teeth, wondering if he would first hear or feel the bones break.

"Don't lie to us, Judge," Anson said. He steadied the chair, letting its full weight settle on Whit's knuckles.

"Did a cop once," Mr. Words said. "Never a judge. Cool. Start with fingers."

"I don't have your money."

"Get him into the van," Anson ordered. "You can have your fun with him there." He hacked phlegm. "And it's time for my medicine."

Mr. Words jerked Whit to his feet, keeping an iron grip on his throat with both hands. Whit tried to wrench free, hoping for a weak spot to punch or kick, but Mr. Words was four inches taller and fifty pounds heavier, all muscle. Whit smelled the pineapple reek of cheap cologne, the soft odor of trash from the diner's Dumpster, the goon's sweat.

Mr. Words hurried Whit along toward a dark blue van parked at the far end of the lot with a flooring company name on the side, Anson's motorized chair purring behind them.

"Cooperate, get off light," Mr. Words murmured in a spate of eloquence. "You don't, die in Beaumont. Talk to us. Be cool."

The half million. They think I have it.

As Mr. Words dragged him along by his neck, Whit considered options. A kick to the nuts and about a dozen hard punches to the jaw were the ticket. Actually, a small nuclear device would be the ticket. But Whit couldn't budge an inch. All he could see was the smeary grease stains of the lot, a few flattened cigarette butts, and the dark shadow of the van, barely illuminated in the halo of light from a streetlamp at the corner.

Head held down and stumbling, Whit saw the damage before they did. All four of the van's tires lay flat. He made a noise, and Mr. Words stopped and saw and said, "Well."

Whit, the baby of six dirty-wrestling brothers, just needed that second. He fought just the way he learned at his brothers' knees and elbows and fists. He smashed his heel down on Mr. Words's arch, gouging the foot with the modest heel of his loafer. Mr. Words yelled. Whit slammed a forearm against Words's right arm, then elbowed backward into the thick throat. Mr. Words yelped. Whit spun free of his hold, then drove headfirst into the man's abdomen. Mr. Words staggered back and Whit jabbed hard with two left upper-cuts that sent the kid sprawling onto the asphalt.

"Eddie, get out here!" Anson screamed. Whit whirled, trying to get his breath back. His throat felt like it had been scalded, his fingers felt like rubber, either broken by Anson's wheel or Mr. Words's jaw. *Eddie.*

New plan. Run. He bolted and Mr. Words kicked out, catching both his feet on a muscled leg hard as fallen timber, and Whit slammed hard into the pavement. *Well, you tried.* Fingers closed around his throat again, yanking him to his feet.

Movement came from behind the van. "Eddie's indisposed." A familiar voice. Gooch, holding a sleek automatic pistol, neatly fitted with a silencer. The pistol was aimed at Anson. The grip on Whit's throat tightened.

"Let the judge go, son," Gooch said. "Or I shoot the old man. Then you."

Mr. Words moved Whit in front of him as a make-shift shield. "Or maybe I just break his neck if you don't drop the gun."

"I can shoot you first, son," Gooch said conversationally.

"Or I can shoot Anson. You want to explain to Papa Deloache how you got Anson killed?"

"Let him go," Anson said quietly.

Even when whipped, Mr. Words made an excellent lapdog. He let go. Whit gulped a long sucking breath, one that scorched his throat but his lungs savored.

"Judge, come here by the van," Gooch said. "I don't want you to get blood splattered all over your nice clothes."

"Idiot," Anson snarled. "You mess with us, you don't have any idea what you're buying."

"Oh, I do." Gooch smiled. "But mess with me and you buy a grave no one will ever find. Understood?"

Whit leaned against the van. "He said Eddie..."

"Eddie Gardner's in there. He's catching some shut-eye right now." Whit peered inside; Eddie Gardner lay propped in the back of the van, bleeding lightly from his nose and mouth, but breathing. Yellow rope wrapped around his arms and legs.

"You. Get in the van," Gooch ordered Mr. Words.

The young man stared stupidly.

"Clearly you're no Fulbright scholar," Gooch said, "but do what you're told and you'll be fine. You come out of that van before I say, I shoot him and then I shoot you. You understand?"

Mr. Words glanced at Anson; the old man nodded. The boy climbed into the van next to the unconscious Eddie, and Gooch slammed the door. He then held up a clear plastic bag to Anson: three black pistols, .22s, a switchblade, a blackjack, and a cell phone lay inside. "I don't think I missed any of your toys when I went through your van, Anson. If I did, and Muscles comes out shooting, you get a bullet in the brain."

Whit thought, *No, Gooch, don't do this,* but he said nothing, still rubbing his aching throat.

"I'm old, do your worst," Anson huffed. "I probably get a colostomy bag next year. You think I'm afraid of you?"

"I don't believe you want to die one second before you have to, and I really don't think you want to see Muscles die. Isn't he Deloache's nephew?"

In the dim light Anson's stare narrowed. "Who are you?"

"Why are you following Judge Mosley?"

"Kiss my ass."

Gooch brought the gun up. "How hard are the cops going to look for your killer, Anson? I think not very."

"He thinks I took Pete's half million," Whit coughed. Feeling was slowly creeping its painful way back into his fingers and throat.

Gooch raised an eyebrow. "Anson?"

"I don't feel good. I need my medicine." Moments ago he had been all snarl; now he was all plead.

"I got a permanent cure here if you don't start talking," Gooch said.

Anson shrugged with a baleful look at Whit. "You're like me, aren't you?" he asked Gooch. "Always cleaning up other people's crap. We ain't done anything wrong, we're the wronged ones."

"Oh, I bet," Gooch said.

"Junior gave Pete Hubble a half-mil cash of his dad's money for some adult film series, because Pete promised Junior a percentage of the sales, the starring role, and all the bimbos he could screw. Well, that ain't the movie that Pete was making. He was making some documentary about his missing brother. Junior found out and wanted his—our—money back and Pete balked, kept saying it'd be a much better investment than porn. But Junior hadn't told his dad about this unapproved investment. We got to get that money back."

"And you couldn't find it on the boat, so you figured the judge had it?"

"We been keeping an eye on Pete's boat, saw the judge leave it and head out of town like his ass is on fire. I figured he had it, or knew where it was."

"I don't have your money," Whit said.

"Don't feel bad that it's lost," Gooch said. "He bought it with the veins and noses of kids." Gooch pushed his gun into the old man's face. "Did you shoot at Whit the other night? Threaten him about the Hubble inquest?"

Anson shook his head.

"I don't mean you personally, Anson," Gooch said. "I'm talking anyone you know."

Anson shook his head again. "I...maybe Junior got a guy to come up from Corpus, some local muscle. Just a theory."

"How'd he know about Whit's family?" Gooch snarled, grabbing Anson's throat.

Anson coughed. "Junior...drinks at the Shell Inn. The owner brags about her former stepsons. In excruciating detail. Again, just a theory."

"Ah. Thank you," Gooch said. He eased his grip.

"I don't suppose it had occurred to you that Pete might have spent the money," Whit said. He was surprised at how calm his voice was.

Anson huffed. "Not in a few days in Port Leo. It's still our money. He lied to us and we want it back. I figured either you or that Velvet had it."

"Where's Junior?" Whit asked, a sudden icicle forming in his heart.

"He said he was going to Houston, explaining all this to his dad."

"Bull," Gooch said. "You know damn well where he is."

Whit pulled out his cell phone and dialed Velvet's motel room. No answer. He left another message with the motel clerk to have Velvet call him as soon as she could.

"Maybe Junior's trying to rough Velvet up the same way you roughed up me?" Whit said.

"He's not gonna hurt her. He wants to be in her movies." Anson shook his head. "Blue films. No values left anymore, the world is just going down the toilet. Why Hollywood don't make a nice musical is beyond me."

"Lecture your Sunday school class about it," Gooch said.

Whit played a card. "You know, I just heard on the radio that they caught Jabez Jones and he's talking. He had to get his dope from somewhere, and he might be implicating Junior."

Anson kept his face stone still. "I don't know what you mean."

Gooch laughed, very softly. "Whit, go back to your car. I'll join you shortly."

"What are you going to do with them?" Whit asked.

"Just go." Gooch's voice sounded soft, lazy, as though nothing was on the agenda more compelling than a tall glass of lemonade.

"No. I'm calling the police."

"We're not doing that," Gooch said.

"I'm a magistrate. I'm having them arrested. At the least for assaulting a public servant."

Gooch glanced back at Anson. "What if the next schmuck they come after doesn't have the luxury of me to save him, Whit?"

"If they're in jail they can't go after anyone."

"I can't testify in court, Whit," Gooch said mildly. "It's not going to happen."

"You're not going to kill them."

"May I suggest," Anson said quietly, "a compromise?"

"No," Gooch said. "Shut up."

"Do you think this is how I wanted to spend my retirement?" Anson said to Whit. "Picking up after drunken, clueless morons who think they're tough?"

"Better than retiring behind bars and being sold for cigarettes," Whit said. "You lose those dentures, you're gonna be real popular. What can you give us on Junior Deloache?"

Anson smiled and shook his head. "I ain't giving you item one on Junior, Judge."

"Fine. Then I won't call the police. This isn't my jurisdiction anyway." He knew he'd miscalculated in pulling the moral high ground attitude with Gooch. Anson saw Whit's worry as weakness. He walked away and thought: *Please, Gooch, don't kill them.*

"Wait a second," Anson called, but Whit kept walking. There was only the silence of his footsteps; no sounds of shots, no sounds of screams, no sounds of life ending. The highway gave off a distant rumble of its uninterested traffic. He sat inside his Explorer and closed the door.

Whit waited. And waited. Thirty minutes later, Gooch sauntered from behind the diner with a slight smile on his face. He climbed in next to Whit.

"I'm afraid to ask," Whit said.

"They're fine. They're in custody."

"Whose custody and under what charges?"

"Assault." Gooch shrugged. "That kid and Eddie beat

me up. Anson helped him, you know." He paused. "I think the Feds might be interested in them. Drug trafficking, money laundering, all that kind of stuff. Sheer nastiness."

"I see. Thank you, Gooch. You want to tell me why you followed me to Beaumont?"

"Saving you isn't a good enough reason?"

"Please tell me you didn't kill those men."

"They're in custody, I told you. Go outside and see if you want."

Whit walked to the back of the diner. The van with its four flats was gone. He walked back to his car.

"That diner any good?" Gooch asked. "I'm starved."

35

After leaving the nursing home, Claudia returned to the station. There was a message from David: Jabez Jones remained at large. Of course, no one was looking for Marcy, what with a high-profile quarry like Jabez. Claudia started the tedium of phone work. Buddy Beere was home with a bad cold, but he did confirm the transfers that Roselle Cross had mentioned. He sounded horrible, stuffy and wheezing, and said that he did personally supervise a few of the transfers, when family couldn't be bothered. He couldn't remember ever having hired anyone from Deshay, Louisiana, or having heard of the nursing home there.

"I do remember having made personal trips to fetch clients over the past couple of years," Buddy said. He stopped for three thunderous sneezes. "But other Placid Harbor folks handled transfers, and I can check my files on Monday if you want to know who exactly did what. Or sooner, if this is an emergency."

"That's okay. I hope you're feeling better soon."

"I'm mainlining NyQuil. I hope that's not illegal," he laughed.

"I won't report you," she said.

"Detective? I know you're buddies with Whit Mosley,

but if I win the election, I just want you to know I'll work hard. And I'll look forward to working with you."

"Thanks, Buddy," she said, feeling awkward. "I appreciate that. I'm sure we'd work together just fine."

"Okay. Let me know if I can be of further help." She thanked him again and hung up.

So no connection there between Deshay and Port Leo. She rubbed her temple with her pencil's eraser. But what if there were similar cases to Marcy's? Her disappearance might be part of a wider blanket. Maybe.

So she phoned the Department of Public Safety in Austin, where the state's "missing persons clearinghouse" database was located, and she gave them a set of parameters to check—young women, last seen at places of work.

There did not seem to be a spate of women abducted from nursing homes. DPS faxed her a list of disappearances, and she studied the dates. Odd. She flipped back to her notes from Roselle Cross. A week after the transfer of a client from Port Leo to Laredo last November, a young woman, Angela Marie Norris, had gone missing from a Laredo Taco Bell restaurant after her shift ended. In May, three weeks after a patient moved from Placid Harbor to another facility in Brownsville, another young woman, Laura Janelle Palinski, disappeared from a pizzeria she worked at.

Claudia called DPS back, and they faxed her details, descriptions, and photos of both young women, and she sat studying the pictures. Both bore a passing resemblance to Marcy Ballew with dark hair, round faces, naive smiles, but then they were all of a common type. Nice girls working in low-wage jobs, saving for college maybe, or just trying to live from paycheck to paycheck.

The times when Buddy—or whoever had handled the transfer—had been in the two towns were close, but not the same. And Buddy had not been alone on the transfers, there had been a nurse-practitioner accompanying him. But then, the women hadn't vanished when Buddy had been in town. And Buddy had never supervised a transfer from Deshay, Louisiana.

It was just odd.

She called the police departments in Laredo and Brownsville, got the names of the detectives in charge of the missing-women's cases, and left messages for them to call her back.

She then called Roselle Cross's office.

"I'd like to know if Buddy was at work on these days: November 10 of last year, May 3 and September 30 this year." Those were the days Morris, Palinski, and Ballew had all dropped out of sight.

"Why?"

"I'm just trying to piece together a chronology of where he's been."

"My word. Do you suspect him of something?" The woman sounded appalled.

"No. It's a way to simply get a clearer picture. I just talked with him, he's being entirely cooperative."

"Well," Roselle Cross said, "I'll have to check Monday morning."

"Mrs. Cross," Claudia said, "it's getting late, it's Friday night, I'm sure you want to get home. So do I. You can go check this on a computer in about five seconds. I just need to know if he took vacation or sick time then."

"One . . . moment!" Roselle Cross said with clear peevishness and put Claudia on hold.

A pang of hunger gnawed at Claudia's stomach. She dug down in her purse for a candy bar she usually had stashed away in the depths and her fingers found paper instead. She pulled out an envelope marked OPEN IN PRIVATE. Probably a love letter from David he'd stashed in her purse. She tore it open. Out slipped a copy of a newspaper photo. A teenage Junior, Corey, Eddie Gardner, and a girl holding fat fish. Whit had attached a note: *Not sure if this means a single thing, but thought you should know. Also: I think Junior gave Pete a half million. Maybe Gardner got it back for his old fishing buddy, the tough way. And maybe Gardner ruined those evidence bags as a favor to Junior. Thought you should know. Watch your back. Will call you soon. Be careful. Whit.*

She could have strangled Whit.

Mrs. Cross huffed back on the line. "Buddy was here those days. No vacation time."

"Thank you," Claudia said. "I appreciate your help."

Mrs. Cross hung up without further comment.

Claudia dialed Whit's cell phone and got a message saying the phone was out of the calling area. She left him voice mail. "You better call me back as soon as humanly possible," she said, leaving her home and office numbers. She tried Velvet again at her motel; still no answer. The woman might have decided to leave town once the inquest went against her, but according to the clerk she hadn't checked out of the room yet.

Claudia went to Delford's office. He sat at his desk, his service revolver unholstered, sitting next to an untidy hill of papers. He glanced up at her with a sharp look; she was clearly unwelcome.

"Late night?" she asked, trying to sound casual. The hard look in his eyes made her throat feel thick.

"I just got a complaining phone call about you from some woman over at the nursing home."

"You have bigger problems than me," she said. She placed the photo and Whit's Post-it note on his desk.

"Holy smoke," Delford finally said. Claudia sat across from him.

"I don't understand," he finally said. "You're saying that's Eddie Gardner?"

"I think it is."

"He knows Deloache," Delford said.

"Yes."

"Have you talked to him about this?"

"No. He took off hours ago." She paused. "Did you get a copy of his service record from Houston?"

"Of course. Eddie was as clean as a whistle. References, the whole shebang." Delford pointed at the picture. "Maybe this is just coincidence. Kids go fishing on the jetties, meet each other during a day, then never see each other again."

"Eddie and Junior are both from Houston."

"Them and four million other people. Lots of kids from Houston fish here. Not a crime."

"No, that's not. Dealing drugs and covering up a murder sure are."

"You're just full of serious accusations, aren't you, missy?" Delford squinted at her. "I mean, what's with you lately? You question how I do things around here, you check out files you don't got any business worrying over, you screw up evidence bags and blame a colleague..."

"I don't even know you anymore," Claudia said softly. "Why are you having these meltdowns? Tell me, Delford. I can help you..."

Delford's phone rang and he scooped it up. He listened and muttered "ah, no," three times. Then he hung up.

"We got us a dead one. Floater in the bay. A girl." Delford gulped, clicked his service revolver back in his holster. "She's not . . . whole. Some sicko carved her up."

Velvet came awake suddenly. She had finally managed to doze after a while—time was impossible to measure— after he had finished his assault. Now she felt a wet rag move along her skin, cleaning her legs and privates, cleaning where she had soiled the sheets, removing them and curling towels under her hips. A voice humming "Surfin' Safari," ignoring her shivers of rage and fear.

"Soup, darling?" Corey asked. She nodded, barely.

He spooned lukewarm chicken broth into her mouth. She swallowed it and made herself not cry. *Some last meal.* She heard the spoon click against an empty cup. He dabbed her mouth, replaced the gag, and refastened the lock with a dainty click.

"Sleep now," he said, and she heard him leave the room. The door shut and then there were five or six snicks—with terror she realized they were dead bolts being thrown. She was locked in times six.

Tears would not come. She strained and pulled against the cords, but they were intractable.

I've been raped, she thought in disbelief, and her father's unbending Methodist voice, the pride of an Omaha pulpit, crowded into her head: *Are you surprised? What you do it's an abomination and a shame and you get what you deserve . . .*

No. She shook her head against the imagined voice. Her father never said those words to her. He'd never lived to see

her sink. She shuddered and the tears came in a hot flood.
She cried silently, the tears sopping into the blindfold, a
pool of snot forming at her nose that she blew out to clear
her airways. She wished for a cloth so...he...it...would
not see she had cried.

*Screw a handkerchief. Wish for a gun, so you can blow
the son of a bitch straight to hell.*

She must not crumple. Someone would realize she was
missing and gone, Whit and Claudia would look for her.
Wouldn't they? Maybe she wasn't even in Port Leo anymore. She had no idea how long she had been unconscious.

Think. Think.

He had said he was Corey Hubble.

Pete and that movie. Pete had been too tight-lipped
about his research. Pete *had* found Corey but Corey didn't
want to be found. Corey might be a complete freaking nut,
a drug runner, a smuggler. Clearly he didn't balk at kidnapping or rape. Maybe he hadn't balked at fratricide.

She had to get out. She could not simply lie here and
wait to be killed.

First she needed to see where she was. She needed to slip
free of the blindfold. The restraints on her legs gave way
enough that she could push with her heels and bring up her
knees slightly. She did so, pressing her head down against the
sheets. She felt a knot in the blindfold's side where the fabric
gathered, and she pulled herself down, mashing the pillow
against the fabric. Then she raised herself up again, pushed
back, and tried to drag the blindfold off. Again. Again.
Slowly the knot yielded its position, rolling up her scalp.

After several minutes of steady pushing, all breathless work, she had shoved the fabric up enough—all she
dared—where she could open one eye.

The room was dark; one small lamp in the corner, down by her feet, emitted a feeble glow. The lamp was kitschy, featuring dancing circus elephants cavorting in a circle, the kind of lamp you might find in a child's room.

With the one eye she saw that the room was windowless— or rather that neat planks of black-painted plywood covered where windows had once been. Dingy wallpaper hung on the walls, strips dangling. The paper showed cartooned cowboys riding on the range, lassoes a-whirling, wild ponies bucking in corrals, the antiseptic, 1950s version of the Wild West. A child's room, left to rot.

She turned her head to inspect the cords; thin yellow rope, like the kind she'd seen on boats at the marina, although some softer material cushioned the rope around her wrists and ankles.

The bed she was bound to was metal, an old twin-size contraption. She remembered with a grimace that the springs were noisy.

But metal meant parts. Sharp edges that might cut rope.

Yeah, and I'm Houdini. She pulled again, trying to free one hand, liberate one foot. The tape covering the ropes gouged her flesh. No ease, no relief.

She wept again, hating the rubbery taste of the mouth plug.

So talk him into letting you go.

She stopped crying. She snuffled, not wanting to block her airway.

How was she supposed to work that bit of mojo? She heard her own voice, bickering with Whit in his yard: *I'm superior to any man who pays money for my tapes.*

She knew Whit believed she demeaned herself with her work, but this, this was debasement beyond her dreams.

But she knew: she *was* greater than the men who snuck into the adult bookstores under cover of night, quickly paid in cash to rent her movies, ordered them via Internet anonymity, played the tape in darkened dens, and watched the men and women she arranged act the charades of love.

She knew what would turn her audience on.

What turned on Corey, clearly, was control. Brutality. Hurting her was foreplay to him. Her death would be his climax.

So she needed to slow his madness, subtly wrest control away from him. Her attempts to get him to see her as a person had flopped. He would not call her by name but by his creepy term of endearment. So maybe the solution was in being what he wanted her to be: an object. A nonperson who only existed to satisfy his lust.

But an object who would kill him dead, dead, dead.

Velvet took a deep breath.

"I'm going to kill you, Corey," she whispered.

She would be ready.

36

THE SHRIMPER WAS a thin, grizzled Vietnamese man named Minh Nguyen, and he was unusually calm, considering the catch in his illegal nets—the partial remains of Heather Farrell. The corpse, gutted and slashed, had been collected for autopsy.

"I can tell you the cause of death. A freaking nutcase," the mortuary service driver told Claudia as he and his partner loaded the body bag into the transport, in the bright gleam of the harbor's mercury lights. After one good look at Heather's sad remnants Claudia vomited, leaning against a pier piling and spewing into the greenish gray water. She had never seen such butchery.

You looked for her, you didn't find her. You should have made her stay in a cell, you failed that poor girl. Please let her not have suffered. Claudia staggered away from the pier's end, wiping her mouth, hoping the others wouldn't say a word to her. Two other cops had puked, but they were both rookies.

Mr. Nguyen, the shrimper, smoked a bummed cigarette while he repeated the story to the four officers ringed around the table. He was unflappable and precise about his account, and Claudia wondered if he had seen far worse in his life. The man was in his fifties, certainly old enough to have witnessed the horrors of war in his native land. Besides Claudia and Delford there was an investigator from the Encina County Sheriff's Department and a ranger from Parks and Wildlife, both of whom would be interested in any possible crime committed on the waters of St. Leo Bay.

Mr. Nguyen was trawling on the edge of the bay when his net tangled. Night shrimping was against the law, but no one was debating with him about this at this point. A heaviness caught in one of the sleds had kept the netted shrimp from tumbling free, and when he inspected it he had found the girl's body, her eyes staring up at him from beneath a mask of wriggling shrimp.

It was nearly midnight when Claudia went out for a breath of fresh air. From the police station stoop she could see the curving arc of Port Leo Beach Park aglow in the streetlights, the statue of stern Saint Leo watching over the bay. Autumn moonlight made the small waves gleam. She watched a family, tourists, amble from one of the restaurants down near the water's edge toward the Colonel James House Bed and Breakfast. They seemed uneager to surrender the day. One of the family was a teenage girl, and she shyly waved at Claudia, sitting on the steps. Claudia waved back.

Heather was someone's daughter just like that girl. She had told Delford she would call the girl's family in Lubbock and she had, but there was only an answering machine. The parents, perhaps out late, dining, wining. Not looking for their daughter, no, sir. What did people do who had runaway children? Did their lives resume with faked normalcy? She would keep calling. She heard footsteps behind her and Delford appeared.

He still looked gaunt and pale. "We're gonna find this monster, Claudia. You expect this in Houston, not here." He mopped his brow and she noticed the dark circles underneath his uniform's sleeves. He was sweating as though fevered. "I thought you were taking care of this girl."

Her throat worked. "I . . . she didn't want help. She didn't want protection. I tried."

"Try harder next time."

Silence fell between them, the soft sound of the waves, boats creaking in the harbor a block away. Claudia's heart hammered in her chest.

"Marcy Ballew," Delford finally said. "Maybe this is what happened to her?"

"I don't know," Claudia said. She told him about her research. "I'm still waiting to hear back from Laredo and Brownsville on their missing-persons cases."

"We got a missing girl and we got a butchered girl. And the way Farrell was killed, Claudia. He took out her organs."

"Let's not get ahead of ourselves," she cautioned. "Marcy Ballew could be sitting on a beach in California for all we know. And I think that this might have more to do with Pete Hubble's death. Once it gets out that the girl who found him is dead herself . . . it's an awful stretch for coincidence, Delford. Surely you see that."

He blanched. "She's a transient. They're always easy targets. Sure could be a coincidence."

"Maybe she saw something she wasn't supposed to."

"Pete Hubble committed suicide. There was nothing for her to see. Hell, she was prone to amble at night. She just might have walked herself into some new trouble."

Claudia kept her voice low. "I'm not going to argue with

you, because it seems pointless. But this is not like you, Delford. Bullying me. Sticking your hand in the middle of investigations. Just wait until the press learns the girl who found Pete Hubble is gutted and sliced up in the bay. You tell people there's no connection, you're gonna be looking for a new job. Why are you fighting me every step of the way?" She felt sick, breathless.

Delford Spires sank onto the steps next to her. All the bluster from before was gone, and she saw his hands tremble as he slowly rubbed his jawline.

"Whit Mosley believes—and I'm not sure how, since I can't get in touch with him—Pete Hubble got half a million in cash from Junior Deloache. The money's gone. There's no trace of it in Pete's account. Pete's dead. Now Heather's dead. I think this missing money is at the heart of this, Delford."

He blinked at her. "This'll kill Lucinda."

Claudia cared very little for Lucinda Hubble's feelings at the moment. "It's already killed Pete and Heather."

"You think the mob cut up that girl and dumped her?"

"Yes, I do. At least based on what I know now. We need to find Deloache."

"Yes," he agreed. "I'll talk to him."

"You talk to Eddie yet?"

"Eddie's not answering my calls," Delford said. "I'm gonna go over to his house and see what's up." He turned and headed back toward the station.

Claudia went back inside to the interrogation room. A slip of paper from the girl's jeans was there, secure in an evidence bag. Claudia stared at the phone number that had been tucked in the girl's wallet. It was blurred from the water but still readable. Faith Hubble's home phone. Maybe

Faith had offered to help the girl, given that she'd had the trauma of finding Pete's body. Right. Faith Hubble, good Samaritan.

She turned to the worn, grass-stained duffel. After Heather's body had been found, Patrolman Fox and another officer immediately combed her hangout, Little Mischief Beach, for information. A couple of girls puffing cigs on the beach, transients, knew Heather and when told of her fate, shattered into tears. One produced a duffel bag within ten minutes. They thought Heather had just blown town and you know, they could sure use her stuff if she didn't need it. They'd last seen her on Wednesday night.

Claudia sorted through the contents. A pair of jeans, crusty with sand. A pair of panties. She examined the manufacturer and the size: on both counts, the same as the panties found at Pete's death scene. Claudia let out a long breath. She'd had Heather show that she had underwear on, but she'd been given a bathroom break before and had her duffel with her. She could have changed into a pair of fresh panties before Claudia asked. Maybe she was messing around with Pete Hubble and suddenly had to get dressed in a hurry.

Yeah, if she killed Pete. Or if she was with Pete when he was killed.

She called the crime lab in Corpus and asked them to compare any pubic hairs found in the panties in Pete's case with Heather Farrell's pubic hairs, once they had processed her body. She had a sick feeling that there would be a match.

She pawed through the duffel bag. Two sweaters, threadbare, a couple of T-shirts with Port Leo themes, one for the Port Leo varsity swim team. A small stash of cash:

thirty dollars. A couple of bus tickets to go as far as Houston, unused—the ones the constable had mentioned at the inquest. Who was going with her? A notebook, full of stiff but accurate pencil drawings of whooping cranes, Caspian terns, egrets, and roseate spoonbills. Boats, people walking on the beach. She hadn't been kidding about being an artist. With instruction she might have been quite good. Another page, full of hopeful scribbling. *Heather Hubble. Mrs. Heather Hubble. Heather Farrell-Hubble. Heather and Sam,* the *H* and the *S* ornately drawn together to form a lopsided heart.

Whoa.

The drive to Lucinda Hubble's house took three minutes. Lights were on, both upstairs and downstairs, even at the late hour. Lucinda answered the door, in silk pajamas and robe. The skin under Lucinda's eyes was dark, like a pale bruise.

She tore open the door quickly after Claudia's knock, her eyes wide. Seeing Claudia seemed to make her breath freeze.

"Hello, Senator. I'm afraid I'm the bearer of bad news. Is Faith here?"

"Bad news," she repeated dully. But she led Claudia into the main den, where Faith was speaking softly into a telephone. Faith clicked off the moment she saw Claudia, not even bothering with a good-bye.

"What's going on?" Faith asked without preamble.

"The young woman who found Pete's body, Heather Farrell, is dead. A shrimper's net caught her body out in the bay a couple of hours ago."

The women exchanged glances.

"Was it an accident?" Faith asked. "Did she drown?"

"Hardly. Stabbed, disemboweled, throat slashed."

Claudia let the silence hang. Lucinda sank into a chair.

"There are those who might be tempted to treat this as a coincidence—Heather finds Pete dead and ends up dead herself in a matter of days. I don't believe in coincidence. I don't care how Judge Mosley ruled." She glared at Faith Hubble, then turned to Lucinda. "I never thought your son committed suicide, Senator, and I think so even less now. You have anything you want to tell me?"

Lucinda folded her hands in her lap. "I can think of nothing that could help you. I'm horrified beyond belief that such a crime could happen here."

Faith said, "Let's call Delford," as though Claudia were not sitting there.

That boiled Claudia's blood. "We have another young woman missing, and if Heather's death is not related to Pete's, I think it's related to this other case. Have either of you heard of Marcy Ballew?"

Both women shook their heads.

"She vanished from Deshay, in western Louisiana. She worked at a nursing home there."

Faith shook her head, but Lucinda's mouth worked and she made a noise in her throat.

"Senator?" Claudia asked.

"No, I'm sorry, I don't know her. Or of her."

"In Heather's jeans we found a piece of paper that had your home phone number on it. Had either of you been in contact with her?"

Faith looked stunned. "Lord, no."

"I gave the girl that number," Lucinda said quickly. Faith looked over at her, surprised.

"When did you see Heather Farrell?" Claudia asked.

Lucinda folded her hands in her lap. "I ran into her. On the street on Wednesday, I think it was. I gave her our number in case she needed any help. You know, a place to stay, food, perhaps some clothes or money. I—felt sorry for her."

How did you even know what she looked like? Claudia wondered, but she decided to play this out. She turned to Faith. "Did Heather Farrell ever call you?"

"No," Faith said. She glanced over at Lucinda, and some unspoken code seemed to hover in the air between them.

"I'd like to talk with Sam."

"Why?" Faith asked.

Claudia decided to fish a little. "Heather Farrell hung out a lot at Little Mischief Beach. If Sam hung out there, he might have seen who else was around Heather."

"I don't think Sam knew the girl. I mean, I'm sure he would have mentioned it if he had," Faith said.

Claudia watched her. "I'm quite sure Sam knew her. She left a notebook in her duffel with hearts drawn around their names. Along with two bus tickets to Houston."

Both women stared.

"I think I should call Delford," Lucinda finally said.

"Fine." Claudia smiled. She played her trump cards. "I suspect the FBI will be interested in talking to Sam even more than I am. If Farrell's death is related to Ballew's disappearance, and Ballew was kidnapped and brought across state lines, the FBI takes the case. Maybe even before the election." She let the cold knife sink and twist. "Should I have the agents call you, Faith, or you, Senator?"

"You despicable bitch," Faith said under her breath.

"Faith!" Lucinda gasped.

Faith grasped the arms of her chair. "She's enjoying this. She's wanted to turn the screws on us for a long time."

"You don't matter one iota to me," Claudia said evenly. "But I'd like to talk to your son. Now, please."

Faith closed her eyes and a shudder went through her body. "You can't. We don't know where Sam is."

A minute later Claudia called Delford at the police station.

"Sam Hubble is missing." She told him what she had found in the Farrell girl's belongings. "I just spoke with the senator and Faith. Sam is gone. No sign of him. He took his own car."

Delford wheezed. "You had no right to go over there..."

"That suicide note can't be for real. Sam Hubble faked it."

"You think...that boy killed his daddy and Heather Farrell?"

"I don't know, but we need to find him." She paused. "Did you find Eddie?"

"No. He's gone. His car, everything, his apartment's empty. I...sent Fox over to Junior Deloache's. I just got a call. They found Deloache there. Stabbed to death, stabbed like two dozen times."

Claudia leaned against the kitchen counter, Lucinda and Faith watching her. Sam Hubble, Jabez Jones, and Eddie Gardner had all gone missing. Heather Farrell was dead and her story about Pete Hubble was a lie. Junior Deloache was dead. Welcome to chaos.

"What's happening is that Pete Hubble stirred up the wrong hornet's nest. He stirred up the past. People are dying because of what happened to Corey Hubble all those years ago." She waited for him to react, to speak, and he said nothing. "If there's anything else you can tell me you better tell me right now, Delford."

His breathing grew harsh. "You're leaping to conclusions. No reason to think that note's a fake. Boy might have just gone partying in Corpus. You're making all kinds of unsubstantiated claims, bothering Lucinda. I won't have it, I won't have it from an officer of mine."

She started to speak again. "Delford..."

"Shut up. You're fired, Claudia."

37

WHIT AND GOOCH barreled on deep into Friday night, north, heading for Missatuck, Texas. They had left Gooch's car parked in a brightly lit trucker's stop on the outskirts of Beaumont. The easternmost slice of Texas unfolded ahead of their headlights, an endless ribbon of road bordered by tall loblolly pines. The weather cleared, the cool night the luxuriant reward for a too-long, sweltering summer. Whit drove, and Gooch sat in the front seat, reading a battered Mickey Spillane paperback by penlight.

"I can't read in a car, it makes me sick," Whit said. There had been little conversation between them since leaving Beaumont, although Whit's mind was full of questions over Gooch's ability to make felons disappear.

"I'm highlighting the appropriate tough guy phrases for you so you know what to say the next time you encounter an Anson type. You're a little too Larry McMurtry for that crowd." Gooch glanced. "Although you acquitted yourself well against that slab of a kid."

"I feel like I broke every finger in my hands on his face."

"If you did, you couldn't steer," Gooch said matter-of-factly. "Enough self-congratulations. What matters is that Junior thinks you've got his moolah." He shut the Spillane. "*Moolah,* there's a word that needs a renaissance."

"Perhaps Pete hid the money somewhere before he died."

"For what purpose? Stealing from mobsters, even the IQ-challenged contingent that Junior represents, is an extremely bad idea." Gooch shrugged. "We may be crediting Pete with greater brains than he deserves. He may have only had one large working organ. I think that Junior-boy had Pete killed."

"So where is the money? I would think if Pete doesn't have it, Velvet might."

"I'm sitting in slack-jawed amazement. You generally consider Velvet as some whore with the heart of gold, pardon the cliché."

"If she had the half million, wouldn't she give it back to Junior, having seen what happened to Pete? And if she took it she'd be gone, and Junior and Anson would be off in hot pursuit."

"We don't know Pete ever kept it on the boat, but they thought it was on the boat."

"Where else might he hide it?"

"Gee, in a bank?" Gooch asked. "Has anyone looked in the poor schmuck's accounts?"

"Yes. Claudia researched his bank accounts. It's not there."

"So who could have taken it?"

"Velvet. Anyone who came on the boat…me, Claudia, Delford, Gardner, the other cops. Heather Farrell. Sam Hubble."

"Who do you like?"

"I don't see either of the kids taking it. They were too rattled."

"Didn't you say Delford Spires was blasting you and Claudia?"

"Yeah."

"He's probably threatened by Claudia in that she has twice the IQ," Gooch said. "Unless . . . maybe the Deloaches already had a different purpose attached to the money."

"As in?"

"Drug money. Money that's due to be freshly laundered and shouldn't be given away. Or money to grease local palms, perhaps Delford's."

Whit considered. "Okay. Say Papa Deloache gives poor Junior an operation to run. Off the beaten track from main centers of illicit commerce, like Houston or Galveston. Port Leo would qualify. Not too far from Corpus Christi or San Antonio, only hours from major markets like Houston and Austin."

"And not too far from South Padre, where your seasonal business is. Junior would mix well with the college students, the old frat party guy with a thick wad of cash." Gooch stared out at the darkness, the outlines of the pines etched in black. "Of course, the frat boys and sorority girls would be laughing at Junior behind their hands."

"Are you ever going to tell me what happened back there in Beaumont?"

"Not a hair on their sainted little heads was hurt."

"You've got friends in the police department there?"

"I'm not on the witness stand in your courtroom, am I?" He fell silent; topic over. "So what do you hope to learn from this mystery woman Pete had called so often?" Gooch asked.

"She clearly expected money when she called Pete. She clearly didn't know he was dead."

Gooch cracked a window, and the thick, earthy smell of the pine forests, stirred with the odor of gasoline fumes, streamed into the Explorer. "You want me to drive for a while? You tired?"

Whit nodded. They pulled over and Gooch took the wheel. Whit moved to the passenger seat, feeling too revved to relax. But as the nighttime road unwound, he slept.

Whit and Gooch crashed at a cheap motel off the highway around 2 A.M., rose at seven, and arrived in Missatuck, a town three miles off the main highway with one bumpy major street and two stoplights, around nine Saturday morning. Missatuck was little enough that asking for a local address at the small grocery got results.

Kathy Breaux lived at 302 Cotton Creek Road. The house was a brick duplex in a very modest neighborhood, the only kind Missatuck offered. Ill-kept flowerbeds dominated the yard, and a motley crew of lawn gnomes congregated in one untilled bed.

"Let's be careful," Gooch warned. "Anyone who collects lawn gnomes is not to be trifled with."

Whit rang the bell. No answer. He rang again and knocked. No answer. The door to the other duplex creaked open, and a woman in purple jogging sweats, holding a purple mug of coffee, stepped out onto the concrete slab that served as a joint porch. She was tall and skinny, with raven-dark hair pulled into a sloppy ponytail and a bevy of unfortunate whiskers on her chin.

"Awful early to be pounding on a door," the woman observed in a gravel-bruised voice.

"I'm sorry," Whit said. "I'm Judge Whit Mosley. I'm a

justice of the peace in Encina County, down on the coast, and this is my associate—"

"Dr. Guchinski," Gooch interjected and Whit kept his neutral smile in place. *Doctor. Heaven help us.*

"I'm looking for Kathy Breaux," Whit said.

The woman sipped her coffee. "What do you want with her?"

"A man committed suicide in my jurisdiction, and he had called the phone number at this address repeatedly," Whit said. "We're trying to establish the reason for the suicide, and we thought Ms. Breaux might know his mental state."

The woman blinked. "Who is this man?"

"His name is Pete Hubble. Does that name ring a bell?"

"Well, do you have some identification?" she asked.

Whit produced a laminated card with his name and title issued by the Texas secretary of state. He didn't offer her one of his regular business cards to keep because what he didn't want was her phoning the Encina County authorities. Buddy Beere, if given half a chance, would make widespread hay about any wild-goose chases Whit pursued right before the election.

She studied the card, then handed it back to him. "Kathy's at work, got a double shift. It's about ten, fifteen minutes away. I can give you the address."

"Thanks," Whit said.

The woman returned with hastily scribbled instructions. *Follow Highway 363 to the Louisiana border, where it becomes Louisiana FM 110, go straight until you get to Deshay. Memorial Oaks nursing home is on the left after the second light.*

Deshay, Louisiana. A nursing home. A tremble rose along Whit's spine.

"Thanks," he said.

"She's not in no trouble, is she?"

"No, I don't think so," Whit lied.

" 'Cause she's a pretty good renter," the woman added, as though this were a treasured commodity in Missatuck.

"Promptness with rent is always to be admired," Gooch said. "Thanks again."

The woman shut the door, and they went back to Whit's Explorer.

"A nursing home in Deshay," Whit said. "That's where that Ballew girl vanished from, the one whose wallet they found outside of town. Her face has been all over those blue flyers, Claudia mentioned the case to me. It can't be coincidence."

They drove thirty miles over the speed limit, zooming into Louisiana.

Deshay was the kind of town repeated ten thousand times across America: an unhealthy selection of fast-food chains, a neon-lit doughnut shop, a pair of peeling strip centers, a furniture store with plastic-sheeted inventory overflowing into the parking lot, and five gas stations lining the main road. Memorial Oaks squatted on a corner. Bricks the color of creek dirt lined the concrete walkways and ill-clipped Japanese boxwoods stood beneath the windows. The home didn't look dirty or unhealthy, just glum, a sad coda for lives in their final movements.

"Despicable the way we treat the elderly in this country," Gooch said. "When I hit sixty I'm moving to China, where the old are revered."

"I hate nursing homes," Whit said under his breath. "They're like parking garages for people."

"Would you rather die young? I could call Anson and see if he'll hook up with us again."

When they asked at the information counter for Kathy Breaux, the dour receptionist nodded toward a hall that fed off from the central hub.

"She's down in the television room, probably doing a little feeding," the woman said.

Gooch whispered to Whit as they walked: "A feeding. How evocative. Is there a trough?"

The room was large but fusty, its cornerstone a sparkling new TV that dangled the joys of the outside world. A trashy morning talk show blared from the set, mothers having their mouthy, punk- and Goth-dressing daughters made over into pink-angora debutantes. Several patients watched with blank stares fixated on the lives on the television instead of anything else in the depressing room, blankets covering their laps. An array of shiny black dominoes lay spread out on a table, awaiting players. No nurse loomed to greet them. One patient, in her early eighties, glanced up at them as they came in and gave them an intelligent smile. She was reading *The Norton Anthology of English Literature, Volume 2,* her bony, mottled finger stuck in the mammoth book, the other hand holding a magnifying glass.

"Hello, ma'am," Whit said. "How are you today?"

"Lovely. How are y'all doing?"

"We're fine, ma'am," Gooch said. "We're looking for Kathy Breaux."

The old woman puckered in distaste. "Kathy is no doubt outside, sucking a cigarette down to the filter, as I would if she gave me half the chance. She ought to be back in a minute."

"Which way, ma'am?" Whit asked.

The old woman nodded toward a door that opened into a hallway. Whit thanked her and moved toward the hallway.

"I'll stay here," Gooch said, "in case she comes back." He leaned down toward the woman to see what she was reading. She flopped open her book for him.

"Robert Browning?" Whit heard Gooch say good-naturedly. "You're not wasting your time on him, are you? He's a psychobabble bore."

"Nonsense," the old woman said. "Now, when *I* taught Browning..."

At the end of the hall Whit found a bay of large windows that opened out onto a grove of mossy oaks. In the foyer formed by the windows, a bathrobe-clad crone hunched in a wheelchair while a spare, trim woman, dressed in the bright magenta scrubs of the nursing staff, mopped up around the chair.

"Bad bad girl," the woman chirped in a singsong voice reminiscent of a preschooler ditty. "You keep your hands off your diapy-diap now so I don't have to clean up after you again."

A half grunt, half wail was her answer from the poor old woman in the chair.

"Excuse me," Whit said. "Are you Kathy Breaux?"

She gave him a bright smile he suspected was reserved only for visitors. "Yes?"

"I'm here to talk to you about Pete Hubble."

The smile barely dimmed. "Who?"

"The man who placed several phone calls to your house over the past week."

The grin stayed as fixed as stone. "I'm sorry, I didn't catch your name."

"Judge Whit Mosley. I was a friend of Pete's. He's dead."

Her grip whitened against the handle of the mop.

"I'm conducting the inquest into Pete's death and I'd like to talk to you about why Pete was calling you," Whit said.

"You know, I would love to help you with whatever this is, but I can't talk now. I'm working." She tucked a lock of hair behind her ear with a coy little flick of the wrist.

"Considering this is an investigation into a possible homicide, I'm sure the home's administrators would be glad to provide us with a private office and time alone." Whit kept his tone friendly. He'd heard enough voice to know she was the woman who had called on the boat. "He was shot. In the mouth."

"Please," she said, "let me get her cleaned up and then I'll talk with you." She turned and wheeled the woman around in the foyer, then said, "Oh, why don't you just come with me while I get her settled and then we can talk?" A tenseness framed her face. "Just come right along with me."

Whit got the distinct feeling she didn't want him out of her sight. "Actually I need to borrow a rest room." He had noticed a men's room right off the foyer. He didn't wait for her permission, he turned and ducked into the bathroom. He washed his hands while counting to one hundred, and then came out. Kathy and her incontinent charge were gone. He hurried back to the main room; Gooch was still there, arguing the merits of Victorian poetry with his new friend. No Kathy. Whit wandered back down the hallway, peeking into the rooms. One room was tidy with its lack of occupants. Another held an ancient woman, napping and snoring loudly.

The third room was occupied. Whit peered into the dimness. An emaciated figure lay in a bed, a rope of drool uncoiling from his slack mouth, his eyes at half-mast. His dark hair was cut in a crisp burr, and an ugly scar split the hairline. His skin was sun-starved, his cheeks sunken, but Whit could see the man was young. Too young.

"Oh, my Lord," Whit said.

It was Corey Hubble.

38

Velvet was awake when he returned. Wriggling carefully, she had worked the blindfold back into place. She kept her head turned to the side to hide any lopsided silk.

"Did you miss me?" Corey asked.

"Why do you hate me so," she said, "to do this to me?"

"I don't hate you. Not at all. I love you."

She wanted to scream, *This isn't love, you freaking nut bastard. Even as screwed up as I am I know this isn't love.* Instead she said, "Are you doing this because you've seen my movies?"

A soft laugh. "I've seen your movies. Am I better than Pete?"

She didn't answer.

He touched her cheek. Gently. "Tell me."

"Of course you are," she lied. She heard shoes easing off feet and hitting the wooden floor, the soft rustle of clothing sliding down legs, a jingling of keys tossed to the floor.

"Don't," Velvet said. "Please don't."

Silence again.

"Why not?" Corey finally said, sounding amused. "Since I'm so much better."

"Because," she said, her voice calmed with a mighty effort, "you don't have to. Not this way."

"I need to."

"Corey?"

Silence again, longer this time. She heard the even rasp of his breathing, near her ear.

"What?" he finally said.

"Corey. Please don't." She put even more fear into her voice than what she felt.

"No talking now." He climbed upon her and forced himself on her again. She gritted her teeth, tried to summon memories from faraway sweetness. The tang of lemonade on a summer day, the soft pine-cologne smell of her father's camel-hair jacket, cinnamon and butter pooling on hot toast. Sitting in the quiet dark of her daddy's church on a Saturday afternoon, leaning back in a wooden pew while he practiced his sermon, pretending to snore if the sermon got a little dull, him never getting mad. Pete, bedecking her with roses on her birthday. But all the good failed her and she screamed and cried, muscles aching, body sore. She told herself, *It will be over soon, over soon, over soon.*

It was. He lay atop her when he was done, his skin sweaty and smelling of burgers, her skin clammy. His face was buried in her hair, and she felt him breathing in its scent. Lingering on her, like they were lovers. She so wanted her gun. She would fire a thousand bullets into his guts and brain and what odd lump passed for a heart.

"Why did you kill Pete?" she asked.

"Who says I did?" His voice was muffled in her hair.

"Did you kill him to get at me?"

No answer. His seed trickled out of her and she wanted to vomit.

"Tell me," she said. "Please."

"I didn't kill him. I wanted to, but I didn't."

"Liar." She couldn't hide her contempt.

He sat up, going on his knees, straddling her, and slapped her hard. Once, twice, three times. Her ears rang. Blood leaked from her nose. He stopped; she felt his erection return, pressed into her breasts.

"I thought I was your darling," she managed.

He made a guttural sound. She could feel his legs shivering against hers.

Velvet wet her lips, tasted her own blood. "Pete loved you, Corey. He only wanted to help you."

Another low laugh.

"Do you want me to love you, Corey? Maybe I could." She heard him laugh but not move. "I can't love you if I don't know you, though," she said.

"You love Whit Mosley." His voice grew distant. "I saw you hug him."

"I sure don't love him. I hate his guts."

"Don't hate his guts. I might bring them to you."

Velvet's tongue felt stuck. She expected him to rape her again, but instead he clambered off the bed. She heard him gathering his clothes and then the door shutting behind him. In a minute or so the soft hiss of a shower began to run.

He was gone. And he had not shoved the gag back in her mouth. With its tiny lock. Its edged metal lock.

In the end, of course, she called David.

Claudia awoke early Saturday morning and lay on the futon for an hour, her body stiff against the flowered sheets. She had no job. She had rent, she had food to buy, she had a car payment, she would have no health insurance, she had less than two thousand dollars in her checking account and less in a savings account, she owed six hundred on a Visa card with seventeen percent interest. Twice she reached for the phone to call her mother, but even before she dialed her mother's voice rang in her ear like discordant chimes: *What's wrong with you? You give up a wonderful husband, now you lose your job? What, you want to shrimp with your father? There's a future. Why did we bother sending you to school?* She wasn't up for her mother's blunderbuss catechism. Heather Farrell's face swam before her, dream-edged, and twice Claudia stumbled to the bathroom, surrendering to dry heaves of sick and shock.

So she finally called David, whispering to him about losing her job, about failing Heather. He came over at seven-thirty in the morning, arrived with a bag of breakfast groceries, drew a hot bath for her, made omelets while she bathed and dressed in old nubby pajamas soft as a kiss. She heard him in her kitchen, sliding drawers, chopping vegetables, pouring juice, sizzling butter.

That didn't take long, did it, Miss Tough? You're just gonna let him right back in, aren't you?

She popped open the drain, let the soapy water begin its downward swirl. *Yeah. Maybe I am.*

They ate their eggs and biscuits and juice, and Claudia, rather than talking, went under a wave of exhaustion. She fell asleep curled on the futon, David lying beside her, stroking her dark hair.

She awoke at 10 A.M. Her blinds were lowered, the room grayish dark. She stumbled to the kitchen. David sat drinking coffee, reading the Corpus Christi paper.

He lowered the paper. "Hope I didn't overstay my

welcome. I thought you might want to talk when you woke up."

"Thanks. Thanks for the bath and breakfast and everything."

"But I want to get something straight, okay?" New steel in his voice—she hadn't heard before. "I'm not trying to take advantage of the…emotional train wreck you've just gone through. I'm saying that out loud because I know how your mind works, Claud, and sooner or later you're gonna think I'm trying to tiptoe back in."

"Oh, David, I don't think that," she said, unsure of what she thought.

"Okay. I just don't want you to be alone if you don't want to be."

She got herself a cup of hot coffee—he'd brewed hazelnut, her favorite—and added generous milk and sugar. He had his back to her, sitting at the kitchen table, and she watched the set of his shoulders, his burr of auburn hair, his wiry arms, the constellation of freckles on the back of his neck. She wanted to hold and kiss him and feel him against her, and she nearly dropped her mug.

Carefully she sipped the piping hot coffee, standing in the kitchen away from him. He turned around in his chair. "You want to talk options? Delford can't just terminate you, Claudia."

"He could and did." She shrugged. "It's a right-to-work state, he can fire me at will. I had to go back in, surrender my side arm, my badge. I didn't have a box to clean out my desk, I guess I have to do that Monday."

"Are you going to appeal to the mayor?"

"I'll write him a letter," she said. "But I don't think I'm overflowing with options here."

"Come work for the sheriff's department," he said instantly and then stumbled. "I mean, you're a good investigator. You could work for DPS, too, or Parks and Wildlife, maybe."

"I'm sure something will come up. I can always shrimp with Papa. That should drive Mama into the crazy house a full ten years ahead of schedule." She finished her coffee. "So what about your big Jabez Jones case?"

He shrugged. "He was spotted in New Mexico. I think he's probably heading back to California, where he's got a lot of friends. The DEA agent from Corpus told me they think Jabez's donation receipts don't match the figures in his books. He's gotten maybe thirty thou in donations and three million on his ledgers. Mary Magdalene still ain't talking. Sits in her cell like a freaking Amazon warrior, silent."

"I thought maybe Junior Deloache was bringing drug money into Port Leo."

David nodded. "Probably. With Junior dead, and Jones running, I wouldn't be surprised if there was a connection. That three million, maybe it's Jabez laundering Junior's money."

"I just wish Velvet would turn up," Claudia said, thinking of Heather's water-paled face. "Her car was at Junior's condo, her purse with a gun in it, but she wasn't."

"You think she killed him?"

"No. I mean, I doubt it, but who knows. I don't know her." She gave a thin, nervous laugh. "I for sure thought I knew Delford, but he turned on me quicker than a rabid dog."

David shook his head again. "With all this insanity, I can't believe Delford fired you. He needs everyone he can get."

"Does he? If the crime's this big, the DEA and FBI will take it over. Delford'll just wax his mustache and make press announcements." She retrieved the coffeepot, freshened their mugs, came and sat next to him at the table.

"I don't get how the Ballew girl fits in," David said. "Comes from Louisiana to see Jones, gets involved in this money laundering, and ends up dead?"

Claudia explained what she had found about the nursing home connections. "It's strange, and maybe I chased a shadow," she said. "But I found, well, not quite a pattern, but a couple of odd coincidences of timing."

"Are all your notes at the station?"

"Yeah. But I can get you a copy. I mean, it's really your case."

David phoned the station and got a clerk to make copies of Claudia's notes on Marcy Ballew.

"Ask them if I've gotten any messages from out-of-town police," Claudia said.

He did. He paused, gestured at her for pencil and paper, which she handed to him. He jotted notes.

"Well, this is interesting. You got messages from investigators in Brownsville and Laredo." Neither police department had made much progress on the Morris or the Palinski case. Both women seemed to have vanished into thin air: no witnesses, no evidence.

"Let's call them back," she said.

He reached for her phone. "Not on my unemployed dime," she said. "Let's go over to the sheriff's department."

She dressed quickly and they drove over. David made the calls, asking the investigator on duty if there was a nursing home near either woman's workplace. The Laredo detective said yes, there was a nursing home right across from the Taco Bell that Angela Morris vanished from, Bellewood. It was the same one that Placid Harbor had handled a patient transfer from. Brownsville didn't know if there was a nursing home near the pizzeria; they'd find out and call or fax David back.

So David called the pizzeria to ask if St. Mary's Nursing Home was close by. No, not at all, the pizzeria was at the northern edge of town on Highway 77. St. Mary's was on the east side of Brownsville.

"But 77's the main highway," Claudia said when David hung up. "Anyone going to St. Mary's might still pass that pizzeria. I'd just like to know more about these transfers, about how they work, the time involved."

David set the phone down. "You want to go talk to Buddy Beere with me?"

"I'm not a cop anymore," she said. The truth of it still sounded alien to her ears.

"You are to me. C'mon, you've already talked to the guy. Better than sitting around updating résumés and harboring grudges."

Now she smiled at him. "Sure. Let's go."

The little lock lay in the no-man's-land between Velvet's torso and her elbow, and if she moved her arm slightly, the lock and its strap teased her skin. But she could not move it toward her hand.

She wept briefly in frustration and then she slept again. Sleep was the escape door. In sleep her father's arms enfolded her and he said, *I forgive you I forgive you and I love you no matter what.*

She woke at his touch. She wasn't sure if it was minutes later, hours, time ceased to hold meaning.

"Need to pee?" he asked abruptly.

"Yes, yes," she said. She had peed in the night, like a baby, and the towels were sodden with the smell.

"I don't got no more sheets or towels to put under you right now," he said.

Of course not. Who has time to do laundry when you're busy kidnapping and raping? she thought crazily.

She felt a bag—roomy, made of soft chamois, reeking of dust and fuel—go over her head. He loosened the cords at her feet first, rubbing her ankles for her.

"I'm taking you to the bathroom. Now, you try anything, I'll cut and gut you, you understand?" he muttered.

"Yes. I'll be good," she answered in a timid murmur. *I'll kill you if you give me a moment's chance.*

He slipped her hands free from the shackles. She heard the toss of keys again on the floor. She slowly massaged her wrists.

"Do what I say." He pulled her to her feet. Bolts of numbness shot up her legs. She nearly fell, every muscle screaming. He yanked her forward and the doorjamb brushed her shoulder, and seven steps down—she was counting—along carpet that felt frayed, he steered her to the right. Cold tile prickled her bare feet.

He pushed her down onto a cold toilet seat.

She urinated, emptying her aching bladder. He hummed along, a bouncy tune she recognized as "I Get Around."

I am so gonna kill you. "I need to . . . um . . . too," she said in a very quiet voice.

"I'm not leaving."

She couldn't see him with the sack over her face. "Corey. Please."

"No."

"Please, Corey, please!"

"No." He sounded amused again. He wanted her to grovel, wanted her to beg, just so he could say no.

If he kills you now at least it's over. She had acted the dominatrix in her movies, and now she called up that icy, imperial voice. "Do you get off on bathroom functions, Corey? How sad. I thought you were a real man."

A long silence and she thought: *Either I got you or you're about to strangle me here on a toilet.*

He said, "I'm not some freak. I'm normal."

His denial almost sent her into peals of hysterical laughter. She gripped the cool bowl of the toilet.

"I know, Corey," she made herself say. "You're normal. And a normal man lets a lady go to the potty in private." She paused. "You do that, and I'll show you fun in bed you've never, ever seen before."

Long silence. She prayed a true prayer, for the first time in a dozen years. *Please, God, please help me now. Please.*

"All right," he said. "I'll wait outside. But don't try anything."

"I won't."

She heard him step out and the door gently close.

She yanked off the cloth hood and ripped the silk blindfold from her head. The bathroom was small, decorated in sea-foam green tile at least thirty years old. The shower was a stall, and the shower rod was bolted to the wall.

There was a small bolt on the door. If she locked it he would hear.

"Hurry up," he called.

"I am!" she yelled, putting a teary tone in her voice. She groaned, as if troubled by a pained stomach. "Just a second." If he heard her rummaging he'd crash in. She almost wept in anger. Nothing, nothing to fight with.

She knelt, gingerly opening the cabinet under the sink. Cotton balls. Toilet paper. Disinfectant spray.

Yes.

He shoved the door open. She sprang to her feet and jetted disinfectant hard into his eyes. He shrieked and fell back.

"EEAGGGGH!" he screamed, clutching his face.

Velvet shoved past him and ran down the hallway. To her left the hall opened up into a den and she saw a front door. She threw herself at it.

Locked.

"YOU BITCH." He staggered to his feet, clawing at his seared eyes.

Six locks on the door and three were dead bolts. These she clicked open and tried the door again. Still locked. The other locks required a key.

Where would he keep the keys? Fighting a surge of panic, Velvet scanned the den. Nothing on the table except a plate dirty with sandwich crumbs and a milk-smeared glass. Nothing on the small kitchen counter.

She had heard the jingle earlier when he tossed the keys on the bedroom floor.

She turned and he charged at her, his face set in fury, his eyes red slits.

She grabbed a lamp from a side table and swung hard. It nailed him on the shoulder. He went down, and Velvet raised the lamp to smash it on his head.

He seized her legs, trying to topple her, and she slammed the lamp's base against his neck, then against the back of his head.

Don't let him get you down. He wins if he gets you on the floor.

Teeth closed around her ankle, biting hard and deep, down to the bone.

She screamed and fell to the floor, kicking him. His teeth tore the flesh of her ankle.

She grabbed the fallen can of disinfectant and fogged him again, trying to loop the lamp's cord around his throat. He sobbed and lashed out with a punch that caught her hard in the windpipe. She gagged, gasping for breath. He swung the lamp hard, connecting against her skull, the lamp breaking, and she went down, eyeballs rolling up. Her final thought was, *Not like this, no.*

The Blade stood, then sank down again. His eyes burned like she had poked hot matches into the irises. He crawled to the sink and splashed water repeatedly into his aching eyes. She hadn't gotten him so good with the last cloudy burst of disinfectant, but the first had been unadulterated hell, toxic waste hitting his eye tissue.

She might have blinded him. Maybe even caused permanent damage.

He puked into the sink. He rinsed his eyes for what felt like an eternity. The pain subsided down to a dull roar, enough to where he could read the instructions on the disinfectant. Call a physician. Not an option right now. Oh, he would make her pay. He went back to the rinsing.

Thirty minutes later, his hands still shaking, he could see well enough to relock the dead bolts and to drag her back to the room. Her left ankle was a meaty mess and she wheezed, but she was still unconscious.

This is what being nice brought, he thought. But none of the others had fought him so hard, and when the pain faded, that fire of hers would make punishing and crushing her sweeter than killing Mama. Oh, the fun. He hardened at the images, even with the pain in his eyes and his head. He'd hold her eyes open and spray till the can was empty. He put on his knife sheath so she could see what waited for her after their chemical games.

He choked down a half-dozen aspirin and slung Velvet over his shoulder. He tossed her onto the bed and started to retie her to the posts.

A knock pounded on the front door.

39

YOU'RE IN A bad situation," Whit said softly.

Kathy Breaux sat in one corner of Corey Hubble's room, watching Whit. Her soap-roughened hands lay in her lap, fingers laced together. Her fingernails were short and bitten, and she smelled of the antiseptic that wafted through the home like souring perfume. Hair dyed a slightly too-bright red, a starved look about her face and hips. Gooch had left them alone, to go perform an important errand at Whit's request.

Kathy said, "I don't know what you mean."

"There's several different ways this can play out," Whit said. "Pretty much all of them involve me calling the police. And me calling the FBI. What happens between now and then will make a big difference."

"Look, I just work here, okay? I just do what I'm told." She kept her voice hushed, accustomed to talking around the napping old. She glanced at Corey, propped up in the bed, eyes shut, breathing slowly, abandoned to a world of his own.

"Just following orders? That didn't work at Nuremberg, why do you think it's gonna work here?"

"What do you want?" she asked.

"I want to know how this man got here."

Kathy swallowed. "John's been here at least five years. I don't know much about what happened to him."

"John?"

"John Taylor."

"I think his name's Corey Hubble."

"I said I don't know what you're talking about."

"I want to see his files. Go get them and bring them back here."

"I can't do that."

"I can either tell these folks you attempted to extort money from Pete to reveal his brother's whereabouts, or I can tell them you discovered this man's real identity and sought to help his brother find him. Your choice."

Kathy Breaux stood and said, "I'll be right back, then." She hurried out the door.

Whit got up and went to Corey's bedside. He took Corey's hand; it was limp and bony and pale. Someone had created a new identity for him. Someone had financed his care all these years. That narrowed the suspects considerably. He had trouble visualizing Junior filling out insurance forms for a guy he turned into a vegetable.

It had to be the Hubbles. He tried not to think of Faith's face on the pillow next to him, smiling, tracing his lip with her fingernail.

"Hey, Corey," Whit said quietly. Corey gave no answer. A thin dribble of drool collected in the chapped corner of his mouth, and Whit wiped it away.

"I don't suppose you're gonna tell me what got you here," Whit said.

Corey kept his silence. The vicious trench of scar on his head looked like a bullet wound, long healed. Corey had

been shot. The bullet must have obliterated his mind but
not his functions, trapping him in this limbo.

If someone had tried to kill him, why keep him alive?
Attempted homicide made no sense. It must have been an
accident. But then why the secrecy? Because the accident
and its circumstances, if revealed, must threaten someone
powerful.

He searched Corey's room: neatly folded sweats from
Walmart, white tube socks, vanilla-scented hand lotion,
an uncracked Bible. In the back of the closet lay a plastic
bag of new sweats, also bought at Walmart, a sales slip still
inside. Paid with cash, but bought twelve days ago. He figured that was a Monday, an exact week before Pete's death.

He had no idea about Lucinda's schedule, but it would
be easy enough to find out if she was out campaigning
and where she was. Or where Faith was. He pocketed the
receipt from the clothes bag, careful not to get his own
prints on it.

So what did he owe Faith? A consideration phone call?
*Honey, I'm about to reveal to the press that your long-
missing brother-in-law isn't so missing anymore. You want
to tell me what you know before I call the cops?*

If he cared for her, he owed her this. Didn't he?

Corey lay in the bed like a broken dream.

Not yet, he couldn't call her. He would need more proof.
Fingerprints. Dental records. The business of proving who
lay in this bed meant more than simply picking up a phone
and summoning the press. They wouldn't run a story without harder evidence, and he had none.

Gooch came back into the room. Whit tucked Corey's
cool hand back under the sheets. Corey moaned, rasped, a
shuddery breath.

"Any trouble?"

"Nope. The local drugstore sells them." Gooch produced a cheap disposable camera from the bag and began to snap photos of Corey from various angles. Whit had thought it an appropriate precaution. He told Gooch what Kathy had said.

"So what are you thinking?" Gooch asked.

"I think Lucinda put him here."

Gooch gave him a disbelieving squint. "I don't like her, but if her child was hurt, she'd want him taken care of."

"He *is* taken care of. And his brother tracked him down here—he at least was in contact with this nurse here—and dies."

"You're suggesting Lucinda killed one son because he found out about her other son?"

"I don't know. And that missing girl, Marcy Ballew? She worked here, then she vanishes from Port Leo. She has to be connected to this somehow."

"Consider this," Gooch said. "Kathy knows that John Taylor really is Corey Hubble, long-missing son of a prominent politician. Maybe she wants to sell that information to Pete. And maybe the Ballew girl was in on the scheme. She goes to Port Leo to deal with Pete, loses her wallet, and ends up missing or on the run."

"If Pete thought Corey was in this town, why not just come here and get him and publicize it? It doesn't make sense," Whit said.

"Maybe he didn't know. She's calling him from little Missatuck, Texas. Corey's in Deshay, Louisiana. Who knows what story she told him." Gooch finished his roll of film.

Whit ran a finger along the burr of hair and scar along Corey's scalp.

"So you think Lucinda shot her own kid and set him up here?" Gooch asked.

"No," Whit said, "I think Delford Spires shot him."

"Why would Delford shoot a teenager?"

"Before he disappeared, Corey told Marian Duchamp that he was going to kill Delford Spires. I think Delford and Lucinda were involved—he is still extraordinarily protective of her—and Corey found out. That weekend he vanished, I think he headed north to Houston, to the conference his mother was attending. Suppose Delford's shacked up there with Lucinda. Corey finds them, there's a fight, the gun goes off. Corey's wounded."

"They would rush him to a hospital," Gooch said.

"You'd think. But maybe Delford's worried he'll lose his job. Maybe Lucinda's worried about the political ramifications of her lover shooting her son. Obviously they chose another route."

"How would they have taken care of him, though, if he'd been shot?"

"She's an RN. I saw her diplomas in her office, it got mentioned a lot in the papers when she first ran for office and she was big on health care, nursing home reform." He shook his head. "I don't know, Gooch, but this *is* Corey, and he got here with a new identity."

"So how would this Kathy have found out about Corey?" Gooch asked.

"A website about Pete Hubble included a picture of Corey and the number to Pete's answering service—sort of an online milk carton. Kathy might have seen that and realized she was sitting on a financial opportunity."

A jowly man with reddened cheeks and wispy blond hair stormed into the room. He wore a short-sleeve button-down shirt crisp with starch. A succession of chins nearly hid his tie's knot.

"I'm Felix Duplessis, the chief administrator here. Who are you people and why are you terrorizing my staff?" he demanded.

"We're not terrorizing anyone," Whit said mildly. "I'm Judge Whit Mosley, from Encina County, Texas, and this is my associate, Leonard Guchinski."

"A judge?" Duplessis blinked. "One of our nurses said you're bothering this patient."

"Good," Whit said. "It's about time someone bothered about him."

"I'm asking you to leave."

"We're not going anywhere," Whit said. "This man has been missing for years and he's just been found, and we're calling the police and the FBI."

Duplessis gaped. Whit explained. At the mention of Marcy Ballew's name Duplessis grew gray-pale. A return to the main office of the nursing home showed Kathy Breaux was gone. Duplessis paged her over the intercom.

"What can you tell us about John Taylor?" Whit asked.

Duplessis shook his head as he dug through a file. "Not much. He's our youngest patient by far. He's supposed to be transferred today. We just received a call this morning."

Transferred. Someone wanted the evidence whisked away, dumped in a fresh bed. "How is his care paid for?" Whit asked.

"A trust fund pays for what the government don't." Duplessis pulled a thick file with TAYLOR, JOHN on the tab.

"Who administers this trust?"

"A woman named Laura Taylor. From Texas. Austin, I believe."

Faith worked out of Austin as Lucinda's chief of staff. "Does she ever visit?"

"Rarely. She was here, oh, a couple of weeks ago."

"What does she look like?"

Duplessis shrugged. "Big old girl type. Early forties, tall, heavyset, pretty hazel eyes. No nonsense."

Pretty hazel eyes. Faith.

Whit flipped through the file. John Taylor, thirty-two years old, born in San Antonio, Texas, suffered severe head injuries in a car crash sixteen years ago and vegetative since the accident. He had been moved to Deshay six years ago from a home in Texarkana, where he had spent the past ten years. At the back of the file were the transfer papers from Texarkana, the signature at the bottom a loopy scrawl with the name typed beneath: Buddy Beere.

"Oh, no," Whit said. "Oh, no." He reached for the phone.

40

DAVID KNOCKED ON the door again. Claudia stood at the porch's end, watching the oaken limbs sway in the wind.

Yeah, stay out of the way, because you're not even an officer anymore, just a tagalong. Give David a peck, send him on his way, get on your own feet, find yourself a job. Maybe out of Port Leo.

"Mr. Beere?" David called through the shut door. "Sheriff's department, open up, please." He gave Claudia a half smile, warm, just happy she was there. She half smiled back.

They had driven out to Buddy Beere's address in David's cruiser, outside the Port Leo city limits, cutting through a grove of bent live oaks, and driven into a small clearing, studded with a few laurel oaks and a tidy cabin. A van was parked next to the cabin. Beside it was a shanty garage, tilting slightly with age. The cabin faced away from the road, faced away from the direction of town and bay, as though the little house had turned its back on the world.

"Anyone home?" David called. "Mr. Beere?"

They heard movement inside then, a scuffling sound, someone hurrying across a wood floor. Locks unlatched slowly—six of them—and the door creaked open an inch. A brown eye—oddly reddened and squinting—peered out at them.

"Mr. Beere?" David said.

"Yes?"

"I'm Deputy Power with the Encina County Sheriff's Department. This is Claudia Salazar, you spoke with her on the phone yesterday." Claudia nodded, not drawing closer. She wasn't here in any official capacity and didn't want to give the wrong impression to Buddy that she was still an investigator. One hint of that and Delford, in his current mania, would press charges against her.

The eye blinked. "Hello. Yes. Sorry it took me a while to reach the door, I was in the bathroom."

"Not out campaigning today?" Claudia asked in a little too-bright tone from her end of the porch.

"Oh, no, not today," Buddy said.

"Over your cold yet?" Claudia asked.

"Mostly. Thank you." The door did not open any farther. "I don't want to give my cold to y'all."

David cleared his throat. "We don't mind. Your boss is helping us with some inquiries. We're reviewing when certain patients were transferred into your nursing home."

Buddy opened the door a little wider, and over David's shoulder Claudia could see his whole face now, round, soft, some slight scarring from old acne, a puzzled look. He wore surgical scrub pants, the kind she'd seen at the nursing home, a thick T-shirt. He slid his hand up along the locks set into the door.

"Transfers? Gosh, all those records would be at Placid Harbor." He opened the door a little more. He was stronger than he looked, stocky, arms and chest thicker than she would have guessed from the hunched way he bore himself about town.

"Okay, Mr. Beere, would you mind stepping outside here for a moment?" David asked. "So we can talk?"

"Sure. Let me get my sandals. There's splinters on that porch," Buddy Beere said, reaching by the door. "Just a second—"

David turned and took four steps toward Claudia, shrugging, a question forming on his lips: "You wanna ask..." and then a blast of thunder exploded from the door. David fell, blood and flesh flying from his shoulder. Buddy Beere stepped entirely out of the door, bringing the shotgun around and up. Claudia threw herself off the porch as the barrel roared again and little meteors screamed past her, heat cutting near her throat, her hair.

She had no weapon. She scrabbled to her feet and ran for David's cruiser. Another blast and the cruiser's windshield dissolved into pixie dust. She was a clear shot in his sights. She swerved left hard, running low, putting the corner of the shanty garage between her and him.

Another blast, into the cruiser's hood. He was laughing. No, giggling.

He's killed David.

Claudia hunkered down by a corner of the weathered garage, trying to guess which approach he might take. There was a rifle and radio in David's cruiser, but it was twenty feet away and she imagined Buddy Beere, the gun steady in his hands, watching for her to stick her head out as a sweet target.

The garage might offer a weapon, but once she went in, she would be pinned. The doors were antique, opening in the middle like a horse's stall. Unlocked and slightly agape.

Running across Buddy's acreage offered little in the way of
cover, beyond the motte of live oaks situated on the wrong
side of the garage. To the other side seacoast bluestems
grew thick but only thigh-high. Not enough. He could take
a leisurely bead on her head and fire at will.

She heard the kick of his feet coming along the side of
the garage, between her and the police cruiser. She made
her choice.

She slipped inside the garage. It was neatly kept, small
windows offering a hint of light. Tools were aligned along
the back wall, a broom, a set of fishing tackle, an old sky-
blue Volkswagen Beetle parked on the right side, cramped
in the space. A trailer, carrying a small fishing skiff, was
next to the Beetle. She hurried to the back of the garage,
squeezing between car and boat. Her eyes ranged along the
back wall of the garage: screwdrivers, wrenches, a pair of
wicked-looking gardening shears.

"Claudia?" she heard Buddy's voice ask. He said it
Clau-di-a, the honeyed singsong a child might use in playing hide-and-seek, hoping to lure a playmate into the open.
She grabbed the gardening shears and hunkered down
behind the skiff; it offered the most immediate cover. But
it gave her the least room to run or fight. She crouched, the
shears heavy in her hands.

Shot pummeled through the doors, just in case she'd
been hiding there. Sunlight glowed through the frail, splin-
tered wood. Silence followed, and she saw one of the doors
creak open.

"You know," Buddy said, almost conversationally to
the empty air, "John Wayne Gacy invited the surveillance
cops to breakfast at his house. That's when they noticed
the funny smell and found a basement full of dead boys.

I always thought he should have killed the cops—how stupid just to cave. Dennis Nilsen pointed to where the chopped-up remains of his darlings were when the police came knocking. He should have at least killed those cops, gone out with a bang."

Kneeling, breathing through an open mouth, she saw his feet paddle past the other side of the Beetle. "Come out now," he called. "I don't want to shoot up my nice car and boat, and I'll make it quick."

She didn't move.

"That other cop, he's messy but still breathing. Come out or maybe I go back up there and make sure he stops."

She didn't move. He began to walk toward the back wall. A few more steps and he would be able to spot her. She braced herself.

As he turned, the barrel swiveling toward the ground, she launched herself up, slamming her forearm against the blued bottom of the shotgun's barrel. It swept right, exploding, cannonading into the garage wall. She pistoned her legs, driving Buddy hard into the side wall of the garage. She dropped the shears, both hands grabbing hold of the shotgun, trying to wrest it away.

He slammed the shotgun barrel against her head, hard, twice, stars and sharp pain blurring her vision. Shoving up with her arms, she got the gun above her head and powered her knee square into his gut.

He squirmed back, gasping, still holding the gun, and she kicked, hammering him in the mouth. Teeth broke and lips opened under her boot's heel. Buddy staggered back, blood bursting from his torn mouth. She pulled hard on the shotgun. It discharged once more in the air, deafening in the small space of the garage.

With a scream he yanked the weapon free from her
grasp and swung it at her head. She fell to her knees, duck-
ing, taking the blow on her shoulder. He pulled the gun
back to its firing stance, squeezed.

Nothing.

Empty, jammed, she thought. Buddy charged at her,
raising the Model 870 like a club, and she plowed back
into him, knocking him to the dirt floor. She scooped up
the fallen shears and vaulted into the narrow skiff to clamber toward the garage doors. He rammed the side of the
light boat with his body, and she fell from the prow, diving
headfirst, scraping her back against the trailer hitch, hitting
the hard-packed dirt. The shears were beneath her and she
twisted, trying to free them from her own weight. She saw
Buddy squeezing through the narrowed space between the
tipped boat and the Volkswagen. He tried to vault it, land
on top of her, but he tumbled headfirst as she scrabbled out
from underneath the boat.

He grabbed her ankle.

Claudia screamed, trying to kick him again. He tugged
her back toward him, the shears slipped from her grasp,
and she saw him pull a long brightness from a shoulder
sheath. Bowie knife.

He slammed the knife into her calf, and she screamed
her throat raw in one second. She felt her own flesh tearing,
the knife colder than ice. She kicked hard with the other
leg, impacting collarbone, and pushed away, frantically
grabbing for the shears. She smelled her own blood as her
fingers closed around the shears' handle. Pain—beyond
pain—raced along every nerve in her body.

He lifted the knife from her flesh.

"Quit fighting, quit fighting!" he yelled. He climbed on

top of her and lifted the reddened knife. Claudia rammed the shears into his gut, hard, feeling Buddy Beere's innards part before the points. She surged to a sitting position as she pushed, felt the blades slide along rib bone, and the shears vanished into him, all the way to the hafts.

Her face was an inch from his. She felt the Bowie knife tear into her shirt below her arm, the blade catch in the fabric, its edge whisper along her skin.

Buddy did not scream. He fell away from her, hands slapping the shears' smooth handles. Blood seeped from him and she crab-crawled backward, smelling his blood, her blood, kicking the dirt between them. Buddy lay on his side, blinking at her, mewling.

"No...Mama, help..." he wheezed.

Claudia hobbled to her feet. Agony lanced her leg, blood greased her skin. She staggered toward the cruiser and threw herself inside, glass from the broken windshield crunching under her. Buddy Beere still lay on his side, the shears protruding from his stomach, mouth a wet ruin from her kick, eyes dimming of life.

Claudia flicked at the radio. It still worked. "Officer down...help me...this is Claudia Salazar...with David Power. Officer down...officer down...He's been shot, gunshot...I've been stabbed...suspect is Buddy Beere... I think I killed him...officer down...we're at Buddy Beere's house off FM 1223...couple of miles past Port Leo on the right...4704 FM 1223...hurry, hurry."

She clutched her leg. Movement at the edge of her vision. Through the shattered windshield she saw a woman, stumbling from the house, naked, bruised, her face a mass of blue.

The county dispatcher's voice blared on the radio, telling her to hold on, help was on the way.

"Velvet!" Claudia called. "Velvet!"

Velvet limped toward the car but saw Buddy collapsed in the shadow of the garage. Claudia, clutching her leg, pulled herself out from the cruiser. Velvet stopped, stared at Claudia, then stared back at Buddy.

"Velvet, honey, it's okay…" Claudia gasped. "It's gonna be okay." She hoped. She wasn't sure she could stay conscious much longer. *And David, oh, babe…*

Velvet knelt by Buddy, yanked the shears out with a decisive pull, tore open the scrub pants, and began to perform crude surgery. In the distance sirens roared in their approach.

"Velvet! Stop! Stop!" Claudia called.

The blood flew upward with Velvet's blows, dotting her face, and soaked the ground.

41

I NEED TO TALK to Claudia," Whit said into the phone.

"She don't work here no more, Judge," the weekend police department dispatcher, a lady named Trudy, told him. "Delford fired her. She went and raised holy hell with the Hubbles, and he canned her."

"Over what?"

"That girl they pulled out of the bay . . . the one that found Pete Hubble's body, apparently she had something going on with Sam Hubble and Sam's disappeared, although Delford don't want to put out an APB. I heard him and Claud arguing about it. Delford's furious with Claudia, I don't even dare say her name aloud when he's around." She quickly told him about Junior Deloache, Heather Farrell, all the whirl of death since he left town.

"Oh, man." Claudia fired. Heather and Junior dead. Sam missing. His stomach tottered on the lip of a pit. "I need Spires's home and pager numbers."

Trudy gave him the numbers.

He dialed Delford's number. No answer. He tried the pager number, keyed in the nursing home's number, hoping for a quick response.

Think. Think.

Buddy Beere knew about Corey Hubble. Perhaps even assisted in the grand deception. Pete had found out where Corey was and Buddy silenced him. Perhaps silenced Marcy Ballew as well.

But how did Buddy learn that Pete had found Corey? Who knew what Pete knew? Not even Velvet, he'd kept even her in the dark. Not Kathy...killing Pete meant no money, and Whit didn't even know if she knew Buddy Beere.

"They authorized him to be moved," Felix Duplessis said again, sitting in his chair, staring at Whit. His face sagged with the worn look of someone who suspects a good day will not come in the immediate future. "The call came this morning. She insisted he be moved to a home up in Shreveport immediately."

"She?" Gooch asked.

"John's trustee," Duplessis said. "Laura Taylor."

"Let me have her number, please," Whit said. Aside from the Austin number was a 361 area code: Texas Coastal Bend.

Duplessis clicked on his speakerphone, and Whit dialed. The phone chirped and a woman's voice answered.

"Hello?"

Duplessis said, "Miz Taylor?"

A pause. "Yes, this is she." She sounded tired, anxious, and exactly like Faith Hubble. Whit leaned over the phone, still silent, his eyes closed.

"This is Felix Duplessis at Memorial Oaks in Deshay. How are you?"

"All right. Have you moved John yet?"

"There's been a delay here, ma'am."

"He has to be moved immediately to the home in Shreveport. That's what we pay for. Immediately."

"Well, yes, ma'am, but we've had a problem," Duplessis said. "There's a gentleman..."

Whit stood by the speakerphone and leaned down. "Faith. It's Whit. I'm here. I found Corey."

No answer from the other end of the line.

"Faith?" Whit tried again. "Are you there?"

"I'm here," she finally said.

"Why does Corey have to be moved so quickly?"

"I..."

And as soon as he asked the question, he saw his own logic misfire. Pete had died because he learned the secret. The secret the other Hubbles had cultivated and manufactured. But neither Faith nor Lucinda knew of his plans for the movie, that he was bloodhounding Corey's trail.

Pete would have had only one confidant, one person he needed to turn against the Hubbles.

"Is it Sam?" Whit asked. "It is. Sam."

"He's run off. He may be on his way there." Her voice broke. "Whit, don't let him do anything...stupid. Please."

"He killed Pete," Whit said. "He killed his own father. Faith. You knew?"

"If Sam is there...please don't hurt him. Don't hurt him!"

Whit turned to Felix Duplessis. "We need to move Corey...I mean, John. Or get guards here, one of the two. Now."

"Now, wait a second, we just got to get this sorted out..." Duplessis said, and through the blinds Whit saw a BMW slide crookedly into a parking space, bumping a van. A lanky figure loped toward the nursing home's front door.

"Faith, he's here," Whit said. "Sam's just pulled up. Do you know if he's armed?"

Gooch bolted from the room.

"Don't hurt him!" Faith screamed. "Please!"

Whit ran out of the office. He spotted Gooch heading toward Corey's room, pushing the wheelchaired patients back into their rooms, telling the aides to get them out of the hallway. The aides, collecting the breakfast trays, began to argue with him.

"Call the police! Now!" Whit yelled back at Duplessis. His yell made the hallway go silent.

"Whit!" Faith screamed from the phone. "Don't hurt him, he's my baby, don't..." and her voice vanished as Duplessis jabbed a button and dialed 911.

Whit reached the lobby just as Sam Hubble, wearing a denim jacket and dark glasses, left the information desk with a nod, heading toward the north ward of rooms.

"Sam!" Whit yelled.

Sam Hubble turned.

"You." Sam reached behind him, pulling a Ruger from its tucked spot in the back of his jeans, hidden by a baggy T-shirt. He pointed it at Whit's head, six feet away. The woman at the information desk screamed and ran down the other hallway.

"It's over, Sam," Whit said, holding his palms up. "It's over. I just talked with your mother. She wants to talk to you. Give me the gun and let's go to the office and talk with her."

"You screw my mother so you think you can tell me what to do?" Sam narrowed his eyes into a hateful stare. "I don't think it works that way."

He knew, oh, damn. He knew like Corey knew, years ago. "I don't want you to get hurt. Your mother's on the phone, she wants to talk with you."

"I hate you," Sam said. "Why did you have to come here, drag her into this?"

"It's over," Whit repeated. "The only person Pete would have trusted with the whole story of what he found was you. You're the only one he would have told, because he wanted you to be with him. He had dirt so bad on your mother and your grandmother that he actually might have won custody from them. So he told you what happened to your uncle Corey, but you decided to side with the home team. Your grandmother and your mother. You didn't want Pete ruining their lives, so you ended his." He softened his tone. "It's over, Sam. Put it down."

"Shut your mouth." Sam gestured with the Ruger. He glanced at the others in the lobby: a woman visiting a wheelchair-bound man, both cowering by a coffee table. "I start shooting and maybe I don't start with you."

"There's no point in hurting anyone else. The police are on their way. Give me the gun and let's go talk to your mom."

"No." Sam backed down the hall, keeping the gun leveled at Whit. Whit followed him, slowly.

"Pete told you what he thought you should know about your perfect family, all to convince you to be on his side."

Sam hurried down the hallway, residents and aides and nurses scrambling and screaming, hurrying into rooms. At the end of the hall Whit saw Gooch move out from Corey's room, then duck back in.

"He was lying," Sam managed. He bumped into a food tray trolley, shoved it over. Fish sticks and macaroni greased the floor. The gun shook in his hand. The boy began to cry.

Whit kept his voice even, his movement even with

Sam's, close but not too close. "Monday night he thinks he's spending it with you, he sends Velvet away. And maybe you call, tell him you need some time to think. He's alone. Your friend Heather goes to see him. You hide out on an empty boat nearby, maybe. Had she been befriending him for you, spying on him? They drink, she flirts. Maybe she sets up the camera for him. You sneak aboard. He strips and gets on the bed, maybe she strips, and you come into the room, shove the gun in his mouth, and fire. Or she does. Which was it?"

"Heather didn't do nothing," Sam whispered. "Stop saying that."

"He's dead, your family's safe, and you found a bonus: a half million in cash. You've also got his computer and all his notes on Corey. Heather pretends to find the body, but when your father's other relationships start producing questions, you produce a suicide note. And Pete conveniently confesses to his own brother's accidental death. Just so no one bothers to pick up looking for Corey."

Sam stopped. They stood ten feet away from the end of the hall, near Corey's room. The screams had died down as the terrified clients took cover, except for one rasping old woman's voice calling from a nearby room, "Nurse? Nurse?"

"I couldn't let him...couldn't let him do this to us." Tears streamed from Sam's eyes.

"I know you were just trying to help your grandmother, Sam. Your mother's on the phone, down at the office, she wants to talk to you. Give me the gun and come with me. We know how all this happened. There's nothing to be gained from hurting Corey or anyone else."

A shrill of sirens screamed in the parking lot. A hard light gleamed in the boy's eyes.

Sam muttered words Whit couldn't hear and Gooch launched himself from the door, pile-driving the boy down, smashing a fist against the boy's wrist. The pistol fell and Whit grabbed it.

Sam wriggled beneath Gooch, cursing, crying. Gooch yanked him to his feet, holding him with one massive arm.

"You okay?" he asked Whit.

Whit watched Sam's face. "Yeah."

Officers charged into the hall, demanding all three of them lie facedown. Whit put the gun on the floor as ordered and put his face on the cool tile. Duplessis hurried among the police, explaining, telling them Gooch and Whit were okay.

As the Deshay officers pulled Sam down the hall, he sobbed, "Let me call Heather. Please let me call Heather."

He doesn't know.

Whit went to go deal with the police and to tell Faith her son was still alive.

Hours later, when evening began its soft slide into Deshay, Whit returned to Corey Hubble's room. Corey lay in the bed, eyelids like half-moons, moaning softly. A police guard at the door nodded Whit in.

Whit pulled up a chair next to the bed.

"Well. Hello. It's been a long while. I know you and I weren't close, but I also don't know...what you can hear, what you can understand. I'm gonna assume it's more than we think." He touched the bone-thin arm under the sheet, remembering the smiling boy holding a proud string of redfish aloft. "The fishing's been good this year, Corey, although I sure haven't had time to go. We don't have a prayer in football season this year. The coach doesn't know his butt from a hole in the ground, so we're all resigned to losing. We ought to do better in basketball next spring, one of the Lindstrom boys is six-seven. And would you believe I'm a judge? I know: a Mosley acting all respectable. But it may only be for a little while now." He cleared his throat. "I went to go see Marian Duchamp. She cares about you, you know, even if things weren't exactly running smooth between you…"

The talk went on for another hour before Corey dozed into sleep. Whit stayed by his bed, watching the ghost breathe.

42

---◄●●●►---

THE ONE TRUE suicide note composed that October in Encina County read as follows:

I deeply regret the things I have done and left undone. I murmured that at church each Sunday for the past sixteen years and each time it felt like a bee's sting near my heart and God knew I was a rotten liar. If I make it to heaven I'll know He's forgiven me.

I take full responsibility for what happened to Corey Hubble and in turn what happened to Pete Hubble. I heard as a boy that love made you do great things, but I never figured good love would make you do evil. I write this not as explanation but as apology, and because regretfully Lucinda will not tell one moment's truth.

Lucinda and I became lovers before her husband died. His death from cancer was long and drawn-out, and the love between them faded long before he got sick. We were very careful and discreet, but Corey found out about us after Lucinda's election to the state senate. I don't know how, maybe he started following his mother and spotted us at one of the motels we used. He delivered flowers for spending money, so perhaps he saw us where we shouldn't be. While we were staying at a friend's house in Houston, Corey surprised us. He burst into the upstairs bedroom with a shotgun and we fought. I got the shotgun away from him, but then he grabbed for my service revolver and I grabbed it back and it fired twice, once hitting him in the head. He was hurt, but he didn't die. Lucinda's an RN. She stabilized him but refused to take him to a doctor because she was worried about the scandal. I began to cease to love her then. What kind of woman does that? A kiss can fool you. But I went along with her idea, scared of losing my career, and we drove the boy to Texarkana, where she knew of a nursing home where she could cut a deal. She'd been doing legislation on nursing home reform, so she knew which homes were crooked and might cut her a deal and would benefit most from her protection. Lucinda greased some palms and he got care at the home. We thought he would quietly die but he didn't. We returned to Port Leo late that Saturday, me driving Corey's car, Lucinda driving mine. I took command of the investigation into Corey's disappearance, and I stamped out any evidence that could point to him having fallen victim to violence.

I am sorry to the people of Port Leo for betraying their trust, but I was young and foolish and scared. I have read a lot on head and brain injuries, and they are confounding, unpredictable things. Corey hovered over our lives, not alive and not dead. He haunts me even now.

The administrator at the home (Phil Farr) was a crook, and he'd done Medicare fraud before, creating clients that never existed. After we took Corey there Lucinda protected this home against agency investigations. Farr and this clerk made Corey into John Taylor. This clerk, a man I never met, was suspected at one point of smothering a lady patient at the home, but nothing came of that. Now we know that clerk became Buddy Beere and followed Lucinda eventually to Port Leo, and now he has killed some poor young women. I take blame for that as well.

I thought Lucinda had killed Pete, or perhaps his ex-wife Faith. I did not want a murder investigation centering on the Hubbles. I behaved badly. I am sorry to the people I have hurt. I am not sorry to Lucinda Hubble, and the people of the Coastal Bend should not suffer her one moment longer.

I apologize to the people who have suffered so because of my mistakes, including Claudia Salazar, who I wrongfully terminated and should have her job back. Claudia, don't hate me. I always loved you more than a little. God forgive me my wrongs.

—Delford Morton Spires

He hanged himself with a stout length of rope. His service revolver lay on the floor below his feet, polished and oiled, next to his gleaming badge and his carefully folded uniform.

Claudia and Whit stood on the slope of land leading away from Buddy Beere's cabin, watching the work crew spear the ground with their shovels. The men dug slowly, carefully, methodically unearthing the land around Buddy's house, looking for the mortal remains of Marcy Ballew and the women from Brownsville and Laredo. Claudia stood on crutches, her leg heavily bandaged, her hair pulled up from her eyes. Whit leaned against an old laurel oak. He held blank autopsy orders, ready to fill out in case the searchers found human remains.

Whit watched Claudia. Her face was emotionless. "You sure you want to be here?"

"It's okay. You got to look the beast in the eye, Whit."

"You gonna bring David here when's he released?" Whit asked. David was recuperating at a Corpus Christi hospital, having suffered severe bone and nerve damage in his back and chest from the shotgun blast. He was out of immediate danger, but the road to rehabilitation looked to be long and winding.

"If he wants to come," she said, not looking at him.

"You haven't talked about David much."

"David . . . needs me right now. Badly."

Claudia said nothing for a long while, watching the dirt slowly pile.

A pair of FBI agents came out of the cabin, notepads open, arguing. Buddy's belongings had been boxed and cataloged and no doubt would be sent to Quantico for the criminal psychologists to purr over. All the evidence they would need to scribe their papers on Buddy Beere, add him to the literature of the compulsive killer. Patsy Duchamp, given a meaty story, had delineated most of the facts in the paper, and Whit had read the account with a greasy kink in his stomach: Buddy was born Darren Burdell in Milwaukee, with a hophead mother who disciplined her tot with blades and lit cigarettes. Little Darren killed his mother at age thirteen when she tried to castrate him. He decapitated her an hour after her death, which gave the social workers pause. He spent time at a juvenile home and mental ward, seemed to improve, worked odd jobs. Fell out of sight and headed south, apparently killing the occasional prostitute or runaway. One pundit quoted on television opined that Buddy preferred work at nursing homes since he would get to see people expire on a fairly regular basis. This might also explain his desire to be a rural JP. Serving as coroner, inspecting dead bodies, would have been delightfully stimulating for him. Credit-card receipts showed he had visited Deshay at least twice a year—perhaps treating Corey as a trophy, an example of his cleverness, paralleling the serial-killer fixation on visiting hidden remains of victims. A check of the human resources files at Placid Harbor showed that Buddy, armed with a master password, had altered the personnel records three times to indicate he was present at the nursing home when he was not. The dates were the dates when Marcy Ballew, Angela Norris, and Laura Palinski all vanished.

Claudia watched the federal agents walking around the cabin. "I wonder why he didn't bury Heather if he buried the others," she said in a dead voice.

Whit inched onto the thin ice. "You couldn't have saved Heather, Claudia. You couldn't know she was in mortal danger. Neither did she."

"I could have convinced her to stay in a safe place."

"Stop it," Whit said. "She was a co-conspirator in murder. No way was she going to get close to you or let you help her. You saved Velvet and David and anyone else Buddy would have killed along the line. That has to be enough."

"Delford could have told me." She suddenly shivered.

"He could have turned himself in. He had years of outstanding service on his side. He could have cut a deal, testifying against Lucinda."

"You want pearls with your hair shirt, Claudia?" Whit said. He put an arm around her, and she leaned against him, old friend to old friend.

They watched the work crew begin to dig on a fresh stretch of land, between the oaks. Fifteen minutes later the crew found bones. Claudia stayed in the shade of the trees while Whit completed the autopsy authorizations.

Four days later Whit came home to find Faith Hubble, out on bond, sitting on a deck chair by his father's pool, waiting for him. She wore jeans, a dark blouse, a ball cap, dark glasses. The uniform of the incognito.

"I assume I'm not in violation of some restraining order," she said, not lowering the glasses. "I'm behind on reading my mail."

"You're not," Whit said. "But if my father spots you here I imagine he'll say you're trespassing."

He couldn't see her eyes behind the sunglasses. "I suppose you will say you were just doing your job," she said. "Destroying my son."

"Me? Look in the mirror, Faith."

He saw her hands tremble. "My mother always said I had dreadful taste in men. I think you and Pete proved her point."

"Go see your son at the jail, Faith. While you can. They don't arrange visits between prisons."

"You're a cruel bastard."

"I spent about five seconds feeling sorry for you," Whit said. "Lucinda dragged you into the cover-up, made you dirty your hands instead of her. But you did it, willingly, for years, Faith. If you hadn't, Sam never would have had a reason to kill his father."

"You don't know thing one about my life...what my life has been like..."

"No, I don't. I can't comprehend it." He felt a tremor of revulsion that he'd ever touched her.

She stood. "We have very, very good lawyers. And I promise you, when justice is served and our names are cleared"—a straight reading from their press statement, he thought—"you're done in this town. You won't be able to get a job scrubbing toilets."

"Probably not," he said. "I have a feeling you'll have filled that position."

Selected election results from the November 7 election:

Texas Senate, District 20 (Encina County tally
   only):
Aaron Crawford: 11,587
Lucinda Hubble*: 939
*Hubble formally withdrew from race 10/24
Justice of the Peace, Precinct One, Encina County:
Buddy Beere**: 12
Whitman Mosley: 5,347
**deceased but not removed from ballot

Whit could only suppose those twelve voices of democracy did not read the newspaper or voted strict party lines, death and felonies notwithstanding. Whit watched the results with a somber Irina and Babe, gave Patsy Duchamp a neutral comment for the paper, and went to bed.

You don't act like a judge and you end up getting elected, he thought before sleep claimed him. *Politics is just strange enough for you to stay.*

The Honorable Whit Mosley savored the beauty of the late January afternoon as the borrowed *Don't Ask* puttered out of St. Leo Bay and beyond Escudo and Margarita Islands. Before him lay the wide-open Gulf of Mexico, the sea gunmetal gray, the waves whipped by just-right wind. January had been warmer than usual, the breezes sweet, the sunlight healing. Gorgeous, the fresh air like vitamins sucked straight into his lungs.

"You let me know if you get seasick," Whit called to Velvet. She sat in a chair, face tilted toward the sun. She had returned from L.A. for Sam's trial, starting in two days, and had been quiet since Whit picked her up at the Corpus Christi airport. She had hugged him fiercely but said little, nodding when he suggested spending an evening out on the Gulf and out of the reach of the reporters.

"Just don't steer this leaking contraption like a drunk man."

"Speaking of drunk," Whit said, "where are these legendary margaritas you promised?"

"I knew you'd put me to work." Her first laugh.

He dropped anchor and followed her down into the spacious cabin. She was dressed in casual jeans and rugby shirt, her hair pulled back into a modest ponytail, and skin lightly touched with makeup. This was the Velvet, he thought, that might have been if the cameras never rolled. The Velvet that still might be.

"What can I do?" Whit asked.

"I don't trust you to mix the booze right, but you can

juice me some limes while I work my tequila magic." She inspected the bottles in Gooch's bar. "Don't tell me there's no Grand Marnier in here."

"I strongly suspect Gooch's boat is Grand Marnier–free."

"Shows what you know." She raised a half-empty bottle of Grand Marnier in victory from the cabinet. "Just hiding back here, waiting for me."

She began to rinse out a blender. He sliced the limes. They worked in amiable silence.

"I should hate Sam and oddly I just feel sorry for him," Velvet said suddenly. "He doesn't deserve it, but I do."

Whit poured the lime juice into the cleaned blender she had set next to him. "I thought I knew what family tragedy was. I didn't."

Velvet poured liquor into the blender and turned it on. Whit moved behind her and hugged her, carefully. She leaned back against his shoulder. He felt the flutter of her sigh.

She finished the drinks and he tasted. "Wow, that's good," he said.

"A tart margarita is my specialty." She blinked. "That used to be a joke."

He smiled. She didn't smile or laugh much; he couldn't blame her. They took the blender up to the deck. The two of them drank and played at fishing, caught nothing, and listened to a strange mix tape Gooch had made: Smashing Pumpkins, Italian opera, Patsy Cline, Jimmy Buffett. Sad songs but somehow not so sad they hurt. They sang along with "Margaritaville," and Velvet leaned back against Whit's chest.

The sun sank into the horizon. They cooked steaks, and Velvet blended another pitcher of margaritas. The night air was crisp but not damp, the breeze a constant caress. They talked as the moon rose, Velvet reminiscing about growing up in Omaha, Whit telling tall tales on his brothers, thinking, *This is it, this is life, this is fixing her.*

Sitting on the deck, Velvet and Whit watched the stars glimmer over the Gulf and finished the hearty dregs of margarita. Whit was drunk, pleasantly and amiably so, for the first time since coming back from Louisiana. Velvet leaned back against his chest, her hair scented with the tang of lime juice. The stars, away from the smears of light crowding the coast, were like virgin light glistening in their first night. Velvet started to count them.

"Each one's a wish you get to make," she said.

Whit let her get to a hundred before he kissed the side of her throat.

"Don't," she said.

He stopped. But she didn't pull away from his arms, his lap.

"I'm sorry," he said. "I thought..."

"I know, Whit. You want to make... what happened to me right. I love you for that. I'm not gonna let what that bastard did to me dictate the rest of my life."

He was quiet, listening to the water lap against the hull. "But you don't want me."

She shook her head, turned to face him. She traced his jaw with her fingertip.

"I got a Plan B. I'm going back to Omaha when Sam's trial is done. No more movies for me."

"I'm glad. Very glad. But..."

"And so, I'm kind of taking life slower. If you and me... well, it would just be for the short while before I left. I don't want that anymore, Whit." She laughed softly. "I went so long not saying no, and now I say no to a guy like you. I got no brains."

He kissed her once, softly, letting the boat rock them like a cradle, and finally she fell asleep against his shoulder. She slept in his arms until the morning, and he watched over her, counting the stars for them both.

When his best customer—and friend—is
killed outside his Miami bar, ex-CIA
agent Sam Capra goes undercover to bring
down a criminal family unlike any he's
seen before . . .

Please turn this page
for a sneak peek at

INSIDE MAN

0

THE CAR TUMBLED off the cliff, hurtling toward the distant blue shimmer of the water.

The first, instinctive reaction is to draw in, brace yourself for the impact. Brace, never mind, *survive* the impact.

Next was the peculiar itch in my daredevil's brain, figuring gravity's pull at 9.8 meters per second squared, thinking, *We have five seconds before we hit*.

In the second of those seconds I felt the gun's cool barrel press harder against my temple, realized my passenger was aiming right at my head in case the crash or the water didn't end me.

That is attention to detail. That is commitment.

Three: The water rushed toward us. I moved forward, reaching, the cool steel barrel staying on me, my fingers along the floorboard groping for my one chance.

The sky, the water, my last breath, everything blue.

Four: The gun fired.

1

FOUR WEEKS EARLIER

Y OU'RE SOMETHING, AREN'T you, Sam?"

"I'm just a guy who owns a bar." I slid Steve another draft beer. Someone had left an abandoned checkers game on the bar and I moved the glass around the game. The guys who'd left it might be back tomorrow to finish it. It was that kind of bar.

"But you used to be something."

"A bar owner is being something." Why is there no one-word term in American English for being a bar owner? Publican sounds too English and formal. Barkeep isn't enough. I glanced through the windows. A young couple still sat on the outside couch, a dog at their feet, and I could tell from the angle of their beer bottles as they sipped that they were nearly done. The covered patio of the bar was otherwise empty, a slow Sunday night headed toward empty. I had to close at midnight, and that was twenty minutes away.

"But you used to be *something*." And I couldn't miss the prying hint in Steve's voice.

"We all used to be something," I said. "You too, Steve."

Steve smiled. "The way you move. The way you eyed

that jerk who bothered that young woman in here last night. You didn't even have to raise a fist, threaten to call the cops. Or even boot him. Just the look you gave him."

I shrugged. "Looks are cheap."

"The way you study every person who comes in here, Sam. One glance of assessment. That's a habit of being in tough situations."

"I just don't want trouble and it's better to see it coming than be surprised."

"So the something you were," he said. "I think if you were ex-military or an ex-cop, you'd claim it right away. Proud of it. But you don't."

I shrugged again. Bartenders are supposed to listen more than they talk, anyway. We're not the ones paying. I wiped the bar. Every night was too slow. My other bars around the world were high-end joints but Stormy's wasn't, it was a certified dive. It had been open for years, sliding through an assortment of owners until it came into my possession. The other nearby bars in Coconut Grove were a bit higher end than Stormy's. Scarred bar, couches under a crooked TV, games such as checkers and Connect Four on the little tables. No fancy drinks; beer, wine, and your basic hard liquor. If I told people I owned a bar in Miami they'd automatically assume I owned some uber-trendy nightclub in South Beach, women pouring out of limos in tiny skirts and huge heels. Many of my customers walked to Stormy's from the surrounding neighborhoods in Coconut Grove. We were not a tourist draw.

I wondered why I was bothering to keep this joint open. It was just me and the couple on the patio and Steve and two older guys watching a west coast basketball game on the corner TV; they'd already finished a pitcher. Miami wasn't playing so there wasn't a crowd.

"So. Since you won't claim what you used to be, maybe you can't." Steve kept playing at Sherlock. He could play all day. I don't talk about my past, not my real past, and for sure not to a guy who drinks too much. Even if he was my best friend in Miami.

"You mean like I was in jail?" I said. I didn't smile. I had been in a prison once, but not the kind he thought. A CIA prison is a different proposition.

Steve laughed. "No. Maybe you were working in something you can't talk about."

"Maybe you're just underestimating the skills involved in running a bar." I didn't have a manager in place here, which was why I'd spent two weeks in Miami. Maybe I could offer Steve a job. But that would mean being honest with him about what I did, what I'd done in my previous life, and asking him to stay silent. I wasn't sure he could stay quiet.

I would wonder, later, if it would have all been different if I'd offered him work during the past two weeks. I needed someone to run the bar, and to keep the secrets associated with it, and Steve needed a purpose. If I'd let myself say, *Here's an old friend who could handle the secrets, the tough situations.* If I'd let myself trust him. But I was worried he'd tell my parents. If I had trusted him…then it might all have been different for him, and for me. He might not have kept the job that he did.

"I know what I see," Steve said, suddenly not smiling, serious. "You know how to handle yourself, Sam. I could use some help, maybe."

"Help how?"

"Well, you know I used to work in freelance security." I'd first met Steve when I was fifteen years old. He'd worked a security detail attached to my parents' relief workers team in central Africa. He'd saved my family's lives during a chaotic evacuation from a war-torn nation, pulling my parents and my brother and me from a wrecked vehicle and getting us to an airport to board the final military flight before the rebels bombed the runways. He'd stayed in steady touch over the years: sending us Christmas cards from distant corners of the world, a pen and pencil set for my high school graduation, flowers and a thoughtful note when my brother Danny, a relief worker in Afghanistan, was kidnapped and executed. When I'd come to Miami two weeks ago to address the nagging problems of my bar here, he'd showed up and claimed a barstool the next day. I first assumed my parents had sent him to spy on me; after years of estrangement they'd decided to take an interest in my life. But Steve was living in his parents' house in Coral Gables and was already a semi-regular at this bar. He hadn't done security work overseas in a while. He seemed happy to guard the bar against any potential danger.

But he saw something of himself in me right now. It was unnerving that he could read my past in my movements, my attitude. I thought I had mellowed more.

Part of me just wanted to tell him to forget it, that he was entirely wrong, and hope he'd let it drop. But spies, even former ones, are curious people. We want to know things. Even when we're not spies anymore. I was twenty-six and had spent three years with a secret division in the CIA. I guess it showed. Or did Steve know more about me than he was willing to admit?

"You're wrong about me, but what is the job?"

He looked at me as though he could recognize my little white lie and shook his head. "Am I wrong? Maybe I can tempt you. I could use an inside man." He gave me a smile. I shrugged like I didn't know what the term meant and went to the guys watching the basketball game to see if they wanted anything, which was an unusual level of service here at Stormy's. But I wanted Steve to change the subject. Inside man. To be a spy again. When the guys wanted nothing more, I returned to the bar and resumed tidying.

Steve lowered his voice. "So. I'm meeting a friend here tonight."

I frowned. If I was trying to impress a woman, Stormy's was not my choice of venue, and I owned the damned place. "Uh, you know we're closing in a bit?"

"I just need to talk to her for a bit. You don't have to serve us. It'd be a big favor. You'll be here anyway." That was true. I lived in an apartment above the bar; every one of my bars around the world, they all had living quarters above them. There was a reason for that, and it was the reason I didn't think I could offer my talkative friend a job. But Steve was here every night when I shut down the bar, and we'd hung out and chatted after I turned off the OPEN neon sign.

"I should charge you rent," I said, joking. The couple on the patio left; the two guys watching basketball got up and left. I left Steve for a moment to collect their tips and their empties. I didn't have a server on duty, the one I'd hired hadn't bothered to show up. The staff, the location, the rundown look of the place, the long lack of a manager, all were problems. I owned over thirty bars around the world and so far Stormy's was the divey-est. I didn't live here in Miami and the place was dying of neglect. Hence my past two weeks, trying to decide whether or not I'd sell. If I did, I'd have to buy another bar in Miami to replace this one. I have very secret bosses—who gave me the bars to run—and because this place doubled as a safe house for their operations, I could not sell it and then not replace it. Miami was a town where they would too often need a safe house.

I dumped the glasses and slid the money into the cash register.

"I could pay you, Sam."

"What, your tab? I thought you had a friend coming..."

"No, dummy. To help me with this security job I got." He was trying again.

"Thanks for the offer," I said. "But like I said, I'm not anything. Just a bartender."

Steve studied me. He was older than me, in his mid-forties, burr haircut going silver, a man who had once been handsome and still could be but there had been too much beer and too many fights. He looked worn and beaten down. "You sure? I still think I'm right about you."

"My brother always told me to stay on my guard. I think that's what you see."

"You know how sorry I am about Danny."

"I know."

The thing was—I don't think I'd talked to another guy as much as I had to Steve since my brother Danny died. Most hours that the bar was open, I was here and Steve was here, drinking sodas during the day, tapping at his laptop or reading or watching the TV. My closest friend from my days in the hidden Special Projects branch at the CIA was a guy named August Holdwine, and August and I no longer talked much. We didn't have reason to; and as much as I liked him, he felt like a part of my past I didn't care to revisit. And as far as my friends from my Harvard days went, to them I was a mystery. I graduated, went to work for a London consulting firm that was secretly a CIA front, and had now ended up owning bars. I had fallen out of the drawn lines for what was acceptable success. And I wasn't on social media, posting pictures of my child, recording what I'd eaten for lunch, or talking about my favorite football team.

But every day for the two weeks I'd struggled with getting the bar on its feet again, Steve had been here. So we'd spent those past fourteen days and nights talking for hours, everything from basketball to women to books to movies. I hadn't had a friend in a while. I hadn't had the time for one. And he was someone who had once helped my family during a dark hour. I owed him. Maybe I should listen to his offer, help him. I felt torn.

"When's your friend coming?"

He glanced at his watch. "Any minute now."

Then the woman walked in. Even in the dim light you could see she was striking. Long dark hair, a curvy figure. She wore a scarf around her neck that blocked some of her face and as she unwound the length of red cloth I could see her mouth, lipsticked, set in a determined frown.

She was my age, mid-twenties, and I thought: She's not really his friend. But then, I was his friend, and I figured it was none of my business.

She seemed to give Steve a look of polite surprise. Like she couldn't believe she was here. It was close to midnight and we were in a cheap bar. Who meets at a bar so close to closing?

"Hello," she said, shaking his hand. "Let's sit over on the couches, where we can talk."

She clearly wanted to be away from me. But Steve, ever the gregarious one, said, "This is my good buddy Sam. He owns this dump. I just keep it in business."

The woman offered her hand, and I shook it. She had a confident grip. She didn't tell me her name, though, and I couldn't tell if she simply forgot or she didn't want me to know. Steve didn't introduce her. This was odd; this was off. Something else was going on here. "Hello. What may I get you to drink? We're about to close, but you're welcome to stay and talk."

"I don't want to inconvenience you ... "

"Sam lives above the bar; he can't be inconvenienced," Steve said. "This is a very private place. Like you asked."

She glanced at Steve's empty beer. "Well. All right. That's kind of you, Sam." And her lovely eyes met mine. "Could I please have a club soda? With lime?" And her voice was low and slightly loping in how she spoke, and heating you while you stood there.

"Of course. I'll bring it to you." I muted the post-basketball game analysis that was playing so they could hear each other more easily.

The woman gave me a grateful smile. "Thank you, Sam; you're kind." That molten voice, like warmed honey.

They headed for the couches and I got her a club soda. I wished our bar glasses were better crystal. I saw her glance at the walls: the vintage Miami Dolphins posters, worn signs from local breweries, a framed photo of the bar's original owner—a famously irascible woman named Stormy who had died a few years back—and Ernest Hemingway from the 1950s. A message blackboard where anyone could write a morsel of wisdom. This evening it announced, in blue chalk: SPECIAL TONIGHT, BUY TWO DRINKS, PAY FOR THEM BOTH. I hoped she'd think the bar was retro cool instead of outdated lame.

I brought her the club soda, with the nicest looking lime

slice in the whole bar, in time to hear Steve talking about his service in working security overseas. He shut up—nothing could get Steve to shut up normally—when I set down the drink. I left them alone, feeling vaguely uneasy. I wondered what kind of job he'd needed help with where he'd need an inside man—someone to go undercover. I knew he owned a security firm and that he'd handled bodyguard duties for celebrities when they came for big awards events, although he hadn't seemed at all busy the past two weeks. He had a house close by, and I wondered why he wasn't meeting his lovely friend there. They spoke in low voices, too low for me to hear, like lovers.

I turned off the OPEN sign, locked the door, retreated back to the bar. I wiped the already spotless counter, working around the checkerboard, and did a quick inventory. Short on wine and beer. I'd have to reorder, eating up the scant profits. And then I'd have to decide if I was going to go home next weekend, to New Orleans, and see my son Daniel. The weekend would be the busiest time, and the bar couldn't easily afford for me to be gone. No one could manage it; the current staff had no stars I could groom. And given that the bar had its own secrets in the apartment above it, I needed a manager I could trust entirely. I could maybe recruit one of the managers from my other bars: Gigi from Las Vegas, Kenneth from London, Ariane from Brussels... The Europeans might particularly enjoy a stay in Miami.

I saw Steve lean back suddenly from his friend. They'd become huddled, her talking so softly that I couldn't even hear the murmur of that honey river of a voice of hers.

I glanced at the clock. Ten past midnight.

He studied a small piece of paper and then handed it to

her and she tucked it into her purse. I heard him say, "Considering what they sent me, you have to treat this seriously."

She said, clearly, "I don't know what they want. I don't understand it." Then she glanced at me, as if realizing that she might have spoken too loud.

And then his voice dropped back down again.

I opened up a laptop I kept under the bar for the extra slow times like this. Keyed it on. Typed in a website and then there was a video feed of my son Daniel, asleep in his crib. His sleep was so deep that for a moment I got worried, and nearly called Leonie, his nanny (of sorts—she used to be a forger and I saved her from her life of crime, long story). She'd set up the feed for me, the traveling dad who had to be away too often.

Then he stirred, that magical breath of life, and I watched my baby sleep.

This is why I can't help you with your security job, whatever it is, Steve, I thought. *I need to stay out of that world.*

"Sam," Steve's voice broke my concentration and I closed the laptop.

"You all want something else?" I asked. The woman was still sitting on the couch.

"I'm going to go get her car and bring it around, then I'm going to follow her home on my motorcycle." Steve lived only a few blocks away, in a nice lush corner of Coconut Grove, near the landmark Plymouth Congregational Church. When he didn't walk to the bar, he rode his motorcycle. "Will you stay in here with her, please?"

"Sure. Has someone threatened your friend?"

"Just keep an eye on her." He turned to go.

"Steve? Seriously, is there a problem?" I raised my voice.

He cracked a smile. "Just keeping her safe. You sure you didn't used to be somebody?"

"Just a bartender," I said, automatically.

He paused, as though wishing I'd finally given him another answer. He headed out the door. Most of the parking for the bars in this part of Coconut Grove is either valet (with several restaurants sharing the service) or individual paid lots of banks or other early-closing businesses scattered through the neighborhood. Stormy's was between a valet station for a couple of nice restaurants, closed by now, and a paid lot three blocks away.

Something was wrong. I walked to her table. "Is there a problem?"

She glanced up at me. "You're a lot younger than Steve is."

"So?"

"Don't you have friends your own age?"

"Yes. Steve seems concerned."

She said nothing.

The spy in me. "Are you in some kind of trouble? Are you his client?"

She didn't answer me. She glanced around. "It's not what you'd call a nice bar, but I like it," she said. "I like that you have left that checkers game untouched. That's some customer service, there." She tried out a smile. It was lovely.

I shrugged. "Every game should be played until there's a winner."

"I agree completely." She stood and watched for him at the window. Steve's motorcycle was parked out front, and he'd left his jacket and his helmet on the bar. I moved them down to the end of the bar and I could hear his bike's keys jingle in the jacket pocket.

I joined her at the window. A block down was another

bar, with no one sitting outside. A moderate rain had started, chasing the Sunday night drinkers inside. Rain was a fact of life in Miami; some days it felt like the humidity never eased. But traffic had thinned, a light mist coming with midnight. The street was empty. "I'll be fine waiting for him."

"He asked me to stay with you," I said.

"That's my car," she said. I wondered why on earth he would have insisted that he bring her car around rather than just walk her to it if he was concerned for her safety. Steve was Steve. It was an older Jaguar, in mint condition. I saw Steve at the wheel, turning onto the street from the prepaid lot, three blocks from us.

He pulled up. He stepped out onto the bricked sidewalk.

Then from the opposite direction, from the road Steve took to his house, a heavy SUV roared down the street, slowed when it reached Steve. He turned to look at it.

I heard a single shot, muffled.

Steve fell. The SUV roared past us.

The woman screamed.

ACKNOWLEDGMENTS

In writing this book, I relied on the kind advice and expertise of many people: Peter Ginsberg, Joe Pittman, Genny Ostertag, Carolyn Nichols, and John Paine; Mindy Reed; Joe Stanfield, George Creagh, Asa Yeamans, and Mike South.

Particular thanks to The Honorable Nancy Pomykal, justice of the peace, Calhoun County, Texas; The Honorable Patrick Daly, justice of the peace, Aransas County, Texas; and Chief Tim Jayroe and Detective Mark Gilliam of the Rockport, Texas Police Department.

Thanks also to Mitch Hoffman, Lindsey Rose, Emi Battaglia, Beth de Guzman, Siobhan Padgett, Sonya Cheuse, Barbara Slavin, Andrew Duncan, Jane Lee, Marissa Sangiacomo, and the entire team at Grand Central.

ABOUT THE AUTHOR

Jeff Abbott is the *New York Times* bestselling, award-winning author of fourteen novels. His books include the Sam Capra thrillers *Adrenaline, The Last Minute,* and *Downfall,* as well as the standalone novels *Panic, Fear, Collision,* and *Trust Me. The Last Minute* won an International Thriller Writers award, and Jeff is also a three-time nominee for the Edgar award. He lives in Austin with his family. You can visit his website at www.jeffabbott.com.

LOOK FOR EVEN MORE
JEFF ABBOTT THRILLERS

Available now